When Raven Dances

WW II Invades Young Lives in Seward, Alaska

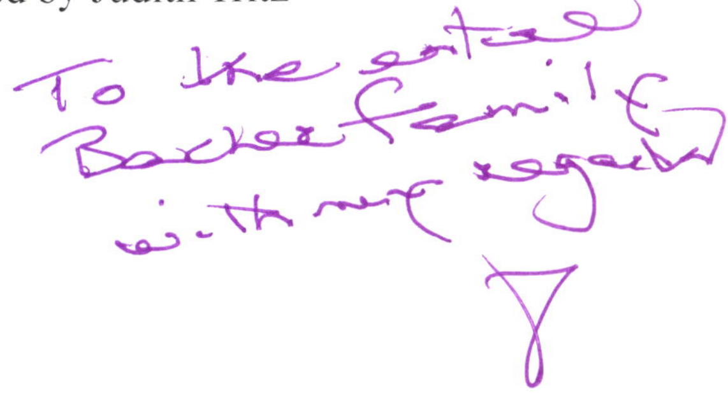

POLLY BIGELOW

Illustrated by Judith Tritz

PO Box 221974 Anchorage, Alaska 99522-1974

books@publicationconsultants.com—www.publicationconsultants.com

ISBN 978-1-59433-414-6
Library of Congress Catalog Card Number: 2013952223

—First Edition—

Illustrator: Judith Tritz

Manufactured in the United States of America.

ACKNOWLEDGEMENTS

My desire has been to tell the story of the crucial role tiny Seward played in the Allied success during WWll. I wasn't there, but I am an army brat, remember what life was like during those years, and hoped that I could make a stab at the task. I needed a great deal of help and there are many who assisted in my effort.

Certainly the first is Mary Barry. Her extraordinarily detailed history of Seward served as my beginning. I read them all, returning to them, especially Volume III, for more information along the way. Beyond that, there still remain in Seward a few citizens who did live during those years and they volunteered details and anecdotes regarding life at that time. They include Nancy and Jack Sadusky, Beverly and Willard Dunham, and Jack and Betty Skinner. Jean Schwafel was supportive of my efforts as well. I thank them for their patience.

I have from the first received unqualified support from Qutekcak in Seward, specifically Melanee Stevens. The indigenous people in Seward chose the name for my pivotal character, Sava Sahtaii. I also thank Esther Ronne, one of the last residents of the Jesse Lee Home. She graciously gave me an afternoon to talk about life at the Home. I thank Michael and Crista Lee Tritz for taking me out to view Resurrection Bay close-up, for hiking with me, for showing me a WWll munitions cave, and running myriad errands for me.

John Foutz of City of Seward provided an excellent city map and Bill Toskey assisted in locating important sites. Father Richard Tero of Sacred Heart Church has been supportive as well. Of course, the

Seward Community Library and Museum have provided me with excellent historical material and books about Raven's antics.

I can't remember not knowing folk stories and myths of many cultures. I suspect they exist in my DNA. For that reason it is difficult for me to denote what stories I have known since childhood and those I have read, but I list a few books in the bibliography. Since I know that Coyote and Raven are the creators and powerful tricksters in their culture, I felt free to weave them together in this story.

In writing about the strong connection between Athabaskan language and various tribes of the continental Southwest, once again I am grateful to those who mentored me. Robert Johnson, Navajo cultural specialist at the Window Rock Museum assisted me with my Navajo character, Naasha, and her view of the world, as well as certain Navajo words included in the story. His help was detailed and I tried to adjust words and concepts so that they were suitable for a small non-Navajo girl.

Regarding Athabaskan, specifically Dena'ina language, I am indebted to Dr. Siri Tuttle, Professor of linguistics at the University of Alaska Fairbanks, who patiently led me over the mine field of sophisticated language similarities and differences.

Bruce Orton also provided a potential source for language assistance.

Regarding both native languages, and my use of their words, I am a novice and request that those more knowledgeable be patient with my errors.

Katch Bachellor at the Alaska Museum fielded my questions concerning prehistoric land animals and sea creatures in Alaska. My interpretation of that information is clearly my own, but even a cursory look at that subject reveals that dinosaurs did populate the Kenai, particularly sea creatures, and animals of monstrous size have been spotted by radar in Alaska waters not all that long ago.

Library staff in Juneau and Ketchikan fielded my queries and cheerfully assisted. I am particularly indebted to Hillary Koch, who sent me information on Ketchican.

Bora Zipkovic, Blog Editor for *Scientific American,* helped me regarding sleep patterns in Alaska animals. Keith Boggs, Director of the Alaska Natural Heritage Program at University of Alaska Anchorage, assisted me with Alaska flora.

There were those who willingly supported me as I wrote, especially Diedre Bloom, Jennifer Fields, and Angela Dunne. Angela designed the iconic Raven. Patricia Cleavenger served as my thorough and capable proof reader.

I am grateful to Rebecca Goodrich for showing me the road and then making sure that there were plenty of dips and detours along the way. Her patient tutorials made the book stronger and richer.

I thank my daughter, Kate, who was my support and mentor regarding social media. Son, Bill, helped me occasionally with internet problems. Thanks also to Ray Massucco for legal advice regarding the book.

My husband, Jim, became my patient technical assistant and confidant.

Lastly, I am profoundly grateful for my editor extraordinaire, Patricia Fry. Her light touch and incisive insight brought needed clarity to the book.

A big thank you to my reviewers and their kind words.

I am sure there are others I should thank—I have had many supporters. To all of you I offer my sincere gratitude.

Finally, I ask the reader to recall that this is a work of fiction, laid over a few facts about what was the valiant town of Seward, Alaska during the war and throughout the '40s. The town near Window Rock in New Mexico is a creation of my imagination. Those who populate both towns in this novel are, one and all, creatures of my imagination.

Here we are, my brother and I
On our way to "I don't know why."
Filled with the spirit to smile and sing.
We truly have everything.

Author unknown

Where is the way where light dwelleth? And as for darkness, where is the place thereof...hast thou entered into the treasures of the snow?...
Hath the rain a father? Or who hath begotten the drops of dew?
Out of whose womb came the ice? And the hoary frost of heaven, who hath gendered it?

Job chapter 38; 17 through 29

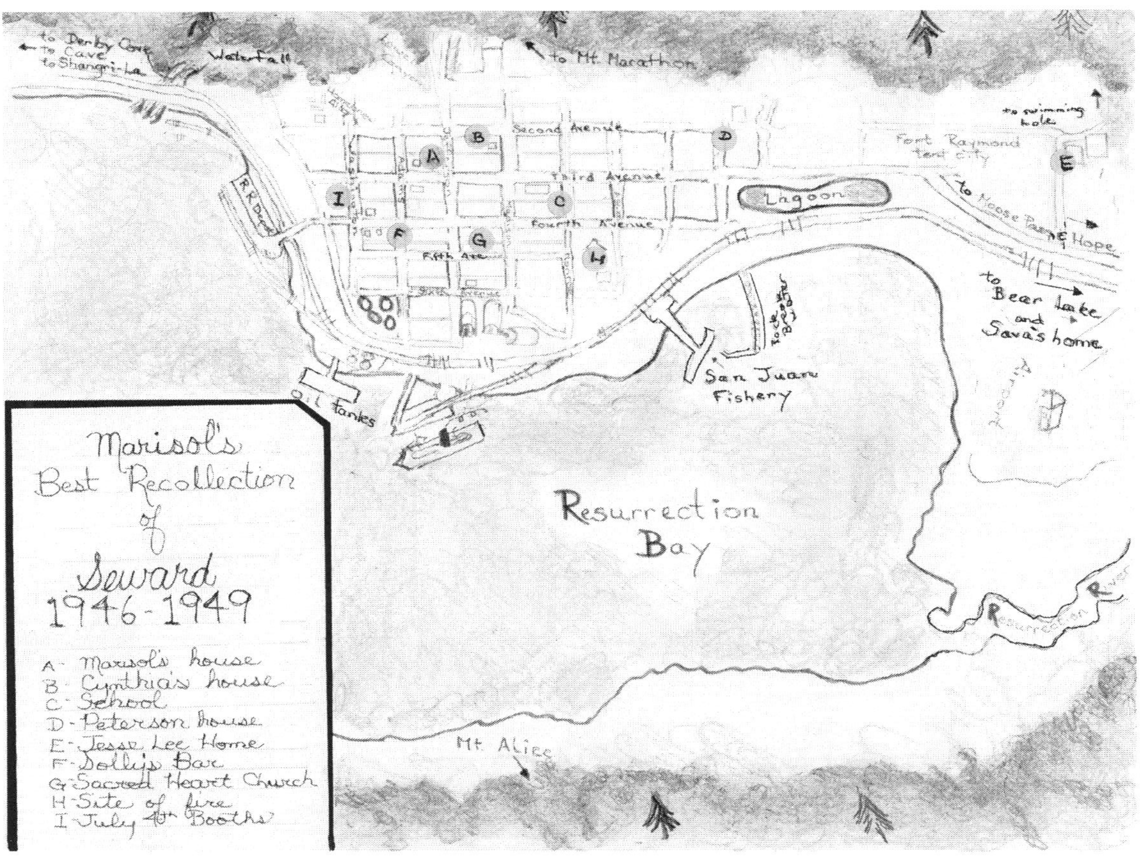

to Derby Cove
to Cave
to Shangri-La
Waterfall
to Mt. Marathon
to swimming hole
Second Avenue
Third Avenue
Fourth Avenue
Fifth Ave
Fort Raymond
tent city
Lagoon
to Moose Pass & Hope
to Bear Lake and Sava's home
R.R. Dock
Oil Tanks
San Juan Fishery
Resurrection Bay
Airport
Resurrection River
Mt. Alice
Marisol's
Best Recollection
of
Seward
1946-1949
A- Marisol's house
B- Cynthia's house
C- School
D- Peterson house
E- Jesse Lee Home
F- Dolly's Bar
G- Sacred Heart Church
H- Site of fire
I- July 4th Booths

SEWARD HARBOR DEFENSE SYSTEM

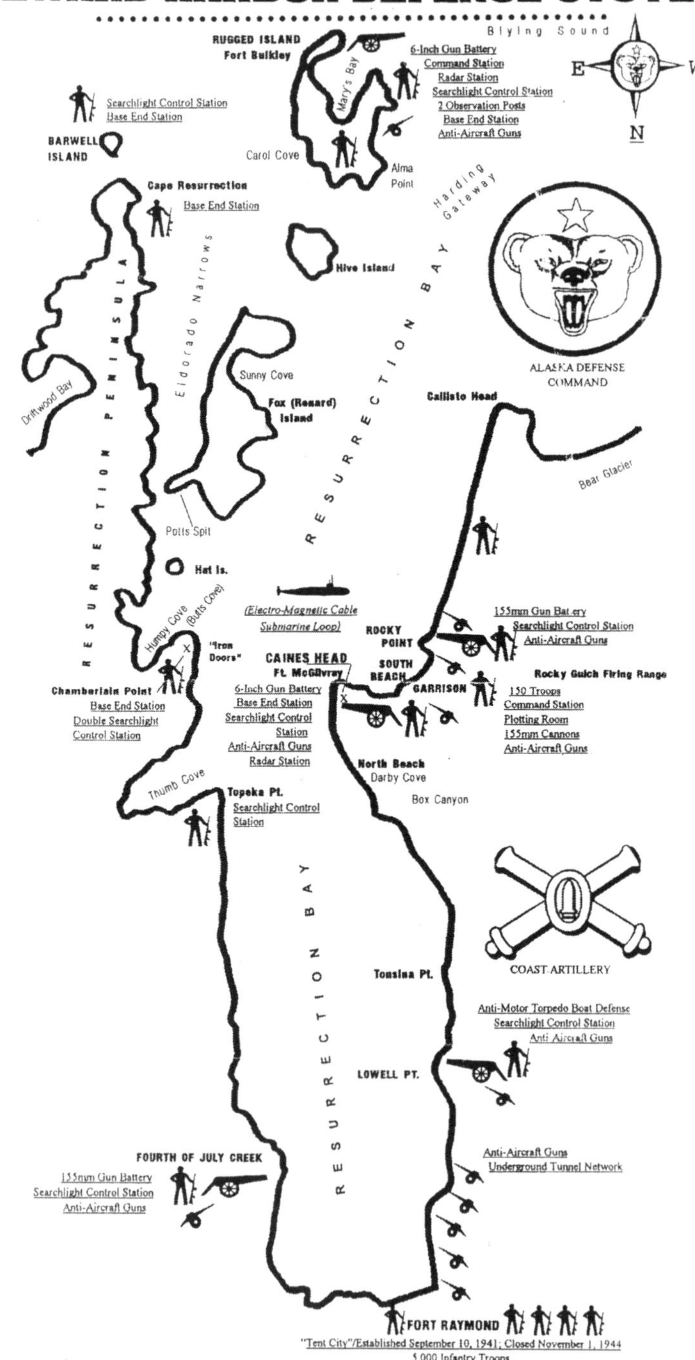

TABLE OF CONTENTS

THE PESKY BIRD PREVAILS

August 1963

I don't want to write this story, but Raven insists.

I sit upon a giant slagheap of mica schist that has exploded onto the hillside, likely from a gaping earth wound, the end product of some lumberman's interpretation of harvesting trees or some miner's effort to locate a promising vein. Stumps remain, occasionally jutting from this burst of shining detritus that I cannot construe to be anything other than the fractured guts of earth. For about half a football field in size, the site festers, quietly sloping at a degree slight enough that I have negotiated it easily by foot in order to survey it.

I have driven gravel roads and hiked about four miles to find a place in these mountains that reflects just how I feel at this moment and this is it.

It is 1963 and I am in Hope, Alaska, just up the road from my childhood home, Seward. My reason for being here is not a happy one. I suspect the *hope* encompassed in that name has to do with the heady optimism felt by scores of miners as they trod these hills searching for the shiny stuff—gold or silver or copper. Most of them scoured this area seventy years ago, with varied levels of success. This wound, this gash in nature's belly, is trying to heal. Many spots are now green, soft to my sight, velvet as the new horns on a deer. Baby aspens and conifers seek to make life out of this ugliness. God bless the moxie of Alaska's

Mother Nature. I have come to adore her and I have come to think my heart and hers are one.

I sit on this velvet patch, among the new saplings, my arms wrapped around my knees as I survey the world about me. I wear well-worn brown hiking boots, a necessary part of my daily uniform. At my feet, flows a rushing stream shining silver in the sun's reflection. It comes to my sight from the right below, arcs around to my left and then winds again to the right and down the mountain, to sites not yet wounded, as far as I know.

High in the spruce tree sits Raven. It isn't enough that he lives in my heart, he has to nag me, to boot. His call is far from pleasant, but it is insistent. I watch as he jumps from branch to branch preening and fussing. Raven has been after me for a few years now. He says the time has come for me to tell my story. For the life of me, I don't know why he thinks that what I have to say matters in the least.

Besides, this is a sad time for me. Most of the time I act on his advice, but this writing thing is tough. He says that if I don't get going, he will pull my hair and peck at my ear until it is raw, and then he will do it again and again. And I believe him.

I could defy him. I have done that before. I could dig in with my boots and fists and just refuse to do his will.

Or perhaps, given my mood today, I will slide down and allow myself to be sliced by these shards, becoming slivers of brown boot, khaki shorts, and blood flowing into that lovely stream. Like colorful Buddhist prayer flags, fragile as a breeze, I could become part of this lovely natural world.

There he sits, perched on the branch over to my left. He hops from branch to branch performing for my benefit. It is his call, his voice that penetrates my head. He clucks, he squawks, he rails at me and there is no denying his demands. All his companions in the forest, including me, give in and heed him. He snaps his wings, he rants, inveighing me to get started. "Tok, tok, tok."

Pouting has never been a major part of my persona, so I give in and do his will.

Raven says to get on with it, and there is no way I can ignore him.

MAMA AND I ENCOUNTER A FLOATING COLOSSUS

May 1946

So I reach deep into my pack for pencil and paper and begin the story of growing into a woman in a magic land of crystal cold and cutting winds. I have been supported by many who showed me the way through the labyrinth, freely sharing their love and wisdom.

There have been so many; but one in particular dominates my mind today. He is an extraordinary person made of Alaska soil and flesh, a man whose spirit is one with everything that matters in this Alaska universe. His name is Sava Sahtaii, and he is my dear friend.

This is also the story of my mother. Her way was not easy, but she was determined to encounter her own future while holding tightly to my hand or my wrist, as I reluctantly stumbled and scuffed along beside her.

It is the story of Cynthia Bergen, my best friend, whose virtues and talents refused to remain hidden within her, in spite of her modesty.

I am compelled to mention Silvio, whose sporadic entrances into my life, followed by his capricious exits, continue to perplex me.

I should mention Matthias, a little boy of modest and questionable provenance who sings like something celestial and is master of an exotic skill.

Others cheered me on, or counseled me on the way ahead. Some threw obstacles in my path, but fortunately those who helped have been many and those who hindered have been few.

Finally there is my father, who left me virtually before my voyage began. He didn't want to leave me; I know that. But leave me, he did. He left me to contend with great sadness—and this pesky, demanding bird. And perhaps some of his kin, to boot.

What I will recount to you begins when I was a little girl, many years ago, and it ends tomorrow, August 27, 1963. That is because Sava will be gone then. I know that because he told me that his breath-soul will leave him then, and it isn't difficult to figure out what that means.

I am Marisol Downey. I am twenty-six years old and a wildlife biologist with the U.S. Forestry Service. I live about fifteen miles from here in the Chugach Range.

1946

In May1946, I found myself in a cab in Seattle, Washington headed for the port. My heart pounded, but that had been happening often lately. Everything I had encountered in the last five days was new territory for me. I sat directly behind a cab driver, his rough wool cap filling my already limited field of vision. I was, after all, only fifty-two inches high and a goodly part of that was legs. Within the last half-hour Mama, the driver, and I had managed to stuff piles of suitcases, cartons and bundles into the trunk and passenger seat of the cab. We scrambled into what space remained. Now the driver slowed, stopped and rushed to open Mama's door and I crawled out after her.

Before me was a long expanse of wet, worn concrete with sides that dropped directly into a leaden-colored ocean. In front of me and to my side wallowed a black and white behemoth, a cold metal giant of a ship. I wanted to bawl. To forestall that potential shame, I stuffed two lemon-flavored Life Savers into my mouth and chewed them with ferocity.

I had to crane my neck to see the ship's top edge. I saw what looked like metal arms of strange, jointed shapes, standing at the ready to achieve feats that I could not yet imagine.

From a rusty hole the size of my Granny's entire dining room, a mammoth black chain spewed, as if it were the tongue of this huge beast—a tongue that reached down into the depths of the fearsome chasm as if it sought a drink of that murky water. The chain and a series of grimy, slimy ropes, nearly as thick as my entire body, held the ship so that its movement was limited at the dock. Even so, it still bobbled and leaned lazily, just enough that I could contemplate my fate if I took just three steps that direction and fell between the concrete and the side of the ship.

I would have become peanut butter with pigtails and ribbons in seconds, and no one would even know I was gone.

"Oh, Marisol, just look at our ship!" exclaimed Mama. I looked up at her expression, something I could not share at this moment. She was excited; I was terrified.

On the back of the ship I saw the words, *S.S. Denali* and I saw that one of those arms had ropes attached to it that had something to do with a flag that fluttered in the slight breeze.

Ahead of us, a white canvas-covered chute shot out from another opening and dropped, making contact with the concrete pier. Above it I read the words, *Alaska Steamship Company.* The whole contraption made me think of the chute made of poles and planks that my Grandfather, Juan Felipe, used to usher his cattle into the corral at his rancho in New Mexico. The only difference, I reckoned, was a fancy canvas cover, but cattle chute it was. I knew well what was to befall the cattle. They were either going to receive a searing, hissing brand on their rumps or they were headed to market to become roasts and steaks.

I was dressed in what was to become my "for best" uniform throughout our voyage, and for the next year—a light brown plaid wool skirt and a brown jacket. On my feet were saddle shoes, barely broken in and long enough for me to grow into. The white parts blazed and the toes curled up already, impatiently awaiting the feet to fill them. My hair was still slightly wet, plaited into two braids and firmly finished with rubber bands and tan satin ribbons. Atop my head, perched a brown beanie with a perky felt heart on the top.

Within the last two hours, I had experienced my very first shower. Until that day, Mama had scrubbed my head in the kitchen sink of our house in Gardner, New Mexico and the rest of me had been routinely scoured and polished in a footed bathtub.

We stayed in a hotel in Seattle last night. When I looked from the seventh floor window at frothy gray ocean, cloud-dotted mountains and the horizon beyond, I was amazed. Gardner had offered nothing like this.

Mama and I were on our way to a strange town called Seward, in the coldest corner of the world I could imagine, Alaska. For weeks I had known this was to be my fate, but that didn't mean I had accepted the idea. I felt as though Mama was forcing me to leave behind my almost perfect life, where I was born and had been a happy little girl.

There, I was surrounded by family who adored me. By the completion of my ninth year, I knew just about every tree, every fence, every corner of town and most of the people who lived in it. I could predict precisely what my day would be like, and I liked it that way.

We were to sail from Seattle to Seward on a steamship, Mama said. That only confused me more; to me steam was something that hissed when Mama pressed Daddy's wool pants with a hot iron and I couldn't imagine how that had anything to do with going somewhere on a ship. The truth is, I was smart enough to have figured it all out, but I didn't want to.

At this moment, my proximity to that dark abyss monopolized my thoughts. I grabbed the edge of Mama's jacket tightly and held on. There we stood among all our mismatched paraphernalia, feeling very inconsequential.

The *S.S. Denali* was as long as a football field and at least five stories high. Its open belly, a great, gaping black maw, swallowed a line of crates and boxes that looked to me a lot like stained teeth. Workmen shouted and grunted, jamming those teeth into any available crevasse they could find.

A group of green-jacketed men marched past us playing horns and beating drums. Then, a tall imposing official approached us in a white and gold uniform, pen and list in hand. He waved us on toward that white chute and we were too stunned to disobey his order. He motioned to a worker who dealt with our suitcases and trunks. Laden with our few small packages, we ascended the gauntlet. I thought about my grandfather and tried to assure myself that we were destined for something more cheery than the branding iron.

Mama's family had lived in New Mexico for centuries. In 1611, the Spanish King Felipe III granted land in this territory to the Spanish

Duke of Vasques Alvarado. My grandfather's, grandfather, many decades back in time, Manuel Fernandez Vasquez del Pedregál de la Luz, was a nephew to the duke, who granted him land in 1618 with instructions to establish a ranch. At that time, their neighbors were gentle Hopi natives, jackrabbits and rattlesnakes.

That site, known as Rancho San Pablo, was Grandfather's land where his family still raised sheep, cattle, and wine grapes since before many of the original colonies even thought about becoming states.

Not too far from the old well on his property, an ancient cork oak grows. It's still a source of Grandfather Felipe's pride and testament of family loyalty to their roots in Spain. Grandfather continued to harvest cork from that tree occasionally to seal his bottles of wine from his own grapes. Grandfather was proud of just about every part of his life; his wife, his daughters, his animals, his small garden where squash and corn grew. I could almost measure his pride by how deeply his thumbs hooked into his leather belt, as he surveyed what pleased him. So I can tell you that he took great pride in his *huerta,* his orchard just beyond the cork tree. At harvest time when he gazed at the almond trees and his beloved fat clusters of deep purple grapes, his thumbs didn't just rest in his belt. Occasionally they tapped a light tattoo on his slightly expanded belly. reflecting his gratitude and satisfaction with what life had given him.

I loved visiting and playing at that old rancho house. Around the front and sides of the house wrapped a long, terraced veranda that was embraced by Abuelita Clara's garden filled with cactus, azucenas, scarlet poppies and black-eyed Susans.

For awhile it became my habit to bring all my retinue of dolls to the house. On many warm afternoons we sat in a line swinging in the timeworn wicker swing.

The only impediment to my joy was to be found in the hall. If I came into the house through the heavy main door, hewn of solid oak planks, I found myself immediately in the hall. I much preferred entering the house through the kitchen, where I could count on Abuelita Clara's kitchen servant, Alma, handing me a freshly made *bunuelo* or a slice a ripe peach. But even then, there was no way to get from the kitchen to anywhere else without going through that hall, where on the wall hung an imposing portrait of Doña Inéz Albuerquerque del Vasquez.

Over the years, an "er" in her aristocratic family name had been lost, but on the polished brass plate below her portrait, the ancient "er" still remained. As I passed her, Doña Inéz always stared down at me, her thin eyebrows frozen, framing her icy imperious black eyes that seemed to follow me wherever I went. Her skin was powder white and her thin, dark red lips were set in prim disapproval. Her neck was long, wrapped in a high white lace collar and, at her throat, she wore a garnet and pearl brooch. A high amber comb held her hair in place. Framing her head was a gossamer short mantilla. Her dress was velvety black, and in her lap, her hands held a burgundy and jasper-colored fan.

Mama told me I was related to her, but I didn't want her to be my ancestor. She terrified me and I was glad she was imprisoned in that ornate golden frame, unable to step down and smack me with that fan in her bony bejeweled hands. She knew I stole grapes from the arbor, dusty, warm and delicious, and she begrudged me every single one.

***

I held on to Mama's jacket as we found our way to an upper deck. There we stood looking down at the busy pier, once again feeling no less inconsequential. Mama handed me my brand new Brownie camera from her purse and I began to snap my first pictures.

In one photo, Mama is in shadows. She stands leaning against the railing, a slim, pretty lady hugging a blue topper coat about her. A soft felt hat perches at an angle on her head—more rakish than was her usual style. As I look at that photo now, I suspect that the tilt of her hat reflected her nervousness that day. When I think about it, she was about the age I am now, and I wonder if I would have been as brave as she was then. Today she would brush off any mention of bravery; she had no choice, she would say, and that she had to move on. As usual, she was right. Nevertheless, her rueful smile in that photo seems to say, *Oh Marisol, what have I gotten us into?* What indeed?

***

In the year of my birth, 1937, civil war blazed in Spain. Mussolini's troops marched into Ethiopia. Nazi bombs destroyed Guernica. The entire world seemed determined to destroy itself, and the destruction continued into the next years. Japan's armies pillaged China, Hitler's tanks overwhelmed most of Europe…

The date that changed my life was March 1944—a date now seared into my soul in vivid Technicolor.

An unusual spate of rainstorms had soaked New Mexico's soil over the last two weeks. Immediate and intense, the water came in wind-blown gusts, falling in sheets. Within minutes, the torrent pervaded every available crack and crevasse, creating gullies and streams that rushed into dry, dusty flatlands and cut across roads.

We all feared and respected the *cienegas*. Those wild, powerful, dangerous, short-lived flood waters could pick up an automobile, twist it and turn it over completely, potentially rendering it a thick, muddy tomb, which could suck away any life force instantly.

Those rains also enabled long-latent seeds to germinate, sprout, and blossom. Their life was brief; their blossoms erupting, maturing and expiring, creating new seeds that would lie dormant in dry clay until the next capricious drenching—perhaps years away. We New Mexicans never knew when we would see another display like the one that spring, so we appreciated its spectacular splash for as long as it lasted.

I recall seeing banks of blossoms, deep pink, gold, and lavender, that day as I walked home from school. Often I skipped home, and there would have been no reason why I would not have done that on this particularly fine day.

I went up the steps, past the huge pottery jug Mama kept on the back porch that contained a hardly-ever-used umbrella and Daddy's walking stick—his *shillelagh*, he called it.

The instant the screen door slammed behind me, I sensed something different—something wrong. It was written on Mama's face. I took a deep breath as I looked at Mama. She clutched a yellowish piece of paper. She was weeping so hard I thought she might collapse. I looked at her hands and thought, absently, that they looked like the claws of a hawk grasping a small critter. My Tia Susana's arms embraced Mama, her head on Tia's shoulder. I hadn't yet let out that breath I realized.

"What?" I whispered softly, my eyes moving from Mama, to Tia, to that piece of paper.

Susana released Mama and reached out for my hands. "Marisol, my dear child." She swallowed and stepped toward me. "Marisol..."

Mama sat down hard in a kitchen chair. I could hear her continuing sobs.

Tia grasped my hands, gazed at them momentarily, then looked into my face; her face puffy and red like Mama's. "I am so very, very sorry." She swallowed and continued. "Your daddy is gone, honey. He, won't be coming back. He was killed in battle in Anzio, Italy."

I was not there, I was in some other place looking at my Tia, but I was not hearing the words, those choked words that came from her mouth mixed with all manner of additional sounds that I wouldn't hear...couldn't hear. What was battle? I thought. What was Anzio? Where was Italy, for that matter? My throat began to burn. I remember saying, "Why?"

Susana just shook her head. I began to cry, I think. I could well have stamped my feet or kicked a chair, I really can't be sure. My head felt as if it would explode. I ran over to Mama and buried my face in the apron in her lap, sobbing.

Mama began to stroke my hair, humming quietly, her finger tracing the circumference of my ear over and over. I still remember her repetitious croon; I opened my eyes and saw before me only the brown checks in the apron fabric, seemingly huge and out of focus, and I smelled doughnuts and fry bread, worn into the threads of that apron. For just a moment, I considered pretending we were in a brown-checked tent and what seemed to be happening really wasn't so and Mama was just cooking and we would fly into the sky and disappear or dissolve right into that apron. As far as I was concerned, that would have been all right with me.

NAASHA'S NAVAJO WORLD

My thoughts snapped back to reality when a ship's officer, dressed in a crisp bright white uniform passed behind us, hesitated just slightly, then stopped and offered to take a picture of us both. Before he moved on, he handed us several rolls of colored paper streamers.

"When the ship pulls away, feel free to throw them," he said. "That is a proper nautical way to say goodbye." He smiled and walked on.

Those were the wrong words to say to me at that moment. All I could think of was my Daddy and the last time I saw him. I thought again, what I had thought many times before. I must not have given him a proper goodbye, because I lost him.

***

In spite of a world in turmoil, my birth was met with joy and pride by my parents and all manner of family, both Daddy's and Mama's. At my arrival, I became everybody's darling as I cooed, cried, crawled, walked and chattered my way through early childhood.

New Mexico sun reigned supreme over my little yellow adobe home, in our often cloudless, startlingly colorful sky. Sometimes deep azure, at other times cobalt blue, at sunset, amethyst, coral or violet, that sky could just as easily become glistening ink black, as dark as a child's image of doomsday. Always intense to my eye was that sky.

Some of my first innocent memories involve riding in Little Lulu, our dark blue Chevrolet sedan. I sat in Mama's lap, Daddy at the wheel driving roads, string-straight and flat, cutting through biscuit and bronzed soil, baked for time interminable by the sun's intense rays. That soil, lashed and punished by winds and leading to the cusp of the horizon, lay straight ahead and farther. Daddy would begin a tune as he drove and we would begin to sing in probably nowhere near the right pitch, but always loudly. Somewhere along the way, Daddy would sigh and say, in his affected Irish brogue, "Ah, it is a long, sad road that has no turns."

And I would groan and say, "Oh, Daddy! Do you see any twists in this road? That's just the way you say it was back in Ireland!" Little did I realize what import that phrase would have in my life.

Even though there was a war going on somewhere, it affected my life very little. On Saturdays, when Mama, Daddy and I went to see a movie, the news reviews showed battle sites, bombs exploding in places with exotic names like Casablanca and Tripoli—places that were far away from me and Gardner, New Mexico. I continued purchasing my little stamps at school and pasting them into my little booklet, assuring myself that I was doing what I could to win a war somehow—a war that didn't seem to belong to me.

The war had caused slight changes in our lives. The grocery store manager, the barber, and some of our school teachers left and came home wearing uniforms. Daddy's brother, Kenan, came home in a navy officer's uniform and left for duty in the Atlantic. When our second grade teacher left, Tia Susana filled in for him.

One morning, Daddy sat Mama and me down at the kitchen table and explained that he, too, would be leaving. Just for a short time, he said, and when he came back he would be wearing an army officer's uniform. How was I to know how important that conversation would be in my life?

Gasoline became a precious commodity, purchased with funny-looking tokens. For that reason, Little Lulu languished most of the time in the garage behind our house. Rancho San Pablo seemed to have enough tokens. Grandfather had to deliver animals and produce, so with good planning, we managed to go everywhere we needed to go.

Mama kept a can with a filter on the stove, and every drop of grease from the kitchen went into that can for the war effort. I learned to save every little piece of soap and metal, including tinfoil from my gum wrappers. Just like a lot of kids, I piled newspapers and magazines into my little red wagon and lugged them to the community center each Saturday morning.

Sometimes, when Mama needed sugar, or the butter dish was empty, she looked cross. And once in awhile she said that she would sell her soul for a new pair of stockings.

I recall that Grandfather was often grumpy; I saw him mumbling and pacing on the patio grousing in Spanish about the fascists and communists in Spain and Mexico; he thought I couldn't understand what he was saying, but I did. That is, I had no idea what those fancy political names meant, but I understood the words for *scum* and *assassin*.

Daddy had left and come home wearing, as he promised, khaki pants and shirt and on his head he wore a cap sort of like an envelope that had a silver bar pinned on it. Then, after what seemed like just a few days, he was preparing to leave us again.

I still recall that dreadful night. Dusk was just overtaking the sky as he drove Mama and me in Little Lulu to the airport in Albuquerque. Mama sat beside him and held his hand as I sat in the back, elbows draped over the front seat, chattering away.

He drove us to a spot on the tarmac apart from the main airport building, where a single airplane waited, propellers turning, engine idling *clankity, clankity*. A door opened onto a set of metal stairs.

He got out of the car and reached into the back for his green jacket. This time, he put on a billed cap with a big gold eagle on the front. I looked up at him, so handsome, and I swear that from my diminutive point of view, a thin line of gray clouds balanced directly on his head. A tear rolled down my cheek and I wiped it away with the back of my hand. He leaned over and picked me up.

Besides Mama, Grandad Cormac and Granny Bridey, Daddy's sister Maureen was there, and Susana, Grandfather and Abuelita Clara, standing in a loose circle, all talking quietly.

The plane engine noise became louder, more insistent, and that was Daddy's cue to board. He kissed the ladies and me. Putting me down reluctantly, he made me promise to take care of Mama. He hugged Grandad, shook Grandfather Felipe's hand, hugged and kissed Mama again and again, and finally picked up his bag, resolutely walking into the gaping, dark doorway of the plane.

Just like that, the door closed and snapped shut, the plane flew away, and Daddy was gone into the evening sky. Tall as the bottom edge of that New Mexico sky, my Daddy was, and now he was forever gone from my life.

***

That's it, I thought. I must not have said goodbye properly. What should I have done differently? I pondered, knowing that I had thought through every possibility I could imagine. The purser's innocent remark made me realize how wrong I was.

The ship began to move away from the pier. That was our cue to throw the bright streamers over, peppering those people waving to us from the pier.

That was also my cue to weep. Quietly, but desperately, I wept, I couldn't help it.

The officer returned.

He led us into the maze of light gray halls and ushered us into our cabin. A heavy chrome handle on a very heavy door opened to reveal bunks against one wall, dressed in tightly turned sheets, dazzling white—whiter even than my saddle shoes.

The officer left us and we busied ourselves counting suitcases and filling drawers with underwear and clothes. Folded away in a small closet, we found blankets, some deep gray, some army khaki in color, a small reminder that this ship had, until recently, plied these waters carrying troops and war supplies. We had our own sink in our room and found that we would share a bathroom with two other passengers.

Suddenly we heard what sounded like xylophone music, like this—*BING BONG BING!* We opened our door to see a man dressed in starched, white pants and a short jacket playing those notes on a small metal instrument he carried, perhaps a little bigger than a cereal box. *BING BONG BING!*

"Lunch will be served in fifteen minutes!" the white-pants-and-jacket-man declared as he marched on. *BING, BONG BING!*

"Lunch, Marisol!" Mama cried. "Let's go see what it is all about!"

"I can't Mama," I said, and I meant it. My heart was sad and my stomach was boiling. So with reluctance, she left me to unpack as she ventured forth to discover lunch.

Now I can appreciate how much she needed me, but I just couldn't go with her. Mindlessly, I unpacked more clothes. Pajamas, and sweaters and socks put away, I came upon the doll our Navajo friend Naasha made for me. I began to cry again, gathering one of those khaki blankets and pulling it around me. I hugged my doll and thought about home.

***

Just about every week, Naasha visited our house, carrying a large basket filled with fry bread, blue corn pudding, and rabbit, freshly stewed with juniper berries. She and Mama had laughed and gossiped together for years. Shorter than Mama, she was shaped rather like an eggplant enshrouded in her full pleated skirt and blouse and wrapped in her traditional woven shawl. She wore a heavy silver necklace and a woolen scarf that covered most of her dark hair, framing her face and accenting the creases in the center of her forehead. The arrow-like lines at the outer edges of her eyes indicated to me that shy laughter was part of her persona bespeaking her opinion that her life was generally quite worthwhile.

Her hands were strangely large in proportion to her body, and they were callused. She often sat on Mama's white metal step-stool and stretched out her legs, emitting a tired, but happy, sigh. Sometimes I sat on the floor near Mama's chair while Naasha and Mama talked, and from there I could see Naasha's soft rubbed-leather shoes, well-creased and stained from wear.

She called me *Ma'ii,* little fox, ever since I was a toddler, because of the color of my hair and the way I skipped and tumbled over my feet. Actually there was another word that went along with Ma'ii, but I couldn't say that word and finally Naasha laughingly settled for Ma'ii. For my fifth birthday, she presented me with my small stuffed doll. Wispy brown pigtails radiated from a wheat-colored buckram head. Onto the face, she had embroidered two huge brown eyes with eyebrows that occupied the middle of her forehead. That was it—the doll had no mouth. Her arms jutted out of a cocoa-colored leather dress, and her feet were wrapped in scraps of brown rough-woven fabric. Created just for me, to this day that doll is my loved and loyal companion. At some time, Daddy had attached his worn rabbit's foot to her arm, and I rubbed that foot often for good luck.

Naasha loved to tell us stories about her family and her ancient ancestors. I sat entranced while she told us how her people had struggled, walking their way from someplace far away through four worlds, finally crawling from a hole in the earth into what they called the Glittering World, the White World.

She told us about Coyote, who came into this world right along with First Woman and First Man, and how, in a fit of anger, he shook a blanket and had caused the stars to be scattered across the sky. She told us of Spider Woman and how she taught her people to weave.

One day when she joined us for a ride, she pointed out the shiny obsidian lava flows just outside of Grants. Now solidified glass, their black edges could cut, and they shone sharp and cruel. They were really the blood of the Evil One, she said, changed to glass when he was destroyed by the protectors of this world. The hair on my arms tingled and I hoped I would never have to encounter that Evil One or be cut by that dark glass.

As she talked, I watched her face and I never doubted she was telling me the very truth as she knew it.

She would arrive at our house at the end of her day, and it was a good thing because she often stayed into the evening. She usually left on foot to catch the bus home, but sometimes it became so late that Daddy or Mama or all of us would pile into Little Lulu and drive her to her home on the reservation.

Sometimes, as we drove her home, we saw a coyote or two slinking through the dry grasses, hunting prey for dinner. Always, if one approached us on the road, she made us pull over and look away from the animal. "Don' look at coyotes. We wait. If it go across an' we there, bad luck. Bad luck."

On nights when the moon was nearly full and covered with wispy, translucent threads of cloud, Naasha said, "Moon fuzzy tonight."

She'd sketch her finger back and forth across the sky. "Fuzzy 'cause see, Coyote hung his coat on it."

Once, we spied one coyote intently chewing on the cadaver of a small hare, shaking it from side to side. Another coyote sat in silhouette, resting, not interested in us at all. "He busy now, his fur make cloud on the moon. He wait to take his fur back from moon," she said. "We don' bother him, 'cuz he still have looong time to wait for his fur I think, an' not so good for you an' me to look at moon for long time."

Near the coyote chewing on the cadaver hopped a lively, sleek black bird. "That just *gaagii*—boy raven," Naasha remarked.

For the most part, we obeyed her about the moon. But once, I stole a quick peek at the swath of stars beginning their nightly light show. And then it happened.

I spied a star as it fell away from its companions, and took an arching path toward earth. Behind it came a few more stars, arching as if they were swallows headed to water. They continued their flight, slowing as they approached the coyotes. Seemingly on cue, the coyotes looked up and those stars just dropped from the sky and into their eyes, where they sparkled for a tiny instant, before melting into golden liquid. By the time the sentinel coyote turned to look my way, his eyes had solidified to amber glass. Startled, I looked away, and gasped, "There, did you see that?"

Naasha, Mama, and Daddy looked my way. They had been busy conversing, talking about something else entirely.

"Did you see the coyotes' eyes light up?" I asked.

The adults had no time for my silly chatter. They kept on talking. My eyes remained on the sky, and I spotted another star that came nowhere near the coyote. Instead it veered into the horizon, etching an arabesque line across the sky until it finally burned out.

At that moment Naasha looked my way and nodded, as if to say to me that that kind of thing was as natural to her as boiling water.

I remembered our trips into the desert scrubland when she wanted me to see things she thought would be important for me to know—things she felt would help me endure the pain of my loss and make me strong enough for Mama's plan for our future.

"You know, *Ma'ii,* you gotta work to forgive your Mama," I remember her saying. "She need you so much to stick to her, to help her go on. And you, too. You gotta go on. You know, our men come back from the war to us on the reservation too, hurt. Hurt inside and outside bad. They need medicine bad, they say they gotta find way and get better. And kids, too. If you a girl in my village, shaman put you out by yourself 'till you see the way. Not good kicking feet and sticking out lip. No good, *Ma'ii.* No good, Little One."

I listened, and I knew she was right.

***

The rhythm of the ship ceased being my enemy, at least at that moment. I was drowsy as I thought about Naasha's farewell gift to us. She had lovingly woven a small rug for us and the main motif was a coyote that she declared would protect us and give us luck. Mama beamed happily as she accepted it, but as we packed it, she told me, "Consider this thing yours. I don't care if I ever see it again." So the pelt became mine.

I heard Mama return after lunch. She slipped off her shoes and quietly crawled into the lower bunk. The warmth of the blanket and the doll in my arms had lured me into a happy sleep.

"Mama?" I mumbled.

"Hmm?" she replied.

"I'm sorry I couldn't make it to lunch," I whimpered.

"It's all right, little girl, it's all right. We'll talk later."

We both dozed toward a well-deserved nap.

THE TERROR OF WAR

When I awoke Mama requested tea and toast and they seemed to settle my tummy. She sat me on her bunk, still wrapped in my blanket, and related to me her experience having lunch,

"Honey girl, I miss all those people we just left, too. I miss them so much I could cry. But I can't. I have to remember that if we stayed there, their overbearing love would make me dry up inside. I was already feeling helpless. Sometimes I wanted to go in the bathroom, close the door and scream. I know that your Daddy understands and approves of what we are doing. And I say this now and I will say it over and over—I can't do this without you. We are a team, you and I."

"I do feel better, Mama," I said.

"So you think you can make it to dinner?" Mama sat cross-legged on the bunk. She grasped my shoulders. "Oh, Marisol, you will be amazed with the dining room. I've never imagined anything like it in my life. It is like the dining car in our train to Seattle, but better four times over. The waiters and the tables—and the food! Oh, Marisol, please try to enjoy it with me, because I am really happy about our trip so far."

To see her so animated made me smile. At that moment nothing could have prevented me from accompanying her to dinner.

"We sit at a table with some of the most fascinating people I have ever met! There is this family who just returned from Italy!" She reached over, covering my hand with hers and squeezing. "That means that they lived there throughout the war, and if the Germans had known they were Americans, well, they would probably be dead by now. Can you imagine? I don't know if they just got caught in Italy, or if they were spies—but we don't dare ask them about what they did because the father just might have been part of the underground. But I have to say, they are, they are—exotic!

She continued sharing her excitement. "Oh yes, there is another person. He is a surgeon and he wants to start a practice in Juneau, so he can fly out to people needing help in what he calls *the bush.*"

We laughed. To us *the bush* was a scrawny thing that struggles to subsist in the desert.

"He is handsome and has a moustache, and he is interesting, but—he is boring compared to the Neroli family. Especially Mrs. Neroli."

Mama's hands shot out at her sides and she worked them as if she were dancing. "Her face is stunning and she sits stick straight, and her hair—oh, Marisol, she is glamorous, and seductive!" Mama drew her hand slowly under her chin, and then made her fingers dance as she described her.

So we prepared for dinner. Even though I had been well-scrubbed early that morning, I got what Mama always called a *spit bath* in the sink. Face washed until my cheeks were rosy, hands and feet scrubbed, Mama held me at arm's length and seemed pleased at what she had created. She slipped into her high-heeled shoes and we headed, careening slightly along a path that Mama seemed to have already memorized, toward the dining room.

My eyes opened wide at what I saw. Crisp white tablecloths greeted us, white napkins stood at attention at our places, just to the left of our plates. Waiters were poised against the walls, smiling and awaiting our arrival, to appear in an instant as we approached our chairs to sit down.

I had first encountered the word *menu,* and all it entailed on the train that brought us to Seattle. That meant dinner menus with words written in letters embellished with fancy curls and swirls. I had negotiated that minefield of new foods and considered myself a sophisticate by now. But the ship's menu came to me in an imposing leather folder almost as big as I was, and it was freshy printed each day, with words like minestrone, bisque, eggplant, lamb cutlets, boullion, and soufflés, written like this—Blancmange avec Sauce de Framboise. I was dizzy with choices.

Mama sat to my right at each meal and the doctor sat to my left. He charmed me, talking to me as if I were a real person. He explained his dream to me, to buy a plane so he can serve people living in rural places all over Alaska. I liked everything about him, his slim face, and a shock of dark blond hair often escaping the confines of its proper place. I even thought he looked dashing with his mustache. He wore silver-rimmed glasses which he often cleaned on his napkin. When he wanted to look at me or Mama directly, he would always remove them completely. Every evening from then on, dressed in fresh, starched shirt and jacket, he would ask me, "Now Sugar, just what did you do today to make the world go around?" And I would blush.

We would see him on deck in clothes that seemed somehow soft and comfortable. That was an apt description of him. Comfortable. As he walked, his hands in his jacket's deep pockets, he often whistled a breathy, quiet tune.

My description of our other tablemates tracked with Mama's description, with certain glaring differences. I found Mr. Neroli to be jovial and handsome, but reserved. I found his son, Silvio, to be startlingly good looking, with an impish look which implied that he might be clever and capable of mischief. Two years older and taller than I, he had his father's dark brown hair and his mother's jet-black eyes. I immediately wanted to know him better and fate had dealt me a good card, since we were the only children aboard. Yearnings for my New Mexico pals began to fade.

While Mr. Neroli and Silvio spoke English, Mrs. Neroli did not. They would translate for her and she would smile or frown appropriately. I felt that she had no real desire to communicate in English, though I suspected she understood more than she revealed. *Bicketa dobickita badila picola* is what their words sounded like. She was, as Mama described, exotic.

Her skin was without flaw, with only a light covering of makeup and a hint of rouge. Her teeth gleamed within the confines of her deep red lipstick when she smiled, her earrings danced as she moved her head, and her long, deep red fingernails gestured or tapped the table more often than I liked. I was fascinated by a delicate cameo ring, carved to resemble a tiny rose blossom nestled in gold braid, on her pinky finger.

It is true, she dazzled us all and I decided I would reserve my judgment of her until a later date.

Mr. Neroli was born in Boston and he had worked as an engineer in Italy with his family during the entire war. Without any questions from us, he told us that they had lived on a large farm north of Rome that belonged to Mrs. Neroli's family for a century or so, and Silvio had attended the Catholic school in the village. We all knew there must be stories to tell, about Nazis and Fascists walking the streets of their town, but we were gracious. We demurred from any interrogation.

I set out to become Silvio's pal as soon as possible. First of all, I just plain wanted to, and secondly curiosity concerning his life in Italy was devouring me. I asked him if he liked to play gin rummy; he did, and we made plans for the next day.

I thought he was a little bit amazing. For one thing, he was quick and clever, even though I could beat him in gin rummy. So he taught me another card game he knew, and the truth is, I could beat him at that too, sometimes.

I discovered that he was born in Boston, too. But for as long as he could remember, he had spoken with his parents in Italian. During their entire life in Montepavone, his parents had warned him of the danger of ever speaking English in Italy or talking about living in the U.S. He had arrived when he was four, so he witnessed from a child's point of view, the rise of Mussolini. He saw children not much older than he was marching about with rifles, dressed in black shirts and tormenting the people in their village. He saw the arrival of German troops and knew too well the location of mass graves not very far away.

These things he readily told me, after swearing me to complete secrecy, something I was delighted to comply with. That made me important to him. I somehow felt I was circumventing his mother, and that already pleased me.

He tentatively mentioned he had an extensive set of miniature Italian cars and trucks, thinking, perhaps, that I would think he was too young to play with such things. Not me. I encouraged him, and, over the next days we set up and tore down our world using those miniatures in the ship library. Worn volumes and playing cards became archways and walls, rolled magazines became tunnels, napkins made caves. Chair cushions piled one upon another became mountains with twisty roads. We filled our world with super-heroes and roaring creatures. Soon it became easy to talk as we zipped around in our miniature world. Whenever we found ourselves revealing too much of ourselves, or become angry about something, we could just dive off a cushion cliff or crash into a wall.

One morning, as Silvio and I were constructing our town, I took a deep breath and disobeyed Mama's request. "Silvio," I said quietly, seemingly concentrating on balancing playing cards on a shaky playing card wall.

"Hmmm?"

"In all the years you lived in Italy—were you ever really afraid that you were going to die?"

"Oh yeah," he said. "Lots of times. I knew all the kids in Montepavone. They were my buddies. Sure, we fought sometimes, but I knew they would never betray me. Besides they were afraid, too. Nothing seemed to make a lot of sense to us, and we were always scared. And hungry."

He sat back against a currently cushionless upholstered chair, his arms around one leg, the other splayed out in front of him. "You know, nobody talks about the orphaned little kids that suffered so much. People talk about the bombs and the shooting, and the fear that some night a German truck would drive up to your door and take you away. People talk about how we were hungry all the time—"

"Really hungry?"

"Oh, yeah. We lived with my Nonna on a little family farm. We were lucky. We had olive trees and an apple tree and a few animals, so we could get along, sort of. But we hadn't eaten sugar for a long time, and at the end we ate olives and goat cheese and a lot of polenta. An egg once in awhile. We traded and shared with our neighbors and tried to get by. And we really guarded our beehive, believe me…but today nobody talks about the starving orphan children. Just thinking about them makes me feel guilty."

"Why would you feel guilty?" I asked. "You were hungry too."

"Oh, I dunno. Maybe it's because I couldn't do anything for them. Maybe that's what war does to people, makes everybody feel like dirt."

He had more to say: "Anyway, those children were everywhere and what gets me is they could just as well have been me. They were all little, about five or so, and they were all ragged and dirty, and always hungry. They all had big jutting stomachs and bony tiny legs, and I swear I will never forget their huge sunken eyes. It seemed as if nothing was alive behind those eyes."

By now he wasn't looking my way; he was seeing those children, and I didn't dare break the spell. "My Nonna would shake her head and call them *povere piccole vitteme,* poor little victims."

"How come they didn't have homes?" I asked.

"I guess their parents had been killed, or their family just left them. I don't know." Silvio shrugged his shoulders. "They never talked. Little pitiful ghosts, separated from anybody who cared about them. There was one who came around the farm. Sometimes we would see him sitting under a tree or in a field, and I would always run to the house to find something for him. But sometimes there just wasn't anything to give him. Some dried apple slices maybe. We called him Pietro, but we never really knew his name, and he never would come near the house. If we tried to approach him, he would run away, kind of like a wounded dog.

"Except this one time. Early one morning Nonna went to the barn to feed our goats and she was shocked to find Pietro in the pen with the goats. He was probably trying to stay warm with them, but he was as surprised as Nonna and he jumped from the pen. He must have felt trapped, afraid she would hurt him, or tell on him, because he sat facing her at the edge of a big pile of hay and tried to dig his way beneath the hay with his heels while he stared at Nonna. Anyway, she began to cry and ran into the house. She swore she saw him trying to disappear into the hay. She wouldn't go back out without me, so we wrapped up some bread and cheese and returned to the barn. But he was gone. We looked all over, but all there was to see were deep divets in the dirt where his heels had scratched the soil, and an indentation in the hay pile in exactly the shape of that little boy."

I frowned. "Are you trying to fool me, Silvio?" I asked.

"No, I'm not, honest.

"And so what happened?" I said.

"That's it. I don't know what really happened, Marisol. All I know is that Nonna refused to go back into the barn for weeks. And we never saw Pietro again."

I rubbed my arms, wishing the goose bumps away.

BUBBLEGUM, POOKAS, AND A WHISTLE

Now, as we began to function according to the pitch and yaw of the ship, we learned a bit more about our surroundings, and memorized our way to and from our cabin. We stumbled and staggered at first, from one side of those gray metal corridors to the other. I was still intimidated. Doors were so heavy, I could barely open them. And nearly every threshold was as high as the middle of my lower leg. It seemed that everywhere signs were posted warning us of instant death if we didn't obey their demands. *WARNING! 440 VOLTS! DO NOT ENTER! PREVENT FIRE!* All were accompanied by sharp arrows or symbols of jagged lightning bolts.

On the day we departed, Mama and I had seen those praying mantis arms pick up two Packard automobiles and gingerly place them on the front deck. Now, as we explored the deck, we encountered them again, covered with canvas and secured with cables and ropes. We laughed as we wondered what their future would be in Alaska.

Skies were clear, though we fought wind constantly. The *whoosh* sound of waves breaking as we plowed northward through dark and cold seas, became our intimate companion, as well as the groan of wind as it whirled about, testing and embracing each item on the deck, including us.

Each night, the muffled rhythm of the ship's engine joined the other sounds. They became a sort of lullaby.

The ship passed massive tall trees crowding the shore, climbing the cliffs, scrambling up until they reached hardscrabble soil, their feet buried in well-worn spring snow. One afternoon, a passenger shared his binoculars so we could see a mother and baby bear scurry up a snowy cliff face. That image alone, impossible for us to imagine before, was adequate for us to wonder about our future.

Mama and I began sharing our experiences on the ship. She, too, had decided that the library was a cozy place to relax. We wondered what my grandparents would think of seeing these chilly shores. She had come to agree with me about Dr. Evert; she, too, now appreciated his soft and charming characteristics.

"He reminds me of Bing Crosby, Mama," I said, and sang, "Night and day, ba ba ba buum..."

She laughed, as I knew she would. I could always make her laugh if I sang a song in a silly way.

We still disagreed about Mrs. Neroli. She still found her to be vivacious and electric; I said she reminded me of the slinky seductresses in the Charlie Chan movies. "I don't think she approves of me, Mama. How can somebody not like a kid as cute as me?" I was clowning again, but fleeting thoughts of Doña Inéz entered my mind.

"I think you must be imagining it," she replied, laughing softly and roughing her fingers through my hair.

"You just wait and see, Mama. To me, trying to figure her out is like playing catch with a sunbeam."

Mama laughed again and changed the subject.

That night's dinner conversation surprised us all. We were beginning to feel at home with one another. Perhaps that was the reason it happened, but we will never know. Gradually on this evening, Mr. Neroli had become downright garrulous and the rest of us did nothing to stop his chatter, except Mrs. Neroli, whose tapping fingernails expressed disapproval.

Mama, Dr. Evert and I sat slightly slack-jawed as Silvio's father began to tell us a story about Silvio and the bubblegum.

A major question, still unresolved, was how in the war torn world he had come upon it, but the fact is, he did, in a tiny corner store in Florence. He then spent hours teaching himself how to create the biggest bubble, the loudest bubble, the quickest bubble—all the skills any kid needed to have.

That night, they were celebrating an uncle's birthday with friends in the village bar on the *piazza*. No one went out at all anymore, he explained, and a glass of wine together would be a huge treat. They had just sipped their first taste of wine when a number of German officers came in, sitting down near them. Everyone there became tense and fearful; by now the war was not going well at all for the Germans, and they were more testy than usual. If Mr. Neroli's group could have become invisible, Mr. Neroli said, they would have. "You just didn't know what would set them off."

We were silent, our attention riveted on him.

"Everyone knew the Allies would invade," he said He took a sip of wine, looked at Mrs. Neroli, and laughed sardonically. "The only thing we didn't know was when and where." Mrs. Neroli smiled quietly. Silvio looked toward me, put his fork on his plate, his hands in his lap and looked down.

"So we tried," his father continued, "to continue with our little celebration, when someone at our table, seized in mute surprise, shook a pointed finger at Silvio and began to laugh. Silvio had blown a huge bubble that softly popped and spread all over his cheeks and mouth!

"Everyone in the restaurant looked toward him," he chortled, "and I was frankly terrified," he continued. "So terrified, I couldn't speak. It was as if time just froze for a few seconds."

He looked at the three of us, and then at Silvio, whose eyes continued to search his lap. "Finally I sneaked a look over at the Germans. They were Gestapo, and for a moment even they didn't know what to think."

He was clearly enjoying telling his story; he had everyone's eye. "They were looking at us. Oh, how I wished I could have stuffed my son into my pocket!" he exclaimed. "Everyone froze. No one could find words," he continued. "Can you imagine an Italian not being able to find words?" Everybody but me laughed. As usual I didn't get it. Mr. Neroli continued,

"Then the wife of my colleague broke the spell. 'Oh, please,' she said, 'Silvio, my child, may I blow a bubble?'"

Silvio looked at his father as he tried to imitate the lady's voice.

"And what she did, she made the terror go away! Silvio dipped his gum into my wine and passed it ever so delicately to our friend." He gestured with his fingers how he held the wad of gum in order to blow a bubble. "She blew a fine bubble. And then she dipped the gum into her wine, and passed it to her husband, who in turn chewed, and so on, and so on, until we all had become giggling bubble blowing experts."

He had us all at the table laughing, too.

"And as they chewed, I asked our waiter for the check and pulled out my money. Then I saw in front of me this expanse of gray wool trousers and I looked up directly into the face of the German Gestapo major."

He certainly had our attention. We hoped the outcome would be good, but at that moment we began to doubt.

"The major stood ram-rod straight in front of me and asked, 'May we please have the opportunity to have a try at the bubbles?' I nearly fainted," he said. "But who would ever dream of denying his request?"

We laughed. Mr. Neroli continued: "I asked the waiter for a small glass of schnapps, and I put the gum in and gave it to the major. Then, as they began to chew and make their bubbles, I paid our bill and we got out of there!"

We all loved the story, and Silvio finally looked up, his face a rosy picture of chagrin.

Unfortunately, there were no more stories, that night or ever. The next morning, Silvio beat me soundly at ping-pong. Then, we each got ourselves a Pepsi and sat on deck chairs outside.

"Hey," he said, "tell me about your family."

"Oh," I remarked, "my life isn't nearly so exciting as yours. I mean, I have a great family and all, but it doesn't compare to yours."

"So tell me anyway," he said. We took our Pepsis into the library and plopped onto the soft couch.

"Okay. My parents have always meant everything to me. You know Mama. I don't ever remember when she didn't smell like Ivory soap and apple blossoms. I remember her standing next to Daddy and her head came just to his shoulder.

"Daddy was like a lanky tower. His trousers were always cinched into place by a leather belt and he had dark red, curly hair. His gold-rimmed glasses often sat on his straight nose. Let's see, what else. He liked to putter in his work shed and one day I remember he made me a pair of funny spectacles out of bottle glass and wire."

I quit talking, thinking that was enough to divulge at one time.

"So tell me more about him," Silvio said.

"Okay." I paused. "This isn't so easy for me to do."

Silvio propped his feet on the coffee table. I took a breath and continued. "Every night he told me stories his mother, my Granny Bridey had told him when he was a boy. Irish stories of faeries and little people and wicked banshees and the pooka…"

"Pookas?" he asked.

"Yeah. They change their shape and carry the children away into the deep, deep bogs. His people came to New Mexico from Donegal, Ireland years ago, and they have lived in Gardner for a lot of years."

"And what did your dad do in Gardner?"

"He worked with his father, Cormac Downey. Grandad Cormac started his own insurance agency a lot of years back, and I guess he was pretty good at it because he has tons of friends and they all respect him. *Cormac Downey and Sons Insurance* the sign said. Daddy, Kenan, and his sister, Maureen, grew up in Gardner and, when Daddy finished college, he came back to work with Grandad in the agency.

"Aunt Maureen is the baby, and I think she is quiet and beautiful. Kenan is Daddy's older brother and they were best friends. He is shorter than Daddy was, but he reminds me of Daddy a lot and I like him."

I looked over at Silvio. "Are you sure you want to hear more right now?" I asked.

"Sure. Unless you don't want to talk anymore," he said. Just then someone came in pushing a vacuum cleaner and the sound drove us out onto the deck for a few minutes. We stood, leaning absently on the wood railing.

"So?" Silvio said.

"Okay, right after he came back, Daddy met Mama, and they were married in a traditional New Mexican wedding. I look at the photos a lot and, even though they are in black and white, I don't have any trouble imagining the bright colors there. And Abuelita Clara's tamales and *puerco adobado*, and dancing. Lots of dancing. The family still laughs about Daddy and Kenan playing fiddles as the mariachis played their *corridas.*"

"You should see an Italian wedding," Silvio said. "The invitation is engraved on really heavy parchment or something, and the bride always wears a long lace veil. And the mass is long, oh my gosh. But I have to say it is pretty, and then the party afterwards lasts forever, with lots of wine and so many kinds of olives, and cheese, and ravioli, and cannoli…"

"What is ravioli?"

"Oh, Marisol. there are so many kinds of ravioli I can't tell you all of them because I haven't eaten them all! They are little pockets stuffed with chicken, or cheese, or mushrooms, and they are all delicious. *Molto buono,* we say. But right now, let's go on about your family."

"Okay then. Are you sure?"

"Yeah, go on."

"Okay. We lived close to the agency and I spent a lot of time there while Mama worked as part-time office manager. In summer, I often sat and drew pictures in a certain chair near Mama's desk. My feet were always swinging, and I think I left permanent gouges on the rung of that chair. Once I sat there with a wet bathing suit and I can still hear Mama fussing at me that the stain would never come out of the cushion."

"Did he like to do anything but make bottle-glass glasses?"

"Oh my gosh, yes. I told you he loved music, especially Irish music. He played the Irish whistle as well as the fiddle. After dinner in Granny Bridey's house, the men cleaned up the kitchen and I loved to sit at the kitchen table and listen to them sing Irish laments and rowdy bar songs. Sometimes Mama and Maureen would sneak in and we all would sing with them, 'I had a dreeeam deeear, you had one too.' Sometimes they sang about a ship captain who…"

"Holy cow, Marisol, look at that!" Directly below us in the frothy water there were two, no six, no ten happy orcas putting on a show, arching and diving, sometimes nuzzling one another. We watched, fascinated for minutes, until they finally became tired of us and shot off together to another location known only to them.

IN THE BELLY OF THE WHALE

Our ping pong battles were becoming ferocious and we were gaining onlookers each morning. Silvio was getting to be a better player, but I could still beat him because sometimes his serve was mushy. Besides, he now had an excuse. He had the sniffles.

One morning after our workout, we sat in deck chairs catching our breath. He had lost that day, so we sat while he made a tiny ceremony out of blowing his nose. It was on that morning, I think, that I realized I was feeling terrific and having a good time on board the. *S.S. Denali.*

"So, Marisol," Silvio began, "how did you get your name?"

"Oh, well when I was born, my parents knew that both grandmothers wanted *Mary* in my name somewhere, and everything Irish they could think of was too long. Now my actual name is Spanish—Maria Soledad, which isn't exactly short, but the nickname, Marisol seemed to fit me. So that was it, and I love my name, especially the Sol part, because the sun has always been a part of my life. That is a given in New Mexico."

"How come your mother lived in New Mexico?"

"Oh my gosh, Silvio. New Mexico soil is in her veins. Grandfather Felipe's ranch has been in his family since the 1600s. He is related to the Vasquez Alvarado family and once in awhile he pretends that he is somebody important, but nobody pays any attention to him. Sometimes he stomps and rants, but the truth is he is as softhearted as a dumpling. During the war, he vouched for the families of the Japanese who worked on his ranch and they were never shipped off to a camp. He and Abuelita Clara have two girls, Mama and Susana, and they expect them to do something with their lives. Grandfather never treated them like boys, but those two girls know how to help with the ranch animals and how to compete at everything. But they're best friends. I just love my Tia Susana."

"Your grammas must have been sad when you left. My Nonna cried so much. She was afraid she would never see us again. That's kinda true, isn't it? Hey, you want to play a quick game of rummy?"

"Naw. Anyway, I know Grandfather's heart was broken when we left, and Grandad Cormac's too. At first they thought Mama was crazy when she wanted to buy a house in Alaska. But Tia and Aunt Maureen stood strong with her with the information about Seward. They pointed to the papers, saying, "Just look at the price for this house! And people need places to live!" And Mama was determined to do it, no matter what they said or did. I think they both shake their heads in secret once in awhile, but they have come around, though, and they support Mama and what she hopes to do. You should have seen us when we left. What a couple of vagabonds. Even though we sold everything we could, and stored more in Granny Clara's cellar, we still had so much stuff that Grandfather Felipe had to drive us to Denver to catch the Seattle train in his farm truck."

"By the way, last night at dinner, when your mother whispered something into your dad's ear, did she say, 'My love, you have eggplant in your tooth?'"

"How did you know that?" Silvio gave me a querulous look.

Grandfather Felipe doesn't think I understand him when he growls and grouses in Spanish," I said. "But I do, and the words your mother used sounded so familiar."

"Smart girl, I'm impressed. Hey, come on, let's get out of the wind and play a couple games of rummy before I have to be back in our cabin."

As we headed toward the library, Silvio suddenly stopped. He grinned and looked around, finally saying, "How brave are you? Let's go check out some more of the ship we haven't seen."

"How do we do that?" I asked.

I swear I saw the gears turning in his head. I protested, but not very hard. So that's what we did, poking around, peeking under covers and opening doors, doing things I would never have done without him. We began back toward the promenade deck, dodging crewmen who were busily sweeping, washing, polishing, and painting. As we walked on, pretending that we belonged where we were, we encountered wires, and even more ropes as thick as my body, serpent-curled and ready for action. Just above our heads hung canvas-covered lifeboats, suspended from ropes that allowed for very little slack as they swung from side to side. We lingered patiently in that area while workers finished chores and moved on. When they were gone, Silvio held me up so I could peek into a lifeboat. Grit and droplets of water cascaded down on me as I shouted down to him, "A bunch of life jackets—oars, yeah, tied to the sides—canteens, jugs—a couple of yellow life rings."

Silvio let me down. "No dead bodies or rats, huh?"

I shuddered, glad I didn't meet a rat and hoping we wouldn't have to use those things in the lifeboat. I knew that the waters ahead could be mean and treacherous, already serving as marine graveyards for rusty hulks and skeletons of more than one hapless ship.

At the very top of the ship, we investigated the black, monstrous tube, an oversized tuba really. Its steady, mournful moan had signaled our departure from Seattle, and its sound would be our companion for many days and nights to come.

Somehow Silvio had forgotten his cold, for the moment, at least. He pushed on a door not far from the horn. With effort, it opened, so he signaled for me to follow him. This is where, if it hadn't been for Silvio, I would not have had the courage to invade an inch further. Inside, a constant moan pervaded my body and it became more profound as we descended, the monotony broken by an occasional *clank!* or the sound of metal gears chattering against one another, a grinding noise that became deeper as we descended. But on we went, down tight staircases, through small doors, ducking ledges, past walls with those terrifying warnings, until we came face-to-face with a crewman. Husky and bearded, a toothpick in his mouth, he was dressed in well-worn denim, not the sharp, white uniforms we were accustomed to seeing. He was as surprised to see us as we were to see him. His furry face revealed in quick succession, surprise, bewilderment, anger. Then at last he grinned. "Gor, what the hell is this?" He growled. "Aw, I remember I was a kid once! But you two have no business down here with all this dangerous stuff. So you just be heading back to where you belong."

We were mute. He turned us around, with no resistance from us, and marched behind us through more corridors and stairs and finally through a door, where he bid us farewell, saying, "So, you find your own way from here. If I never see you again, I promise I won't tell my chief that I found two scared little rats scurrying about down in the hold."

He waved to us; a stub was where his middle finger had been. He closed the door very firmly and we did as we were told. We found the library, got ourselves a Pepsi and spoke about our adventure in excited whispers.

"That's exciting enough for me," I said.

"Nah," Silvio said. "But it's enough for this morning." He checked his watch. "Oops, I have to run. My mom doesn't want me to get any sicker, and she wants me to spend time reading Italian each day. She's afraid I'll forget how. See you later."

I went to our cabin to find Mama. She and I took a walk, and I said nothing as we passed doors I had recently entered. Today was Memorial Day and all the passenger areas were dressed in red, white and blue, which brought about thoughts of the war. We weren't very good company for Dr. Evert, who had come upon us and joined us.

Mama and I had begun to think about Daddy and she said she was beginning to have a sore throat. She decided to skip lunch. The truth is that she did have a sore throat, but I knew she had other things on her mind, too.

"Well then, come along, Sugar," Dr. Evert said to me. "You will be my dining partner for lunch." He grabbed my elbow and off we went. He knew I wouldn't refuse his invitation, and lunch turned out to be just fine. Mrs. Neroli actually smiled at me, and I smiled back at her.

But eventually I returned to our cabin, lay on my bunk and I, too, thought about Daddy. I had endured many of the steps that are part of grief, but I found myself still deal-making with God.

***

There had been a time when I thought I would never feel anything… that I was an empty shell. That was how I felt when, just a week before Easter 1944, two soldiers came to our door with a large box that Mama called a footlocker. It was a dusty-green color, with white letters on it that said, **1/Lt. Liam J. Downey 018775**. They carried it into the living room and, when Mama invited them, they took off their caps and sat stiffly on the couch. They called Mama *ma'am* and said they were sorry a lot of times.

When they left, Mama opened the footlocker. Inside was a box labeled **War Department** and inside that box was a letter from Daddy's commanding officer lamenting Daddy's death. Below that box, she found Daddy's clothes; undershirts, pants and trousers, all folded with more care than anything I had ever seen before. Among them were two pairs of khaki wool trousers and two long-sleeved wool shirts.

Neatly placed inside one of the trouser legs was a package wrapped in woolen flannel. Within the folds of cloth rested a shiny pistol with a brown handle, and on the handle was stamped Luger P 08. Its starkness seemed to radiate a peculiar beauty and the thrill of danger at the same time. Mama hesitated and finally picked it up, gingerly turning it over in her hands. She looked at me and I'm sure my expression mirrored hers. We quietly replaced it in its own secluded woolen lair, far from our sight and thought.

Continuing, Mama lifted out small items that belonged to Daddy: his jet bead-and-silver rosary, his Zippo cigarette lighter, his Army ID card, a metal dog tag, a small framed photo of Mama and me sitting on the front porch of our house, a photo of Granny Bridey, Grandad Cormac, Kenan and Maureen. And then she found wrapped in Daddy's handkerchief, his well-worn tin whistle. That was the moment I discovered that I couldn't cry. I understood that I was still sad, but it was a sadness beyond words. I felt as if I was floating in a dream, that there were no tears left, and I wondered if I would ever feel again.

Uncle Kenan seemed to understand as well as anybody. He had tried very hard to help me when he came home on leave and again when he returned from the Pacific. Once he took me hiking, where we encountered a whole bunch of baby rattlers. Mama wasn't too happy about that!

One evening, he took Mama and me to the community hall where he played in the band when he was home. But he could see that Mama was miserable, so he put his fiddle down, took us home. We never did that again.

***

It was on that afternoon on the ship, lying in my bed and thinking about Daddy, that I realized I was beginning once more to have feelings and I liked it. I was going to have to work hard, I realized, but I thought the day was coming when I could be happy again.

It was my turn to leave Mama to grieve alone. I slipped quietly into my Keds and headed to the library to see if Silvio had broken away from his mother. He had, and together we created our miniature world for the afternoon.

There came a moment when he said, "So I know how rough today is for you. I'm sorry about your dad, Marisol. I lived with death and fear every day in Montepavone, but we were so lucky the Gestapo didn't come to our door."

Silvio sat against a wall Indian style. I guessed he wanted to talk and I sure could listen.

"Funny, there was this boy in my school and he seemed to always be in competition with me, playing games, exams, in classes. That is, he thought he was in competition, I didn't. I didn't dislike him, but he sure made me nervous. He began to do everything he could to look at my examination papers, so one time I wrote in a mistake on purpose. The answer to the question was Vivaldi but I wrote down Verdi and it was such a stupid mistake it had to be clear to the, how you say, *professore,* just what was happening. The boy had this pouty look. He was really a pill: somebody I never would want for a friend. But I never could figure him out, and I knew if anybody would tell the Nazis about me, he would be the one."

Silvio pulled his other leg up and hugged them both rubbing his calves occasionally. I waited patiently until he began again. "And sure enough, the day came when the Gestapo arrived at school, but they didn't take me, they took that boy away. Not me. I was so scared. That boy, can you believe it? Turns out his father was a *partisan* and they took his father out with a bunch of other people from the village and just shot them. Just shot them. God, that was a terrible time."

"Why did they do that?"

"There just seemed to be no why then. The Germans were retreating and they destroyed people and things just to be mean. In fact, when they finally began their retreat, they came through Montepavone and killed every farm animal they encountered. The cow at the monastery; shot it. One afternoon about nine German soldiers marched up our road when just Nonna and I were home. She told me to hide in the broom closet and I could see her through the window standing in front of the house, her hands on her hips. One soldier pulled out his gun and shot our goats. Then, as they marched on, two soldiers picked up our chickens, swung them by their necks in the air, and then tossed their dead bodies on the ground, and never looked back.

He paused, gazing past me for a moment, and then he pinched his nose to dam any tears that might belie his bravery. He looked up at me and beyond me. "That scared me. Yeah, that scared me." He paused, concentrating on something unknown by me. "You know, when I left, I gave my radio to that boy at school. I mean, he was still a jerk and a pain, but I did. Why did I do that? The war was over and I didn't fear him, and I never liked him. But I just…just gave it to him."

Silvio was looking at me, but I don't think he expected an answer from me. I gave him one anyway. I even surprised myself. "Maybe," Silvio, you felt sorry for him. Or maybe you felt happy that your dad wasn't the one getting caught."

"Yeah. Or maybe I was still scared, somehow."

"Nah," I said. "I know you and you don't scare easily."

"Maybe," Silvio said, smiling at me, "maybe I knew I was on my way to someplace where there would always be plenty of food."

We both smiled and were silent for a moment. We had talked enough about that, I decided. I purposefully crashed my silver sports car into his ambulance. Our attention now on the car crash, I asked him, "By the way, Silvio. What is a *partisan*?"

He smiled at that, and said, "Mama Mia, Marisol. We'll talk about that tomorrow."

"Okay," I agreed, "but will you answer me one more question?"

"*Va bene*," he said. He tried to smile. "What is it?"

"How far away was your village from a place called Anzio?"

He took a deep breath and explained, "That's near Montecassino. And a lot of your American soldiers died there I know."

We returned to our miniature world, but our hearts weren't in it. Finally, he said softly, "I am sorry about your dad."

It was my turn to stare into space for awhile. "It's okay, I think," I said. "I told you I think I'm doing pretty well. What bothers me now is this move to Seward. How do you feel about living in Juneau?"

"I'm okay with it, really. After living in Italy, I want to try something new. It can't be so bad, I think."

"But you lived in fear for so long. I lived in a place I loved where people loved me, and I was safe every single day."

"Didn't you know about the war? How could you not know about that?"

"Sure, I did. But until it hit me in the face, it was always so far away. All the movies started with news of the war…"

"Like Palermo and Napoli," Silvio commented wryly.

"Okay, I know now that I was innocent. But I was just a kid. At recess, we always talked about it and we thought we were bound to win."

"There were times when I wasn't so sure," he said softly.

"So," I said, "what you are going to say is that I shouldn't worry about this move?"

"Hey, I don't know what the answer is for you, but I can't wait. I'm gonna learn to fish, and play football."

"My gosh, it took something really big to finally convince me to move to Alaska. I sure got enough advice about believing in Mama and leaving New Mexico and I began to think nobody was on my side.

I told you that we had a good Navajo lady friend. Well, there came a time when Granddad Cormac had a heart attack. He was always busy in the community helping the families when the husbands or brothers went off to war. What was tougher, he insured the lives of a lot of them and, when they were killed, he had to go and console the family.

"And then, when Daddy died—well, it just seemed to take his breath away. That was when I was being selfish, not supporting Mama at all. But I swear I couldn't help it.

"When Grandad was in the hospital, Mama needed to be with Granny Bridey and, as it happened, Naasha was at our house when Aunt Maureen called with the news. So Naasha said, 'I stay with *Ma'ii'* and Mama quickly accepted her offer and was gone. I thought about Grandad a lot, and I prayed for him, but I loved being the center of Naasha's life for those couple of days. We played a game with the small bones she carried in her pocket, and we ate the tamales she had brought a few hours before.

"That night, she slept near me on my bed, but not under my covers. She spread her shawl over her half and tossed the pillow onto the chair nearby. We lay there, her big brown eyes staring at me and telling me stories that alternately amazed me and made me laugh. She told me about her uncle who had an eye that turned in, and how that eye caused the rain to come in buckets for days and days."

"Not really?" Silvio queried.

"Well, you'll just have to decide what you believe. I learned not to doubt her a long time ago. She told me how Coyote and Eagle put the moon and the sun in a box because their people needed fire and light. But their curiosity made them open the box and the sun and moon saw their chance for freedom and flew away, leaving Coyote and Eagle with nothing. She talked and talked, until I fell fast asleep.

"The next morning, she packed up some fry bread and fruit and we walked a long ways out of town on the Piñon Camp road to a spot where a shallow *arroyo* touched the road. 'Gotta show you a very nice thing I see yesterday,' she said to me as we tromped along a path. We turned right onto pebbly soil, and followed the *arroyo* to a low *mesa.*"

"What's a *mesa*?" Silvio asked.

So I told him it was a flat place higher than most of the ground near it, and continued, "The dry river's path got deeper and narrower, and we followed it around, and then we climbed on up to the ledge of a higher tableland."

"There aren't a lot of trees there, right?"

"Not where we were. I mean there were some, but it is dry there. There were bunches of sparrows and crows chirping and darting in and out of the scrawny junipers and sagebrush. Anyway, Naasha gave me the quiet sign and we climbed scrabble-dry rocks and flattened ourselves on the top of the ledge."

I must have been telling a pretty good story, because Silvio was quiet as could be, staring at the pattern on the rug. "We lay on our bellies," I continued, "and let the slanty sun bake our backs. Once in awhile, we heard a dove wail while we ate apple slices very quietly, and watched.

"Then she touched my hand and pointed toward a spot below and to our right, near the base of the tableland. I looked hard, but I didn't see anything until, in a thicket of juniper I could just barely see motion, fuzzy motion. And then I let out a gasp. I could see four coyote babies sniffing, making baby growls, stumbling over each other, snapping at each other's tails!"

Now Silvio's eyes were on me.

"Naasha frowned at me and gave me the quiet signal again," I said. "Then mama coyote arrived, and the pups scrambled to get to mama's belly. Oh, Silvio, they were adorable. They turned into one ball of wiggling fur-padded paws and elbows, fighting for their fair share of chow. We watched for a long time and then, on Naasha's signal, we backed away slowly and silently on our bellies down the slope.

"'Good to see that, huh?' She asked. "So we scooted down the bank on our bottoms and found some place to eat our breakfast."

"I think your coyotes must be like our foxes," Silvio said.

"Well, maybe," I said. "But I don't think coyotes are as pretty as foxes. And they can be sneaky."

"So can our foxes."

"Well, anyway, I was telling you about the coyotes, but as we ate Naasha began to talk about another adventure. When she was just a little girl, she saw a big black sow bear and her baby walking around that same place where we saw the coyote family. She said she was terrified and knew she had to get out of there. And she knew she'd better never, never say that Navajo word for *bear*.

"I asked her why, and she made such a face. I begged her to tell me why and she finally gave in. She said that in her culture it's forbidden to say the word for *bear* because one will follow you the rest of your life and bring you sadness."

"So?" Silvio asked. "What is the word?"

I gave him a long look and then started moving my truck into a garage.

"Hey," he demanded, "what's the word?"

"I promised her I would never say it."

Silvio began to laugh, almost a belly laugh, until he saw that I was serious. Then he stopped and spoke to me seriously, "Aw, okay, okay, Marisol, please tell me the word and I promise I will not tell it to anyone."

"You have to double-dog promise."

"I double-dog promise, like you say. Here, let's shake hands on it."

He reached for my hand and we shook. A sincere shake.

"All right," I said. I got up, approached him and whispered into his ear, "*Shash.* That's the word." And I went back to where I had been sitting on the floor.

"That's the word? What's the big deal?"

"Believe me, Silvio, I have always been careful to remember that word, and never say it out loud because I don't want a bear to come after me."

He looked at me from the side of his eyes.

"I am serious, Silvio, and you better not ever say it, either, especially where we're going! You promised!"

It was getting late. We began to clean up and put away our cushion and magazine world. Silvio reached over to pick up two of the cars. He looked directly at me and said, "Shh..."

"No! Don't you dare! That's not funny!" I scowled at him.

"Okay," he laughed. "But I don't believe a bear is going to come after me."

"You just don't know, Silvio."

"All right, all right, if you say so."

He was still grinning as we walked back to our cabins. I was just a little bit hurt. I felt like saying that I didn't believe his story about Pietro. But I did.

***

As I lay on my bunk, I continued to think about those days before we left Gardner. There were two people who didn't think it was such a good idea for us to leave. One was Uncle Kenan. When he came home for Daddy's memorial service, he came over and talked to Mama for a long time. I remember hearing their voices get a little angry and I wondered what they could be arguing about. When my uncle left, he slammed the front door. I waited for Mama to mention why he was so angry, but she didn't. Then he went back to a ship in the Pacific near Midway and Okinawa and I didn't see him again until the war was over.

My other supporter was my third grade teacher. "You are taking that bright little girl to a frozen wasteland?" she remarked to Mama. Finally she sent home with me a large satchel of books, muttering that she was sure I would never see a school again.

I recalled that one night while Grandad Cormac was recuperating, I had a dream. In the dream, Naasha and I were napping and I awoke. The air was still and warm, but what would have been dust in the air were specks of something that made the air look shimmery. I began to walk toward something like a cave. On the ground just to my right, a huge, long snake slithered by, his head well past me. I took in a big breath and stood there until the snake moved slowly on. I had no idea if he was a rattler or a bull snake, but it didn't matter because he had no interest in me at all.

A man approached me. He was dressed like a shepherd and he looked down, urging his animals to walk in front of him, but instead of lambs, he pushed along the baby coyotes with his shillelagh. I bent down and the coyotes cried and licked my face, and curled up around me. He pulled out a cloth and opened it, to reveal Naasha's game bones. He urged me to pick them up and shake them, but before I could, they began to shimmer and they flew into a dark sky and became stars.

Now, when I looked back at him, he squatted down to my level and I knew instantly it was Daddy! I was profoundly happy—a happiness I can't describe. And then he spoke to me. In a voice as clear as can be, he said, "Oh, 'tis a long, sad road that never turns."

That was the moment I knew Daddy really did approve of what we were doing. I would accept Mama's plans without any more doubts.

***

Tonight was to be a special dinner, the culmination of Memorial Day events. Mama was well fortified with aspirin to fend off her sore throat and we were both scrubbed and ready to make our entrance. I wore a green and white jumper that Tia Susana had made for me. It had a tiny edge of lace around the straps of the jumper, and I wore a cotton blouse underneath. Mama looked positively radiant. I could see that the trip was wearing well on her, too; it had been a long time since I had seen her smile so much. She wore a black linen skirt, full and ankle-length, and her blouse was satin and puff-sleeved, with a mandarin collar. At her throat, she wore Abuelita Clara's garnet and pearl pin, and she looked very pretty.

We had roast beef, potatoes and peas for dinner; a meal I will never forget. During the meal, I labored to be grown-up, concentrating on cutting up my thick slab of delicious beef. In my enthusiasm, I caused a bite of meat to slide precariously close to the peas, and one single pea fell onto the bright white tablecloth next to my plate. I looked around to see if anyone had witnessed my gaffe, and then shoved the pea delicately under my plate—a perfect solution, I thought. Until, that is, when the waiter removed our plates. There it sat, now huge and glaring at me and potentially everyone at the table. I was mortified. I know my face colored, but our gallant waiter quickly whisked a napkin across my place and magically the errant pea was gone. I thought I had been saved from eternal shame, until I looked across the table and saw Mrs. Neroli looking at me. She smiled, her perfect eyebrows arched, and I swear there was a tiny, smug twitch at the corner of her mouth. She saw it all, I was sure, and I felt strangely ashamed.

Dessert arrived on platters, carried on heavy silver trays from the kitchen by the waiters and chefs, in their high, puffy chef hats. Baked Alaska was to be our treat. In the high peaky center of the snowy mountains of meringue, silver sparklers flashed and flickered. Tiny paper American flags circled the edge of the tray. We cheered. Eating it was like tasting crusty, cool fluff.

The meal complete, we continued celebrating in the ship's saloon. We sat at a table, the six of us, and the adults ordered drinks, while Silvio and I drank root beer. A trio played Hoagy Carmichael tunes.

Sometime during the evening, Dr. Evert produced a bottle of Benedictine that he declared would help all sniffles and bad throats. "One of the primary herbs in this," he explained, "is Angelica, which grows in Alaska."

"Really?" Mama asked. "That's something new to me."

"Really," Dr. Evert asserted, "the native people use it to heal wounds." He passed tiny filled glasses around, and we two children got our watered down version.

The Nerolis stood to dance and at that moment Dr. Evert held out his hand to Mama. I watched, holding my breath, not knowing what she would do. After a moment of hesitation, she took his hand. They walked toward the floor and off they went. I was so happy for her! I don't think she had danced since Daddy left us.

As for me, I watched and thought about the times when Daddy was playing at the community hall dance. He'd step from the bandstand to put me on his toes and we would twirl around the room. In those moments, I felt as if I were a princess and everyone in the world envied me.

YET ANOTHER GOODBYE

The air had a chill to it now, three days into our trip, even when the sun made its presence known. Just before we arrived in Ketchikan, the fog embraced us, which meant the peaceful day and night was broken incessantly by the deep, sad wail of that horn.

Days lengthened, light came early wrapped in fog, that accompanied us as we slipped among islands barely visible in our effort to reach the town jetty. Mama, in a heavy sweater with wool scarf around her neck, and I stood taking in the totally new sights. So far I had avoided getting her cold.

We watched, fascinated, as sea otters floated near us, diving, rolling onto their backs, cracking open some unfortunate sea creature, scraping it from its shell with their sharp teeth, and then wiping their whiskers contentedly with their paws. One in particular paddled back and forth in front of me. I swore, by the way he surveyed me and worked his mouth, he was wondering why I didn't have whiskers and what use were those ribbons that dangled from my braids. Eventually he paddled on, probably thinking, *What a silly, useless creature that is.*

Frenzied seagulls swarmed and squawked, scrounging fish guts tossed at the shoreline by fishermen cleaning their day's catch. Only when the fog chose to allow it, would we catch a glimpse of the town. Tired, teetering frame buildings clung to wooden pilings, seemingly clutching the massive spruces near shoreline just to avoid slipping away into the frigid gray waters.

Silvio and his father came to the rail beside us, and eventually Mrs. Neroli joined us. Silvio was as warmly wrapped as Mama; he blew his nose incessantly.

Stocky Aleuts, wrapped in fur parkas and wool capes lounged around the docks, watching silently and expressionless as the big ship slipped into port. Assorted sailors and soldiers, remnants of busy wartime days, lazed about the main street railings, which they shared with the boots of grinning sourdoughs. We saw only a few women that morning; they too were sweatered, some wearing scarves, as they walked along, intent on finishing their morning errands.

The ship disgorged some of its passengers and took on a few new ones, while assorted dock workers quickly removed Ketchikan's cargo and lugged aboard more crates, intended for destinations yet to be reached.

We prepared to move on; the bulkheads closing fast. Ropes were loosened and rewound, and we cast off. The horn sounded one long wail, the ship's ear-jarring monotone recessional indicating that we were again at sea, wrapped in heavy mist and northbound once more.

Tomorrow's port would be Juneau and, though no one spoke of it, we were all aware that our tablemates would leave and all our lives would adapt once more.

Mama had an idea, "Since the weather isn't cooperating, why don't we play cards? We all agreed; somehow that seemed a solution for some of our few hours left together. I ran to our cabin to collect our cards. When I arrived at the library, two square tables had been united and chairs pulled into position. Rummy was the game of choice, with two decks of cards, and even Mrs. Neroli appeared to be having a fine time. As I was already aware, she had a very discerning eye and, on two occasions, she caught us up, shouting, Rummy! But the way she pronounced it was more like, "Rroomi." We all laughed at her prowess and her pronunciation, and she actually laughed with us. There was hope, I decided.

We responded to the lunch call, and, after lunch, I sensed that I was getting a sore throat. Whatever my problem, I didn't feel like playing any more cards. It was as if the morning had worn me out. So Mama—smart Mama—suggested that we three sick ones go back to the library and she would read to us. I had always loved it when someone read to me; I feel that way even today. I wasn't sure about Silvio, but he seemed to want to join us. So that is what we did.

Mama puzzled over what she would read. She was reading an Ellery Queen mystery, and that didn't seem suitable. I was plowing through one of the readers my teacher had given Mama for my edification. But Silvio had been reading *White Fang* and that is what she read to us. We all enjoyed that, until there came a moment when the rhythm of the ship overcame us and we became drowsy.

Mama closed the book and pronounced, "You two are about to fall asleep in spite of all this adventure! So, how about if I tell you one of Marisol's father's stories?"

I don't know how much Silvio liked the story, but I sure did. She told us the story of Seamus the Miller and the Jackdaw, trying her best to include some of Daddy's Irish lingo.

A jackdaw is an Irish raven, a familiar and well-loved creature. Over the years, however, I have thought often about Daddy's prescience in bringing that bird into my life when I was so young.

At night when he tucked me into bed, I would beg for those stories and he would groan, rub my head with his knuckles, and tell me for the eleventieth time, one of those stories that Granny Bridey had told him when he was a boy.

"There once lived a miller a long time ago," Mama began. "So long ago it was, that if he was alive then, he would not be alive now."

I grinned. I could hear Daddy saying those very words.

"He was walking along, was Seamus, looking for a stick. What he really wanted to find, I am sure, was one fair and sturdy enough to be a shillelagh."

And so the story would go, about how this scrappy bird landed on his head and how it stole things and tricked people, even Seamus, who he loved, and how he cursed and laughed. Since he was a lazy bird, much too lazy to learn people language, he taught Seamus how to understand Jackdaw language.

Mama did a good job of telling the story, and we listened to her trying to speak in Daddy's lilt. But the moment arrived when I saw Silvio nod off, and my eyes were barely open, as well.

We were awakened by Mr. Neroli who found us asleep, all three. Mama had curled up on the library couch and joined us for a nap.

Dinner that night was not somber, but not far from it, all of us aware that we would go different directions in the morning. There was packing to do and colds to doctor. Our Dr. Evert ended the evening by proposing that we finish that bottle of Benedictine, which he said wouldn't hurt any of us. So we did, and then said our goodnights.

The next morning, we arrived in Juneau. Mama and I ate little at breakfast and we were at the railing as we arrived. We were becoming accustomed to seeing weathered and soiled snow cover on huge peaks along the shore and Juneau fit the established pattern.

Juneau seemed to be a real town in comparison to Ketchikan. It, too, hugged the shoreline, but homes and businesses spread out with a bit of comfort. American flags hung in abundance in Juneau, reminders of the recent Memorial Day celebrations. Along the lengthy concrete wall were piles of machinery and equipment left over from the war. Huge fishing nets hung drying on the dock. Tugs and small fishing boats rested nearby, tethered and dancing in the ripples. Sleek porpoises tucked and rolled near the ALASKA COAST LINES dock, home to a multitude of colorful seaplanes that bobbed in the water. I suspected Dr. Evert was salivating at the sight.

The docking and loading proceeded as we had become accustomed, with one exception. This time, as Mama and I watched from above, the long skinny ship's arms lifted those Packards from the deck and placed them gingerly onto the pier. Since there were no roads in Juneau to speak of, we laughed and wondered just where those automobiles would be driven. Workers unclamped hooks and wiped down the cars. Those automobiles, among the first manufactured after the war, were magnets for every man and boy in the vicinity,

The water in the bay was a new sight for us. Aquamarine and translucent, the color seemed something out of a picture book to me.

The ship purser, standing beside us, explained, "That color comes from all that glacial soil that washes into the bay," he said.

But I wasn't so sure. I rested my chin on the railing, lost in thought. The water looked like the opal in one of Mama's rings, reflecting light to a depth such that I wouldn't have been surprised if a whole other world had lived under that water. I sure could see it, a deep perimeter seemingly marked by mirrors, scores of mirrors, reflecting a swirling place of enchantment filled with dancing ladies and princes and an occasional mermaid. Were those glimmers of honey-and-amber-gold I saw or just my imagination at work, I wondered.

Our friends stood near us, jacketed arms full of boxes and bags. We watched their luggage being carried off and set onto the pier. Assorted people stood, seemingly awaiting them. The moment had arrived and I was having a difficult time saying goodbye.

I pulled out my Brownie camera and took pictures of us all, in different configurations. That seemed to break the tension a bit. We talked about future visits, and I asked Silvio if he would write me. Mrs. Neroli grabbed my shoulders, air-kissing both my cheeks. Silvio and I just stood there looking down, looking at people, looking away.

Dr. Evert surrounded me in his arms and held me. Next, he lightly embraced Mama, held her away, gave her a long look, and pulled her to him again. Finally, frowning slightly, he released her, turned and descended the gangplank, followed by the others. They descended the gangway and were enveloped by people who appeared delighted to see them. From the deck we heard their busy chatter and saw pointing arm gestures ushering them to waiting cars, and then they were gone.

***

The departure ritual was repeated as in Seattle and Juneau. And the ship headed north again, gliding toward Glacier Bay. As we pulled away, Mama encased me with her arms as her hands held the railing. For a long time, we watched together, lost in our thoughts. The sun filled our pallet of sky that afternoon, affording us a full view of the blue-lavender-gray-white other worldly bay. Whales cavorted perhaps fifty feet from the ship and dolphins dove around us, all framed by the beauty of that eerie snow and ice.

An odd sound caught our attention, startling us. At first we heard a slight whine, then a profound, pitiful groan as we witnessed the glacier to our right reluctantly release a huge, thick slice of ice and snow that plummeted, tumbling into the sea. We held our breath, heard a thundering, *whoosh!* And water shot up, sending out an explosive wave that caused our ship to wobble and rock.

The ship rejoined the open sea. The days had already become very long and evening finally arrived wrapped in dull gray mist and rain. Mama and I had stood quietly at the railing for a long time contemplating our arrival in Seward and our future, but the chill reminded us that it was time to move inside. We went to our cabin and began to pack. Our date to depart was quickly approaching.

The water became rough; an angry rain storm lapped and buffeted us, and we traded our preoccupation with our sniffles for worries about queasy stomachs. We had little appetite that night. I finally turned toward the wall, hugging my little doll, angry at myself for feeling sorry about our friends who had left us today. I fell into an uneasy sleep.

In the very early morning hours, the rain abated and fog set in again; the ship's engine set the constant rhythm and the foghorn provided a solemn accompaniment. The ship churned the sea inexorably carrying us toward Seward.

A FOGGY, MONOCHROME BEGINNING

Once more Mama and I leaned on the rail as close to the bow as possible, anticipating our first view of what was to be our new home. We were cold to the bone, shivering, but dressed in our best for our arrival in Seward. A stylish cloche hat hugged Mama's face, her scarf still warming her neck and throat. I wore my skirt and jacket, but a turtleneck sweater covered my neck. The brown beanie once more sat atop my head. Months and years later, when my body had lengthened and thickened, and the skirt and jacket no longer fit, the beanie stayed with me for longer than I would have wanted.

We squinted our eyes and could see almost nothing; our view was arbitrarily rationed by wet, cottony fog. For a few seconds, a sliver-moment of clarity allowed us to see pewter-colored water lapping against the ship. Farther ahead, a darker, denser band of clouds enveloped mountains that I could only imagine. The ration for us was limited to sharp bluffs and escarpments caparisoned in lichens, grasses, scrub mosses and pines. Then, within seconds, fog surrounded even that portion of land.

Earlier we had slowly passed the wasted metal skeleton of the *S.S. Yukon*, a recent maritime victim of treacherous sea shoals. We were aware that all passengers had been rescued and treated at the Seward Hospital. But, as we slipped quietly past the rusty cadaver, there seemed to be, among us, a compulsion to maintain a sense of respect and mourning for the ship's demise. Gulls screeched and battled for a resting spot on the rusting dregs and I heard a quiet groan as some part of the wreck adapted to its grave. Meanwhile our ship's engine continued its barely audible *chug chug*—the lone rhythm—as small waves, ripples really, careened from the ship's side and slapped at the pebbly shore.

We heard the engine ramp up just slightly and the *chug chug* became more insistent as we began our entry into Resurrection Bay. At that moment, we could make out craggy islands, their knife-sharp bluffs shooting skyward, their caves and crevasses fostering throngs of red-billed, red-footed puffins that dove here and there to grab their morning meal from the water. Below us, schools of tiny fish darted and divided crazily just beneath the water's surface, closely pursued by hungry dolphins.

The edge of the mist filled my line of sight, giving me such a limited window, I wanted to reach out and pull the mist away with my hands so I could see what lay ahead. The sun began furtively to sever the curtain of fog, and I glimpsed water, one moment deep green, then turquoise, and next powdery blue through the mist.

A tug approached, its engines contributing to the ship's lazy rhythm. It turned, slowly eased aside the ship, and began to guide us toward the dock. My heartbeat added a syncopated beat to that rhythm. My cold had slipped to the bottom of the list of important things at that moment. We were nearly there!

I could now see portions of the rugged coast to my right and left. A bald eagle left his perch in a tree and dove toward the chilly waters, causing fish to scuttle in frenzied effort to avoid the eagle's deadly claws. Nonetheless, he grabbed his intended prey and flew off, carrying a flash of silvery squirming life to his nest in the nearby trees. I heard water cascading into the sea, but I couldn't see it. A waterfall perhaps?

To our left, a long wooden pier jutted into the bay. It was tiny and fragile compared to the one in Seattle. As we neared the pier, I glanced up at Mama; her chin was firmly set and I suspected I knew what she was thinking. She started the day fiddle-string tense; I knew that because, when she fixed my hair that morning, she made my braids so tight I felt as if my eyebrows were now in the middle of my forehead.

The tugboat slowly, deliberately turned our ship toward the pier and, beyond it, I caught my first look at Seward. A jumble of bland one-story frame buildings greeted me, most shoved up against the base of a mountain still shrouded in low, soggy clouds. The buildings competed for space with piles of somewhat orderly clutter, apparently left over from the war. Crates, fashioned of raw wood, stenciled with numbers and letters, army jeeps and trucks, lined up for some imminent destiny other than Seward. I spied a military bucket loader, stacks of ammunition boxes in front of a Quonset hut, a scattering of the leavings of war—tires, airplane propellers, all standing at ease, awaiting their fate.

Directly ahead, a few modest buildings proclaimed their identity. One was a fishery, another the DREAMLAND MOVIE THEATER, and farther on, a wall declared KENAI LUMBER COMPANY. Scattered among the buildings were vacant areas and building remnants, still black with char and ash. Was this war damage? I wondered.

I was trying to be positive, but my first impression of this place called Seward, beyond its pervasive wet chill that morning, was that it was grim and colorless. Its buildings seemed surrounded by mucky mud, at times laced with dirty snow; sometimes colored cocoa-brown or dingy runoff—no matter, it was still mud, and it seemed to rule the town.

Rail tracks ran directly in front of us left-to-right along shore and then curved away, embracing the tiny town, separating the buildings from the sea. The train engine, painted bright blue and yellow, impatiently awaited its orders to move out. Busy workers hoisted, pulled and pushed crates and boxes, as the train engineer stood alongside, the smoke trail of his cigar evaporating into the mist. That train, with its brightly painted cars, provided us the only color to be seen in the entire town.

I looked up at Mama again. I swear I saw her jaw twitch just slightly, but it was still squarely set. If I doubted Mama's wisdom, I knew better than to say anything.

The sea, the trees, the birds, the sea animals—they were fascinating, but I had seen them now. Were they worth forsaking our warm, sunny life in New Mexico?

Thoughts of family in Gardner poured into my head. My cherry red and pink quilt on my bed, my roller skates and the marks I had gouged with them on Grandfather's veranda. My pet turtle, who slowly circumnavigated his glass world each day, the neighbor's lilac bush, which welcomed my pals and our dolls for hours of pretend play; I missed them, and I said a little prayer. "Dear Lord," I whispered, "forgive me. I didn't choose this place, and I don't think I like it."

And the Lord answered firmly, "So? There are a lot of things that my children don't like.

Get over it."

So I did. I set my jaw just as Mama had set hers and told myself that we would be all right. I told myself what I had said many times recently, that together we could do anything. Even this.

With one substantial thud, the ship came to a stop and the pier burst into frenetic activity. Crewmen rushed about securing thick ropes, opening doors in the hold area, jiggling and shoving the gangway into place for our debarkation. Here the huge crates were marked, *Perishable* and SAN JUAN FISHERIES. Directly below me, two sea lions cavorted among the pilings. For the first time, I came to know that they have an aroma all their own, and it is not pleasant.

On the pier, a small collection of musicians in army uniform assembled to play a tepid rendition of *For He's a Jolly Good Fellow.* "I wonder if they can play, *Oh, Susanna,"* I mumbled and Mama squeezed my hand stiffly. I was trying to make her smile; she ignored me. Yup, she was nervous.

On the pier, assorted town residents stood around, shifting from one foot to another, hands in pockets, staring shyly at us—a soldier, hands on hips, surveying the activity, a sailor brushing something from his Dixie Cup hat, a few fishermen, children of varied sizes and ages pushing, whispering, waving, carbon copies of the people we had seen at our other stops. In their midst, we beheld a portly female in a green print skirt and gray wool coat, her feet encased in sturdy brown oxfords. Short bluish curls and bangs defined her round face, her eyes encircled by brown plastic glasses. She held a white handkerchief high in her hand that she waved toward the ship enthusiastically.

That was our introduction to Dotty Etta, who was to be our first real friend in Seward. We soon discovered she was much more than the scatterbrain she first appeared to be on the dock. A long-time citizen, she volunteered to be the first town librarian and, long ago, she had decided that someone needed to meet each incoming ship, and she appointed herself to be that someone.

She had lived for many years in Seward with her daughter, Maudie, who worked for the mayor as the town clerk. Everyone knew them, of course. If not for their idiosyncrasies, they were known for the huge carpetbag pocketbooks they carried. Dotty Etta's bag could be bright, or printed, or striped, and always full. Maudie's bags were bold prints, also filled to the brim. But that didn't seem to allow adequate space for what she needed, because Maudie often stuffed smallish things into her ample brassiere—paper receipts, lipstick, lunch money, cough drops—often giving her an iconic silhouette.

Over the next weeks and months we found Dottie Etta to be a source for information on just about any subject, including the coming and going of any citizen of the town of Seward. Weekly, she visited the SHEAR JOY SALON where she and her beautician Joyette shared all the gossip while Joyette cheerfully applied bluing to Etta's bob and bangs.

Dotty Etta was the person to ask regarding anything, whether factual, spurious, or shocking. But we also found her to be a staunch friend—one whose mouth was locked shut regarding secrets of those who were dear to her.

Dotty Etta was also the keeper of Alaska stories related to wispy phantoms, bizarre deaths, and prehistoric monsters and she had a strange sense about things that had not yet happened. But I am getting ahead of myself.

From the ship's bow, we saw our higgledy-piggledy mismatched trunks and boxes piled onto carts, and we scurried to disembark in order to catch up with it all on the pier. We looked around, took a deep breath, smiled and waved at the people who looked back at us, and stumbled along behind our luggage carts. Our luggage filled one cab and spilled over into a second. We squeezed in, bosses of our own gypsy caravan, and rode up the hill to our house on Third Avenue. To this day, I wish I had taken a picture of that. Our cabbies helped us lug our belongings onto our very own gravel driveway.

"Here we are!" said Mama, and she clapped her hands together—before knitting her eyebrows and emitting a quiet, "Hmmmmmm."

This time I did think to grab my camera and I snapped a picture of Mama with a wry grin on her face, surrounded by luggage, boxes, trunks—everything we owned, which was not much. I think she had so many things on her mind that she forgot about her sore throat.

She turned, slowly surveying our new home, and began to laugh from her gut, laughing hard, her hands on her knees finally trying to catch her breath. At least I hoped she was laughing. I wasn't sure at first. But then I began to laugh, too. It seemed like the thing to do, better than any alternative I could think of.

Mama then grabbed my camera and snapped a photo of me when I carried a box to our front door. In the picture, my saddle-shoes had transformed from bright white to brown-on-brown, in the short time it had taken to walk from the driveway to our front door.

My photos show our house, a frame structure shaped like a narrow shoebox with a roof sloped just enough to allow most Seward snow to slide to the ground. The entire house needed a coat of white paint, which it would get in spring. Nearly covering the front of the house was a series of windows, enclosing what may have once been a screened front porch.

Mama stood with my camera, her open-toed shoes soggy conduits of silt and black soil. She plunged on, determined to take a walk around our new home. We found an opening underneath the house where we suspected coal had been delivered at one time. At the back, stood a frame shed, sturdy but shopworn. We saw a gravel alley, like the one behind our Gardner house and we figured it served the same purpose. Beyond the alley was an empty lot which meant that, aside from the large cluster of poplars in our backyard and one tall spruce tree, the land around us was empty and susceptible to lots of wind. Mama looked up, surveying the many windows, and grumbled, "I wonder just how I'm supposed to keep this place warm in the winter."

We continued, surveying the circumference of the house. A worn metal tank, perhaps four feet tall, perched atop four slightly splayed legs, was our oil tank, perhaps our major source of heat.

We climbed the front steps, divested ourselves of our soggy shoes, and entered into the spacious parlor-dining room area. Before us we beheld a dusty, but sturdy, dark mahogany dining-room table and six matching chairs. What a pleasant surprise gift! We suspected they arrived on one of those many military supply planes during the war. No matter, it was ours now. The seats were frayed and stained, but Mama knew she could remedy that.

We suspected a wood floor lurked somewhere below the two layers of curling green and black linoleum, but the linoleum would have to serve for quite a few years, until we had the funds to pay for its removal.

To our left was a large kitchen. A white electric Hotpoint stove perched on four chrome legs, and, on its surface, sat three large burners, all of which showed several years of hard use and questionable cleaning. An old Kelvinator refrigerator stood against the once-white wall, and a small wooden kitchen table with two worn wooden spool chairs constituted the only kitchen furniture. Affixed to the walls above the table were pine cabinets, sticky with age and constant use.

Off the kitchen was a dusty pantry that Mama would always call the *bodega*. On its shelves were situated stores of eclectic, zany items, unloved and unappreciated by their former owners and subject to our whim regarding their fate--four boxes of ping pong balls, some yellow, some red; three cartons of powdered eggs; four boxes of powdered milk and seven boxes of Colgate Brushless Shave Cream that promised to deliver a swell shave. There were also seven cartons of canned green beans, a large jar of dried parsley, two huge jugs of undiluted vinegar, a carton containing twenty cans of Ipana tooth powder, several containers of Sal Hepatica, and nineteen rolls of toilet paper.

How could we not laugh as we inventoried the items?

We continued through the house. The room on the left side would become Mama's and my bedroom for a couple of years. There were more rooms at the back of the house, candidates for renters' rooms. Upstairs were more rooms off a central hall, all nearly identical, all having one window and a small closet. One had its own bathroom.

"Kinda like a barn," Mama remarked. Again she mumbled, "Heating this place is going to be a problem."

"Weeell," we both said, looking at each other. That was the cue to get busy. We took off our coats, wiped down the kitchen table and chairs and sat down to contemplate our immediate future. We dragged in a box labeled "kitchen," and found a can of tomato soup, which became our first meal in our new house. I doubt that it had magic properties; all I know is that our colds disappeared. We didn't have time to be sick.

In one bedroom downstairs there were two single metal beds and mattresses dressed in black and white ticking fabric, not so soiled or worn that they couldn't be used. We carried the mattresses into the yard, grunting to avoid dropping them in the soggy soil, hung them over our clothesline and beat them as best we could, while simultaneously nearly exhausting ourselves. We washed down the bed frames, unpacked sheets, cleaned the kitchen and bodega shelves, and unpacked the hodge-podge of items we had brought—a process that had a Christmasy aura to it. Perhaps we would make it after all. This was sort of like camping, we thought. Sort of.

The next day we found the grocery store, and the army surplus office. We bought blankets, dishes, pots and pans, and four pillows, covered in the same ticking fabric. We became frequent customers of that surplus store. Its shelves contained a multitude of items needed and appreciated by desperate people like us.

By evening, we were exhausted, and allowed ourselves a few moments to relax—do what we pleased. Within the first few evenings, it pleased me to write letters. I had never written a letter before, except in school. So those first ones weren't exactly polished. But I persevered. I wrote my Tia Susana, Aunt Maureen, Grandfather Juan Felipe and Abuelita Clara. I also wrote Grandad Cormac and Granny Bridey, my Uncle Kenan, and Silvio.

Mama wrote Tia Susana, Aunt Maureen, her parents, and Grandad Cormac and Gramma Clara.

MAKING THE HOUSE OUR HOME

Every inch of our house needed some kind of care, calling for daunting chores—scrubbing linoleum, dusting and scrubbing walls, beating rugs. Sure enough, when peeling back two layers of linoleum we could see a cedar plank floor, and we dreamed of the day when we could uncover it and let it display its beauty. But that time was not to come for a few years. Mama purchased a wringer washer that dwelt just inside the bodega when it was not being used. We found that our windows were covered in assorted rectangles of insulated board, meant to keep wind, ice and snow from entering. Behind those rectangles, we found heavy felt covers, rolled up onto thick dowels until they would be called upon for additional insulation. Nearest to the inside were brown, deep velvet-like drapes, heavy with years of dust. They were among the first items to get a thorough bath in the washer, and it took Mama and me both to push and pull each panel through the wringer and drag them outside to dry. Next, we cut them into strips and we braided them into rugs for our floors. We worked frenetically, determined to attract at least one boarder as soon as possible.

As we washed and dusted every cranny, we came upon tiny vestiges of the life lived by the prior inhabitants. The now non-existent ping pong table had been on the second floor, we surmised. Water stains on the bathroom linoleum suggested that the officers' bodies didn't fit easily into that claw-foot tub. Liberal amounts of tooth powder were now caked cement-like to the back of a grimy sink and were now fossils, difficult to scrape away. A bookcase against the dining room wall exhibited a deep cigarette burn, and a ragged-edged photo of a pretty lady feeding a banana to a chubby baby was taped to the wall near where my bed was to be. We bought yards of target cloth, a strong slubby homespun fabric from the salvage store, sloshed it around in our washer with sea green dye, and ran hems with Mama's little black Singer portable sewing machine. The result was serviceable curtains for our windows, and bedspreads for our newly-painted lavender metal beds.

My belongings found their special places in our bedroom. My doll from Naasha rested contentedly on my pillow, my trusty rabbit's foot clinging to its arm, and Naasha's woven blanket lay atop my bed, just below my newly-created bedspread. The blanket gave me constant warmth, protecting me from chilly air and dangers only Naasha could foresee. Atop our mahogany dresser and mirror, another gift of the U.S. government, sat the glass lamp from my bedroom in Gardner, and my tiny walnut jewelry box with my initials inset in the top that Daddy made to mark my fifth birthday.

As we labored, we came to expect that most days would bring some form of moisture—a soft drizzle, stringy wisps of fog clinging to the mountains, or billows of fog running interference for an impending wind.

I remember one certain morning; the very moment I finished cleaning the porch windows with a diluted mixture of that donated vinegar, the clouds retreated, revealing for us the vista across the bay. There stood Mt. Alice and her mountain neighbors. Electric-white peaks glimmered in sunlight, the town buildings looked scrubbed; the sun's reflections on the water in the bay sparkled, showing off the stark blue of the sky. It was so beautiful I called Mama so we could share the moment. She dragged kitchen chairs onto the porch, while I grabbed a bag of peanuts, and together we sat cracking and munching, as if we were at the movies.

We heard the wail of the train from Anchorage loudly announce its impending arrival, the monotone moan echoing from one mountain to another, to another, WEEOWAA...WAA...waa. We watched it lumber into town, begin its curved path and ever-so-slowly approach the station and the dock.

We were beginning to understand that the train, the frame buildings on Fourth Street, the boats bobbing in the bay, and the to-and-fro jumble of town activity composed an essential part of the heart of Seward for us.

Our preoccupation with our bowl of peanuts prevented us from immediately noticing Dotty Etta and Maudie as they approached, carrying their usual satchels and picking their way around puddles from last night's soaking. Maudie labored along carrying a brown paper bag loaded with what sounded like canning jars clinking against one another. Etta carried something very heavy in her satchel. Our first visitors! We opened the porch door and welcomed them, delighted to see familiar faces.

We were excited to show off our new house. The ladies cooed over our bedspreads and our cast-off metal beds, now given new life. They appeared to appreciate the shine on our government dining room table, the cleaned windows, and our walls newly painted with Government Issue white paint. Their approval elevated our spirits greatly.

Etta declared that her satchel contained a beautiful, large salmon roast and we invited them back to help us eat it that evening.

When they returned, they eagerly surveyed a dish of nuts that Tia Susana tucked in Mama's suitcase just as we left New Mexico.

"Oh my, pistachios!" Etta's voice expressed unabashed glee.

It was a sacrifice to serve those pistachios, but we hoped to use them to bribe the ladies into answering some of our questions about town. Besides, we were still full of those peanuts at the moment. They fielded our barrage.

Why were there so many military people in town, we asked?

"Oh, of course you wouldn't know, would you?" Etta said. With that, she began to share what we were to come to know as some of her favorite stories. "Well," Etta appeared to be settling for some lengthy explanations, so we did the same, "when the war started in Europe, our government may have pretended the U.S. was neutral, but the truth is we were supplying all sorts of stuff to the Russians. Seems strange, doesn't it, nowadays? But the Russians had been fighting German troops for years and they were tired. And poor. At least they said they were. Nowadays, we can't believe a word they say. Of course, we weren't crazy about doing business with those crazy communists, but what choice did we have, when you think about it?" Etta smiled, looking for our reaction to her words.

"All this war stuff," she continued. "And I mean tons and tons of stuff, just poured through here."

Occasionally Mama slipped away to check what was in the oven.

Meanwhile Etta continued. "It all came up this way, by ship, and in pieces. Propellers, fuselages, trucks and tires. On the next ship would come people, soldiers to manage the parts and ship them up to Anchorage and Fairbanks, where more soldiers put the planes together. Our young men tested the planes and taught Russian pilots to fly them to Russia."

"Dinner is served!" Mama exclaimed, and we sat down to fine food accompanied by a concert of enticing smells. We opened Maudie's jar of piccalilli relish to accompany the salmon. As we ate, we urged them to continue with their stories.

"Lord love a duck," Etta continued, stabbing a piece of potato. "I don't know how to tell you all the strange things that came through here." She put down her fork and her hands fluttered, resembling goose feathers from a beaten pillow. "And some strange people too, I dare say," she continued. "We had all manner of soldiers, and sailors, even some Canadians and Coast Guard people."

"Canadians?" Mama asked.

"Sure, enough," Maudie interjected, "Up the streets and down the alleys, I'd say."

We had finished eating, and Mama brought out a tray of gingersnaps. As Maudie took over the narration, she paused long enough to reach into her satchel, pull out a slim brown cigar, snip the end with a pair of tiny scissors, light a match and begin to puff away. Now that was one thing I had never seen before. Startled, I looked toward Mama, who acted as if that happened in her house every day. She pushed an ash-tray over in Maudie's direction and she continued speaking, "The only other way to get those parts and people to Russia was by land through

Canada, and all those experts figured it would be impossible to build a road north. At least that's what they thought.

"Actually the Canadians had already built a primitive highway in British Columbia, and they had built some little airfields for their own backwoods citizens." Maudie paused once more to puff on her cigar, emitting a slim wisp of smoke that curled about slightly before it evaporated.

"That's right," Mama interjected. "The U.S. didn't build a road through until '43, wasn't it?"

Etta, not wishing for even a tiny interlude in the story, took over once more. "Noooo, dear, no," she cooed. "It was started and finished in 1942 and it went from Dawson Creek in Canada to Delta Junction near Fairbanks, and it was a rough, slogging messy job, I tell you, and dangerous as can be. And those dear men did it in the snow, and cold, and ice, and mud."

Her words flew now, and her hands were flitting. "Oh, Lordie, did they work, those dear men, and it was a cooperative thing, Canadian and U.S. soldiers and civilians. Oh, but that was way later than those first shipments of plane parts and people." She was shifting into second gear.

Mama brought out the teapot and as I brought out the cups and saucers, I thought about all that soap and tinfoil, and newspaper I collected in Gardner.

"A little bit of sugar, dear." Etta smiled and took the cup filled with tea from Mama.

"Anyways," Maudie continued. "With all those parts, what we got were big oil tanks, and trucks, and people to do the work, and they came in every size and color you could imagine, and every kind of uniform, and they built some barrack buildings, and had a radio station, and they needed places to live and eat, and…"

"Don't think that they couldn't be fun, too, right Maudie?" Etta giggled slightly. "They could laugh, and they knew how to have a good time."

Etta had picked up her cup and moved from our dining room chair to the only overstuffed chair we had. Mama filled our cups while Maudie picked up the story again. "You know, sometimes we don't remember that Canada was already at war with Germany, but they were. Canada declared war just after England did, in 1939. So people living on the west coast of Canada already were on alert for an attack by the Japanese."

"No kidding?" I said.

"Ohh yes," Maudie continued. "The Canadian government had moved a lot of people to the interior from the islands, including Native people. And so did we Alaskans. Hundreds of people on the islands were moved inland.

"So, when the Japanese attacked Pearl Harbor, everyone in Seward—well…we were sure we would be the next to be bombed. In a way, we were surprised, but, you know, we really in our hearts had been prepared for a long time."

"From Hawaii to Seward?" Mama queried. Spoons stirred and rattled. I passed the gingersnaps.

"You just consult your map, dearie, and you will see that Alaska is mighty close to Japan." Etta sat back while three of Maudie's fingers made a circle in the ashtray, rubbing out the stub of her cigar. She then continued. "And, since Seward was on the coast, and helping Russia in the war effort, we were sure we were next." She paused for effect, looking to see our reaction. Satisfied that we were appropriately amazed, she continued, "So, it was the funniest thing, half the town population disappeared in hours, just disappeared… and the rest began frantically digging bomb shelters."

"So that explains that big hole down the street! Right next to where they are putting the military chapel from Fort Raymond!" Mama said.

"And the ones all over Seward," continued Maudie.

"And it explains the camouflage on the walls of the Jesse Lee Home, and it explains why your windows come with all sorts of covering to use during our blackouts. We had blackouts every night, and the headlights of all our vehicles were painted to muffle the light."

"And all the burned buildings and charred lots in town—the oil tanks—were they bombed?" Mama thought out loud.

"Now that is another story altogether!" Etta interjected. "In November of '41, just days before the Pearl Harbor attack, a terrible fire broke out in town. Can you imagine?" She sat forward in her chair, planting her feet on the floor, her hands folded in her lap. "It was really a frightening thing, I tell you! We still wonder just how it started," she mused, looking toward her daughter. "But it started on Fourth Avenue and it just roared through downtown. Oh Lordie, we were all terrified. Snow and ice didn't hold it back at all, no indeed, it just made it harder for the firemen to put it out. Oh, my. It was so bad, really…" She slowed for a moment of contemplation. "A good bit of downtown burned. The oil tanks exploded, and, by the time the fire was extinguished, a lot of people were burned out of their homes. We lived over that way then. We had to live in the roller rink for a couple of days after that. Lordy, lord. Can you imagine? Whew!"

The ladies were both close to tears at that moment, and we were shocked to contemplate the devastation.

"Wasn't that a time, Mother?" Maudie broke the spell. Her hands fluttered in her lap. "The Jesse Lee Home took in a lot of people, too. Our town was a disaster. We all thought, if the Japanese flew over Seward, they would just turn around because they would think the town had already been bombed!"

Maudie sighed, and a renewed Etta took over. "But then, after Pearl Harbor, the push was on to get all those children in the Home to other areas—places where they would be safe. Those poor children."

A snippet of a thought of Silvio flew through my head. I remembered him saying those same words.

"Oh," Etta paused again, moved by the memory of those days, "it was simply horrible." Her forehead creased, her mouth was set and firm.

I was beginning to admire the courage of the people who lived in Seward during those tough days.

"That explains it," Mama murmured. "Poor Seward."

I knew Mama was thinking about our first look at Seward, at the charred walls and buildings.

"So," Maudie began anew, "we have arrived at the next chapter in this story. Pearl Harbor made the folks in Washington D.C. realize just how important Seward and Alaska were to the war effort. Oh, it seemed like, immediately, ships arrived with troops and trucks and bucket loaders, jeeps, big guns, little guns, everything you can imagine. Seward fairly buzzed with activity, I tell you. Ft. Raymond was where most of the soldiers lived, in tents on the platforms you still see, and in Quonset huts, too…wherever the soldiers could put them. We never knew what a day would bring, did we, Mother? The army took over buildings, dug ammunition caves into our mountains, put chains across the harbor, built artillery sites up at Caines Point, …I suppose you know there were some officers who lived here for a couple of years."

Mama had been told that when she bought the house.

"And the army finished the road with gravel, at least to Moose Pass."

"But it still isn't much of a road, even today," Etta laughed and picked up the story. "Ooh, yes, dearie, if you think there is a lot of mud in Seward now, just imagine…and so many people! Suddenly we had a hospital, a bit of an airfield, a movie theater, a USO, and Officers' Club, tons of bars and, glory be, everything that comes with it."

Maudie reached for a cookie; Etta continued, "Now, Seward hasn't ever been a dull town, you know, but you believe me, it wasn't then, for sure! We had dances, and drinking, and road houses, and local girls smooching with the soldiers, and blackouts every night, and thefts, and even murders!"

Her hands began fluttering again, and she ceased chattering momentarily. Etta seemed to have drifted to another place entirely. Mama and I waited silently. Finally she began to speak as if she were confiding in us, her tone clearly darker than it had been. "There were some bad people walking our streets then, I tell you. I swear they came in with the winds. We have lots of wind here, but you know that already. I swear, I felt that there was anger in that wind, anger that groaned and stayed, and it just has never left this town. It came in cold, from the west, and it carried mischief and lunacy with it. And I think it still does. Yep, sometimes it's still here, it still lingers. Wouldn't you say, Maudie?"

"I would, Mother," Maudie averred. "Mischief and lunacy—but I think it is getting better..."

If the ladies thought we knew what to do with this new information, they were wrong. If we should have said something, we didn't. Etta returned from her reverie. "You're probably right, dearie. And from it all we got a newspaper, and a radio station, and now, you know." She suddenly looked at her watch and pushed herself up from the comfort of our big chair. "I think we have just about worn out our welcome, Maudie! Let's give our neighbors a break and let them get to bed."

That was to be the end of the stories for that night. Etta's words led straightaway to mutual goodbyes. Chatting still, they collected their belongings, and headed for the front door.

"Glory be, we had better be going, daughter. Oh," Etta said as she picked up her satchel. "I have a book for you that may help you understand a bit about this place that you have decided to live in."

She handed Mama a slim book titled, *Our Beloved Alaska.* "There aren't too many copies left around, but this is our gift to you."

"I can't, really," Mama sputtered.

"Nonsense," Etta spoke firmly. "You'll need it."

At that moment, Etta was the voice of sensibility that we were to come to know. To many, she was an inconsequential town fixture, one who had been here forever, and she did little to sway their opinions. But we were to know the cast-iron core of her character. After many years of knowing her, she shared her reason for coming to Alaska, of her confrontation with her parents when she found that she was expecting a baby.

While her love—her brave knight—waited on the porch twisting his cap in his hands, her father took out his willow whip and switched her breasts and back, and her arms, too, as she tried to protect herself. While her father regaled her with sharp words she had never heard before, she saw red beads, no, bubbles of blood, arise in odd lines and begin to drip down her arms and soak her cotton print dress. She was too preoccupied to notice that her swain, her gallant hero, had thought better of confronting her family and, instead, jumped the porch railing, skirted the vegetable garden and ran for the hill and the train tracks beyond, to never be seen again. It was with her mother's help and money from the sugar tin on the top shelf in the kitchen that had been squirreled away over the years, that she made her way to a spot as far away from her home and father's wrath as she could get.

"By the way," she said before leaving that night, "if you'll come by tomorrow, I have a chiffonier you can have for one of your bedrooms."

"Oh," said Mama, "we couldn't inconvenience you."

"Nonsense! This isn't an inconvenience," Etta retorted absently. "It is a gift. A gift freely given. We insist."

They bustled out the front door, retreating as noisily as they came. As the door closed, Mama and I shared looks of surprise and disbelief.

"Mama, what is a *chiffonier*?" I finally asked.

"I have no idea, Marisol," she said. "But I guess we can use one!"

We left the cups and saucers long enough to consult our newly unpacked dictionary. They were right. We could use one.

"It's just a fancy word for a dresser, huh? I have dibs," I declared.

A SEWARD FOURTH OF JULY

Summer 1946

The train's routine entry and exit sounds became our familiar friends over the years. There were rare occasions when the arrival of Seward's train was delayed by a recalcitrant moose on the track, or by a winter avalanche. With those exceptions, however, our daily activities were gauged in accordance with that long, low wail and the soft grumble as the cars approached their destination near the pier each morning.

The evening routine was normally marked by the train whistle sounding once more, signaling its departure for Anchorage, carrying travelers and goods newly arrived and destined for other parts of Alaska.

Sometimes we would have finished our dinner by the time the whistle sounded, and sometimes we were very close to relaxing over our evening meal. Typically, however, the whistle meant that it was time for Mama to read from the book Etta had given us. We would clear the dishes from our little kitchen table and she would read:

> Alaska's story began eons ago, at a time beyond our contemplation, when centuries of snow and ice encased the land. The cannon-shot crack of a glacier calving and the whine of wind were the only intrusion into timeless silence. Even then, this icy land, seemingly incapable of supporting life, did just that. Prehistoric beasts foraged along the bare hardscrabble green selvage--

"Prehistoric beasts?" I asked absently. "What kind of beasts? Dinosaurs?"

"Darned if I know," Mama commented. "You'll just have to learn about that in school or ask Etta." She resumed reading:

> Glaciers hugged the shore and gigantic prehistoric water beasts swam in the glacial waters, thriving in this seemingly inhospitable environment.

Mama looked up at me. "Okay, so maybe there were dinosaur whales, do you think?" Mama shrugged her shoulders and began again:

> At last snow and ice capitulated to light and warmth. On the Kenai peninsula a splash, a trickle, became a flow of water cutting a valley between mountains, crushing and carrying along whatever prevented its rush toward the bay. The water deposited layers of pebbly, slick moraine, the matrix of what would someday become Seward.
>
> The ice sheet, now called Exit Glacier, retreated miles inland, its waters splintering and braiding in accordance with the water's whims.
>
> The result is many things, not the least of which is a song, a constant, gentle pastoral sonata.

"That sure describes the Resurrection River, doesn't it? At least what we have seen of it." Mama said. She got up and foraged in the cabinet for a couple of gingersnaps, handing one to me. Munching happily, she continued:

> Soon birds, shelled creatures, and then land animals arrived that supplied Food and pelts for warm clothing for the native people, who came to hunt, trade, quarrel, and nearly always move on in accordance with the rhythm of the season. At least one of these tribes called this area, *Qutekcak.*

"Qutekcak," we said. We rolled the strange sound around in our mouths and wondered if we ever would understand this land that was to be our home.

***

It didn't take us long to realize that the amount of daylight changed significantly each day. As summer continued and our days became very long, I imagined that Mother Nature was playing a cosmic game with her Arctic days, a game that went like this:

> Sun: "Mother, may I take a giant step across the midday sky?"
> Mother: "Yes, you may, my sun.
> Sun: "Mother, may I take a bite out of nighttime today?"
> Mother: "Yes, you may, my sun."

We ate dinner in light that made us think it was noon. But the train whistle served as our moment of constancy. And, still, after dinner Mama continued to read from Etta's book:

> At a time when colonial fathers were beginning to consider separation from England, a Russian ship sailed into the bay on Easter Sunday 1792, and the captain named it Resurrection Bay.
>
> The fur trade became a Russian mania, and resulted in disaster for the land and its people. After depleting the animal supply the Russians departed and nature began to reclaim its own.
>
> When gold was discovered in Alaska the human scramble began. Miners, entrepreneurs, con-men, railroad man, pastors, and snake oil salesmen headed for Seward, and then to Hope and parts inland.

"That sounds just like some of the characters we see in town, huh," I said. Mama nodded and she skimmed to find our place.

"In 1903 a working port was established…railroad...no road, no need for one, and no promise of one…" Mama looked up, closed the book and declared, "You know what? Etta brought by a sack of shelled pecans, and that means we have all the ingredients for a chocolate pecan sundae!" She didn't have to convince me. But when we finished every morsel we still weren't sleepy even though it was ten o'clock. The evening light still entered through the windows and outside there existed a strange luminosity that stayed with us until two or three o'clock in the morning. But we knew we had to rest. So, we closed those new lined curtains, and forced ourselves to sleep. That night I awoke and padded onto the front porch.

"Mama!" I called. "Come and see this!"

A huge, liquid amber moon filled nearly the entire sky and lingered at the very edge of the land, seemingly dragging itself along the peak of Mt. Alice. We sat, amazed at the sight, and I quietly sang, "Shine on, shine on harvest moon…" Mama hummed along, Eventually even we wearied of such beauty and tumbled into bed, assured that we were in for moons like this many times in our future.

We came to know that the jarring hoot of the ship's horn marked each Tuesday morning. Sometimes Mama and I walked down to watch the hive of activity at the pier, to see the members of the band and predict what wheezy tunes would greet the voyagers. We could count on Dotty Etta being there, smile and handkerchief at the ready.

The pier was always a site of bustling activity. Fishing boats jostled, contending for berthing spots, weathered fishermen hauled in their harvest, occasionally throwing fish guts overboard, causing fierce squabbles among gulls and sea lions. Harbor employees repaired worn timbers and swept away debris, and tug boat workers prepared for the next ship's arrival. On occasion, a Coast Guard tender cruised the bay, leaving a frothy line in its wake.

Meanwhile, oblivious to it all, Garbage John, one of the town's ancient and crusty loners, would inspect every pile of rubbish looking for a good warm shirt or a part bottle of gin. Or he might dip his line into the water, hoping for a hit this time. Some said that he was Russian, but the only time I conversed with him, I had no trouble with his accent. On my encounter, he was drunk. But that comes later in the story.

Sometimes we stepped onto the beach, Mama and I, our feet sinking deep into generations of shells, mussel and barnacle, causing us to feel as if we were the first people to walk there, ever. If we watched patiently at the spot where the waves lapped gently onto the shore, we could spy sea anemones and crustaceans tucked up against the rocks.

If we crossed the street and walked toward the railroad station, we encountered men tussling with huge peeled logs, fresh from the lumber yard, which they lifted by winch and manhandled into the hold of the ship. They were joined by stacks and bundles of timber, newly sawn into regulation sizes. Next, crates and pallets of canned fish products would be coaxed into the ship's hold, becoming part of the ship's ballast.

We began to know the people who were to become our friends and neighbors through shopping expeditions. We bought vegetables, and chairs, and sheets and bowls; we tried local pastries and we ate moose stew and salmon chowder.

***

It wasn't long before we knew that something exciting was in the wind for Seward. The general pace in town took on a different tone and the reason was soon clear. The Fourth of July was coming. Now that alone is a good excuse for any citizen to celebrate, but in Seward, where summer was short and the summer days were long, the Fourth has always been a really big deal.

Citizens scrubbed and painted; potholes were filled, sidewalks swept. Banners decorated balconies, swags of red, white, and blue nearly covered the railroad station, and just kitty-corner from it, a grandstand was being constructed.

Mama and I walked by the city hall one morning when Maudie came rushing out the door, headed for the courthouse with her arms filled with papers. She spied us and shouted, "You two stay where you are, I'll be back in five minutes."

Off she scurried, hugging her papers which upon occasion refused to remain within her grip. I gathered them up. When she returned, she gratefully accepted my papers and took us each by the arm, guiding us toward the partially constructed grandstand on Washington St.

She wanted to introduce us to someone, and that someone was, at this moment, standing nearby, his back to us.

We beheld a tall, husky army officer, hands on hips, dressed in khaki shirt and wool army drab trousers tucked into brown boots; a cap perched on his head. He was preoccupied with the men doing the construction.

"Major O'Keefe," Maudie shouted over the din of hammers and saws. He turned to face us, paused, smiled, removed his cap, took

Mama's hand and said, "Keith T. O'Keefe, ladies, and if I knew you were coming I would have worn my dress uniform."

That did it. I grinned outright. I was smitten. I could tell Mama was delighted to meet him and was intrigued by this larger than life charmer, but not smitten.

There he stood before us. Other than dark brown curly hair and black-brown eyes, just think Van Johnson and you understand what I mean. It took his entire name, Major included, to embrace the totality of Keith T. O'Keefe.

We chatted for awhile—that is, Mama, Major Keith T. O'Keefe, and Maudie talked. I just squinted up at his face, the sun behind him, and grinned.

He asked Mama if I could join him that afternoon. He had helpers already, but he wanted me to help decorate the grandstand. Of course she agreed. Eventually Mama headed home. Major O'Keefe introduced me to four kids who seemed to be about my age, one of whom was Cynthia Bergen. I had been told that I was little for my age, but compared to me, she was diminutive…in height, that is. Her body reminded me of a small, very full Christmas tree; or perhaps a morel mushroom in trousers. At the apex of her form was a face, comprised nearly entirely of big grin surrounded by short, light brown curls.

I liked her immediately. We seemed to understand what the other was thinking and quickly set about becoming friends. We braided strips of crepe paper into long bright chains, gathered and pleated sheets of colored paper, and we stapled our creations to the poles alongside the platform. There came a moment when Cynthia sat cross-legged near me to my right. I was on my knees, and began to stand to grab a bolt of cloth when the two-by-six beneath me, which had not yet been nailed to the floor beam, gave way. It plunged as the other end rose, and I became a gawky, ungainly bundle of elbows and knees tottering toward disaster. I stumbled to my right, staggering in front of Cynthia, as she impulsively reached out and grabbed the seat of my cotton pants with both hands and held on, her elbows both slamming against the floor, but saving me from a five-foot head-first fall into plywood scraps and nails. Stunned, people rushed toward us, a motley scrum of arms and legs. We were frightened, but fine, we proclaimed, except for Cynthia's skinned elbows, my bruised shin, and my damaged pride.

Major O'Keefe appeared with chilled orange soda bottles in hand. He surveyed the circumstances, handed us the drinks and suggested that we take a break.

"Let's go over to the waterfall." I suggested.

"Over by the shore?" Cynthia asked. "That isn't really a waterfall. It's not so exciting as that, but I love to listen to the water anyway and stick my feet in the water until they get so cold I can't stand it anymore. Let's go."

"That water comes out of a diversion channel," she explained, sticking her bottle of soda into the flow of water. Mine soon accompanied it.

"But where does the water come from, and why has it been moved to here?" I asked. My hand went into the flow and chilly shots of water spattered onto my face.

Cynthia sat on a stone on the beach Mama and I had walked recently, just across from the high cascade of water. "Well, I don't know how much you know about town. Do you know the area at the base of Mt. Marathon that is shaped like a saddle, with rock cliffs on each side?"

I wasn't sure enough about town to say that I did or I didn't.

"Well, it isn't far from where we live now, and sometime I'll take you over there. Anyway, that's where the glacier water from Lowell Creek used to flow down to the bay. It cut the town in two. Man, I can still remember when the water came through town. There were two bridges over it, I think. But sometimes, when we had a warm spring, the creek would burst its banks and flood everything. So finally some army people came and built the tunnel that carries that water over here to where it dumps into the bay. Can you imagine? With all these soldiers and jeeps, and trucks, can you imagine what a muddy mess we would have been in if they hadn't built the tunnel?"

She paused to take a swig of her soda and returned the bottle to the water before continuing. "And they filled in the riverbed, and made it Jefferson Street, so now the town isn't divided in half anymore. I was in first grade when they did it, and I guess I'm happy about it. Lowell Creek wasn't just a little creek, after all. It could be scary--how does your shin feel?"

I had forgotten all about it. Our toes were chilled to the bone. We rubbed them, encouraging blood to return. We returned to find that other hands had completed our decorating chore, so we walked toward my house. On the way, I told her about Gardner, and Daddy, and what Mama and I wanted to do with our house.

She had an older sister and a little brother, and her father was the finance officer at the fishery. Her mother taught piano, she said, and they had lived here throughout the war. She also told me that she was Jewish. I had no idea what Jewish was; she may as well have said that she was Martian for all that meant to me. I thought her family was brave to have endured those scary days during the war. I was thinking of questions to ask her, but more than anything I was happy to know someone who was my age. We made plans to meet again, probably on the Fourth downtown.

Midmorning on the big day, Mama and I walked to the Brosius Building to witness the parade. Streamers and rosettes decorated the occasional charred wall, left over from the 1941 fire, as well as newly painted ones. The flag on the firehouse flagpole fluttered gently. VFW members, the ladies of the churches, the town leaders, all stood behind tables, purveying Alaska delicacies—moose pot pies, smoked halibut, bear stew, and king crab cocktail.

It was a great day for a parade. We stood with those few remaining citizens, who were not serving food or would not be sitting on a float, to await the parade. In time Cynthia joined us, with her little brother in tow. Major O'Keefe appeared, Crackerjack boxes sufficient for us three children in his hands, and he stood beside Mama.

At last we heard thin strains of a Sousa march, and then we saw two fine, spirited horses approach, their male riders sporting black cowboy shirts with white trim, and KENAI LUMBER COMPANY emblazoned on the back. A contingent of members of the Oddfellows marched by, throwing candies to the audience. The school band approached next wearing frilled uniforms and marching proudly, drums tapping out a quiet tattoo. Next came a number of floats, including one advertising JESSE LEE HOME 40TH ANNIVERSARY. "That's the home for the orphans and abandoned native children," Cynthia explained, munching her caramel corn. "They're going to come back this summer from all parts of inland Alaska. Most of the people in town don't mind but the snobs don't like that at all."

She then turned to her brother, "Aaron, I told you to quit throwing corn on the sidewalk!"

"Where are the children?" I asked. "Why don't they want them here?"

"The children were moved out early in the war, along with people from all the islands, like Attu and Kiska. The government was afraid they'd be killed or become prisoners of the Japanese. You do know the Japanese bombed Dutch Harbor? Well that scared us a whole bunch. Anyway, the children are coming back now and I bet some of the same stories are going to start." She tipped her head from side to side as she mimicked the voices, "'Those kids are sick, they have influenza germs, they shouldn't be able to mix with the people in the town.'"

She reprimanded her brother again, "For pity sakes, cut it out! Don't spit!"

I had just met Aaron. He was mischievous, there is no doubt. But I liked him from the first moment. There were only three things you needed to know about Aaron—he was very smart, he didn't miss anything, and he had a dimple in his left cheek. Oh, and if you play chess with him, prepare to lose.

Cynthia's comments about the orphans and the townspeople made me think about the Navajo children in Gardner. They always seemed to have runny noses and they never looked you in the eye. For the first time, I wondered about the attitudes of the people in Gardner and in Seward. It made me feel uneasy.

"Hey, look!" Cynthia blurted, holding up her Crackerjack surprise. "I got a flag pin!"

"And I got a ruby ring in my box," I exulted.

The parade continued: a curried and combed goat named Sergeant Bill approached wearing a big striped ribbon around his neck. Next came the tomato-red fire truck, the marching military police squad with white gaitered legs, and finally the police car, its siren shrieking. That signaled the end.

Cynthia was to meet her mother and sister at the USO booth, so she set off, Aaron in tow. I walked with Mama and Major O'Keefe toward the grandstand. Across the street, I spied two girls, perhaps two years older than I, and much more grown-up, even sophisticated. They were pretty and totally involved in their separate, happy world, which I doubted would ever include me.

We turned and walked toward the train station and it was there that my eyes took in a sight totally alien to anything I had ever encountered before. A spotless white Cadillac sedan passed us and stopped about fifteen yards ahead. A spotless car in Seward was itself a rare phenomenon, so when the driver, in a tan suit and derby hat, with skin the color of a Snickers bar stepped out, my jaw dropped. He opened the backdoor and offered his arm to a lady who grasped that arm and headed toward the railroad station. Attired in a patriotic red skirt and jacket, feet shod in white pumps, she carried a small white leather purse in her left hand and clutched what looked like a pair of white gloves. White shoes and gloves in Seward? I was spellbound. On her jacket blazed and dazzled a large pin encrusted with red, white and blue stones. Her hair, swooped up and piled on her head, was barely darker than bright red. It was an amazing sight. I thought she was glamorous, in a ragged kind of way.

"Mama!" I whispered. I knew better than to point, so I motioned with my elbow toward the lady. "Look at that lady! She's really pretty, don't you think? You could wear your hair like that and you would look beautiful!"

Mama looked over to see what had caught my eye, looked back at me, pushed my elbow down abruptly, gave Major O'Keefe a look I could not fathom, and said quietly, but firmly, "When pigs fly, sweetheart." She grabbed my hand and we began walking at a brisker pace.

"When pigs fly, Mama?" I sputtered. "I don't understand—" I struggled to keep up with Mama as she pulled me along.

"Exactly," she said, as Major O'Keefe burst into a long and hearty laugh.

SETTLING IN

One early August morning a half-ton army truck pulled into our driveway, and two uniformed, wearing those envelope caps like the one Major O'Keefe wore, soldiers knocked on our door to inquire if they could drop off some salvage beds and mattresses. We quickly assented, and in they came. Of course I immediately thought of the two who delivered Daddy's footlocker, but the difference was that this time I didn't want to cry. I said a little prayer of thanks for whatever this strength was that had been delivered to me, and started wiping down the beds.

"My goodness, thank you, young men!" Mama exclaimed.

"Don't thank us, ma'am, thank Major O'Keefe."

So we happily walked to town immediately and did just that.

"Well, I tell you, ladies," he smiled down at us, "you are very welcome." He then suggested that we take some wood from the piles behind his office, and arrange to have some furniture made of it. "Good lumber," he remarked. "No sense to waste it."

So we did that, too. We hired the town woodworker, Mr. Menamin, to fashion furniture for us from flooring planks, salvage studs and plywood. His first creation was a fine pine wardrobe for our bedroom. Next, he built side-tables. In the parlor, on one of them, soon sat a framed photo of Daddy. Next to the picture sat our new Philco radio, a farewell gift from Tia Susana. Resting at its base sat the rock containing the footprint of a pterodactyl Daddy had found on one of our treks near Gardner and Fort Busby.

Our daily life in Seward took on a semblance of routine. We became addicted to WVCY, Seward's very own radio station that brought us local news and news from what we called the lower U.S. We listened as Russia clamped down on its satellite countries, President Truman desegregated our army and navy, and the U.N. Security Council met for the first time.

We also listened to our own music program, presented by the Triple Triad, the local singing group. They sang everything and their be-bop wasn't bad. On Saturdays, we planned our meals around *The Shadow* (the adventures of a wealthy man about town, Lamont Cranston, and his lovely friend and companion, Margo Lane). At first, we had already heard the stories, but that didn't matter, we loved hearing them again anyway. In Gardner, when I first heard the program, I was enchanted by the name Margo, and I still think Margo is the most sophisticated name I have ever heard.

We posted a notice in the post office and in the grocery store, *Pleasant, Hospitable Lady desires respectable tenants. Bedroom/bath and supper daily. Price reasonable. Come by 3rd Avenue across from the Lutheran Church.* To the notice I had added a few little flowers in the corners, brightly colored and quite imperfect.

Soon we had our first tenant. Miss Mary Ruth Tenney arrived on the ship in early August. She was to be the new first grade teacher, but she quickly became more than a tenant to us. She took care of her own breakfast, enjoyed helping Mama in the kitchen, and they became friends—a friendship that still lasts today.

Soon our second prospective tenant arrived at our door. He was massive; in fact he filled the entire doorway. He was Mr. Lauber, a carpenter in town. His rugged face sported a short, wiry, light brown beard that made me think of Mama's worn wire pot scrubber. I hadn't heard of Vikings at that age but as I think back, that word would have described him well. At breakfast, when he dipped his toast in his coffee, a gooey crumb or two would stick in his whiskers. When that happened, I was mesmerized, watching those crumbs jump up and down, sometimes cascading onto the bib of his overalls.

Our third tenant would be Mr. Norman, the assistant port manager. He was born in Sweden and, while he could have been a Viking, he was the image of a gentleman. From the first, every day when he left for his office he was attired in a dark suit and tie, and a worn homburg hat on his head. In winter, his attire changed little. During the coldest months, a heavy, long, dark gray, wool coat and tweed scarf were added to his sartorial routine. He must have had to wear boots occasionally, or gloves in the winter, but I only remember that hat, which upon occasion proved to be a source of worry for him as he walked against Seward's often diabolic winds. Mr. Norman took great care with his hat and his mustache. When he came to the table at breakfast or dinner, the mustache was freshly combed down and shaped to curl around the sides of his mouth. He told us stories about his tiny village near Oslo, and his stories, told in his Scandinavian lilt and peppered with an occasional, *Ja, ja,* made me grin.

Over the next years, the members of our boarding house family changed slightly, but the size remained the same.

Once in awhile those two girls I'd seen on the Fourth of July walked down the street past my house. One had dark blonde curls and eyes with long lashes like I had seen only on fancy dolls whose eyes never closed unless they lay under chintz and satin coverlets. The other girl was slightly pudgy, her face seemingly made of porcelain. They often wore full gathered skirts and polished saddle shoes. I wondered how they kept them so clean. I suspected they were wearing lipstick, something I didn't even want to contemplate. I saw sailors in town giving them long looks, too, and I saw them blush and look away. Those girls were of a class not yet in my understanding.

We visited our post office box almost daily, hoping for letters from Tia Susana or Aunt Maureen, or Abuelita Clara. We craved news from what had been so recently our happy life. On our way home, we bought canned food at the Brown and Hawkin store, stopping often for a soda at the Palace Café. Huge heads of lettuce, tomatoes and squash arrived at our door delivered by a booted, pistol-packing lady named Ida Swift.

When a letter arrived from Gardner, I read it over and over, and answered it immediately, practicing my newly-acquired flourishing handwriting style with curls on the ends of my "y's" and "g's". Naasha wrote to Mama and me together; it was a chore for her to write, so we didn't get those very often. But we treasured every one. I wrote to

Silvio again, and didn't receive an answer. I decided that he thought my letters were silly, and perhaps they were. I pretended to be nonchalant and forgiving, knowing that he could never find a friend as loyal as me. The passing of time caused me to think about him less, and hope that his life was going just fine.

We often stopped for cups of coffee and cocoa on our walks and we began to catch some of the local gossip. We heard that George Nishiyama, who had run a noodle shop in Seward before the war, had just returned from an internment camp in Idaho. We knew that could become a problem in town; fury and anger over the Japanese still roiled in everybody's minds, ours included.

While listening to the town gossip, we heard that part of the closed military hospital was reopening to take care of tuberculosis patients, and the bridge at Mile 18 would be finished any day now, and we discovered for the first time, that Seward was supposed to have been washed away by a tidal wave just a few months before we arrived! We didn't mind missing that event.

We were home on a Tuesday morning in mid-August when the children destined for the Jesse Lee Home began arriving in earnest. Of course the ship's horn signaled its arrival, and we could see the children hugging the railings of the ship. Within the hour, they were walking past our house, older children herding the smaller ones, each child carrying a substantial satchel in his arms or on his back. They were quite an assortment; boys and girls, wearing nearly identical shoes, dressed sensibly but adequately. Some had diamond-shaped faces, some long faces; some were dark skinned, some had my coloring. Some had blue eyes and some were tall and rangy. The fact is that they sure looked like the rest of the people in town. I waved to them from the porch and they smiled and waved back. I was curious about them. I knew they must have stories to tell and I wanted to hear them. Two of the children who had recently arrived at the home spoke only Japanese. They had been kidnapped by the Japanese when they took Attu Island.

Mama registered me in the fourth grade at William H. Seward School, two blocks from my house on Third Street. There would be ten fourth graders this year, seven fifth graders and ten sixth graders. Miss Tenney's first graders and the remaining grades would be combined.

Seventh and eighth graders constituted the junior high. They had classes in a separate building which they shared with the high school, which served the thirty students in grades nine-through-twelve.

That made twenty-seven of us in our combined fourth, fifth and sixth grade class. Those two girls were in sixth grade, along with a boy named Andrew. He had lots of friends, but the person he spent the most time with was his little brother, Earl. Actually Earl wasn't little anymore. He was shorter than his brother, but he was built like a fireplug.

Earl would be my first experience with someone who had come into the world with mental difficulties. Something about his eyes led me to know that he was different. But he smiled so much, I sometimes wondered if his face ever ached. He wore all kinds of hats, usually a wool striped cap, or an old leather aviator's cap, but once in awhile he would surprise me by wearing something different. He had trouble keeping up with fourth grade subjects, but he worked so hard at each chore, it was impossible not to admire him as well as like him. In case anybody was tempted to take advantage of him, his brother was always there with him. Andrew called him Early and those two were best pals.

Of course Cynthia was in my class, and I began to feel that I was going to like it in Seward. I connived to sit near her in class. Cynthia's wardrobe in fourth grade was iconic. She nearly always wore a jumper to school which reflected her mother's penchant for green and brown. Her feet were a little longer than mine, and, like mine, nearly always encased in brown oxfords or saddle shoes when weather permitted.

Our teacher was Mrs. Vohlman. We figured she was in her early fifties and tried to be a good teacher, but though we were few, we proved to be a challenge for her. In retrospect, I think we were an unusually bright and imaginative group and therefore difficult to control. We were forever dreaming up projects and it taxed the lady dearly to keep up with us. Since we unkind children thought she must have been a Mrs. for a hundred years, we often pondered just what had happened to Mr. Vohlman. We giggled, imagining Mrs. Vohlman sorting his socks and folding his BVDs over and over, until they were thin as gauze. Perhaps she wore him out, just like his socks and his undies. Or, we thought he might have expired from always sitting up straight and using the proper fork.

Mrs. Vohlman's skinny frame fed our demonic imaginations. We figured she was so old that all her wrinkles and creases would run together someday, and she would just slide under the classroom door and out of the school like a cup of oil, her eyeballs blinking back at us.

Cyn and I soon found that we were fiends with crepe paper, an item which appeared to be abundant in our school storeroom. We gathered the stuff with needles and heavy thread, we pleated it, stretched it, twisted it. We made costumes, decorations, May baskets, blossoms; the truth is we became the consummate crepe paper queens of the school and our talents made us Mrs. Vohlman's little darlings, a relationship we did little to discourage.

The two perfect girls now had names and families. Merrylyn, of the porcelain face, was the daughter of the owner of Kimball Mercantile. Her mother was the town doyenne and she taught dance lessons. Gloria, of the blonde ringlets and the eyelashes, had a mom who was beautiful, always perfectly made up, distant, and unhappy, I thought. I witnessed those girls every day in class and I still couldn't figure out how they kept so unwrinkled.

My school wardrobe consisted of cotton dresses, left over from my New Mexico days. Under them, I wore undershirts and over them I wore sweaters. Within weeks, I launched into a growth spurt and soon Mama was madly adding ruffles to the hems of those dresses. That green and white dress that I wore on the ship was already too tight around the middle. Mama had made it from a dress of Tia's and I would have worn it every day if I could. The problem was that when we jumped rope at recess, the snaps in the back would give way to my expanding body and I would exit the rope with the snaps at the back totally open, underwear and petticoat flying about. I would skip over to the school wall and put myself together again. It didn't bother me at all—I figured nobody else noticed since I couldn't see myself from that perspective. Unfortunately, I miscalculated; I suspect Mrs. Vohlman called Mama because the snaps were soon reinforced with grippers. Eventually, the dress just disappeared completely from my closet. I still mourn its demise.

My Alaska afterschool routine was like this: I would put away my school clothes, don flannel-lined blue jeans, and begin chores—clothes to fold, table to set for five of us, onions or celery to chop. I was also responsible for some of the simple ironing. I wasn't tall enough to do shirts or dresses, but I could iron handkerchiefs, tablecloths, pillow cases and sheets. The truth is, I liked doing it, as long as I could listen to the radio as I worked. All of those chores I would finish as quickly as humanly possible, so Cynthia and I would have some time to play.

Cynthia's house was two blocks from mine and closer to the mountain, on A Street. I came to know Cynthia's routine, as well. She practiced piano, and, when her mother was busy with piano students, she helped prepare dinner. I learned that there were certain foods that her family did not eat, and food preparation entailed care. So that was what it meant to be a Jew, I thought.

I found I was not so advanced in arithmetic as I should be. I had mastered subtraction in Gardner, but my class in Seward began the year reviewing multiplication tables and I was hopelessly lost. I didn't know them at all, and I didn't want to know them. I tried every trick I could devise to ignore the problem, but it was not to be ignored.

Perhaps the same person who called about my dress, also called about my lack of math skills. Mama and I had a very serious talk and for many months, any reading from the book on Alaska was put aside in favor of reciting the times tables. I shared my despair with Cynthia and she volunteered to help me.

On many afternoons when she came to my house or I went to hers, we worked on the infamous times tables. In her bedroom, or as we walked paths at the base of the mountain, she would cue me. Sometimes she made up rhymes to help me, sometimes we marched to the rhythm of, "Seven times nine is—, three times eight is—."

She made a game out of that onerous task; she even found a way to explain to me *why* multiplication was important. She made up quizzes about the things around us, as in, "If there are twelve sets of five jujubes in a package, how many does each of us get?" Important things like that.

One day she told me that in the Bible, Daniel talks about multiplying by fours and I wondered which was more onerous for him—multiplying or entering the lion's den. Finally, I mastered the blasted things.

***

One day when we were walking home I asked, "Cynthia, what was it like to be here during the wartime?"

"Gee, Marisol," she responded, "it was awful. Yes, awful really, and scary. I was little, but I remember people everywhere. Strangers, dressed in strange uniforms, with grim looks on their faces. They all seemed so serious…and in a hurry. They all had rifles on their backs and guns on their belts. I was little and Mother kept me home with her all the time, especially in the winter. There weren't many sidewalks and even those were muddy, deep enough that I could sink to my knees, and they were rutted with frozen snow all winter."

We trudged along, walking over toward the airport. She looked at her feet as we walked and I caught glimpses of her as she continued. "There were these big army trucks, with huge wheels as tall as I was, that would spin and spit out rocks and mud. I can still hear the noise and see the mud." She paused, recalling some scenes and working at finding the right words. "Sometimes my father took us to his office, and from there we could see huge gobs of plane parts come out of the ships' holds, and the ships were painted gray and black, really ugly. Anyway, we would watch that, and there were all these grim people doing grim work.

"I remember the fire in town just before Pearl Harbor was bombed, and that was really scary! The sky was dark, and flames were everywhere."

"What caused the fire?" I asked.

"We still don't know. But it doesn't take much with all these wooden buildings. Anyway, when the oil tanks exploded, I thought the whole world had exploded and I just screamed because father's office wasn't far from there. But it was the Steamship Company that burned, not the fishery. A lot of Fourth Street burned. It seemed so strange that things were burning and still snow was falling all over, white and then gray and mucky with ash. I saw the flames reflected in the melted puddles, making strange designs. Ugh, I will never forget the smell, the smell of burned wood and oil that made my nose clog up."

She looked over at me, and then continued, "My sister Louise was only seven, and I remember she just started to cry and cry, and Father held her and tried to make her feel better. I remember he made tea for both of us, and told us to wrap up on our beds, and he came in and tried to get our minds from the terrible scene outside. He told us stories about his family in Europe, about his crazy cousin Benjamin who put castor oil in the chicken feed."

By now we had turned and headed toward home. We spotted a couple of large rocks and we sat on them while she continued. "Oh, Marisol, we laughed so hard! Benjamin is Father's relative who makes everything into something else—if it is supposed to be a cake, he'll make it a pie, and if it's a box, he'll make it into a lamp. Oh, how Father can make me laugh about Benjamin.

"Anyway, all during this time, Mother was expecting Aaron. Sometimes she tells us how she bumped into walls and furniture with that big tummy, and today we can laugh. But it wasn't funny then. On December first, she went to the hospital and Father came home and told us that we had a baby brother. She came home just the day before the Pearl Harbor bombing."

Cynthia turned to face me, remembered fear evident in her eyes. "I can't explain to you how awful that was—that was a very frightening thing. I didn't understand what was happening. Nobody understood, really. There were no airplanes overhead protecting us, and the only communication we had with the outside world was the telegraph, and that was sketchy at best. Suddenly everyone was leaving, and in a big hurry. Everybody in town was sure we were all going to die the next day, so they piled out of town on the train as fast as they could go. I was afraid, but I didn't know what to be afraid of. And anyway, where would we go?"

We had begun to walk again and we came to my house. But Cynthia wanted to talk some more; I'm not sure she even knew where we were. So we walked on, and still she kept talking. It seemed as if she needed to do that, so I didn't stop her. "So we stayed, and we prayed," she continued. "We covered the windows day and night and sometimes there was no electricity even if we did want to turn on a light. And it was bitter cold. The trucks drove with their headlights barely shining. They were painted with blue paint. I remember that, and I remember Aaron crying a lot, and mother worrying about washing and drying diapers and whether we could keep the house warm, and if we would have food to eat. We filled jars and bowls with water, just in case. Oh, I remember we spent a lot of time in front of our little kerosene stove. Just beside the stove was a box of asbestos blankets for us to wrap ourselves in if we caught on fire."

The thought of my friend catching on fire frightened me to the bone. We kept walking and I said little. By then, we had walked past her house. "My sister read to me a lot, and we ate out of cans. Have I told you that she is a real pill? Well she was still kinda nice back then. That was the time for Hanukah, our feast of light, and I remember Mother saying something about being grateful that light was the only thing we didn't have."

Cynthia's mood lightened as she talked about light, I swear. We turned back toward her house. "I remember lighting those Hanukah candles in the kitchen, with the door closed so they couldn't be seen. I remember lighting the candles and my parents singing."

We arrived at her house. "Oh!" she blurted, "come inside, I want to show you something!"

She led me to the hall closet, pulled out a cardboard box, and, with a quick flourish, slipped on her very own gasmask. She clowned about, dancing like an otherworldly creature, but I couldn't think it was funny. That thing was grotesque and terrifying and I'm sure my face reflected that thought. Saving soap and grease and newspapers were such trivial sacrifices, considering what my friend's family had endured.

***

Although evening arrived sooner each day, most afternoons Cynthia and I still found time to walk and explore. New buildings sprang up as charred debris was cleared away. The Alaska Shop was nearly rebuilt, as was the building next door. We visited the Kimball Mercantile more than once trying on their wool caps and sunglasses, testing the patience of the saleslady and hoping that Merrylyn's father didn't know who we were. Often we spent our allowance on jawbreakers at the Palace of Sweets.

Saturday was Cynthia's Sabbath—a time she usually spent with her family. But on Sunday afternoons after mass, we would walk down to the roller rink at the Kenai Trading Post and watch some of the high school girls flirt and skate with the soldiers. On one Sunday, we saw a ninth-grade girl kissing a soldier while rubbing his rump. We looked at each other in amazement. That was a sight we were not ready to cope with. We pondered what her parents would do if they knew. But now, looking back, I wonder if we both kind of wondered what that would feel like.

We walked to Lowell Point where the ground was lightly covered with a skiff of snow already peppered with grit, ruts, and pebbles. We leaned against a large rock, looking out at the eagles as they grabbed the day's catch, and concentrated on our jawbreakers.

"Look at all these paths, and the tiny gravel road," Cyn pointed. "See all the ruts around and the junk still here?"

I looked toward where her finger indicated.

"Now I remember more of the changes here," she said. "All of a sudden, after Pearl Harbor, there were hundreds of soldiers instead of a few, and they plowed the trees under, and built that huge tent city they called Fort Raymond. See, that's what is left of it."

She pointed toward a pile of wood pallets and poles. "About three hundred men lived there, and they plowed up the sides of Mt. Marathon, and blasted holes in rocks all over here to make hiding places for their big guns. There were guns over across the bay and near Humpy Cove too, and on Rugged Island, and there were radar stations and huge search lights."

"Hundreds of soldiers?" I asked.

"Yeah, more than you can imagine, really. Most were in the Coast Artillery, and there were other uniforms, and sometimes there were tribal people here, too. I remember they came in on their snowshoes, and sometimes the ships would load them up and take them south to get them out of danger."

As she rattled on, I remembered seeing the blank faces of those people at the dock in Ketchikan. Eventually, she had finished talking about that subject, I figured. As we headed home, we chatted about our jawbreakers and school. There would be other opportunities for me to learn more about Seward.

***

On an October day, Cynthia and I set out for town. Alaska winds blew in off the bay, through town, and points north, bringing snow, too. But so far, we could still negotiate the roads, even though sometimes the wind blew us places we didn't want to go.

We ambled toward the diversion channel. Nearby gray waves washed ashore carrying froth and foam, whipped up by the wind. The waves lapped vigorously onto shore and out again, revealing shards of soft, pale colored glass, worn by decades of wave motion. We could see tiny limpets holding onto pebble and glass, still determined to survive in spite of their chilly, watery world.

"Along here somewhere," Cynthia remarked, "was the spot where the Russians built their ships. Built their *ship*, rather. They began to fight with each other, so their activities ended quicker than they wanted."

We walked on. By now, our gloved hands in our pockets, our noses began to drip. We were near where I had seen the lady in the Cadillac. "This street used to be called Homebrew Alley," Cynthia said. Actually it still is, I think. Some busybodies tried to rename it Champagne Street, but that sign didn't stay up for long."

"Why?" I asked.

"Well," Cyn continued, "Mother says that it started before my parents arrived in Seward. There was a time when people made their own booze. Miners and trappers and railroad workers have to have their liquor, you know. Then when all the soldiers came to town—"

"How did they make it?" I asked.

"I don't know, really." We stopped just long enough to dig out handkerchiefs for our noses. "But I think it had to do with tubes and big copper pots and fires. Father says that there are lots of tiny stills between here and Moose Pass even today. Father even made some wine one year in one of Mother's big crocks."

She paused and then pointed, "Over there, look. There used to be a soldier standing all the time, with a rifle. And there were others all over, especially on the other side of the bay. There were military police, two together always, walking through town, night and day. But, of course, the days were really nights. Oh, and did you know there were Japanese submarines in the bay? People say they came in twice, but we didn't catch them."

I tried to imagine what a Japanese submarine would look like.

"Cynthia," I whispered, changing the subject completely. "Have you ever seen a lady who drives around in a Cadillac and she…"

"Has a colored driver with a derby, yes I have seen her, but all Mother says is that she's a rich lady in town. That's all she will say."

It was clear that she didn't have any more for me on that topic.

***

For all of September, the Seattle dockworkers had been on strike. That meant that ships didn't arrive with fresh food; and, by now, certain foods were scarce. We all became creative in order to survive, and we learned to share. Mama utilized some of those crazy items we found in the bodega, and elk and deer meat became daily staples. We grabbed any canned food we spied at the military salvage store. Mama mixed store milk with powdered milk and Ida brought us a bit of cream along with her cabbage and carrots when she could. Mama began growing chives, oregano, and parsley in jars on her kitchen window sill, and we didn't throw away anything that could be mixed with something else for another meal. Citrus fruit was nearly impossible to find, but one day Cyn and I found a lone, dried lemon at the grocery store. We bought it, split it, sprinkled it with salt, and devoured it. The enamel on our teeth may have suffered, but the lemon was delicious, skin and all.

Over the days and weeks, Cynthia pointed out what the people in town called *sourdoughs.* Some were miners or trappers, in town for the winter, or here to replenish their supplies before they headed out again. Some were done with their days of trapping or mining or hunting and they got by, like Garbage John, checking out trashcans, or sleeping by the railroad station or wherever they could find some comfort and protection from weather. Disreputable as they looked, and unpleasant as they smelled, they were a harmless part of the town color. Their faces might change, but there always seemed to be at least five or six and they congregated at Solly's Bar. We never understood where they got the money to buy booze, but they hung around there just about any time of day, in particular in the afternoons and evenings.

Cynthia pointed out one called Charlie Coyne. We watched him one afternoon, arms and legs flapping about, entertaining anyone who would listen. I don't know how many pairs of socks he was wearing, but I saw the tops of at least three different colored designs curling around the tops of his weathered boots. He must have had a protruding chin because a dark, whiskbroom beard jutted from his face which looked for all the world like the cowcatcher on the front of the train engine. So I called him Cowcatcher Charlie.

We found that nobody paid much attention about what they said around us—we were just kids after all—so we caught bits of gossip as we walked through town, more than people would expect us to know. We heard the whispers about the high school girl who had to get married, about the high school boy who took the change from the cash register at the grocery store, about the children at the Home who had measles, about the army officer who had a heart attack. We heard a couple of nurses *pfrump* about Port Captain Pumphrey who thought he had to go south to find himself a proper bride, and we heard that the German prisoners of war, still incarcerated on Excursion Inlet just south of Seward, were on strike.

***

Cynthia's home was different from mine and it intrigued me. My nose took in exotic aromas from the kitchen; dark wood floors always shone, books on shelves filled an entire wall, white linen lacy cloths covered many surfaces, and, on the dining room sideboard, stood a polished candelabrum which Cynthia called the menorah. Near the Bergen's front window sat a baby grand piano, proud and lustrous, absorbing much of the living room space. Often I sat listening while Cynthia played, sometimes accompanied by Aaron on the violin. Occasionally, they groaned when their mother insisted that they practice, but not often, because they really loved to play. But I never heard Cynthia's older sister play anything. She had mastered the art of shrill off-key whining, instead.

"Just a few weeks ago Louise declared that she would never play the piano again," Cynthia told me.

Louise honed her skills at being a difficult teenager and she was good at it. She wore down every creature who had to occupy space near her, even the family dog. I began to watch her behavior when Cynthia and I did our homework together. We could, if we wanted, view her through her open bedroom door, surrounded by fashion magazines and listening to her recordings of Frank Sinatra and Perry Como. She had hopes of being a cheerleader next year, and sometimes we could see her practicing jumps, checking out her figure in the mirror. That body was ripening to perfection and she knew it. It was fun to catch her when she didn't know anyone was watching; she sucked in her nonexistent belly, checked out her silhouette and pursed her lips. Even then, she pouted. Cynthia said she thought her sister was unhappy because she had been too young to attract the attention of the sailors and soldiers who were here during the war years.

One afternoon while I was there, Louise came into Cynthia's room and took a scarf from her drawer. When Cynthia protested, she said, "Don't get all upset, Useless One. Maybe I'll let you borrow something someday." She blew her sister an air kiss and pranced out.

"She *borrows* money from Aaron too," Cynthia said. "The only thing is, she never pays it back."

I knew that she had closed Cynthia's fingers in a door last year. "She apologized," Cynthia said, "in front of our parents, and then came into my room and told me she wasn't sorry at all. My fingers swelled up and my fingernails turned black. I was afraid I wouldn't be able to play piano ever again. But they got better." Cynthia shrugged, as if that was something not to be concerned about anymore.

Louise's lodestar, her very reason for life itself was her newly acquired boyfriend, Byron Peterson. Byron was the tall, too-handsome only child of one of the few wealthy families in town. He was the kid who, with his father, rode those beautiful Appaloosas at the start of the Fourth of July parade. He was a rising star of our football team and president of his eighth grade class. The junior high girls swooned over him, with his fetching lock of dark brown curly hair that fell across his forehead at just the right moment. His darling pouty mouth betrayed weakness, I thought, even meanness, and a lot of kids thought he told the truth only when it suited him.

Louise doted on him; in fact she did most of his homework for him. I don't know if he ever cared about her, but I suspect that he loved himself so much there was no room in his teeny heart for anybody else.

MAMA AND THE BRIDGE LADIES

I am at our Seward home now, the one Mama and I worked so hard to make our own. I sat on that hillside in Hope as long as I could, but I was finally chilled through and through. So I packed up my notebook and all the pieces of paper I had brought with me and headed down here. I can smell the aroma of my pot of coffee brewing; I'll continue writing as soon as I grab a cup and a decent pencil.

Once a month, I drive down the Seward Highway from my apartment in the Portage Valley and it is always comforting to return home, even when it is empty. Mama lives most of the year in Anchorage now and, at this moment, she is visiting Susana and her husband in South America.

I have just spent some time wandering about, checking for mice and break-ins. When I do that, I always find myself thinking about our first years here in Seward. I gaze through the porch windows at the late summer sun's rays; they are canted and the leaves on the aspens quake crazily when the wind gusts. In Seward, these are friendly winds, so far not insistent. I sense no portents which would make Dotty Etta shiver.

Cynthia arrives tonight. She is flying to Anchorage from Toronto, where she teaches advanced math at the University of Toronto. She is also a resident guest pianist with the Toronto Symphony Orchestra. I feel pleased about her well-deserved success.

Okay, Raven, wherever you are, here I am, ready to go. A pile of paper beckons and pencils are sharpened. I have decided the time is right to talk more about a person very important in my life, Mama.

As I remember her in Gardner and our first years here, she had thick, dark brown hair which she pulled into a bun at the nape of her neck each morning. By midday, misbehaving wisps of that hair would threaten to break loose into curly waves across her forehead and the nape of her neck. I can still relate the litany she would mumble as she tried to shove and coax those locks of hair back into place. Finally she would give up, exasperated. Then her smile would return and the crows' feet between her eyebrows would vanish.

She grew up on that rancho in New Mexico surrounded by animals, servants, friends, and a very loving family. I have talked about her father and I mentioned that he was *exijente*, demanding. That is, he expected much of her and expected that she would have a mind of her own. In 1935, she finished her second year at the University of New Mexico and returned home for the summer. Within weeks, she met Daddy and her career plans careened in another direction.

"My life just took a *desvio,* a detour," she used to say.

Daddy had recently graduated from the University of New Mexico and Grandfather Don Juan Felipe Fernandez was one of Daddy's newly assigned clients. He often talked about the day he drove out to the rancho to introduce himself. As he pulled up near the house in his new blue Chevrolet sedan, dust flying behind him, he saw Mama standing on the patio, and she saw him, too.

At that very moment, as they both would say, that was that. Mama was totally smitten by the tall red-haired Irishman with the wide Will Rogers smile and freckles that danced across his nose.

Mama tells me that sparking is a word for courtship; well, they sparked, all right. Mama's thoughts of returning to school were forgotten and the lovers succeeded in eventually wearing away Don Felipe's resistance. My grandparents and Tia Susana told me stories of the wedding day, and photographs reveal a bright sunny day and a traditional Chicano wedding. I still swear I can hear the mariachi croon *Por tu amor.*

The new couple bought an adobe cottage in town and began their happy life together. Mama worked as secretary in the insurance agency, soon becoming office manager. In good time, I came along and we became a trio. Now, isn't that a perfect picture?

Then came the day we lost Daddy. Sometimes I dawdled walking home from school, picking up bugs, or measuring my steps so I didn't ever step on a crack. I knew, though, that when I opened that screen door, I would find that ever-present personal treat from Mama's oven—some kind of delicacy redolent of cinnamon, or lemon, or chocolate. It was always part of my happy, predictable life.

When I cried myself to sleep, Mama carried me to my room and left my little lamp on, creating a diminutive haven of safety around my bed. She must have been exhausted. No one stayed to console her; she had only me. I remember once, in the early hours, I awoke, my heart pounding. Something was squeezing my chest and I screamed, "Mama!" I grasped the edge of my mattress and held on. Shadows and shapes grabbed at the circle of light surrounding my bed and my eyes searched every corner for anything that would steal my life from me. "Mama!"

Immediately she came, clutching her chenille robe around her. She held me and I held her and we wept, we two, hostages to our misery, bound by our heartache which would never end. I begged her to sleep with me that night, and she did, and I finally slept again cradled in her arms.

Mama was my bedrock. We began to drag ourselves through each day, and hoped that the next day would be a tiny bit easier to bear. Her pain must have been beyond comprehension, but I was hurting so much that I couldn't help her, and, frankly, sometimes I didn't even think about helping her.

Eventually, the days weren't so miserable. Life went on. On the outside I guess we looked the same. We still lived in our perfect little stucco house. Three times a week, a pint of thick cream and a quart of milk appeared on our back doorstep. We ate, we even began to laugh once in awhile. We worked at being happy.

Now I realize how young she was when she was forced to begin making those tough decisions for us, and, for awhile, I didn't make it easy for her.

Only once have I known her to stumble, and she was wise enough to rely on our God and her good sense to help her find her way. But we will talk about that later.

During our first days in Seward, she forged a friendship with Miss Tenney which was long-lasting. Their shared interest in cooking brought them lots of laughs and praise from those who devoured their food. We were the beneficiaries of their experimentation. Mama's Irish soda bread was tough to beat, as was Miss Tenney's gingerbread. Their goulash and gnocchi were unqualified successes. But their Navajo fry bread was just passable, and we had to be content just remembering Naasha's blue corn tacos.

Mama was never sure why she was invited to join the neighborhood ladies' bridge group, an established conclave of ladies of the town; she just said that she would love to be one of them when she was invited. The group included Merrylyn's mother, Gloria's mother, and Byron's mother. Mama told me she considered herself lucky that the ladies cared enough to include her and she planned to enjoy the hours she spent with them. But that meant that Mama might not be home on Wednesday afternoons when I got home from school, and that I would have a few more cooking chores to do that day. But Miss Tenney assured her that we could fill the gap.

Once in awhile Mama was hostess for the bridge club. On those occasions, I hung around just to study the ladies and listen to their talk. Merrylyn's mom was sort of jolly, and laughed a lot. She wore makeup to cover up large pores on her nose, tending to blend the color out even onto her ears and down her neck, but sometimes she forgot the back of her neck.

Gloria's mom pulled her honey-blonde hair back into a sleek chignon and painted in stark, brown eyebrows just above her real ones, causing her to look as if she were always about to ask a question. She kept a mock tortoise-shell compact in her purse and often pulled it out to dab her nose and cheeks with powder. At the conclusion of the game, as the score was totaled, she would open her teeny silver engraved lipstick case, and a pop-up mirror appeared, just the size of her lips. With it in hand, she carefully repaired her Marlene Dietrich smile, checked her teeth for errant smudges, closed the case, and smiled broadly at everyone, including me. She never really asked a lot of questions, in spite of her eyebrows.

Mrs. Peterson, Byron's mother, just played occasionally. With her light brown hair in waves caught in hairpins close to her face, she was a no-nonsense lady with a deep no-nonsense voice. She wore well-made, but plain wool skirts and jackets, and her shoes were always classy leather—very sensible. She always had something nice to say to me, and I had to wonder just how she could have produced a kid like Byron.

Oh, the stories Mama came home with about the ladies and the town! She would share some of them with me, and more with Miss Tenney, which I would overhear, accidentally, of course. I heard who said nasty things, and whose dog had dug up whose summer strawberry patch, who had flirted with whose husband, and who would chair the next church charity. I began to have a perspective of the citizens of Seward different from most other nine-year-olds.

Those bridge ladies were fun, and they didn't seem to mind our eclectic mixture of furnishings. I have memories of giddy laughter among them, occasionally peppered with gasps and screams when someone bid and made a slam, whatever that was.

Always the afternoon ended with a gooey sugary snack and coffee, served on pretty plates and cups. Mama used her wedding gift porcelain ones, and there were no morsels left on those plates when the ladies left.

Though it was unsaid, Mama knew there was a limit to the extent of the ladies' friendship. Mama was pretty and Mama was charming, and she understood that she was viewed as a potential threat to other peoples' husbands. She was single after all. So she was sometimes not included in their domestic soirees. I mean, just how do you set a fancy table with one extra person? Mama didn't mind, and she told me she had too much to be happy about to be bothered by an occasional slight.

Besides, she had come to enjoy the company of Major O'Keefe. Once in awhile he took her to dinner and a few minutes with the slot machines at the Officers' Club. Or they would go dancing at a roadhouse near Moose Pass called the Nobby Club.

Mama's tenants kept her busy, especially Mr. Lauber, the carpenter. He was blustery, and he smoked a lot, particularly cigars. But his cigars didn't smell as good as Maudie's little brown ones. Under his amazingly short, stubby thumbnail often lingered a glob of dirt and he laughed just a little bit too quickly and too loud. It was difficult to explain, but he tested Mama's patience, and made her nervous. Occasionally he went out in the evenings and returned after we were in bed. But his return was quiet, and he never forgot to lock the door; his trips just became part of the normal rhythm of the household. As long as he kept his smoking in his room and paid his rent on time, Mama stifled her doubts about him.

Mr. Norman's personality was just the opposite of Mr. Lauber's. He was a source of delight as he told us how he missed eating salt mackerel and pickled beets, and once in awhile he invited Mama out to dinner.

She was thriving on our modest success, and for the most part she liked the people she met. She knew the Inkvals, who ran the bakery, and Anna Felch, who published the paper. The manager of the Liberty Theatre, Mr. Tecklenberg, was her buddy, and she knew the manager of the roller rink, and the bowling alley. In fact there weren't many people she didn't know already. You could easily think she'd lived in Seward her whole life.

Then there was Major O'Keefe. He had become something of a fixture in our lives. He seemed to fill any room he was in, and he brought happy excitement with him. He fussed over me. He played rummy with me anytime I asked, and always had cookies or gum in his pocket.

His job in town was to coordinate the continuing breakdown of the residual military installations that remained. Whenever he came to our house, he arrived with some commodity that had become exotic to us—cans of applesauce, or mandarin oranges—all food we craved during our food shortage. We just thanked him and never asked about the source of the things he brought.

Somehow, somewhere Major O'Keefe discovered a large carton filled with old movies left over from Seward's military heyday, and he arranged for them to be shown on Thursday evenings at the Liberty Theater during the short days of winter.

He decided to make the showings a big event, and, of course, Mama was his date. I remember watching Mama as she dressed to go. She tried to pile her hair together, pinning it on top of her head and, at first, it looked lovely. Then, within minutes, the hair at the base of her neck began to slip out and behave as it wished, which I knew it would do. I watched her slip on stockings and high heels that night, something she did rarely. I thought she looked beautiful and, of course, when she hugged me, I smelled soap and apple blossoms. When Major O'Keefe arrived, he hugged me, helped Mama with her coat and held her arm as he walked her from our door to his military jeep, washed clean for the occasion. It was fun watching Mama negotiate that gravel driveway in her heels; and I was glad she would encounter a sidewalk in front of the theatre. I was happy for her and I wished that she would have a good time—but I also remember asking her what time she would be home.

OUR FIRST WINTER IN SEWARD

Winter 1946/7

Citizens of Seward, especially the feminine kind, were becoming downright snarly over the ship worker strike. Lettuce, green beans, even Spam had long ago disappeared. The newspaper featured recipes for creative ways to fix moose, caribou and bear meat.

Their total fixation on food appeared to be why the first snowfall caught people by surprise. Silly, isn't it, since it happens every year without fail?

By November, in the late morning, the sun plays tricks on your eyes; the weakened glow of the sun brightens for perhaps three hours until around three p.m., when it becomes a coral smudge in the sky. Then it gently retreats, and is gone before you are aware of it. In those rationed daylight hours, the sun's beams cast a sideways ray that makes bizarre shadows on the entire area—the snow-covered mountains, the leaden-colored sea, the deciduous trees, bare and still. Tomorrow, the shadows will return even later and exit even earlier.

On those bare branches, the eagles sit by the hour, bodies attentive, seemingly inert, and watching. They sit for hours, their silhouettes blending into the branches, and the salmon-colored sun behind them making them appear black to my eyes as I watch. At my feet their shadows, grotesque lumpy gray cartoons of the bird, appear on the uneven snow banks. Their shadows seem tangled in a web of jagged lightning bolts which shoot out in every direction. Suddenly the eagles spot their prey and pounce, skimming the water's surface, grasping in their talons the unfortunate creatures destined to be their next meal. I have watched this winter ritual often. Whenever a rogue school of herring would enter the inlet on their way up the river, eagles were never far behind.

Eagles are carrion eaters as well as raptors. In winter, when food is less plentiful, they will devour, any kind of carcass, bird, fish, or animal.

As cold winds arrived, Mama began to worry anew about heating this frame barn which was our home. We covered windows with thick, insulated boards called Celotex and cardboard, which we hid behind our double-lined target cloth drapes. Our pot burner stove would be our central heating. Enthroned in the center of our living/dining/parlor area, it was fed by tiny drips of oil, which created heat as they exploded. The stove had a disposition of its own—cranky, smelly and demanding. It got tender and constant attention from us; without it, we shivered and if it didn't get precise nighttime care, it could explode and burn down the house.

Our living room was, by now, reasonably furnished. A Victorian fainting couch was now covered in new government issue mattress ticking. Two high-backed spruce chairs with cushions newly upholstered in burgundy-dyed target cloth helped fill the parlor area. The chairs were carved in a sort of Alaska primitive style. A large braided rug, created by our very own fingers from scraps and drapery fabric, covered the dining room floor and extended to the couch and occasional chairs.

Daytime hours of darkness and cold precluded any thought of adventure outside of town, so home and school became my center of activity. The school held a Ginger Bake Sale where assorted baked creations, all lovingly made by the school mothers, were bought, sold and traded for the benefit of the school treasury.

With Thanksgiving in mind, Cynthia and I created cornucopias out of brown paper bags from the grocery store and we filled them with our painted papier mâché apples, pears and bananas.

Mrs. Vohlman read Washington Irving's *The Headless Horseman* to our class each day after lunch, and Cynthia and I were enchanted. Dotty Etta, was thrilled with our interest in this book and prattled on, encouraging us to read *The Tales of the Alhambra.* "The words will sometimes challenge you girls, but I think you should at least try it," she said, handing the book to me. "After all, it is written by Washington Irving."

We opened the book to see words well beyond our ken, but we agreed to try. We scurried to Cynthia's house and began our narrative adventure. As Dotty Etta predicted, we struggled with the language, but we persevered and soon we were transfixed with the adventures those pages offered us. We read each adventure aloud in the safe environment of her bedroom or mine; our eyes widening as we imagined worlds filled with mysterious hooded hermits, valiant knights, cavaliers seated straight and smart on silver and leather saddles atop their trusty steeds, falcons standing guard on their shoulders. We imagined dreamy, doe-eyed ladies wrapped in shimmering chemises, glowing embroidered silks, and tiny velvet slippers. We held our breath as bandits and slaves escaped across steep cliffs and icy streamlets. We met people with exotic names like Boabdil, Zorayda, and Sanchica, and cried real tears when the princesses languished helplessly in the tower, sighing, alas, never to experience the charm of the winsome, lovesick prince. We read of lacy alabaster arches and deep magical caves. We witnessed ghostly apparitions and imagined damsels dancing the fandango with bright ribbons in their hair and tiny golden bells attached to their woven belts.

It took us a very long time to read that book. We devoured words such as, falconry, cuirass, and Saracen, and charged on through the entire book, wishing it would never end. We dressed our dolls as close as we could to reflect the stories, and the adventures continued for many dark winter afternoons. Each time the library book became due, we begged Etta to renew it.

As Thanksgiving Day approached, Mama set out to create a new table covering. With checked fabric and wide white lace ordered from the Sears, Roebuck catalog, she went to work hemming and stitching with her portable sewing machine.

We decided we had to have a fine meal in spite of the strike, but it took real moxie to plan it. Miss Tenney had made other arrangements, but the rest of our tenants would come, along with Major O'Keefe, Dotty Etta and Maudie.

In September, Mama and Miss Tenney had thin-sliced two of Ida's huge cabbages and crammed the result, well mixed with kosher salt, into one of Etta's crocks, covering it with a large plate. They put a well-washed rock from the driveway on top, and covered the entire mixture with cheesecloth. For a month, we endured that putrid smell while daily scraping away scum and sopping ooze. Now would be the sauerkraut's debut, if Mama could find a good recipe.

A large turkey appeared on the porch just before the special day. We asked no questions about its origin, instead busying ourselves picking and cleaning the bird until he was perfect. Then we put him in a pan, covered him, and stored him in the bodega where he would stay chilled.

Now, the day before Thanksgiving, we opened two quarts of our cabbage brew, drained off the brine, rinsed it just a little to remove some of the salt, and put it in the oven to slow cook with bacon, onions sautéed in butter and brown sugar. We added a few cranberries for color and flavor, and began to pray for decent results.

We mashed potatoes in a casserole, baked apple pies, and made stuffing out of dry bread, onion and the assorted herbs Mama grew in the pots on her windowsill. To that concoction, we added fresh pecans, sent to us by my Abuelita Clara. On the special day, the bird, packed with stuffing, went into the oven. Soon that aroma, universally familiar and welcome, overpowered all others and filled every corner of the house. I remember feeling smug that Mama and I had done this together on our own.

I polished Mama's silver flatware and set the table. Forks sat on napkins carefully folded. In the center sat one of our handmade cornucopias, all sorts and sizes of pinecones filled any vacuum. Ruby-colored water glasses sat at each place, a farewell gift from Daddy's family. I made place cards from my construction paper and wrote each name in my most florid penmanship.

Mama was alternately frazzled and radiant in a new turquoise and black wool dress, for the better part of the day covered completely by a cotton frilly apron. The gold earrings Daddy had given her adorned her ears. I had been thoroughly scrubbed for the occasion—my braids crossed the top of my head and were affixed with dark blue grosgrain bows directly above my ears. Blue wool socks covered my knobby knees and, on my feet, were my polished saddle shoes, which now pinched my toes.

Major Keith T. O'Keefe arrived dressed in a gray suit and tie; in his hands were two bottles of burgundy, two small boxes of frozen green peas, a jar of pickled peaches, and hugs for both of his girls. Maudie and Etta slipped off their galoshes and put on their spotless oxford shoes. Their satchels contained a jar of tiny sweet pickles and a large can of black olives.

Just before we sat down, I looked at the sleeve of my new blue blouse. There, bold as could be was a smudge of dried tooth powder and spit. I prayed no one had noticed and quickly went into the kitchen, turned the spot to the back of my arm and pulled up my sleeve so it couldn't be seen under my sweater. Yes, even though toothpaste was now the new fad, Mama mandated that we would use up the Ipana tooth powder. She gave it away as bridge prizes and convinced her friends that it was their civic duty to help us use it up.

We sat down together, Mr. Lauber in clean wool pants and a plaid flannel shirt. His huge, rough boots were newly polished and his fingernails were stained, but almost clean.

Major O'Keefe carved the turkey as Mr. Norman told stories about holidays in Oslo. We didn't have wine glasses, so we drank from our matched set of jelly glasses, which sat next to the ruby ones. I drank my little bit of wine, well diluted with water, and remembered family times in Gardner. Abuelita Clara fixed turkey the old way, *adobado* and served it with fresh white rice speckled with carrots. But on Granny Bridey's lace-covered table would stand at least three sizes of beautiful glasses—thin, etched with delicate flower designs. I smiled as I recalled the holiday cleanup ritual when Daddy and the men would sing and play their Irish tunes. My favorite tune was one that described a beautiful woman. The words were like this:

"The captain fell in love with a lady like a dove—."

I loved that tune and I wondered, with the way my feet and legs were sprouting and my middle was thickening, if ever anyone would think of me as a lady like a dove.

I snapped back to reality and our table. Everyone seemed to be having a very nice time, and I was proud and happy for Mama. Our table was no banquet table in the Alhambra, laden with roast pheasant and candied pomegranates, but the meal was a memorable occasion.

Almost perfect; unfortunately marred by just one factor. As dinner progressed, Mr. Lauber helped himself to more than his share of our wine. While the grownups talked and laughed, the contents of the bottles disappeared well before dessert time. Our gentleman guests were judicious about what they drank; Etta and Maudie didn't drink and Mama drank very little, that meant Mr. Lauber was taking more than his share. As the meal progressed, his stories became louder and longer, and repetitive. He also enjoyed his own jokes far more than any of the rest of us did. Just a little too soon, people excused themselves and our feast ended. I knew Mama was dismayed.

Major O'Keefe stayed to help us clean up. Mama stood washing the dishes and we wiped. We heard the sound of the front door opening, closing, and from the kitchen window Mama could see Mr. Lauber trudge through the snow down the street toward town.

"Going to the bars," said Major O'Keefe, and Mama didn't argue with him.

I wasn't so young that I couldn't sense tension. It prevailed in that kitchen.

CHRISTMAS IN SEWARD

Dull Alaska skies were as close to ink as they could become. Sometimes, when murky fog dominated our world, it took real commitment to walk out the door. At the point of the slimmest sun-slice, we were all sorely in need of a festival of light.

Though massive snowdrifts impeded all efforts to go anywhere, a sliver of amber sun presented itself every day, indicating meekly that life's daily errands must go on. Before we knew it, that small slice began to gain strength and credence. Each day was brighter, the sun's rays penetrating the surfaces of our glaciated and benumbed town. Nature's promise that new life would come again was becoming reality.

Christmas was coming—our holiday filled with promises. Mama and I knew this one would be different from any other we had experienced. We would be away from all the people who had been our family circle, in that sunny place called Gardner, New Mexico.

Perhaps that is why both of us were so set on making sure this would be one to remember. As Christmas vacation began, Mr. Norman arrived at our front door with a majestic eight foot spruce, his face one large grin. I took it all in and gasped, "Wow!" And a great puff of steam escaped my mouth. There may have been trees like this in the New Mexico mountains, but the trees I had known in Gardner were runts in comparison to this Alaska beauty. Mama clapped her hands in delight at its elegance and immediately made a spot for it at the front window. Ida brought a huge wreath of cedar and spruce branches for our door when she delivered our weekly hothouse vegetables and Cynthia and I painted cones and bottle caps for ornaments.

Mama wrote Christmas cards and I added my note to most of them, including those to Dr. Evert and the Nerolis.

At Thanksgiving, I asked Etta to help me find a native-made basket for Mama. Her umbrella and Daddy's shillelagh now were housed in an army salvage trashcan, painted white. I had been saving my allowance and I hoped I could supply her with a finer home for them.

We shared an evening of Hanukkah celebration with the Bergens. We arrived, wrapped and rosy from the cold, peeling off our crystal-covered winter accoutrements at the door. A basket of soda bread and canned pineapple, surrounded by my handmade little ornaments and cones were our house offerings.

Mr. Bergen welcomed Mama, his open hands reaching for hers, and Aaron sat us around a table where we played a game using a wooden top he called a driedel. Candles reflected happy faces at that table, especially Cynthia's, content to share her holiday with us. We devoured potato latkes laced with tiny specks of carrot, and warm honey cake. So this is what it means to be a Jew, I thought.

Barely before Christmas, the forlorn wail of the ship's horn signaled good news. The longshoremen strike must be over. We all salivated at the thought of fresh oranges and tomatoes and we rejoiced at this pre-Christmas gift.

I was old enough to know better about Santa, but I thought ruefully that Seward must be just about the toughest place he would have to visit. At least in our house, we had filled every crack and crevasse with Celotex or tape or woolen scraps to prevent the entry of wind and ice.

Mama and I had attended Sacred Heart Church since we arrived. The parishioners were kind and helpful, and we were beginning to feel like real members of their tiny community. Mama worked when she could with the ladies in the church and sometimes they socialized with the Episcopal Womens' Auxiliary. We loved our priest, Father Paul.

He encouraged us to help in planning the Christmas events. It didn't take much encouragement for me to jump in. Did they need any painted pine cones or papier mâché fruit, I asked. I was nominated to be Mary for the live crèche at Christmas Eve Mass.

Mama fussed over me, releasing my braids and brushing my hair until sparks of electricity shot through it. At the appointed time, she dragged her nervous daughter to the church. Yelping at the bitter cold, stomping through piles of new snow, we dashed to the sanctuary where a coterie of church ladies bedecked me. Wrapped in a light blue shawl which covered nearly all of my electric hair, I was placed in a large gold-painted picture frame, a sweet blanketed baby doll in my arms. There I sat, and I sat, as still as I could, maintaining my best adoring expression.

Worshipers arrived, shook off snow, brushed boots and settled in for the service. I sat. And sat.

The smell of moist wool abated; Father Paul had dressed the scene with candles that exuded a pine smell. Every kind of voice began to sing the familiar tunes beloved by all of us.

"Silent night, holy night; no crib for a bed; oh, come ye joyful and triumphant—"

I came to be aware of my central role in the night's story and I smiled, perhaps more than I should have. I thought about the large crucifix that hung well above me and to my right; I contemplated how cold that bluish, nearly translucent form of Christ must be in that chilled arctic chapel, and wished I could wrap Him in the baby's blanket and give Him my blue shawl.

I pondered what it would be like if His heart could begin to beat again. He could do it; He had the power, after all. What if those eyes became real? What would Jesus see as He looked out at us? Bundled worshippers, beaming faces, some weathered and shop-worn, some sporting wild beards, some with runny noses. Some ladies in proper hats, some in black veils, some with thin wool scarves. Two black faces looked up at Him, and a few black-eyed and tawny ones, wrapped in heavy leather and beaver skin—each one His child, warts and all, offering real love to Him on this birthday night.

After the carol service, reduced to my human status was once more, I was wrapped in my warm, worldly garments, and we trudged the short distance to our house.

Before we left home that evening, we had taken a last contented gaze at our tree now loaded with decorations—some sparkled and shone, some given to us by new Seward friends. Chains of hemlock cones draped the branches I could reach, painted and strung with care by Cyn and me. All softly glowed, reflecting the light from a nearby lamp, our heating stove, and the mellow love of that special holiday.

In honor of the occasion, Mama had made Granny Clara's soda bread, loaded with caraway seeds and raisins and she put a loaf on the kitchen table with a candle to keep it company. This was to be Jesus's treat in case he needed to come to our house, and this would be our Christmas Eve treat when we returned home from church.

We came home hungry. The candle, which had been placed in a small bowl of water while we had been away, was our light as Mama cut into the loaf, carving off two very generous slices, and then slathering them with fresh butter.

"Well, kiddo," Mama announced, sweeping bread crumbs into her cupped hand, "We had better get to sleep if we ever hope that Santa will find this place."

We started toward our room, but not before another glance at our beautiful tree. There hung one of my baby shoes, and the glass wreath Daddy had given Mama on their first Christmas together. There hung a deep red ceramic cross, and a tiny woven figure Naasha had given us. We turned out all the lights we could; Mr. Lauber would be the last one in. With memories of Daddy and our New Mexico family, we toddled off happily to bed. So far we had done as well as we could have hoped.

Mama woke me early. I don't know how, but Santa had found our house just fine, bringing me badly needed winter school clothes, cotton and wool underwear, and bright orange galoshes. He also brought my first Nancy Drew mystery, a Monopoly game, new rummy cards and a Mickey Mouse watch. Packages from Gardner yielded one Navajo blanket, dozens of cookies, Chen Yu lipstick and nail polish (dark red), one very large *ristra* (a string of dried chile peppers), paperback mysteries for Mama, bags of pinto beans, a bunch of mistletoe gathered with a silver bow, stationery, and pictures of everybody (Grandad Cormac and Gramma Bridey standing tall, and Maureen and Kenan making faces). In Tia's photo she held a plate of fresh tortillas.

On Christmas Day, Mama cooked her first bear roast, laced with garlic and onions, covered with oregano and paprika and braised with some of Major O'Keefe's Irish whiskey. Miss Tenney had baked cookies and rolls for us with newly-arrived flour and sugar, and Major O'Keefe brought his usual collection of exotic additions, one of which was a small jar of kumquats in heavy syrup. Dotty Etta and Maudie arrived with a large box wrapped in green tissue paper and curly ribbon. I was thrilled; I knew what it was. Mama opened it in front of all our guests—a lovely basket woven of birch branches dyed in natural colors. It had a stout base and stood about two feet high, just right for Mama's umbrella and Daddy's shillelagh. She seemed delighted, placing it near our front door where the shillelagh, our protector, took its proper place.

After dinner, feeling splendid and filled with the seasonal spirit, some of us decided to try our best at Christmas caroling. Wrapped up and shod in our arctic paraphernalia, enjoying the light flakes twinkling in the town lights, and ignoring the wind that caused the snow to fall at a rakish angle, we trudged to our neighbors' homes and returned, feeling happy and silly, and chilled throughout.

Mama came in last, and, as we peeled off our damp winter coats and hats, I saw that her face had taken on a quizzical look. Her eyes were on the dining room table. Mama's pretty lace tablecloth had been pulled askew, one corner nearly touching the floor. We looked quizzically at one another. Who would have done such a stupid thing? Such a small matter was not meant to compromise the revelers' happiness; Mama straightened the tablecloth. We each filled the tiny spaces left in our tummies with hot chocolate and more cookies and soon our satiated friends began their chilly trek home.

Mama and I picked up the dishes and headed for bed, but not without another glance at our tree. Every tree is pretty, we knew, but this one was ours and it was beautiful. Glass ornaments sparkled, the ceramic red cross from Santa Fe glowed next to a scuffed, creased baby shoe. But hanging next to it was something neither of us recognized. It was a delicate spun-glass angel playing a flute. We looked at each other; we couldn't help but be teary. Where did it come from? We asked about, we inquired, but whoever donated it wished to remain anonymous. We would be content to be grateful. Whatever had caused the tablecloth incident, it paled in comparison to our new angel ornament, and the happiness of the day.

Thank-you notes were our first post-Christmas chore. This time I had to write my own. One of the happiest ones Mama wrote was to my third-grade teacher. In the note she included a copy of my first report card from William T. Seward School which included a not-so-good grade in arithmetic, but an A+ in reading. She also slyly mentioned that I had finished reading *The Alhambra.*

Soon after Christmas, Mama contracted with the woodworker who had made our tables; to make us a sideboard and cupboard for our dining room. Mr. Lauber heard about what Mama had done and he soon made it known he was not happy about it.

Mama and I were sitting at the table when he came in the kitchen. He stood at the doorway, his countenance looming over us, hands absently pulling on his broad suspenders, speaking shyly. "I can do that work for you, Mrs. Downey," he said, "And I will do it for half the price, whatever it is," he said, his beard making a slight up and down motion.

"I really appreciate that, Mr. Lauber," answered Mama. She stood up to face him, looking very diminutive in comparison. "But I have already made a deal and I don't want to go back on my word," she continued, grasping her hands behind her, her fingers lacing and unlacing. "But I tell you what, how about you build some shelves for us in the laundry room?" She cast her eyes about the kitchen, smiling, her eyes dancing. "I really need some, you know, and then when the weather breaks, you can build us a new set of steps in the front!"

Mama finished with her most charming smile, which didn't completely obscure her fear; nonetheless she had indicated to him that she was finished with this subject.

That seemed to placate him; he rocked up and down on his toes a couple of times, rubbed his hands together, nodded his head and finally backed out of the kitchen. The entire conversation didn't last more than a minute, but it seemed like ten, and Mama was on edge. Finally, slowly, she exchanged her unease for a smile. "Well!" she said, turning to me and rubbing her hands together, "what were we talking about?"

That evening, as he had on other evenings, Mr. Lauber set out for the bar, returning past midnight.

***

Eventually, the sun, with determination, began to chase away some of the chill of the season. Icicles began to drip before freezing again, shortening them but sharpening them all the while. Mama could begin to relax, knowing that her efforts to heat our house had been adequate It was during this time that all of Seward was gossiping about the nearly naked hunter. It seems that two sourdoughs, who had been prospecting for gold for a number of months about five miles this side of Ptarmigan Creek, decided that their food larder was low. On a morning more dark than light, in fog which could be cut into cubes and after partaking of their alcohol-laced breakfast, they set out to hunt whatever small critters they could scare up.

Feet in snowshoes, brains insulated with gin and coffee, shotguns in hand, they began their hunt. Their first kill was a porcupine, not a hunter's favorite meal, but better than nothing. Once they gutted it, the stalwart hunters left it hanging in a tree and set out once again. Sure enough, after a few minutes, one saw a moose, got a shot off and informed his pal that he had hit "a big'un".

Now there are those who say that shooting a moose with a shotgun would be somewhat like shooting a hippo with a B. B. gun, but that didn't sway our determined hunters. They set off after the wounded animal, trying to locate a blood trail, but without success. Eventually they gave up, starting back toward their stake, tired, chilled, thinking about a meal and, just perhaps, some more liquid stimulant.

At length, they approached their porcupine in the tree, to a sight that froze their hearts and fuzzy heads more than their noses. Just barely they could make out a grizzly sow standing near the carcass, rubbing her eyes and looking around. Likely aroused from her winter slumber by the shots and by the smell of the porcupine guts and blood, she was now confused and angry at being interrupted. She spied one of the miners, who commenced to yell and raise a racket, firing a shot or two her way. But she was not in a mood to retreat. Instead, she moseyed up and took two swipes at one of them, bloodying his face and lower body, just about removing his clothes. In response, his fearless companion bellowed and beaned the sow numerous times over the head with a snowshoe and a gun butt. At this moment it was as if they had declared a truce. The sourdough caught his breath warily watching his adversary. The sow gazed at him, and finally elected to amble off, confused and slightly sore.

The hunters, clearly shaken, staggered back to their lair, where the unscathed one quickly wrapped his wounded friend in blankets, settled him onto their sled and began pulling him toward the road, a good mile or more away, always watching for the sow.

There, they flagged down a trucker headed for Seward, who piled the wounded one, sled and all, into the truck bed, wrapped him in more blankets, gave him a shot of rum, and rushed toward the hospital in Seward.

At the hospital, the nurse began peeling off blankets, coats of winter gear, shredded clothing, each layer releasing a wave of body aroma, ripe and well-aged.

At last she reached his hide. She was startled to discover, she said later, that among the bruises and claw scratches left by the bear, there were three significant gunshot wounds right there, smack in the center of one cheek of his derriere.

His pal and hunting companion stood near his side, eyes wide in realization.

"Well I'll be," mumbled the wounded one, "I did thank mebbe I felt a sting back thar."

"Hot bedamn, Clyde," his companion exclaimed, "I'm right sorry. I shore thought ye was a moose!"

***

Every Alaskan learns quickly about the many natural dangers which are part of living in this land, and they learn to give them respect; a major one is bears. It is their home territory, after all. They can be anywhere, anytime, and they don't like to be messed with. Bears in Seward come in two colors, black and brown and in two sizes, big and gigantic. Any sensible person avoids all of them. While an encounter with a brown bear is a terrifying experience, one swat from a grizzly paw could break a person's neck, and they don't mind making a meal of arms or heads.

During the war, when the town grew from tiny to substantial, waste and garbage became a real problem. When the snows came, and their food sources were sparse, the bears discovered the town garbage pit, and it was not unusual to see bears loping down Main Street or visiting anybody's trash can. They scavenged wherever they wanted. They could open doors or windows whenever they chose to.

We carefully kept our trash in cans with lids, closed in our storage shed behind the house, and we closed that door tight every night. Even so, one October evening we heard a huge crack and clatter behind the house. A grizzly sow had demolished our shed door, and sat herself down to enjoy a leisurely meal of variegated garbage. Next, she swiped her massive paw and all the hand tools on the bench flew across the room, electrical wires scattering as if they were sewing thread. Eventually, she became bored and left, munching on a butter wrapper. The next morning, we gazed at the damage done by her raw power and strength. We learned something that night. We began keeping our trash in containers with heavy duty clasps, just inside the back door of our house.

Just after Thanksgiving, a male grizzly made a dramatic entrance into town. Witnesses saw him amble among the flat shoals of Resurrection River, across the covered bridge and along the shoreline, and they declared he was at least nine feet tall. His body was massive, the stunned witnesses said, and behind his huge head was a mammouth hump of fat and muscle. He had a wisp of whitish hair just above his eyes that made him resemble a grumpy old curmudgeon. He quickly gained legendary status and he deserved it. He became known as Old Gnarly.

The police arrived and tried to convince Old Gnarly that he would be better off someplace other than in town. They threw firecrackers at him and shot rifles in his direction. At last he decided to bolt, scurrying back up the shore, past the covered bridge, back against the mountain, and up the cliffs. For two or three months, nobody even caught a glimpse of him.

Then he made another visit; he was spotted lunching at the trash dump and a picture of him with his particular eyebrow markings, licking peanut butter from a jar, made the front page of the local paper.

CYNTHIA DISCOVERS SHANGRI-LA

"Father calls him, 'Golem,'" Cynthia laughed. We had been talking about Old Gnarly at recess.

"What is Golem?" I asked, perplexed.

"Oh...," Cynthia paused, and continued, "he is a creature in lots of old, old Jewish stories. He was made out of mud and sticks hundreds of years ago, to protect the Jews when they had no hope for help."

"Why would that be?" I queried.

Cyn's face clouded as she went on. "Marisol," she paused, took a breath, and let it expire slowly, "lots of people think that we deserve to die because we killed Jesus."

"That's crazy!"

"But it's true. And every once in awhile they have come after us with hate in their hearts. When that happens, and it has happened a lot, Jews have had to do what they could to survive."

I was stunned.

"And on one occasion hundreds of years ago, they made this creature, this huge, ugly creature. He has no brain and he can only do what he is told, and he saved the Jewish people. But the problem then became, what do we do with him? After all, he can't think, and he can really get in the way. So they figured the only way he can be destroyed is to dissolve him, break him up." She paused for a moment. "And then we have to think about whether we will need him again," she continued. She was nervous, seeming to wish to change the subject. "So Father said, and he was kidding, that perhaps some army people made a Golem and stored him in one of those hidden ammunition caves, just in case the Japanese invaded."

"Well, we certainly have plenty of mud and sticks," I laughed.

"And plenty of caves, too. That was why Father said maybe he woke up and came to town. Just a silly thought." Cynthia's voice trailed off.

I then got Mr. Bergen's little joke. But after that, I thought about people wanting to kill her people. We would talk about it often, but I can't say that I understood. My friend was smart, very smart. But now I knew she was wise in ways I had not yet had to fathom.

I could understand the danger of bears, though, and now we began to think about what we would do when the air warmed and the snow began to disappear. It was retreating each day; the days lengthened and we were sure the sourdough miners and lumbermen were in the wooded areas nearby already. Surely bears had awakened from their winter sleep and headed up into the mountains to forage, away from anyplace we would be interested in exploring. Each day was warmer, and each day Cynthia and I worked on our parents relentlessly. Finally, in late May, we gained uneasy permission to hike up in the Lowell Point area.

Dressed in what was to be our uniform—rubber galoshes and jackets—we prepared for the muddy paths. We had made lemon Jello in paper cups, and egg salad sandwiches. We were ready for adventure! We marched, no slogged, up the path playing mind games and singing the latest tune we had heard on our radios, something called "Buttons and Bows."

"East is east, and west is west, and the wrong one I have chow-wwse," we twanged as we climbed, keeping a serious lookout for bear sows and cubs or any other variety of critter who would not have our welfare at heart.

Every plant we encountered was greening and budding. Where white spruce and willows offered protection, we spied blueberry and rose bushes covered in sweet blossoms, their feet still buried in small, soiled patches of snow. On the mossy edge, we unwittingly flushed nesting birds. They fluttered up wailing, infuriated at our intrusion, making a racket and putting on a show to divert our attention from their hungry babies.

Suddenly, directly in front of us in the mud on the path, we spied a dead sparrow, its feathered remains weathered and flat, eye sockets vacant. The sight of it was enough to break the hearts of us young girls. We were resolved to give it a proper burial. Just off the path, before a weathered stump, we scratched out a fairly rectangular hole in the semi-frozen loam, and, with somber ceremony, we sent the bird off to Bird-Valhalla. A smooth stone, plucked from the mud, covered the grave and, just behind the stone, we placed a cross of twigs tied with grass stems and new vines. Over the years, we were to repeat this ecumenical ceremony often.

To our left, at the base of the cliff where we stood, was the sea; Fox Island jutted from the water perhaps a half-mile away.

"Did you know that there is an elevator carved into the rock cliffs of Fox Island?" Cyn inquired, leaning against a large stone, taking a drink of water from her thermos.

"No!" I exclaimed. "Why?"

"Well," she began. I sat next to her, gulping water, as well, "those cliffs are so steep, that was the only way the army could mount a big gun at the very top. We can't see it, but there are big holes cut into the rock where the guns could point at the Japanese either coming in from the ocean, or if they had gotten into the bay."

She took another swig of water. "They found a body up there in the caves."

"Who was it?" I asked.

"Never knew," she continued, placing her thermos back into her canvas bag. "And I have never heard anything more about it for a long time."

"Hmmmmm," said I. I could imagine all sorts of scenarios.

We could smell the ocean and hear waves lap against the rocks, but our view was slightly impaired by a thin stand of pines. Refreshed, we began to walk again. The path turned slightly up and to the right, bound for territory less protected from the wind. We encountered heather and high bush cranberry bushes greening and growing among the crazy overgrowth of vines and prickles. The path continued to veer right, and soon we were beside a fair-sized bracken of fiddle fern. The only trees here were spindly little things, barely taller than the huge devil's club, leaves tangled and intertwined with sprawling salmonberry and raspberry vines, all growing with abandon in the lengthening days. On the path ahead, two grouse observed us, and chose to ignore us as they waddled up the hillside into prickly weeds and red-stemmed alder trees. This was, perhaps, a clearing a few years back. Vines were coming to be thick and jumbled and we could see small animal trails, tunnels really, bored by tiny critters, beneath the underbrush. To our right, vines, ferns, and stunted shrubs clawed and climbed to the mountainside where their progress was thwarted and they retreated along their former path, doubling over their own growth and crisscrossing the growth below. It didn't take much for us to imagine mystical creatures dwelling in those tunnels. Our boots crushed bramble and vine as we waded in, and at each step we felt guilt for the damage we were doing. Soon our legs tired of slogging. We uncovered a stump and sat, savoring the site before us as we pulled out our sandwiches.

Just then, Cynthia gave out a small gasp of surprise; she was pointing toward a bump, nothing more than a slight protuberance in the brush. She went over to it, perhaps four yards away, and began to pull away growth from what we could see was an opening in the vegetation. We both were excited and a little bit nervous. I joined her and together we pulled and yanked, uncovering what once had been a carpenter's wooden sawhorse, perhaps four feet long, now weathered and patchy-black from mildew and mold. Once vitally useful for someone cutting or joining or nailing timber, probably when the military site was constructed, it had been abandoned. Such ignominy was not to be, we decided. This would be our own secret Shangri La. We busily cleared the space inside, then scooted and scooched our backsides into our secret spot, facing the meadow before us and the few sparse sentinel pines which obscured the shore of the ocean beyond.

We continued our lunch in our refuge, loving every moment of it. As we munched, we imagined stories about our sawhorse haven. Perhaps the soldier who used it was suddenly transferred to Guam or Midway Island and didn't have time to take down his sawhorse. Perhaps he had died and his faithful sweetheart, living in Arkansas had vowed to never marry, like the maidens in the Alhambra castle.

We could hear the caterwauling from the bird rookery on Fox Island's cliffs. Sometimes we imagined the fretful activity over there, roiling with life while we munched crackers, and planned our next visit to our secret sanctuary. Then, when the warm sunshine caused us to become sleepy, we wound branches and leaves into pillows and took a nap.

When we awoke, the sun's rays had lengthened; we reluctantly prepared to leave, carefully covering our spot with the original vines and some of the neighboring greenery, as well. Our camouflage complete, we backtracked through the weeds and headed home. Upon arrival at our homes, we could barely hide our smugness. We were the owners of a secret hideout. We were sure our faces betrayed our happy secret, but no one in that world seemed to notice.

We returned to our little spot often, usually on a Sunday, sometimes with comic books, sometimes with a deck of cards, and always with a snack. One time we brought binoculars. We negotiated the thicket to the line of pines and the cliff below where we sat, and watched scores of silly puffins waddling about caring for and feeding their brood. We could still hear the racket on Fox Island as kittiwakes sailed and swooped, teasing and jeering, creating rowdy disorder.

On another visit, as we stood so close to the edge of that cliff that our mothers would have been furious, we spied two moose munching away in the mossy bog below, their huge hooves plodding in a mucky world of beech, rye, and goose tongue.

We began to leave an item or two in our sanctuary—crayons, pencils, paper, all stored in a cracker tin. If animals had investigated our trove during our absence, they appeared to have no interest in our meager belongings. Each time we returned, our treasures awaited our arrival.

Meanwhile in town, that place where we lived our day-to-day lives, Old Gnarly visited again. At midday in late May, while pruning her rose bushes, the lady who lived on the corner of Van Buren and Third Avenue called the police to say she had spied what she described as a huge, brown monster lumbering in first gear past her fence. She said she cowered among the bushes and saw the mammoth creature lope along the shoreline, leap over a huge berm and swing up onto Third Avenue, moving fast toward town.

Farther down Third Avenue, as the sixth grade students were outside practicing the Virginia Reel for the spring school festival, the bear strode toward them, seemingly in a hurry for an appointment. Music abruptly ceased, and the sixth graders froze in terror.

The principal ran out blasting on a bullhorn, another teacher beat on a bucket, and a third blew a shrill whistle. Gnarly abruptly stopped, scratched, emitted one huge, horrid growl and a fart, shook his huge head, turned and retreated toward the shoreline.

At this point, those who took it to be their responsibility to protect the town populace decided Gnarly had overstepped his welcome. They chased him out of town with siren blaring. They tracked him, determined to do away with him for good. But Gnarly was not ready to be assassinated. They followed him for days, well back against the base of Mt. Marathon, perhaps three miles into the wilderness, where his tracks disappeared in a path of shale and the river's stony scree.

The next week, they dogged him; they spotted him clawing his way up a cliff. One man took a shot and swore he hit the grizzly, but he couldn't be sure. They saw Old Gnarly continue his climb up the steep cliff until he was out of sight and out of rifle range. He seemed to have gotten the message, because he wasn't seen again, and everyone was grateful. Nevertheless he wasn't forgotten; the entire town had a measure of real respect for the huge canny creature.

A TREASURE PRESENTS ITSELF

Summer 1947

Seward was in the midst of a heat wave. That meant that I could comfortably wear a shirt without a sweater, or even a pair of shorts once in awhile. Days were long and we had returned to our routine of reading from Etta's little book on Alaska. Mama read about the settlers' dreams of a railroad, and its eventual construction, and the building of Seward's first buildings.

In the meantime, Mama had taken the time to ruminate, reflect, and make a difficult decision. She would ask Mr. Lauber to find a new place to live. She had told me that she was out of patience with his nighttime trips, and she suspected he was the one who pulled on the tablecloth as he headed for his room. She had decided, and she would not be moved, but she wanted Miss Tenney and me with her on the day she told him. She was prepared for the inevitable confrontation; if he was displeased with the news she had arranged for him to stay at the Brown and Hawkins Hotel for nearly the price he paid for his room with us.

The truth is, I wasn't going to be sad to see him move on. Our new curtains in his room now reeked of cigars. He had begun collecting old, rusty carpenter tools in a wooden box in the corner of his room. I knew I would find at least three empty gin bottles in his trash basket when I cleaned his room each Saturday, and that sour-sweet alcohol stench clung to his sheets and towels. Now Mama was no prude about drinking; she loved her glass of beer or sherry on occasion, and when she and Major O'Keefe went out some evenings I know she drank, but she knew when to stop.

Mr. Norman always kept a bottle of aquavit and a small glass on his dresser, but that wasn't the same as what went on with Mr. Lauber. I didn't know what was more disgusting—the smell of his sheets, his ashtrays overflowing with cigar butts, his tin cans filled with his gooey chaw of chew, his rusty tools, or the fingernails and toenails he ripped off and scattered onto the floor.

When Mama gave him the news, we were there with her. She charmed him, she nearly flirted, but she made her position clear and would not budge. She stood near the dining room table and she could have leaned on it for support, but she didn't. Instead, her hand gripped the rail of a dining room chair, and she gripped it tightly. She voiced the words firmly, all the while the silver cross necklace she wore at her neck rose and fell just a bit faster than usual. He would have to leave.

In response, his face flushed apple-red; he pushed his huge fists into his deep overall pockets, stood first on one foot and then the other, looking at the floor and then staring past Mama. We stood there also like sticks, silent and nervous, watching him watching her. He absorbed the news slowly, rocking a tiny bit. He turned to leave, and then turned back. I saw his hands straighten in his pockets. He stared at Mama, who stared back, smiling, and did not move. Miss Tenney and I held our breath, seemingly forever. Finally, he turned and lumbered into his room, slamming his door. We three caught each other's eyes and grinned; the worst part was over. But the tension in the house continued to be overbearing until, two days later, he left. I know Mama was relieved to see him go; I had never seen her jaw so set since she made the decision to leave Gardner.

***

July and constant sun allowed for every summer aspect of Alaska's nature to exhibit its beauty. One day, with lunch and our Nancy Drew books in a canvas bag, Cynthia and I headed downtown to spend some allowance money. While we were there, we saw Byron Peterson riding his beautiful horse near the lumberyard.

Lemon gumdrops and bubblegum tucked into our pockets, we began our hike up into the hills. As we trudged, we talked about the most recent fire in town, this one at the tuberculosis sanitorium. "You would think a nurse would know how dangerous a croup kettle is," I remarked.

"Yeah, but wasn't it lucky that she caught it before anyone got hurt?" There were more than forty patients in the "San" at the time.

Next we talked about our new Nancy Drew books, *Mystery of the Moss Covered Mansion*, and *Mystery of the Tolling Bell.* We dreamed about what it would be like to be as clever as Nancy, have a glamorous lawyer for a father and a sporty roadster to zip around Larkspur Lane. We giggled, contemplating what a roadster would do in Seward where paved roads were few and gravel roads could take us only to Bear Lake, Moose Pass and Copper River.

"But we do have taxis," remarked Cynthia. "By the way, did Etta ever tell you about the mysterious footprints on a cliff on Mt. Marathon?" Cynthia asked absently.

"No!"

"Yeah. Well this was during the war, of course, and someone saw strange tiny blinking lights up there. We were all so scared and nervous then."

"So," I demanded, "what happened?"

"Well, the military police, and the intelligence people and I don't know who else climbed up there, and, sure enough, there were sets of footprints. But they just didn't go anywhere."

"So what do you mean they just didn't go anywhere?" I interjected.

"How do I know? That's all we were told. I guess I think what my mother thinks, that the Japanese got up there with ropes, made some signals or something, and then let themselves down to a boat or a submarine, and it never happened again."

She pointed and continued, "There used to be a big, huge searchlight on one of these cliffs, and a sentry post next to it. They turned it on only a couple of times, if I remember. By then, the Japanese had invaded Attu Island and Kiska, and attacked Dutch Harbor, and ships were in and out of here all the time as our troops headed up north."

"Geez, Cyn that is really spooky."

"It really was. There were snipers on duty day and night. I remember Father doing everything he could to keep our spirits up. Once when I was crying, he said, 'But we will get through this just fine; we will just put one foot in front of the other, and we will deal with it one day at a time.' And that is what we did."

"I think some of those days must have been pretty long."

"Yeah," Cyn continued, "even before Pearl Harbor our days were nights, remember. And they were so dark. Then when the long days came, we felt like sitting ducks…"

Suddenly a flash of motion scrambled across just inches in front of us…jet eyes, apricot colored fur. Red fox, vole in her mouth. Here and gone in an instant.

Shocked into instant awareness once more, we decided we had better reserve our thoughts to the present. We both knew better than to let our heads wander. We were not in our home territory, after all. We wore whistles on multicolored braided lanyards around our necks, but they would be of no use if we weren't aware of our surroundings. Now, for some reason, we were not only alert, but on edge. What was it that caused our discomfort? All we had seen was the little fox, but still...

We looked about, our senses on alert, but we saw and heard nothing unusual.

We approached our little refuge, pulled away the vines covering it, scooched inside on our rumps, and gazed once more at the sight before us. In our safe spot we relaxed once more. We read, we ate our lunch, and drew ball gowns for our paper dolls..

We began to feel silly about our unease. At length we decided to go exploring. We had heard that mountain goats had been spotted somewhere near here, so we trudged through the vegetation in search of them. We tromped up the slope, now deep in thorny devil's club stalks and berry vines, until vegetation stopped at the base of the mountain.

There we began to climb and even that was not an easy venture; the base was a scramble of shale and stone outcroppings. Scraping our boots and knees as we sought footholds, we climbed, to spot the goats, or whatever, was supposed to be on the other side of the outcropping. We continued, turning, choosing our footholds judiciously, and then we paused to catch our breath.

"Look!" Cynthia gasped, her breath still heaving, "Is that an opening to a little cave?"

We headed toward where she had pointed, hugging rock protrusions and digging into hardscrabble soil until we arrived at what certainly was the mouth of a tiny cave. We squatted to peek in.

We were, at this point, wary again, watching for critters of any size who might call the cave home. We got out our flashlights and peered inside. Darkness. We listened. Silence. We became resolute; we gathered all our nerve and crawled in. Cyn went in first, squatting as close to the fetal position as boots would allow; I followed, moving in a tight squat. We squirmed about; we must have resembled a couple of nesting pigeons. Finally we sat, crammed in side-by-side, facing out.

My hand searched for an edge so I could sit more comfortably. Instead my hand found the opening of what was a slight crevice in the interior of the outer wall, no more than a slim chink in the inner face of the rock, perhaps ten inches wide. Cyn held the flashlight and peered into the fissure, reaching across me as I leaned back to give her a view. I couldn't see what she saw, but I could see her huge eyes, and hear her breath, just inches from me. She could barely make out some straggly pieces of something, perhaps dried grass. My elbow was still pressed to my side, but I managed to reach in and pull out the something and examine it with fearful, trembling fingers.

It looked to us to be part of an old woven basket. I reached farther into the opening. I could touch something hard, with shape. The flashlight revealed something brownish-black, covered with fungus, a box perhaps, old, very dirty and dusty. Two corners looked as if a rodent had patiently chewed away at it, finally giving up in frustration. It appeared to have endured reasonably well in its dank sanctuary—but for how long? we wondered.

We couldn't even make a guess. With some reverence, or fear, I pulled it out and put the box into Cynthia's lap. She paused and sighed before she slowly, gently, carefully opened it.

Could ancient spores lurk inside, waiting to attack our lungs we wondered? Or perhaps some ancient malevolent spirit would emerge and spit a curse upon us. Our eyes met; we were in new, uncharted territory. Adventures from many Nancy Drew stories roiled in our brains. Our imaginations were in overdrive. We were spooked.

We carefully extracted an ermine pelt, and unwrapped a small piece of pottery with blue patterns on a white background. The second item, wrapped with the same care, was difficult to describe. It wasn't cold like metal, more like a bone, but slightly curved, like a shell with some letter-like scribbles incised into its interior finish. On the very bottom, on a bed of soft fur, lay a strange heavy stone tool of some sort, deep gray in color, with the face of a bird carved into one end. We examined it, rolling it over in our hands. Perhaps it was a hammer, we thought. They looked like this.

Heavy Stone Tool 10 inches

Shell with Etched Letters
5 inches X 4 inches

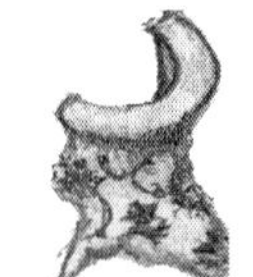

Porcelain Fragment
4 inches X 3 inches

Bentwood Box
14 inches X 14 inches

Basket About
16 inches Diameter

Don't think for a minute that our hearts weren't jumping nearly out of our bodies. We spoke in whispers, fearful that a phantom, or an evil genie, would swoop down and strike us at any moment.

We were now custodians of something special, but what was it and what were we to do with it? We were two very perplexed girls. We decided to put all the items right back into the box and then into the space where we found it, summoning, in those moments, all our reverence and ritual we had ever displayed for our dead birds. We carefully replaced the shreds of basket in front of the box. Next we gently stepped away from the cave, scurried and slid down the cliff, and picked our way through the brambles, too afraid to turn around for a last look.

We returned to the sawhorse, gathered our canvas bag, and quietly covered up our spot.

Then we scrammed outta there as fast as we could.

What, we wondered, would Nancy Drew do in a situation like this?

MY FIRST REAL JOB

For the next weeks, thoughts of our discovery in the cave never left our minds.

"It's as if I have an earthworm niggling around in my head," Cynthia whispered to me one day. "It just never leaves me."

"I know," I whispered. "It is driving me crazy. What are we going to do with those things?"

"Well, maybe we should find a way to forget them. After all, they've been there a long time."

But we knew we could never forget about them. They seemed to be our responsibility now. Surely they must belong to somebody, we thought. We discussed and pondered what to do about them.

Other than that, I suppose our day-to-day lives proceeded according to the season's rhythm. Our long days peaked and threatened to shorten once more. At home we now had a new boarder named Mr. Meninski, one of the town barbers.

By now, Mama and I had established a routine regarding care of our tenants. Washing bedding for five beds was a hurdle. During winter, Mama took the sheets to the town laundry. But that was a hit to our budget, so, whenever weather allowed, we used our wringer washer. The old machine grunted and sloshed away in its corner of the bodega. We manhandled the sheets and towels through the wringer, plopping them into our hefty wicker basket, and dragging the basket out the porch door and to our laundry lines. Sheets snapped when we took them down and folded them, and they smelled of fresh natural air, a smell that still is at the top of my list of favorite scents.

One morning, we awoke to a brilliant summer day. The wind blew away all vestiges of clouds. Though it was Mama's bridge day, we decided we couldn't afford to lose the opportunity to enjoy this fine sunshine. We were up and feeding those sheets into the washer by 6:30 a.m. With effort and luck, we reckoned we could get sheets and towels washed and dried by the time the ladies arrived.

It was a rush, but we succeeded. Mama folded sheets and towels while I began preparing for the ladies. I squeezed every drop of juice from a dozen fresh lemons. I poured the precious liquid into Mama's glass pitcher, added sugar and left it to await water and ice until just before the ladies arrived. I placed the pitcher on the sideboard alongside tall glasses and that was when I heard her call for help with the basket. We groaned, labored and lugged, hiding the basket just inside our bedroom door, minutes from the time for the arrival of her guests.

Mama checked her watch and exclaimed, "Holy heavens, little girl. I just have time to bathe and change. Can you finish getting ready for the ladies?"

"Sure."

I put Mama's china dessert plates, white linen napkins and polished silver forks on the kitchen table, ready for brownies which she had baked while the washer was sloshing away.

We had moved the radio into our room so I could listen to my programs. My plan was to iron while the ladies played bridge.

I was growing, but I still wasn't very tall. My feet continued to lengthen though, and that portended possible height in the future. Even so, I was tall enough that the light ironing was getting easy for me, and I was happy as long as I had the radio to keep me company.

Today Mrs. Bergen would substitute for Merrylyn's mother. The rest would be the usual group—Gloria's mother, Mama, and Mrs. Peterson. The ladies arrived, bringing animated, ongoing conversation with them. Gloria's mom was, as usual, pretty in a severe way, and distant--the antithesis of Mama, who had hurriedly pinned her locks into a ragged twist, that failed to constrain her still damp, frizzy curls.

Chatter filled the parlor; "Did everyone see the engagement pictures of Princess Elizabeth and Philip Mountbatten?"

"Did you hear that George Nishiyama is doing very well with his noodle shop in the Brosius Building? Police will have to keep an eye out for him, still such bad feelings about the Japanese."

"Did you see the pictures of killing and suffering in India and Pakistan in *Life* magazine?" Yakita yakita yakita.

I retreated to the bedroom where I could listen to, *Pepper Young's Family* and the news from the U.S. According to the newscaster, strange lights, looking like saucers that fly had been sighted above Roswell, New Mexico, and Jackie Robinson, the first negro to play on a major league baseball team, was batting well.

While I worked away, each lady came in as they needed to use the bathroom.

Mrs. Bergen was first and, on her way out, she chatted with me for a moment. "Cynthia is home doing chores, too, Marisol, and I want her to practice her piano forty-five minutes this week." She looked over my pile of ironed pillowslips, "But I suspect she would rather do what you're doing rather than practice for that long!" I didn't argue with her, but I suspected Cyn was doing just what she preferred to do.

About a half-hour later, Mrs. Peterson came through, and remarked, "You are doing a fine job there, young lady. Do you really enjoy doing that?"

I told her that I did, strangely enough, "As long as I can listen to the radio."

Finally Gloria's mom came in; in fact she came in twice by the time the afternoon game was over, and each time she left behind her wafted an ethereal, alchemic trail of White Shoulders perfume and whiskey.

"Mama," I asked absently, while we cleaned up after the ladies' departure, "why does Gloria's mom smell of whiskey?"

"Well, honey, she's what I call a sipper. She starts in the morning, I suspect, with a shot of something in her coffee, and I'll bet if you searched her purse, you'd find a lovely flask buried at the bottom. It's sad, isn't it?"

Mama and I flitted here and there, cleaning ashtrays, wiping silver. She continued, "I can't say I understand, really. She just can't seem to find what is meaningful to her, I guess. She apparently needs the liquor to make her feel good." I watched Mama, her face in silhouette as she washed the teacups and placed them gently on the drying rack. Her eyes remained on the teacups.

"But Mama, she's pretty, and smart, and they have enough money—my gosh, did you see that pearl ring she had on?" I wiped another teacup, and then a saucer.

"That's the thing, sweetheart; she doesn't have something, and I just don't know what it is," Mama said softly, sighing, "All I know is that she is wound up as tight as a clock inside and I'm afraid someday she's going to break a spring. I would ask her if I could help if I just knew how."

That entire matter continued to puzzle me. I couldn't understand the problem, much less the answer, and I had to wonder just how tough this must be on Gloria, the girl I thought had the world by the tail.

One day Mama got a telephone call from Mrs. Peterson. Just hearing the telephone ring was still a thrill for us; telephones had just been installed, and we still treated it like a new fun toy. Mrs. Peterson wanted to know if Mama would let me work for her once a week or so, doing light dusting or ironing. You could have knocked me over with a feather. As I look back, I always had the feeling Mrs. Peterson liked me rather like a friend, and kept a friendly eye on me once in awhile. That made me feel strange at first, especially since I didn't have much good to say about her son. But that feeling disappeared. She always treated me well; like the friend she still is today.

I was elated when Mama approved of my working at her house. The next Saturday, a routine began that lasted pretty steadily for the next number of years. Early morning, in fog, snow, rain, or sunshine, I walked to their house. I went alone usually except during those winter months when Mama accompanied me, or Major O'Keefe drove me in his jeep.

In August, getting up early was a cinch; my companion, the sun, was waiting for me like a faithful puppy. My walk took me past a fine view of the bay and the marina, already buzzing with activity my first morning. Trawlers headed out searching for halibut or salmon, motor-boats puttered about; the Coast Guard cutter began its daily watch.

The Peterson house sat at the base of Mt. Marathon, looking out at the lagoon and bay.

It was a large old log home. If I could have imagined a perfect home for me, this would have been the one—beautiful walls and roof, sturdy, enduring testaments to some craftsman's finest work. The walls were log upon log, now dark with age, each carefully routed to fit snugly atop the one below. Plaster filled the seams from the inside, presenting a formidable barrier to transgressing Alaska winds. Resting on the logs were huge beams, entire logs perhaps twenty feet long, spaced about three feet apart, and from there rafters reached up to a rakish point. They, in turn, supported more logs, split to support a thick shake roof. Inside, wide plank floors glistened, finished so that the grain shone through. Huge woven wool rugs covered expanses of the floor.

The kitchen always welcomed me. Mrs. Peterson usually greeted me with peanut butter and bacon toast and chocolate milk. On a polished wooden counter sat a tray with four painted ceramic root beer mugs. Just above them, on the window sill, was a copper planter of parsley. In Mrs. Peterson's kitchen I first encountered shiny rolls of crinkly aluminum foil and I imagined lots of things I could do with that.

Outside the house and to the right was a small barn surrounded by a split wood corral, the home of those pied Appaloosas I had seen around town. Fine, frisky and proud horses, named Daisy and Buck they were, and I was thrilled to make their acquaintance. I talked to them, and I caressed their noses and manes. They struck me as first-class creatures and I imagined they were fine Arabian stallions galloping about the Andalucian countryside carrying gallant knights and rescuing desperate maidens, their silken veils cascading in the wind.

These were my chores at the Peterson house: I folded any laundry left in her basket, I ironed the flat things, and I changed the beds. I dusted sometimes, or put dishes away if she wanted.

Usually, but not always, somebody was home. I liked talking with Mrs. Peterson and I truly admired her. If Byron was home, he just ignored me. He was, after all, five years older than I and lived in a world headier, more sophisticated than I could even aspire to, and I didn't aspire to much.

He could be surly. His parents patiently endured his often stiletto sharp words. He let me know that to him I was an inconsequential gnat on his horizon. Our relationship would morph over the years. There came a time when we clashed and I prevailed, and a time when he stunned me. But that is a story still to come.

I was ready when school began once more in September. The fifth graders had a new teacher named Miss Shaw. She and Dotty Etta could have been sisters, except that Miss Shaw spoke in a southern accent. And she spoke a lot. She wore glasses far down on her little straight nose, and often she would reach into her blouse to pull up her bra straps. We students, angels that we were, would wager how many times in a given day she would reach down there. We tittered and smirked, darlings that we were, and I confess that I was one of the ringleaders. One day, when I insisted on speaking out, Miss Shaw came to the end of her patience.

"Now Marisol, you just hold your tongue!" she demanded in her southern drawl.

So I did just that. Then I waited and waited, my fingers in my mouth until she would call on me, but she never did. Whether she caught on to my pesky plot, or tired of my silly antics, I was not to know. I was forced to suffer my self-made discomfort until I became bored, and pulled my gooey fingers from my mouth and sought a tissue from my pocket, in total defeat.

The truth is, Miss Shaw taught us a great deal that year. She taught us that homework was something to take seriously. In geography she insisted we learn U.S. states and capitals by heart and that was just the kind of thing Cynthia and I, proud and precocious darlings, excelled at. Cynthia told me with glee that she could drive her sister, Louise nearly crazy when she would rattle off the states by regions faster than Louise could file a fingernail. No matter what Louise did, Cyn wouldn't stop until she had finished them all. I'll bet that today she and I could still recite them, along with a verse or two of, *The Owl and the Pussycat.*

Miss Shaw also taught us about our language, how words had jobs to do, that adjectives could paint pictures and verbs could make a sentence dance, or fly, or cry.

She also began to teach us a bit about the realities of the democratic system. We ran our own class activities that year, or at least she led us to believe that we were the bosses. We nominated and elected class officers. When I think back on her influence on us that year, I'm ashamed at my dumb antics.

We fifth graders shouldn't have expected many class offices. After all there were still sixth graders ahead of us. But I nominated Cynthia for treasurer, and I did it because she was a whiz at all those skills having to do with numbers, and everybody knew that. But Cynthia was not elected and I was amazed. A sixth grader won, but didn't people know how smart Cynthia was? I wondered.

That girl was quiet in school, but always right when she answered. Absolutely always. I suppose to others she appeared shy, but I knew better. She was just modest and serious and I knew everybody liked her in spite of her continuing resemblance to a Christmas tree.

Just what was happening here? Why didn't everybody agree with me? I just couldn't get the matter off my mind. I felt bad for my friend, but even more I couldn't imagine why everyone didn't think the way I did.

When I confided to Cynthia, she said to me, "It's just a little thing, Marisol. It isn't the first time and it won't be the last." She looked down and then away, past me. "Forget it and let's just go on," she said, her jaw set just a tiny bit more firmly.

Now that was a strange reaction, I thought. But I never mentioned it again, at least to her. We did go on, but I kept thinking about it. Was it that she was a Jew? I couldn't imagine that. None of us even knew much about the differences between one religion and another, I was sure. She and I talked about it once in awhile; I was Catholic and she was Jewish; but so what? As I look back, it seems that we talked about it only when our religion became a pain and got in the way of what we wanted to do.

Life was certainly becoming more complicated, I realized; and my friend seemed to know a lot more about it than I did.

One day the gym teacher called Cynthia and me Frick and Frack. I had no idea what that meant. All I knew was that the name made me feel uneasy, as if he was saying something bad about us. "What does it mean, Mama?" I asked as I sat at the kitchen table and she sliced apples; I was puzzled. Patiently she put the paring knife down and sat with me.

"Well," she sighed, "Frick and Frack are two ice skaters, Marisol. Funny men who perform on ice, that's all," she explained. "Get me the bag of sugar, please."

"And people laugh at them?" I asked, bringing the sack to the table.

"Yes, they do pratfalls and somersaults," Mama explained. "People do laugh at them, but I think the audience laughs with them as much as at them. People admire them too, because they're good skaters, and people love them, in a way," she mused.

"So do you think he was saying something kind, or something bad?" After all, I thought, Cynthia and I were always together, and I guess we were a bit obnoxious because we always knew the answer to any question. But we laughed a lot, too, mostly at ourselves.

"Perhaps he thought that you two are a good pair," she said.

"So okay, it's all right to be half of Frick and Frack, and I won't let what he says bother me," I resolved.

"Good decision," Mama agreed. "You may never really know what his motives were, but the important thing is, whatever they were, they just don't matter unless you let them matter. I remember Eleanor Roosevelt saying that nobody could hurt her unless she let them hurt her. She wasn't exactly a pretty woman and people could be unkind. Remember what Naasha used to say, Marisol? 'Be like the wise willow and bend with the wind.' In the long run, you will be the winner. Oh, and Marisol," she said. No matter what, you kids did something very right."

"Yeah?"

"Yes. You elected Early to be your Sergeant-at-Arms." She then returned to slicing more apples, adding dashes of cinnamon and nutmeg to the mix.

WE MEET SAVA AND RAVEN

October 1947

In early October, those few remaining leaves on poplars and aspens surrendered and fluttered crazily to the ground. The wind, not always a welcome companion, had arrived and determined to be a force demanding of respect. Perhaps we would be in for those malevolent winds Dotty Etta had described. I shuddered at that thought. For the most part, the wind already blew in from the bay and fairly propelled me toward the Peterson house each Saturday morning. Occasionally, a roaring gust assailed me and I would find shelter by a tree trunk and watch steel gray waters in the bay churn frantically, throwing gobs of froth and foam onto the marina piers and the far shoreline. By late October, those winds had delivered freezing rain and sleet that coated the gravel streets and every structure's southwest wall.

Having accomplished that, the winds often capriciously turned warm, bringing about mush and puddles, and then, just as arbitrarily, froze them again. Freezing rain dripped from the eaves that grew into long icicle stalactites, beautiful but treacherous to life and limb. Each morning, the sun lagged farther behind and morose darkness elbowed its way in. What would this winter bring? we wondered. I thought of Dotty Etta's words about anger in these winds and mischief in the salty grains that pelted our houses. Then I thought about the treasure in the cave and I would fret. What should we do?

My legs had begun to lengthen. By now, Cynthia's shoes were tiny compared to my leather canoes and I had no problem negotiating Mama's and Mrs. Peterson's ironing boards. My sweet red wool leggings and coat with velveteen hood that had come to Seward with us, would not carry me through this winter. I had already begun to wear a thick cotton undershirt under my school dresses, and long wool socks covered my legs. It was impossible to pull last year's Christmas galoshes over my school shoes. The truth was, I wouldn't miss them. They had chafed against my legs, leaving raw, red lines. I donated them to Aaron.

We decided the time had arrived to open Daddy's footlocker, which long ago had been painted yellow and served as my bedside table. We removed the top and pored over those items still carefully folded and placed there, as they were the day the footlocker arrived at our home in Gardner. Memories flooded our minds and tears flooded our eyes, but on the whole I think we both did quite well. We calmly sorted through his clothes, pretending that we did this kind of thing every day. Olive drab woolen trousers and long-sleeved shirts seemed to beckon to me. I tried them on and they fit rather well. Mama set new hems, took tucks in the sleeves, and they became Marisol's toasty warm winter uniform.

In the fold of one set of trousers still lay the Luger pistol, silent, waiting patiently, for what? we wondered. How could something so unobtrusive, almost lovely, be at the same time so ugly? We debated about its future and could only come to immediate decisions: It belonged to Daddy, and so we were to keep it and care for it.

In Mama's top drawer was a department store gift box where Mama kept her silk scarves and handkerchiefs. *The May Co.* was written on the top. Into the box, into a soft nest of color and apple blossom scent, went the gun, and we promptly put it out of our minds.

At the army surplus store, we found leather boots for me and I couldn't wait until I could wear them. I may not have been a beauty queen in those clothes, but I was warm and content with them, along with my new sweaters, dark blue and deep pink.

When Mama wasn't braiding a rug, she knitted. She seemingly knew how many stitches to cast on to form the neck of anything and when or where to cast off for sleeves. All winter, her needles clicked and chattered frenetically, and I was usually the recipient of her projects.

One afternoon Cynthia called with exciting news. Her mom, far and away the best piano teacher in town, had been invited to give a piano concert at the Jesse Lee Home. "My mom is excited and oh, Marisol, just think, this may be our chance, finally, to get to visit those kids!" Her voice was excited; I imagined her rising up on her toes as she spoke.

"My mom is going to perform and she invited Merrylyn, Aaron and me to play, too. Ooh, Marisol," she nearly cooed, "I think this is going to be fun! At last I get to play in front of a real audience!"

It was about time, I thought, and I began to plot just how I could get an invitation, and I prevailed.

The concert date was set for an afternoon in late October. We couldn't wait! We were so curious about those kids.

By then, biting flurries of swirling snow arrived regularly. Concert day brought gusty winds and freezing rain. Already the lakes near Seward were frozen. Main roads had been plowed, encased by a ragged selvage of gray residue. Major O'Keefe drove us to the Home in his jeep. Though the roads were peppered with gravel and dirt, new drifts presented new obstacles.

Wrapped in layers of winter garb, we tumbled out of the jeep and trudged into Jewel Guard Hall, the main building of the Home complex. The director warmly welcomed all of us—Mrs. Bergen and her bundled, retinue of curious kids with runny noses. We were swept inside where a frenzied world of happy children swarmed around us--Aleut children, Athabaskan children, children from Nova Scotia, Norway, and Wasilla with names like Salaktuna and Walker. Whatever their origin, we decided, they appeared to be happy, busy, and pretty much like us.

The director ushered us to the auditorium. On the way, he constantly pushed his glasses back onto the bridge of his nose as he introduced us to teachers and staff and we stole glimpses of children busy learning and doing.

"We have invited one of the local native elders to attend the concert," the director chattered. Cyn and I listened, but we continued to ogle; we didn't want to miss anything. "And he will be telling stories from his culture after the concert," the director continued.

Our ears perked up.

"Would you be interested in staying after the concert to be part of that?" He asked. Would we!

"Yes!" Cyn and I blurted, not hiding our enthusiasm. I caught her eye and I knew we were both thinking about that cache in the cave.

The auditorium was jammed and noisy, children sitting on chairs, seated on bleachers, some on the floor. When a level of order among the children was achieved, the director introduced Mrs. Bergen and brought her onto the stage. The room became quiet then. Here was a new and different adult, and the children were curious.

Then she began to play. She played familiar classical tunes, jigs, and polkas, and they seemed to love them all. But they liked to hear the young people play most of all. Merrylyn played, then Aaron, and finally Cynthia. She played Steven Foster tunes and the children cheered and clapped happily in unison. This was at least something different for them on a miserable winter day.

"More!" They demanded, and Cynthia happily complied.

Finally the students were dismissed and filed out, a parade of foreshortened legs hugging chairs and cushions. Major O'Keefe took Mrs. Bergen and Merrylyn home.

In a large classroom Aaron, Cynthia and I joined a passel of children already seated on the floor. On a bench before us sat the indigenous man I had upon occasion seen in town, sometimes with another lady, sometimes with a couple of children from the Home.

Wrinkles at the edges of his eyes, seemingly carved with a filleting knife, others jagged from his nose to the outside edges of his mouth, precluded any hints of youth. His tawny face was angular and strong, his wide cheekbones protruded, his weathered skin stretched tight over them, his jaw line was firm, straight to his ears. His hair, dark brown to black, was loosely gathered with a leather cord at the back of his neck. Bony, callused hands held each other in his lap; he wore a dark green flannel long-sleeved shirt, and well-worn wool pants; attached to them at the waist front to back were wide, black suspenders. His trousers, slightly wet from snow, were tucked into two damp and much worn dark brown work boots. When he unwound the scarf from around his neck, I could see patterned evidence of additional shirts under the one we saw.

That describes Sava Sahtaii, a Quht'ana, a leader of his people. Rather, that just begins to describe him, a human being who came to occupy a significant place in my life.

Cynthia and I looked over at each other; she smiled and I knew what she was thinking. We evaluated Sava as he evaluated us.

Obsidian eyes surveyed us, his cragged grin welcomed us, and I found myself grinning at him. I tried to guess at his age; he could have been forty, he could have been sixty, or seventy.

He began to speak and I was spellbound.

He asked if we knew who Raven was. We certainly didn't, and if we had, we would have been too nervous to say anything. He surveyed each face carefully; a couple of children giggled. Finally, slowly and absently rubbing his thumb with his other bony fingers, he began: "I am a Quht'ana. Me and my people, and we call Raven, 'Ggugguyni.'" He encouraged us all to repeat after him; "'Ggugguyni.' Can you say that?" We tried, and laughed. "Now with a deep voice, down here," he growled. "'Ggugguyni' eh? That is better." He smiled and paused, looking at each of us.

"Raven is my friend and mebbe you dunno it, but he is friend to you, too." Sava leaned forward, hands on his knees. "He make all this world, and us, too." His arms opened wide to take in all they could, and his deep eyes sparkled. "So we have to give him respect, even when he is naughty," he continued, smiling, his face a puzzle of leathery lines and wrinkles. "And he can be naughty. And impatient. And he make alotta demands." He paused. "But he loves us. He really loves us. So, we gotta love him back!

"But, you know, he is not perfect. Just like us," Sava continued. "You perfect?" He asked, grinning at one of the front row boys. "He love to play tricks and we need to keep an eye there, you know, on him," he said, his finger touching the edge of his eye, "so he don't play tricks on us. Sometimes somebody catch him doing something a little bit bad, sometimes he is maybe too much curious, sometimes he is lazy. But he loves us and he gives us e-v-e-r-y–t-h-i-n-g important we need. You remember that." This was his story for that day:

So you want to know about Raven, huh? You may not know, but you really already do know. You always know. But maybe now, with me, you are ready to know more. How do you like that, huh? Raven always live here, he make this place we live in his home. He look down one day (Sava looked down at his feet, moving them in separate circles) and he take the mud and rocks and he roll them around with his feet, like this. (Next he scuffed his feet.) He scratch out the dirt and rocks and pick and roll it all around with his feet. (He looked up at us and a sly look came onto his face.)

But sometimes Raven, he is not patient, he want to do things FAST and go on to do something else. Very soon he get bored maybe. He began to get hungry I think, and so he left his big, big ball he was rolling with his feet and, um, he just left it. (Again, feet in circles.) Can you believe? Yep, I think he was hungry. So he goes off to find himself some salmon flapping around on the sand by the ocean and he like the look of that fish, so he ate it. That was a big fish! (His arms stretched out as far as they could.) He ate more, and more. He ate a lot, and berries too.

We call most of our berries, *gega*. Can you say *gega*? We have many more names for them, too, but I don't remember what kind he ate. Perhaps *k'enełch'aq'i*. (He paused, took out a plaid handkerchief and blew his nose, then put it back in his pocket.) Anyway I think he sleep, too, maybe, because his gut was sooo full. But I don't know about that. People never talk about Raven sleeping, but how can he not sleep? He have to sleep, but he always, always watching. What do you think?

But anyway, maybe he is not sleep, but he goes away for awhile because his ball got all dry, and hard. Very, very hard and bumpy. (His face contorted, his mouth pursed, hands touched his cheeks.) Oooooh, he was mad. He push at it, he scratch at that ball and he was mad because of all the big bumps and holes he left there. But that was it, he was stuck with it.

He walk around, he pick at it, he kick it, but he was stuck with it. So he get mad, he get angry and all of a sudden he put it in his mouth and spit it into the sky 'way, 'way up there (arms in the air, face turned up) and it rolled around and around and around, 'till

> now it is our land! Fine, he said, we can work with this anyway. So anyway that is how he made our land, and all those sticks and bumps? They are the mountains and the lakes and the rivers. I think he did a pretty good job. He did not think so, but I think so, do you? I think what he did is swell, that is what I think. We call that land *Qutekcak,* and we love it.

"Swell," I thought. What a fine word to describe his story. "I like you, Sava Sahtaii," I said to myself.

I am sure he talked about other things, but that story is all I recall from our first meeting. At last he stood up, and with slow deliberation put on his scarf, his jacket, and a black derby hat. He hugged some of the children, smiled at us, and then he ambled from the room and he was gone.

We filed out, chattering and happily surprised that Major O'Keefe had come back for us. We climbed into his jeep, still excited about the afternoon's events—the children, the concert, the Steven Foster songs, and about this intriguing man and his stories.

More important to Cyn and me, we hoped that he could help us with the treasure in the cave. In Cynthia's bedroom, warm and cozy, she and I did some serious talking. I was sure we could trust him, but Cyn suggested we be patient. I agreed that we should proceed slowly, but we were getting anxious to be rid of the responsibility of the treasure. We waited, not knowing when we would see him again and the wait wasn't long.

Within the week, the Home director asked Cynthia's mother to teach piano to a few of the children. Now that was great news and we always invited ourselves to the story sessions.

Sitting at Sava's side at the next visit was a boy, perhaps three years younger than I. He was skinny with dark brown hair; deep, soft black-brown eyes; tan skin, his expression often serious, almost too serious for his age. Eyebrows usually knitted, he was dressed in what the boys at the home wore—sturdy brown shoes and dark socks, heavy cotton pants and long-sleeved shirt. In fact, he was entirely a study in shades of brown. Throughout the story, his eyes remained either on Sava's face or his own shoes. Here is what he and all of us heard from Sava at our second visit:

> He gave us light, you know, this Raven. Oh, this is so much a great story of my people, I do not know how you do not know yet. Story is old, old, older than time. Raven, he got a look at this thing we call light and he liked it, oooh he wanted it—but there was somebody who wanted to keep it, hide it just for himself, can you imagine? Oh yes Raven was mad, and when he get mad, he thinks. (His middle finger touched his forehead.) He goes up on a branch and he goes from foot to foot rocking like, and he thinks. (Sava's fingers walk on his knee.) He thinks, how am I gonna get that light I like so much? And really I think my people gonna like it, too. Do you think the people like it, huh? (Sava looks at us and we nod our heads.) They can use it and keep warm, Raven think. Like on days like we have now, they wanna keep warm. (His arms hug himself.) So Raven, he hears noise, like 'Mma, bu, guba, na,' like that. Real deep that sound. And he looks around but he can not see nothing. Not nothing—because it is soooo dark. So he listen even harder and he jump from branch to branch turning his head one way and another way. (Sava's fingers jump, his head flits from side to side).
>
> One way and another way. He hear humming. Like this, 'Hmmmm, eh oh eh. Hmmmmm.' He look through the smoke hole of a *nichil q'a.* I told you this is old, old story, older than time. And the old ones, they make house different then. They dig out big hole and put on wood roof with a hole for smoke to go out. So Raven hear that 'Hmmm" sound come from that hole. Raven look and he see a fisherman and his daughter. The fisherman, he 'hmmms' because he is so happy. He have a pretty daughter and he have lots of pretty boxes, some big, some small. The fisherman think, 'Oh boy, I have everything.' (Sava rubs his hands together) Raven watch; watch, from the tree in the dark world. He see through the smoke hole like this. (He makes circle with his fingers and looks through, winking at one of the girls.)
>
> Many, many days he do this, and he see the fisherman open his box, and then find another box inside, and then one more, until he

> have many boxes. And then he open the tiniest box and flash! (His hands open.) Raven see light! Light is in that box! Oh boy, think Raven, I gotta have that. (He rubs his hands together.)
>
> He is thinking and he see the pretty daughter go out with her basket. She want crowberries and roots. (He looks from side to side.) She walk some and then she gets thirsty, you know, and she dip down to take some water in her hand from the stream and QUICK as can be, (He snaps his fingers.) Raven make himself into a teeny little finger fish and Gulp! The pretty daughter drink the little fish up just like that. I think it was what we call, *lch'eli,* fish.

My attention was riveted on Sava. But there came a moment when I felt a small set of fingers connected to a small girl and they were crawling onto my hand. I looked over at a sweet face framed by a halo of wild, short brown curls. Young eyes looked at me, seeking approval for what she had done, and I answered by smiling and grasping her hand firmly. That was the beginning of my friendship with eight-year-old Paulette. We both returned our attention to the story. Sava continued:

> Well, pretty soon, the daughter's belly begin to swell and sure enough she has a baby!
>
> Oh, what a baby. Kinda funny looking baby with yellow eyes that see every place and feet to hold anything. A funny looking baby, you bet, but the daughter and the fisherman think, hmm, he still be a nice baby and they love that baby sooo much that the baby hang around that winter house, that *nichił q'a*. Raven, he don't mind all that attention neither. That 'baby' have a lot of pride and he like how they pet him and fuss over him. He is really Raven, you know. But he remember, he never forget his people and he know he will leave soon, but how? He gets mad when the fisherman play with his boxes and look into his boxes.
>
> So he tell the fisherman, 'I want that box'. (Sava speaks in a high, whiny voice.) First the fisherman say no, but Raven, he just act very bad, very naughty and so the fisherman say, 'Okay, Okay.' Raven is smart and he play very good with the box, he push it, soft and rub his skin on it, soft like.

> So soon, when he cry, the fisherman give him one box more, and one box more 'til he have just the tiny box left. Slow, slow, slow Raven work now. Soft, soft his words when he beg the fisherman for that last box until finally the fisherman, he say, 'Yes.' Then Raven GRAB that light quick as can be and he change into Raven again and he fly out the smoke hole with it in his beak. 'Owwieh,' he think, 'I got it!' He take it to his people and they thank Raven always for that. So Raven walk around with the head high and proud, he happy and proud. Now his people have light.

I loved hearing that story, I knew it well already; Naasha had told it to me, only it was Coyote doing all those naughty things. So those two must be in cahoots, I thought. Or maybe they are one and the same.

One student asked Sava, "You tell us that Raven talks to the people and the animals, but we don't hear that talk."

"Oh you do," said Sava. "But he is not to blame that all we hear is, 'Gga.' He say much, much more." (He smiles and looks around at everyone.) "You believe me, no?"

At last Sava stood, and we knew it was time to go. We stood and Aaron approached the serious boy with the soft brown eyes near him. "Hi, I'm Aaron," he blurted. "What's your name?" Aaron was not exactly shy.

The boy grinned and said, "Hi. My name is Matthias Corbeau."

"Matthias Corbeau," Aaron said, "Well Matthias Corbeau, I live here, not far from the Home. Umm, do you think maybe we could play some cards or checkers some day?"

"Sure," grinned Matthias, and an enduring friendship was begun.

That afternoon we had to get ourselves home on foot. Mrs. Bergen awaited us at the door of our schoolroom wrapped and suitably shod for our walk home. Just a few words with the director arranged for the boys' first checkers match and then Mrs. Bergen led the way into the nearly dark afternoon toward home. Just the slimmest sliver of opalescent light shone over the bay, the waning residual sun. We trudged along, noses wrapped in scarves, complaining about the ice. Surfaces were glazed with ice, polished by the wind so we slid the better part of the way home. The wind had temporarily blown the fog and flurries away, but the temperature was so cold that the stars shivered in the sky.

I loved this Sava; at first I wasn't sure, but now I was sold on his being the very person to share our secret with, but Cyn had not yet agreed to my plan and there had been no opportunity to discuss our secret with him.

SAVA SHARES A MEAL AND MUCH MORE

"Raven stole the sun and brought it to earth today, Mama, to give it to his people!" I rattled on to her as I hung my heavy jacket, wool cap, and scarf on the wall hook near the porch door and pulled off my boots. I kept my sweater on and slipped on a pair of leather mukluks.

"His stories remind me of Daddy's stories about the jackdaw, and some of them remind me of Naasha's stories of coyote. But here in Alaska they call him Raven."

Late fall brought chilly temperatures which pervaded our house. Mama wore a jumper type apron on top of a wool dress and cardigan; she was cutting up stew meat and carrots. In the kitchen, my snack of cookies and canned pears welcomed me.

Mama listened patiently as I rattled on. "I want you to meet Sava, Mama. I don't know how to explain him to you, all I know is that I am so glad to know him and I like him a whole lot, and I want to know everything he has to tell me."

Mama, of course, had seen him in town. "All right with me," she smiled. "Let's have the Bergens over for Saturday lunch and ask him to join us."

That was easy, I thought. I was still rubbing my toes, encouraging warmth to return. "I don't think the Bergens can come on Saturday because of their Sabbath," I managed to speak while simultaneously wolfing Oreos. "But maybe Sunday? That would be better anyway because the boarders fend for themselves on Sunday."

A quick, furtive telephone call took place between Cyn and me; we agreed to find a way somehow to approach Sava about our treasure as soon as possible.

Plans were made for Sunday dinner. Mrs. Bergen was sorry, Louise had plans to go roller skating with Byron, but the rest of the family would love to come. I stood by her side as Mama asked Mrs. Bergen to arrange an invitation for Sava. He lived near Bear Lake, but he and his sister visited the Home often and the director would relay our request. A phone call from the Home confirmed our plans; Sava would be happy to join us, and he would bring his sister, Elsie.

Our initial excitement soon morphed into concern. What should Mama and I feed our guests, we wondered? What foods would our Jewish friends and a native elder be able to share? We fretted, and finally decided on a venison roast with tomato-basil sauce and baked potatoes and turnips in a honey flavored sauce. We would have frozen strawberries from the grocery store for dessert and we would offer water, tea, or grape juice to drink.

We fretted about the roast. We browned it carefully, added garlic and bay leaves, put in some water with salt and pepper, just a tad of cinnamon, and let it simmer slowly. We tested the flavor occasionally, and Mama felt something was lacking. "Wait just a moment!" she said, heading for the bodega. "This should do it!" She poured a bottle of beer into the mix, and the brew bubbled along, the flavor improving each moment.

The moment came; the Bergens arrived, dressed in their best. Sava arrived wrapped in a long wool coat, gray and well-worn, with mandarin collar and no buttons. The usual thick tan scarf was tightly wrapped around his neck, his derby on his head. On entry, he removed his boots, pulled fur-lined deerskin slippers out of his pocket and slipped them onto his feet.

Elsie was encased in a splendid thick caribou skin cape with three buttons sewn at the front edges. A long gray woolen scarf covered her head and tied at her neck, the remainder draping below her chin. She removed her cape to reveal a thick black wool cardigan that she wore over a deep brown wool ankle-length dress. Bright blue glass beads and tiny seashells decorated the collar. She placed a large leather bag on the floor near the door, removed her fur mittens, and she, too, exchanged her high-laced, fur-lined boots for leather moccasins, beaded with bright colors. Her hair, sleek and dark, was parted in the center, drawn toward her ears, and secured with red wool cords. While we gazed at her she took a deep breath, looked around, smiled a very shy smile, and then clasped her hands together.

We all stood silent, nervous smiles on our faces, looking at each other, not sure what to do.

"Well!" Mama exclaimed, nervously clapping her hands a couple of times. "Let's all sit down and have some tea!"

Our living room had been arranged to take advantage of every source of heat available. Our pot burner stove blazed away. Kerosene space heaters provided additional heat this winter. The severe cold caused all pretense at civility to give way to survival—in all areas where the floor met the exterior walls we had stuffed strips of army blankets. Mama and I pulled a few of our dining table chairs into the group and we all sat as near the pot burner stove and the kerosene heaters as possible.

Stiff from nervousness as well as cold, we warmed to each other slowly. Words were stilted at first; pauses were long. Then Sava, seemingly remembering something, looked toward Elsie, pointing at her leather bag, speaking in his native tongue in a low tone.

As he spoke, Mama's face lit up with shock and surprise; she drew in her breath with an audible gasp. "Sava," she said very slowly, her head tilted just slightly in his direction, "did you just say the word, *person* to your sister?"

Now it was Sava who was surprised. He nodded his head, looking quizzically toward Mama.

"That sounds somewhat like the Navajo word for *person*!" She said slowly, grasping the edge of her chair.

They certainly had all of our interest by now. We were bewildered. All that is, but Sava and Mama.

Sava slowly nodded, frowning slightly, "I seem to know there come time when many of our brothers walk down into a place far away, I dunno how..." He seemed to feel his way through his words for some moments. "We say they talk in a way like us still. I think we maybe can sometimes understand each other today." He began to grin. "They live in a place very dry now and some learn to do farming things. But they still use words like our words."

"No kidding!" blurted Aaron.

"The sound…" Mama said, "the way you say your words, that is different, but some of the words—Sava, I have a Navajo friend, and she used words a bit similar to yours!"

The rest of us sat stunned, still as mice.

Again Sava smiled and nodded. It didn't surprise him, this matter of how his brothers in the south talked. He was remembering. He spoke again to Elsie, using the word, *shash,* and, at that moment, I nearly jumped from my chair. "That's a word you shouldn't say, Sava, or the bears will come!" I think I surprised myself; I certainly surprised Mama and startled everyone else.

"How did you know that?" she queried.

"Naasha taught me, and she said that I should never say it."

"It is okay," Sava said, chuckling. "We have enough bears that they not gonna be mad if we say the name. Now porcupines—that may be another story. Our people have many words for bear. *Shesh* is black bear. That word *shesh* really belong to our brothers who live a little ways from here." He paused and continued, "But my mama say that word, so I use it always too." He mouthed the word again, paused and smiled. "I think those Navajo need only one word for bear, you think? They don't have so many bears down there mebbe. *Shash, shesh*--those are Dena'ina words now I think…you know, words that in our talk and their talk still live."

"But it was a black bear that Naasha saw…"

"You and Naasha saw a bear?" Mama asked.

"No, Mama, no. She told me about it. It happened when she was little, and she just whispered that word to me." Mama looked relieved.

Sava continued, jet-button eyes dancing, "Now here I have one more word that I think belong to us. I do not think that those Navajo brothers need canoes, huh? But they use our word for *traveling quiet in the water in canoe* when they say how their owl fly in the night air."

"Holy cow, no kidding!" blurted Aaron.

"Yup. And still today we call ourselves, *Dena'ina* and our south brothers call their selves, *Diné*".

"I'll be darned," Mama muttered.

"The father of my father many times back, he remember stories about when the brothers go. Not so long ago, you know." Sava paused and pointed toward Elsie, saying, "What I say to Elsie was I ask her to give you this."

He pointed at the elk skin bag Elsie had next to her. Elsie reached into the bag, took out a small package and gave it to Sava. Sava then placed it into Mama's hands. All eyes were on Mama as she unwrapped the package. Inside carefully folded newspaper was a small bag made of fine, dark brown fur; Mama slipped her fingers into the little bag and pulled out a lovely wood carving of a black bear.

"Oooohh," we all cooed. We were all charmed by the tiny creature. At that instant, I thought, even the ice around the window frames must have melted momentarily. The small carved bear passed from one appreciative hand to another among us.

Coming together to eat was easy now. Mama's braised roast, boiled potatoes, and fry bread gave rise to looks of contentment and satisfaction from Elsie and Sava. The whipped cream served on top of strawberries was a new experience for them.

Isn't it wonderful, I remember thinking, how eating together brings such joy?

Smiles, handshakes and bows marked the end of our afternoon repast. As the door closed for the last time and we were once more saved from becoming popsicles, Mama sighed, threw her arms out and grabbed me, dancing and laughing. "We did something good, didn't we, Marisol?" My head came up to her nose now; she grabbed my face, rubbed my nose with hers and knuckle-rubbed my head just behind my ears.

Then Mama collapsed onto the fainting couch, and sighed, "What a thought, Marisol!

Perhaps Naasha and Sava are cousins! Who knows, it could be!"

The day had, indeed, been a success. The lovely bear statuette now accompanied our radio on our new table, and the rock containing the fossil of the pterodactyl foot sat beside the table leg.

The only disappointment for me was that Cyn and I had not had an opportunity to talk to Sava alone.

Some days later, Sava and Elsie came by the house when I was in school, with some celery root and dried wild parsley for Mama. She insisted that they come in for tea, she told me, and she was excited. "Once, when he spoke to Elsie, he used *Vuntda*!" Her eyes danced as she explained, "That means, 'her mother,' he told me."

I was puzzled as to what she was trying to say.

"Don't you get it? He was saying, he was saying--that he thinks of you as a daughter!"

Now that did please me greatly.

"Oh, Marisol, what a fine person he is," she continued. She rubbed her hands together absently. "He said he would take us for a hike sometime when the flowers are budding and then, perhaps, we can go berry picking. I told him as calmly as I could that we would like to do that very much."

And to me she said, "Oh, little girl, I hope he doesn't forget that invitation!"

It would be longer than just a few months until Sava would turn his offer into a real invitation, but in the end, it was worth the wait. That afternoon, as we looked out the window at our foggy, drippy gray and white world, it was difficult to even imagine budding bushes and berries. We had many weeks of dreadful winter weather ahead of us.

That winter, a lot of living took place indoors. For Cynthia and me, finding things to do wasn't tough at all. That winter, we became changelings; one day, we would try to jitterbug, or gush over the songs on the *Lucky Strike Hit Parade.* The next day, we were happy to color in color books. We played with paper dolls, designing paper doll hats, beach outfits, pedal pushers, all the while imagining exotic places for them to live.

We read a lot, I wrote Christmas cards, we even wrote a play, a rewrite of *Cinderella* and we played all the parts. To this day, Mama recalls her favorite line. (Cinderella says to the stranger at the door, *Oh, you poor man, would you like a cup of boolyon?)*

I would see Mama look out the kitchen window and I suspected she was counting the days until Sava could fulfill his promise. What she didn't know was that I was counting days too, until the day we could reveal our secret to Sava.

At Sacred Heart Church, to get our minds off of the horrible winter weather, Father Paul started a youth choir. I joined, of course, along with Gloria, Andrew and Early. At his mom's insistence, Byron joined and brought a couple of his buddies with him. Our debut would be during the Christmas season and we began practice in October. At Father's request we were learning Bach's *Jesu, Joy of Man's Desiring.* It was the first time I ever heard parts sung together, tenor, bass, soprano, alto. I'm sure our singing was pretty primitive, but I loved it.

The church mothers fashioned white cotton surplices to make us all look uniformly angelic. On the afternoon of our dress rehearsal, we were all jittery and excited. The choir director lined us up according to height, standing back to assess her efforts and we stood tall and beamed back at her.

Father Paul approached our director. She turned for a moment to converse with him and at that precise moment a hard object hit my head, and with force. I was startled and stunned and I saw stars. I turned to look behind me, tears in my eyes. Why would anyone do that to me? I wondered.

There, directly behind me I saw a grinning Byron; hymnal still in hand. He didn't even try to hide the fact that he did it. Everybody was quiet for a moment, and then his buddies began to giggle nervously. Byron continued to stare at me, a smug expression pasted on his face. He grinned and rolled his eyes. I waited for someone to speak out, but no one did. There seemed to be nothing else for me to do but bear the shame. What made me furious was I had done nothing to be ashamed of. I was confused and felt very small. Those feelings were new to me and I didn't like them.

But then I remembered what Mama had said about Eleanor Roosevelt. I smiled my best smile, and went on singing.

Christmas was very near. Last year, we hadn't dared to think much about Christmas back in Gardner, but this holiday season Mama and I could allow ourselves a few moments to think about what we left behind.

We talked about the aromas in Abuelita's rancho kitchen by the time we'd arrive on Christmas Eve morning. By then, the turkey would have been slow-cooked with garlic and cumin, and the tamale husks would have been cut to uniform lengths. While I pulled meat from the bones, Mama would begin making the *masa harina,* and we would put it all together, wrapping twine around every closed husk package.

"Oh, Marisol, the smell of the *bacalao,* and those yummy red and green chiles, and those sweet *bunuelos* for dessert."

"And Mama, remember Daddy playing the whistle and Samuel with his harmonica on Christmas Day?" Samuel was Grandfather's negro cowboy on the rancho. I was thrilled that I said all that about Daddy without any sadness or hint of a tear.

This year our Christmas dinner would include Father Paul, but the nucleus would be the same. We didn't think much about it then, but Mama and I were establishing our own traditions.

***

One night an event came about at our house that set us on edge. After everyone in the house was asleep, Mama and I were awakened at the same moment. She sat up stick-straight in bed. The window was so wrapped for winter that zero light entered from outside. Only the soft glow from the space heater allowed me to see her, and I was sitting up exactly like her. We listened, barely breathing.

"Marisol," she whispered.

"What?" My breath was tight in my chest, my fingers dug into my blankets. Surely the air was near freezing. I thought, but that was not my primary concern. I felt nothing but fear.

"Do you hear something?" she whispered. "Like grumbling, or funny voices? Listen!" Her voice was husky. Fear, I thought. I listened like I had never listened before. I wondered if Mama could hear my heartbeat; I certainly could.

There it was—something like an animal wheeze, a cat hiss. Maybe the wind, or the frigid temperature caused this? We listened; heartbeats continuing to pound, but then no sound, no hiss, nothing. Minutes passed; nothing. Still nothing. My heart slowly began to return to normal and I realized that my toes were freezing, even under the covers. But I didn't move a muscle.

After what seemed like a half-second I began to do the same, willing silence from the sheets. The pleasure of residual warmth welcomed me back under the many layers of blankets. We lay there, both of us, heads propped upright, alert, bodies grateful for the blankets' warmth, silently hoping for no additional sound, happy for no additional sound, when, "Whump!"

Something bumped the outside wall where our bedroom was. Up again, my heart thumping. Mama eased out of bed and I could hear her slowly slip into her mukluks, and agonizingly slowly, quietly wrap a blanket around her shoulders.

Summoning all my strength, I tried to swallow some of my terror. But my throat did not cooperate. I got up, grabbed my bathrobe, slipped into my slippers and, afghan over my shoulders, and I am at the window with Mama.

Together, we pull back the heavy lined drape, break away bits of ice, pull off a corner of the cardboard, peel back a bit of the Celotex. We're aware of the noise we are making, but we have no choice now. We look out a lower corner of our window. The moisture from our breathing makes fog on the window, which immediately crystallizes.

The snowdrifts reach nearly to the level of the window sill. A half-moon shines dully through cold, sodden fog, allowing little light on swirling snow, those translucent icicles pointing down like swords from the roofline. We can make out nothing unusual.

Shivering, tip-toeing, we negotiate the frightful few feet to the kitchen window. Mama's nervous hand pulls aside the heavy drape (no cardboard here, Mama insists that she be able to look out somewhere during the darkest days to see even the tiniest, tentative sun's rays.)

We squint, surveying the entire front yard, driveway which is now a tunnel from the road to our door--and see nothing. Snow tumbles and swirls, sometimes at a rakish cant. But we see nothing out of the ordinary, really; just scores of snow swirls, little quiet tornadoes in the wind. The only sound we hear is the creaking of the walls as they give way to the insistent wind.

"Mama," I ask softly, "I'll get the big flashlight…"

"No," she whispers. "Not yet."

Beyond the yard and the silent white chapel across the road, beyond tiny homes hunkered down in deep drifts, an occasional faraway light seemingly sputters in the snow, like a distant star, revealing lonely streets buried in huge drifts of snow. We creep to the laundry room, watching, waiting, anticipating but fearing another noise. Silence. We wait; oh how we wait; but we hear nothing, we see nothing. No sounds, no shapes, no nothing. We are frozen with cold and with fear.

At last we return to our beds, throats still throbbing. Shivers begin to leave us, but sleep eludes us. We finally find courage to speak in whispers. Only questions come to mind.

At last pure exhaustion overtakes us.

I still don't recall falling asleep, and when the alarm clock sounded, my head was erect, just as it was when I nodded off, as if I were frozen on guard.

Up early, as usual and entering the kitchen where bacon was cooking, our boarders mentioned the incident. They heard the noises, but they had no answers, either. Had something blown against the house? we wondered.

When Mr. Norman left for work, he trudged in the snow drifts around the house. Deep, fuzzy indentations still existed in the snow's patina, now filled in with new snow. He decided that these could have been boot prints or animal prints, but it must have been hard for the visitor to get around. Other than those marks, there was nothing out of place in our winter world.

I helped with breakfast and went to school; tea, hotcakes, spelling bee, volleyball all filled my day, but barely kept that night's fright at bay.

THE TOWN THAWS AND THE GROUND GRUMBLES

Spring 1948

The calendar indicated that we could all expect to see those blossoms and buds that Mama awaited, but they were slow in coming. The winter we had just survived was still the topic of everyy-body's conversation. Surely there had been a worse one sometime, but old-timers and newcomers alike would remember the winter of 1947 for a long time to come. It made it into the record books. Temperature at Moose Creek hit eighty-three degrees below freezing. Bear Lake froze to the bottom and Methuselah Spring froze over too. The new road to Turnagain Arm had been smothered by avalanches. Snow banks had topped out at twenty feet in some places.

The townspeople of Seward had had a choice; they could give in to the tortuous winter, or find a way to adapt, laugh, and survive. They had chosen to survive.

We still carried the burden of our secret. As Cynthia put it, the responsibility was five times worse than watching after Aaron. We were agitated, awaiting the moment we could talk to Sava. The right moment just didn't seem to materialize.

Mama's and my nighttime adversary visited us twice more, and we were amazed at his/its capability to move about in the drifts of snow. We were becoming accustomed to the routine; low sounds, rustling noises, a pebble or two against the house, then quiet. By now our intention was to show we were not frightened, while in truth we were terrified. Now, on cue, we turned on inside lights to indicate that we were aware of his/its presence, and usually the noises abated.

The entire household was part of the routine. Mr. Norman remarked once, "I just wish whatever it is had the courage to come in the summer. I'd knock its head off." We all felt frustration, but the experiences somehow united us.

As the nights turned the corner and hints of warm breezes teased us, Cynthia and I began our impatient vigil, watching walls of snow slowly brought low, degraded to mere grimy puddles. People in town warily removed just one layer of clothing, and then another. Lowell Creek swelled; the force of water gushing from the diversion channel became dangerous. Resurrection River overflowed its traditional stony banks, uprooting low bushes, flushing away nature's layer of winter debris.

Regarding our burden, Cyn and I made a plan. We'd retrieve the stone tool and present it to Sava as soon as we could. But we had to wait for that splinter-glow to grow into full light. We had to wait until more snow and ice than we had ever known began to give way to warmth and new growth. The wait was a long, agonizing one.

We watched, we plotted, and pleaded for permission to make a quick hiking trip up the hill. Our suspicious mothers appraised us quizzically, reminding us that spring weather could quickly turn treacherous, bringing thick fog or angry rain at any time. And then there were the bears.

We had to be satisfied with walks into town for now, where our fellow humans began to exit from their hibernation. Soldiers congregated at the roller rink. Once, one even whistled at us. Us? We had no idea what to do the first time it happened except to giggle. The second time, we looked away in pretended disgust. Byron once again rode Daisy along Fourth Street and we began to see the usual group of scruffy miners and trappers collecting near the bars. We saw Charlie doing his favorite thing, telling wild stories, his flannel covered gut protruding well beyond the waistline of his stained and worn britches, his lower jaw packed with a hunk of chaw. We stocked up on bottles of Fanta, packs of Fig Newtons, and jawbreakers in preparation for our initial hikes.

At last, the moment arrived. Permission granted from parents, we began our mission to our meadow, and we were happy, albeit nervous, pilgrims. Beside the path loomed pines and spruces, their branches still laden with wet snow. At their feet lay patches of ooze, supersaturated loam; the path itself was mire and slush, but it didn't phase us. In sturdy rubber boots, liberated at last, we set out resolutely to complete our mission.

Snow grouse crossed our path more than once. Insects struggled to establish new homes. We scared up a doe and fawn resting in the trees, and watched carefully for big animal scat or footprints. Busy bird chatter welcomed us. A passel of large black birds clustered and perched on spindly, spare willow trees, just now showing buds.

We approached our little meadow, stomping on snow as we entered. We plowed past our still snow-covered sawhorse, over downed branches, and on to the base of our mountain. Then, struggling and slipping, we began our ascent.

Grateful to find our cache secure, we quickly, but carefully, removed the heavy stone object, wrapped it in a diaper doll flannel baby blanket I had stuffed into my jacket pocket just for this event and placed it into Cynthia's canvas bag.

We stood pondering what to do with the remainder of the treasure, when we both sensed motion under our feet and heard what seemed like a barely audible moan. What on earth could that be? we wondered. Our impulse was to run. Without thinking, we grabbed the remaining treasure, scurried from the cave and to the sanctuary of our sawhorse hideaway, where we wrapped the box filled with the other items in another doll blanket, placed it in a metal tea bag tin, covered the tin with pine twigs and leaves, covered the area with fresh vines and hurriedly began our return hike.

Only then did we discuss what had just happened at the cave. Our nerves had surely overtaken us, we thought. Nevertheless, as we started for home, we began to sing to keep our knees from quaking.

"I'm looking overrr, a four leafed cloverrr." We belted out the notes, without considering our dissonance with the critters of the wild. No self-respecting bear would have anything to do with our raucous music, we thought.

Almost home, we spotted Byron and his dad on horseback riding on the paths toward Fort Raymond. We waved; Cynthia had no reason to dislike Byron really, so she waved at him. As for me, my wave was for Daisy alone.

Treasure in canvas bag, we headed to my house and directly to my closet. We took some moments to examine the stone object, turning it in the light and feeling its cold, smooth surface. We got out my diaper doll suitcase, placed it in a nest of doll blankets and shoved it into the back of the shelf in my closet.

We had completed our task and I would like to say that our hearts were in the right place, but they weren't. They were still in our throats. We sat on my bed and tried to express our thoughts. "So," Cynthia said softly, "what was that sound do you think?"

"Sounded like a low groan, sort of," said I. "Sort of like a big tree falling, but bigger, deeper."

We knew we were well away from the source of our fright. At least we hoped we were. But what was it? We sat, our legs Buddha-style, facing each other.

"But was it a painful sound do you think?"

"I just don't know. I swear I don't know. But I kinda thought it was a sound of—some kind of relief maybe? Kinda like a burp."

"I don't know, either. It didn't follow us, though. That's a good thing, right? All I know is I haven't been so scared since Pearl Harbor."

"I'm just a scared as you are, and I have to say, this thing about our nighttime visitor at the house is scary too, 'cause we still don't know when it will end. If it will end. But I have been even more scared one time before."

"Yeah? When?"

"On the train coming to Seattle. I was just a kid, remember, and a train was all new to me. When I had to use the bathroom, I had to go into this tiny room, open and close the door with the train clicking and swaying the whole time. It was bad enough just brushing my teeth. I had to brace my legs, and the water from the faucet only came when I pressed down, and I couldn't do that and hold on—oh, it was awful. But when I had to go, and believe me, I didn't go 'till I really had to go, the door wanted to slam behind me. Then I would have to lock it, and I always, every time wondered if it would let me out. Then I had to sit on this hissing hole and I could see the ground racing past below the hole, and there was this sucking sound that wanted to take me with it. Can you imagine trying to go with all that? I didn't go at night at all. I would have died first." I spoke with all the fervor I had in me as I relived those moments.

"And then I had to pull up my panties, which was not easy in there, and when I hit the flush button I held on with everything in me. I was sure I would be sucked out right there, and I couldn't think of a worse way to die."

We both giggled, and by then we were calm. At least Cynthia was—it may have sounded funny, but the adventure on the train really did terrify me.

"So, you think we are doing the right thing? Taking something to give to Sava I mean," I asked.

"Yeah, I do. But what is going to happen to us when we go back up there?"

***

Thursday next would be Sava's story class; we were committed to find a way to give the stone tool to him, and we counted the hours.

The day we awaited finally arrived. We came early, waited near the flagpole in front of the school, and at Sava's arrival, we two nervous girls nearly accosted him. We poured out the details of our adventure, mentioning only the tool. Then we opened the suitcase, removed the heavy object and gingerly handed it to him, still wrapped in its blanket awaiting his reaction.

Our friend was clearly surprised. We watched his face as he examined the item for a very long time. Silently, gently, he turned it in his hands, nearly caressing it. His eyes glistened. The shadow of a tear fell down his cheek when at last he spoke, quietly and slowly, continuing to stare at the stone object. He explained to us that he recognized it. Not that he had ever seen it, but he knew from the stories of his people that it was, indeed, old—part of a group of items lost to his people so long ago that they say it was part of time itself. His people, he said, remembered the items and mourned their loss.

They arrived from the sea, he told us, gifts over the centuries from Salmon and his people, and were watched over by Raven. He wasn't sure when they were hidden away by his ancestors to protect them from some danger, now forgotten. We told him that the thing was his. His shoulders began to shake. He carefully rolled the blankets around the tool, and placed it in the leather bag he carried that day. He then looked at us for a long moment, took each of our hands, and quietly said, "Swell."

We began to babble, at last able to share our burden. We told him about the remaining items and, as we went on, his hands moved, seemingly without his will; he closed his eyes and pinched the crown of his nose. His head remained down, he seemed unable to speak. Finally, after we told him about the strange moan and our fright, we waited together in silence for a few minutes, hoping Sava could explain the sounds we heard.

Before Sava could respond, Matthias found us and quietly joined us. Matthias had spent a lot of time with Sava over the months. Now he looked at Sava, particularly at his folded hands. Then he looked into our faces. Finally he looked up absently into the fir tree near us, and our eyes followed his.

Perched there, smart and perky, was a glossy raven dancing from branch to branch.

"Gga, gga, gga," his deep voice rattled.

CAN'T WE ALL GET ALONG?

"Hurry up and do your homework," Mama called to me as I came in the door from school. "Major O'Keefe has invited us to see *You'll Never Get Rich* with Fred Astaire and Rita Hayworth! Dinner is in the pot on the stove and Mary Ruth can do the rest. I'll set the table and we can eat later, now hurry!"

Oh boy. A movie and on a school night. Unheard of. I was off in a flash, homework done, face washed, ready to go.

Mama loved the movies. I remember just after Daddy died, we went to see a Judy Garland movie that had come to town called, *The Clock*. It was about two people who fall in love and their romance is just a few days until he has to leave for the war. As you can imagine, he is killed. I knew what Mama was feeling, because I felt the same way. My hope was that this movie would bring her some happiness, that perhaps we would all I laugh.

Major O'Keefe pulled into the driveway.

"How are my girls?" he asked. He hugged us both, helped me crawl into the backseat of his jeep, held Mama's door while waiting for her to get in, and we were off.

Sacks of popcorn in our laps, we settled in. This film was one from Major O'Keefe's stash of old films, part of his special re-run series. It was a romance, of course. Fred is in the army, in the guard house; Rita is a ravishing showgirl smitten with Fred. It was supposed to be gay and uplifting, but it left me puzzled. Now you would think that the guardhouse would be a tough place for those two to dance, but not in this film. That alone was pretty contrived, but that wasn't the worst of it. In the guardhouse, Fred danced on one side of a divided cell, and his musicians, seemingly happy to be in prison, were all on the other side. I was supposed to ignore that they were negroes, and, because of their color, they were separated from Fred by prison bars, and happy about it.

"That's terrible," I murmured.

"What?" whispered Mama.

"Never mind," I grumbled.

"Are you all right?" Mama turned, looking me over.

"It's nothing," I said.

But it wasn't nothing.

After we arrived home, Major O'Keefe shared leftovers with us, played a couple hands of gin rummy with me, and then left. But I was still disturbed. The front door closed, Mama asked, "All right, young lady, what is on your mind? Tell me."

There seemed to be a lot of things happening in my life lately that I didn't understand. Perhaps I was dense, I thought, but how could anyone accept the concept that those men had to be separated from white people even in jail, and that everybody was happy about it? Fred is happy, Rita is happy, the musicians are happy, the music is happy, and we are supposed to be happy. But I'm not.

I hadn't known a lot of negroes, either in Gardner or Seward, but I had known a few. In fact, there were some soldiers in Seward, and by now I understood that they had fought in the war to protect my country, just like everybody else. "Why is it, Mama, that we think it is just fine to separate people by their color, and treat them differently just because of it?"

"Come here little girl," Mama said, patting the fainting couch. "The moment has come for what I call a, 'Come to Jesus' meeting."

I sat next to her, simmering, swinging my feet. I was first to speak. "You know that is kinda like what happened to Cynthia in the election. She didn't get elected because she was Jewish, or a girl, or both. And it makes me mad," I sputtered.

"You just have to get over what happened to Cynthia," she explained, putting her hand on mine. "After all, she wasn't even a sixth grader.

And do you think it is still bothering Cynthia?" she asked, turning my face toward hers. "Come on now, be realistic."

"Well, maybe you're right, Mama," I said, pouting still. "But why do some bunches of people have to think that they are better than others?" I asked.

"Well I just don't know, Marisol," she sighed. "But it does happen, and that is life, I'm afraid. All we can do is try to never think or act that way ourselves."

"People in town say the children at the Jesse Lee Home have to live there because the're sick, Mama, but the children I've seen haven't been any sicker than I am. Matthias isn't sick and he spends a lot of time at the Bergens, and with Sava." Words tumbled from my mouth. "I think it's just an excuse to keep those children separated from the rest of the town."

"Now be fair," Mama said, putting her hand on top of mine. "They do have some sickness to contend with. A lot of their grandparents died in the influenza epidemic and their parents died from diphtheria." She paused, then continued, "But by and large, I'm sure you're right."

"Then why can't we visit each other and play with each other more?"

"The simple truth is that you should, Marisol. And, have you noticed, you already are?"

"Barely, Mama. You mean our story visits? All we do is sit and listen and…"

"Nonsense, young lady. Somehow you have gotten to know Matthias and didn't you say there is a little girl who always sits with you?"

"Oh, yeah, my little friend Paulette. You're right, Mama."

"And it is a beginning. So just be patient. Sometimes the Lord works in strange ways." Mama pulled her hand away from mine and her back straightened, as she continued to look at me.

"But we don't think that way, Mama, and my grandparents don't feel that way," I declared.

"Oh, oh yes they do," Mama said, rising and retrieving a plate containing a few cookies from the table. "Have one," she said and sat down again. "Part of my reason for leaving Gardner was to get away from that issue." She took a bite of cookie, while obviously considering where to go with this conversation. She chewed slowly, resolutely, and then swallowed. "You know that your grandparents love you very, very much.

But to tell you the truth, my father would rather that I had married what he called my own kind."

I was astounded. "What does that mean?" I asked.

"Good question!" Mama chewed on another cookie. "My family's ancestors are supposedly descended from the early Spaniards who came to the New World. What we call the conquistadors. But pretty soon, the new people—the ones the king or queen sent to govern in the new world—had a word to describe us…the people who were born there. At that time they were children of people from Spain, but just because they were born in the New World, they called them *criollos*. Just because they lived in the New World. And the people back in Spain regarded the *criollos* as just a bit inferior to them. Now, does that make sense?"

Her eyes looked closely into mine. "But even the *criollos* needed to be superior to someone. *Criollos* have no Indian blood they said. A person with Indian blood was to be called a *mestizo,* or mixed-blooded one. My father, your grandfather, proudly claims to be a *criollo*, Marisol, but I have seen pictures of my father's grandmother. And I think she was a *mestiza.*"

"Part Indian?" I asked.

Mama nodded.

"She was tiny and her face was diamond-shaped. In the picture, she looks lovely, but she sure looks part indigenous. *Mestizo*; half-breed. Now, doesn't that sound ugly somehow?"

I think my eyebrows rose an inch; my jaw gaped open.

"Yeah, honey, those are the things people think but they just don't say," Mama went on. "But we can't say anything like that to the Doña Inéz portrait, in front of Abuelita Clara and Grandfather, can we? That would never do."

"So if what you say is true, that makes you and me half-breeds, too, just like a lot of the children at the Home, don't you think?"

"Yes, I do think."

"By the way, you know that portrait of Doña Inéz?" Mama asked, winking at me and smiling ruefully. "I avoided walking past her if I could when I was little because I was afraid she didn't approve of me."

"Oh Mama!" I blurted as I reached for her. "I felt the same way!" I didn't tell her about the day I saw the edges of her mouth pucker as I walked by.

"And," continued Mama, "there is another name we call ourselves, we Mexicans who lived on the land that was formerly Mexican territory before it became part of the United States and who today are loyal citizens of the U.S.—we are *chicanos*. Just what we need, huh? Another word to call ourselves. Who needs it?

"And don't you think for one moment that everybody loves Mexicans. They don't. And Mexicans call white people *gringos* and think they are soft and weak and there are worse words too, and it just goes on and on. People can be so stupid. Now if we have a little indigenous blood, and our ancestor lived here when this was Mexico, what are we?"

I wasn't ready to tackle that question, so I opted for a shift in direction. "But Daddy," I said, "everybody liked Daddy."

"Wasn't he a jewel? What a guy. But they didn't necessarily love who he was. Wrong again, sweetheart."

"Come on, Mama! All of the Fernandez family loved Daddy," I cried out, feeling as if somebody was holding me over a cliff and my feet were dangling.

"Oh, my family did like your Daddy very much; very much. But he just wasn't their kind. Perhaps if I had gone to Spain and married a penniless prince or something..." Her words faded, and then she laughed softly. "To tell you the truth, I suspect the Downeys felt that way about me; but those words have never been spoken." She reached for the last cookie and then continued.

"But don't think the Irish have had an easy time of it, either, sweetheart. A few hundred years ago, the English conquered their land and then let the Irish starve. Really starve. They only had potatoes to eat, and when they rotted in the ground, the people just starved. It was a dreadful tragedy and the Irish will never get over it. It wasn't so long ago, you know. That is why there are so many Irish people in the United States now. The lucky ones took ships and they, too, came to the New World."

Mama was quiet. I watched her face and tried to understand what she was telling me. Finally she sighed again, and said, "So there you are. My parents and Daddy's parents worship the same God in the same church, but each thinks the other isn't quite so good as they are. Of course the Irish have one good thing going for them—they are white. Everybody seems to want to be white-skinned. Do you remember what a parasol is?"

"Something for the sun."

"Good girl. It's an umbrella that the ladies used in the colonial days to protect their skin from the sun's rays so they could be as white as possible. Even in Mexico today, the ladies use parasols. Every woman wants to be lighter than the next lady. Don't think Dona Inéz didn't use a parasol! Even in China, the people want to be as white as possible. Isn't that crazy? But that's the way it is."

She laughed, "You know, our skin, yours and mine, isn't quite the whitest, but it isn't dark either, so people don't know quite how to classify us. I think it's fun when people try to figure out how to classify us. Those freckles on your nose and on your knuckles confuse people."

I smiled at the thought.

"We just always have to be on our toes, to remember that all that stuff is junk. I want us to respect everyone, no matter what color they are, as long as they deserve our respect. Okay, sweetheart?"

I nodded my head.

"Good. That is the only thing that's important. Oh! Something else! Everyone likes tall people," she continued, pointing her finger at me. "Don't ask me why, but they do. So don't think I'm not delighted every time I measure you."

She got up to take the plate to the kitchen. "And by the way, someday you might get a break you didn't expect and it might just be because you're tall. Isn't that crazy?"

I nodded.

"So, when I tease you and Cynthia, and call you, 'Maggie and Jigs,' I mean it as a compliment. But I won't be able to say that much longer, because you are getting so tall, you are beginning to look more like Olive Oyl! So that is why I nag you about standing up straight; you need to be proud of your height."

"Mama," I thought aloud, "people can be crazy and hurtful."

"Don't think anybody is guiltless. There are tribes in Africa who kill each other for the strangest reasons." She was momentarily pensive, and then said, "In one of your Daddy's letters to me he said that somebody tried to sell him a black slave when he was in Morocco. Isn't that awful? Can you imagine?"

"No," I said, and I really couldn't imagine.

"The truth is, we are all half-breeds and we have to remember to find a way to love and forgive each other as much as we can."

We finished cleaning up the kitchen, and headed for our bedroom.

"There is one more thing I have to tell you, Marisol." She took a deep breath and spoke, "There will always be people who just don't like you, just for no reason, and you will never know why. Just steer clear of them, and go on with your life."

That was one lesson I had already learned. A crack on the head from a punky coward and no support from his equally cowardly friends still burned in my heart. But it was nice to know that I wasn't the only recipient of that sort of abuse.

Our disjointed conversation was not over yet. "Let's us two half-breeds get to bed now," laughed Mama. So we did.

WE ARE STUNNED AND ASHAMED

That was not the only grown-up conversation we had. This issue of growing up was beginning to insinuate itself into my life whether I wanted it to or not. Part of this business of growing up involved pain, and I had no desire to be party to that.

But in the name of maturing, my poor friend had been cruelly trapped by her mother.

I went to Cynthia's house one afternoon to help her mother treat her to something new called a Toni Home Permanent. Every other woman in town had been extolling this new product, claiming every woman should have one. And they were so affordable!

A new ritual was born. It had become as famous as Dick Tracy and Gravel Gertie. I watched as my dear friend's hair was washed, and then gathered in tiny, wispy bunches, dipped in a liquid that sent me choking, wrapped in tiny papers about one quarter the size of a square of toilet paper, and wrapped around tiny curlers resembling chicken wing bones. Mrs. Bergen pursued this project very seriously, pulling each wisp very tight, until my poor friend winced.

"Now you know how I feel when Mama braids my hair in a hurry," I remarked; I had become unwillingly complicit in this Toni activity, passing the little squares one at a time, followed by a bone-curler.

"I sympathize," Cyn grunted.

After the curlers, Cynthia had to sit for a long time with a plastic cap on, always at the ready in case any of that dreadful smelly stuff should drip down her neck or forehead.

Finally, the torture completed, Mrs. Bergen combed out the ringlets now covering Cynthia's head and wound them onto old bobby socks, finishing each one with a snappy twist.

As soon as I got home, I declared to Mama that I had never so misbehaved that I deserved one of those permanents, and I promised that I never would if she would not subject me to that horrible experience. And I kept my word…for the most part.

As for Cynthia, she came to school the next day with her hair shaped into a rigid, dull pageboy. I think I could have thrown pebbles at her hair and it would not have budged, and the smell endured for weeks.

***

One afternoon, Sava and Matthias came by our house with a nice big spring salmon. They stayed for dinner, sharing the fish that Mama stuffed with seasoned bread, bunches of parsley and dill. Before it went into the oven, she garnished it with lemon and orange slices. During that process, Sava sat at the kitchen table, talking to her in his native tongue, and Mama worked to understand and answer in her elementary Navajo.

At times like this, when Sava was our guest in our home, the saltine can in our sawhorse retreat was very much on my mind. Cynthia and I were alternately determined to retrieve the remainder of our hidden treasure and deliver it to Sava and terrified of what we might encounter. It looked like June would be our first opportunity. The skies became truculent just as the school year prepared to end. Capricious breezes blew in late snow flurries and sleet. They didn't last long, but they were tedious. Sometimes I would tire of this miserable wussiness and I would wish it would just storm and get it over with, like the storms of the Anaye Thundergods Naasha told me about, filled with fearful sound and crackling with lightning.

Finally, after a number of pleasant, sunny days, we headed up the hill, but not without a warning from our mothers. We were cautioned about the temper of the recent weather. We were to be home by 5:30 or they would send out a search party.

We set off hurriedly. A tiny breeze arose; nothing to worry about. Then clouds rolled in a few miles from the mouth of the bay. Our path was rutted and muddy, nothing more than what we expected. We picked up our pace.

Is it possible for our hearts to jump and fall at the same time? As we approached the sawhorse we saw that our carefully crafted camouflage had been pulled away, tossed about. We traversed the muck and mud as fast as we could, our boots restraining our progress.

We feared the worst, and then we knew the worst. Someone or something had intruded into our special spot and had scattered everything we had stored inside; books, pencils broken, papers ripped, soaked and soiled.

It wasn't long before we discovered the culprit wasn't an animal, at least not the four-footed kind. The bentwood box, with its contents, was gone, and in its place was a drawing, done crudely with our crayons. The drawing, known to everyone those days, was a picture of the famous Kilroy. Nothing more.

Who could or would have done this, we wondered, each of us in shock. Some kid? Did a soldier or a sourdough follow us up here? Just who could be bothered with innocuous pigtailed and permanented us? Was the nighttime visitor at the house the culprit? We thought of the moan we had heard. Had it been human after all? We were mystified, deflated and very disappointed in ourselves. Our hearts were heavy as lead. There was nothing to do but start home.

On the way, wind and rain became fierce, gruff escorts, accompanying us on our slippery trip home. Neither of us spoke. How could we face Sava?

OVERNIGHT AT THE JESSE LEE HOME

We dreaded having to tell Sava about our failure. Even more, we dreaded telling him that his beloved treasure was gone and we had no idea how it all had happened.

Strangely, when we told him, he smiled. The items would come back to his people someday, he said. That he knew as a certainty. "Things work out sometime," he said gently, covering our hands with his momentarily, "but mebbe not how we think."

Nonetheless, feelings of shame haunted us. We appreciated what he said, but our guilt continued.

Perhaps Sava arranged for our good fortune that was to come to us quickly, or perhaps fate decided to cut us a break. Either way, we were grateful for the respite and we were in for a real treat, a dream come true. If we could have wished for something and it couldn't be Sava's treasure, this was surely the next thing on the list. We were going to stay overnight at the Home!

I swear I could hear Daddy saying, "Ah, 'tis a sad road that has no turns."

It happened like this. We heard that Benny Benson, the John Benny Benson who designed the Alaska flag, was coming to town, specifically to visit the Home. Benny's father was a Swede and his mother was Inuit. He had come to the Home from Chignik Island when his parents became unable to keep him, many years ago. Benny learned of a contest while he was living at the Home, and he submitted his design.

On a background of deep Alaska night blue he placed the constellation Ursa Major, which we know as the Big Dipper. Since Alaska is bear habitat, he said, that seemed appropriate. He also noted that two of those stars point to the North Star, symbol of majesty to all the native people of this northernmost territory, and symbol of true north. His submission was chosen to be the Alaska flag; it captured the essence of Alaska perfectly in the opinion of those making the decision. Everyone was proud of Benny except Benny himself. A modest, shy person, his fame didn't change him.

He did win a prize and a scholarship. But when he finished school, he felt the need to return to Chignik with his money and assist his family.

The Jesse Lee Home was established by Methodist missionaries in the early 1900s. Determined souls, they set about gathering children from all over the Alaska territory who, for various reasons, were not being cared for. The facility comprised a number of white stucco two- and three-story buildings on some eighty acres of land. The main building housed a large meeting room, a kitchen and dining facility. There were also dormitories that could house up to two hundred children. There was a small hospital, and the large Jewel Guard Room. Besides classrooms for children from nursery school age through eighth grade, there was a woodworking area, a sewing room and more. A vegetable garden, carefully tended, contributed to the children's nutrition. The students and faculty also processed fish and sold it. The missionaries worked diligently and creatively to support the children as best as they could.

Mrs. Bergen had been teaching piano at the Home for a number of month now, and had three students whom she thought had promise. Every time Cyn tagged along with her mother, I tagged along, too, making friends with the children every chance we got.

Benny's visit brought real prospects that we may just get a chance to spend meaningful time at the Home if we played our cards right. The mayor wanted to have him visit the new marina improvement. Or, could he stay for Fourth of July? Benny made his feelings clear. His main reason for coming was to visit the Home.

Mrs. Bergen's students would have a chance to show off their talents for the famous visitor, and they doubled down to a ridged schedule of serious practice. Mrs. Bergen was now a respected member of the staff.

We begged her incessantly to get an invitation for us during Benny's visit, and happily, she was successful. We were invited to stay for the day of Benny's visit and spend a night in the girls' dormitory.

Two jittery girls we were, standing just outside the main door at 7:00 a.m. on a sunny June day, to witness as the boy scouts raised the flag. Within seconds Paulette came flying out the door among a passel of little girls all wearing identical brown shoes. My Paulette, in her light brown jumper and cotton sweater, spotted me and grabbed my arm in a way that I knew meant that her intention was never to let go that day. Lilly spotted Cynthia also, and together we filed into the dining room. We stood at long tables, set with nice flatware, cloth napkins and heavy, sturdy dishes. An older boy led us all as we said grace together. The jarring noise of scores of chairs being pulled out and then scooted in lessened and we dove into a breakfast of applesauce, oatmeal, milk, and a cup of Postum. I mimicked Paulette, putting our bowls at the end of the table and putting spoons into the now empty milk pitcher. Next I was led to her second-grade classroom and I encountered my first obstacle—my assigned desk in Paulette's classroom was a just bit tight for me. A lot of nervous little faces shyly giggled at me as I wiggled into that seat, and I grinned back, my legs spraddled in the aisle between the wooden desks. I had little time to think about Cynthia's fate. Surely she was happily ensconced in another desk, hopefully bigger that mine. I would see her sometime, surely at dinner.

Paulette's best friend was named Dinah. She was a tiny wisp of a girl with inquiring black eyes set just below thick black eyebrows. Dark brown hair had been clipped straight just below her ears. I contemplated, as she peered up at me, what she had already endured in her short life.

We next marched to sewing class. Now Dinah led the way and Paulette held onto me, grinning and looking up at me. I grinned back. Almost immediately the older girls busied themselves on their projects. They were responsible for making many of the dresses for the girls in the home. Paper patterns fluttered here and there as they pinned and snipped. The short spurts of sound from sewing machines filled the room—brrrrrm, brrm, brrrrrrm.

Paulette's group was too young for that task. Instead, they generally worked on smaller tasks. They embroidered table runners and napkins to be sold to help support the Home. That day, though, Paulette and Dinah's task was to darn socks, hers and those belonging to the boys. She handed me what she called a darning egg. It looked to me like someone had sawed off the top of Granny Clara's spindle bed. They didn't need to use one, but I inserted the egg into my sock and it helped me to see the size of the hole destined for repair. I copied what Paulette did, dipping into the threads at the edge of the hole, carrying my thread across to the other side. Then, at her example, I began to work my thread across the ones I had already created. Up and down the needle went, bobbing under and over, until I had created what seemed to be a tiny tapestry that filled what had been a void.

"Be careful to pick up just a little bit of the sock edge," Paulette explained, "or the edge will bunch up and hurt somebody's foot when they wear the sock." She and Dinah began to giggle. "I can think of some feet I wouldn't mind hurting."

Whoever would have thought that darning could be an art? While mine was something I hoped would be serviceable, theirs were really fine little works of jagged-edged art.

Some works of art were more apparent than others, as when they decided to be whimsical and patch a blue sock with yellow thread. A striped patch made its way into the basket upon occasion.

The entire, cavernous room was orderly, even with countertops piled with paper patterns and sewing items lying about. Scores of dresses at varied stages of completion hung along one wall. At the end of class, the girls put their sewing projects neatly into cupboards and set shoe boxes containing their scissors and sewing tools on top of the counter.

Lunchtime brought us back to the dining room where we blessed our meal of canned cherries thickened into a sauce and served on toast. We drank milk and ate sliced apples for dessert. Different, I thought, but the children didn't think so. I liked it.

Outside, we jumped rope, the girls awaiting their turn, holding their skirts to their sides as they prepared to run through. The rope, turned by two of the bigger girls, snapped the ground setting the cadence, and the jumpers joined in chanting, "Fudge, fudge, call the judge, Mama's gonna have a little bayyyybee. Wrap it up in tissue paper, send it down the elevator, First floor out! Second floor out! Third floor out!" On the next snap of the rope, if all went well, one girl would exit just as the next in line scurried in.

Some of the girls played games with stones and string that I wished I understood. These were their games from life back in Kodiak or Chugnik, or wherever their original home had been.

In arithmetic class, I was delighted that I could actually help these little girls. I thought about how unhappy their lives would become when they encountered times tables.

My chance to see Benny Benson close-up came during this class; we stared and grinned, and giggled; but clearly he was as shy as we were. A tall slim man, with sandy hair, he leaned against the wall and watched us as we labored on adding two digit numbers, little hands putting #2 pencils to paper, at least one student licking her lips as she concentrated. Sometime Benny had quietly sashayed toward the door, and waved to us. We waved back, expressing our goodbyes to our local hero, and he was gone.

Late in the afternoon, we filed into the auditorium to hear the much anticipated student concert. By now we knew the protocol for assemblies. Chatter finally settled down and we witnessed children playing their best on drums, horns, and flutes, children dancing reels and native dances. Clearly all of them were having a fine time entertaining Mr. Benson. At last we heard the piano students from the Home play on the stage. Some seemed terrified, some attacked the poor keys, succeeding in punishing them for unknown sins, and some played well. Each seemed pleased to take a bow, some tickled that they had accomplished the task, the rest happy they had survived the experience.

After the concert, Paulette and I peeled potatoes for dinner.

"Come on, Marisol," she chattered, "we need to hurry so we can get the sharp knives." She made sure that we were at the kitchen in time to pick the medium potatoes. The big ones were too much for her small hands, and the little ones were filled with pesky eyes that needed to be removed. Nearby Cynthia shredded piles of cabbage for salad while Lilly's little fingers removed the strings from the green beans. All went into a kettle of cold water destined for tonight's chicken stew. As we worked, strong aromas of bread and pies permeated the kitchen and invaded my nose, piquing my interest in dinner. The kitchen had been a busy place all afternoon, it seemed.

"Hurry up," my little friend whispered. "We gotta get to the front of the school to see the Boy Scouts take down the flag!" She held my hand and we flew, grabbing sweaters on the run. On our way out of the main entrance, I noticed rack upon rack of cubby holes, most filled with galoshes of varied sizes and color—mostly red. While they could rest in June, there they sat in readiness for next winter's mud and drifts of snow.

We washed for dinner and filed to the dining hall once more. Sava and Matthias sat with some of the other boys. Sava caught my eye and smiled. We ate healthy portions of hearty stew, fresh bread, apple brown betty with homemade ice cream. We were to a person, satisfied diners, happy diners, including apparently, Benny Benson.

Homework and showers followed dinner. The shower process was amazingly orderly; each washcloth and towel was the responsibility of its owner. Now as to water being thrown and sprayed on unwilling victims—I admit to hearing an occasional squeal and screech, accompanied by laughter. Bedtime beckoned. The bunk directly above Paulette's was to be my bed. I hung my clothes on one of three hooks by my bed, just as the others did. The other two hooks held my towel and bathrobe. Under each bed sat pairs of those ubiquitous, nearly new brown oxfords. When lights went out, gossip and giggles prevailed. Somebody's secret was revealed, having to do with who she loved that day. We heard scary ghost stories and assorted silly comments about their favorite subjects, mostly teachers and boys.

Out of the darkness came a voice. "Hey, did you get a look at Ivan and the way he looks at my sister Nelly? She says she can't stand him. And I watched him today at the assembly. He was picking his nose and wiping the booger on his shirt sleeve." Everybody exploded in squeaks and guttural caws.

From the darkened room came another voice. "Ugh, what a cull." The room erupted again with a wave of giggles. At the bottom of each apple crate case there would be a handful of scrawny apples too small, too wrinkled, too ugly for just about any use. In the Jesse Lee Home world to be called a cull was the worst insult in this world, a word saved for the smelliest, dirtiest, stupidest of all.

Even the mention of apples caused ripples of giggles throughout the dormitory. Generous, well-meaning Methodists in Washington State shipped tons of apples to the Home every September, in jars and crates and boxes. The children were suitably grateful, but they knew they were in for eating a lot of apples—dried apples, apple pancakes, applesauce, apple cookies, apple cake, apple fritters. When the time came for the temperature outside to plummet, they would put their share of apples on the windowsills, pulling them in at will. That was their apple ice cream.

Cyn and I were quiet at breakfast. We were to leave soon. As for me, I was grateful for even that short visit. To this day I remember many moments and recollect the fun we had with our friends at the Home.

Mama and Mrs. Bergen were at the director's office to fetch us, and as we walked home Cyn and I realized that we had not even thought about the treasure during our entire visit to the Home. We hadn't had time.

GROWING UP

Summer 1948

New experiences marked the summer of my eleventh birthday, most of them having to do with my body and, as far as I was concerned, they were a bother. I was perfectly happy being a kid. All this growing up stuff only brought me moments of confusion, over which I seemed to have no control. There were times when I felt as if I were standing alone in the gray, mucky quicksand on the edge of Turnagain Arm.

Changes befell me; changes in my understanding of life, changes in my body, changes in my relationship with Mama and the people I thought I loved and understood.

At least my birthday party would be one that a kid would love, I determined. I could, at least, control that, still. Cyn and I hatched a bizarre idea; why not, we thought, have a Backwards Party?

Mama thought it was a terrific idea.

We concocted screwball invitations. Cynthia pasted parts of newspaper pages upside-down onto our always handy construction paper. Onto that, we pasted my hand-written message, and this is how that looked:

Please Come to my Birthday Party on Saturday at 2:00. Wear your clothes backwards.
Marisol Downey

The wheels in our minds clicked away; our enthusiasm could not be contained. When the day arrived, everybody had to come in backwards, up the steps of the backdoor entry. As I recall, we played dodge ball with our backs facing the circle, and when that was not very successful, we ran a relay race with upside-down wooden spoon batons, each with a drop of molasses on the bottom side.

At just the proper moment, Mama and Cyn brought in my birthday cake—a pineapple upside-down cake with, “losiraM yadhtriB yppaH.” written in vanilla frosting across the top. Not a small amount of ice cream hit the floor as my pals devoured cake with whatever hand we were not accustomed to using.

When the party ended, Mama clapped her hands and said to Cynthia and me, “When you started this, I thought you two had bats in your belfry. But that was fun!”

So it was, and so was that summer’s unending game of war. A bunch of us thought it up, and Cyn and I were happy to join in. It kept us from thinking about anything having to do with the treasure.

Every kid from nine to thirteen happily participated. We imagined scenarios, bloody and valiant, and then we did our best to act them out. We kids were united as we had never been before. We went home to do chores and eat and then we scurried back to serve in our ongoing marathon martial campaigns. Considering nearly unending daylight hours, our days of battle could last for a very long time. We sometimes called truces just because of exhaustion.

The realism was intense; our battles were ingenious and our wounded were treated in the hospital, neutral territory, where they were bandaged and fortified with Fig Newtons, and given five minutes of recuperation time. Even the beautiful Gloria joined us for a few afternoons. She ran, she fell, she even got dirty, and it was the first time I saw her lie on the ground and belly laugh. The time would come when I wished I could have given her more of those moments.

Summer was quickly becoming fall and my neighborhood friends gathered again for what we knew was likely to be our last "war" of the season. Each side had generals and troops, nurses and medics and cooks and, of course, spies. One day I was designated as a soldier/spy for an army whose headquarters was located behind a raked wall of deep, soft, tiny needles, untold years' slough from the spruce tree close to the alley behind my house.

Across our alley, to my left, piles of leaves under the thicket of aspens had been raked and gathered into a huge, amorphous hill. For some reason, our general decided that Andrew and I would be snipers and hide ourselves in the pile. At the very moment the enemy passed by, we were to pop up and annihilate the entire unsuspecting enemy. I don't recall who our general was or where Early was. Perhaps he was our general; I don't recall.

We obediently crawled into the pile of leaves, our faces planted down, our plastic six-shooters in hand, while our fellow soldiers piled tons of leaves on top of us. At once, it became amazingly quiet down there in those leaves. The conversation of the soldiers covering us became muffled, and then drifted away. I felt as if I was floating in a light golden sea, breathing the musty aroma of the leaves, still newly fallen but already moist and slightly mildewed. An occasional rustle of leaves broke the heavy silence, but it was truly quiet.

Then I did something, and I have no idea why. I let go of my gun and my fingers began crawling, sand crabbing, until they encountered Andrew's hand. My fingers grabbed his, and after a milli-moment, Andrew grabbed my hand back.

Well, now what? I thought. There we lay, face down, in different leaf-compartments, not speaking, not understanding, not saying a word for a long time. How long were we there? I have no idea; time had slowed to a wisp. What had I done? I wondered. Andrew was my pal, my friend. Whatever had possessed me? I didn't understand then and I'm not sure I understand today just what that was all about. When suddenly we heard the voices of our enemy approach; we froze as the enemy, a squad of four, sat down nearly on top of us, taking a break.

Instantly, in our sniper mode, our minds cleared; this was serious. Our adversaries' backs were just inches away from us, unsuspecting,

Whoosh! Up we popped at just the right moment, surfacing from our leafy sea, and with our shiny chrome pistols we demolished the enemy completely. Blam, blam, pop, pop! Victory!

What happened to that strange moment with Andrew? It vaporized, I think. Perhaps Andrew was just as bewildered as I was. But to this day, neither of us has spoken of it. We continued our life of being buddies. We went to school together, sang in the church choir together, shared at least one harrowing, life-changing experience, yet neither of us has ever mentioned that moment.

***

I was flummoxed by the changes in my body. I was certainly no longer diminutive. I would never be a lady like a dove, I was sure. I was forever needing bigger shoes and my legs and arms had lengthened too; so fast that I was soon taller than Mama.

Mama was delighted. She examined me, her arms extended, holding me by the shoulders, and said that I looked more like Daddy each day. That was fine for her to say. She didn't have to live with knobby knees and elbows that seemed to be where my wrists used to be.

About this same time, I noticed that the nipples on my chest would pooch out just a little bit once in awhile, and I didn't like it. I hoped that I could just ignore them and they would go away. So I did, and sure enough, for awhile those pitiful pooches went away.

But not for long. A few days later, there they were, stupidly pooched out again, and then they stopped going away. Those pesky things were there to stay and I sulked.

Next, I noticed fuzzy stuff beginning to grow in the area known universally as *down there.* What a pain. I wasn't ready for this, either. I just wasn't.

What the girls my age did and said was changing, too. Now, when they gathered in town, they giggled and thought they had to talk about these strange changes and boys. To me those palavers were just boring. Sometimes I didn't even understand what they were talking about, and

I chose to put those thoughts in the back of my head, in a mental box, and I vowed to cope with them some other day, a day when they might make sense.

Next, I noticed that the boys began to look at us girls just a little bit differently, and some of the girls began to look at the boys differently, too. I remember the girls giggling over something called a dirty joke on the playground. It was about a man who was attacked by a shark and no matter how hard they tried to explain, I didn't get it. My first dirty joke and I just didn't get it.

During this time, Gloria had her thirteenth birthday party. Cyn and I were invited and this was the first time we saw boys and girls really dancing together. That was a moment for terror—a sense of terror that continued when we were introduced to "Spin the Bottle." I sat there doubting my own intelligence when I understood the rules. But I stayed in the circle anyway. I sat hugging my legs, my head on my knees, trying to be invisible.

Early's friend, Terry, chose me. I became speechless and helpless, I swear. I couldn't believe myself as I actually followed him into the kitchen pantry, where he put his arms around me and he gave me a quick, gentle smooch on my lips. Aarggh. Now that I think about it, it really was a nice little kiss, but at that moment all that spit revolted me, and his breath so close to my face, and his eyes right in front of me—I was frightened and struck stupid. I bolted, pushed against the swinging kitchen door, and walked out, my flushed face set in my best idea of a blazé expression.

My cheeks and ears burned; I told Cyn I had to use the bathroom. The bathroom was down the hall and it was small. Gloria's mother had painted it apple green and decals of rosy cherubim danced around the chrome mirror. The commode was tucked between a pink plastic shower curtain and a small sink. As I sat, directly in front of me to the right on the wall, hung an intriguing picture. In this dreamy scene of willowy trees and vines was a bed and on the bed lay a beautiful pink and white lady. Her hair was golden and flowed almost like water, over the satin and silk bed covers. Her slippered foot draped over the side of the bed and one hand covered her eyes as she rested. Everything was soft and shimmery in the picture, all in shades of pale blue and rose, gold and silver. All this was captured in a thin wooden frame painted burnished gold. She had to be some kind of princess, I thought, in a world I had never seen before.

I finished and noticed a nearly empty toilet roll. I opened the pine cabinet under the sink, where I knew Mama would always keep another roll. Spying a couple of towels which seemingly covered a roll or two, I folded them back and was stunned to discover not toilet tissue, but a half-bottle of bourbon lying in a towel-formed cradle.

In this, the home of one of Seward's elite, the reality jolted me, and caused me to recoil as if I had found a snake. My reaction is difficult to explain; I knew Gloria's mother drank, but encountering that bottle was a shock. It made the entire matter an ugly reality. I had trespassed on someone's private problem and all I could do was cover it back up. I closed the cabinet door, tucking the entire experience of that day into that mental box in the back of my head. That box would fill up rapidly over the next months. Late summer arrived, the time when the professional baseball teams in the United States were competing for a slot at the World Series. I loved playing softball, but I knew absolutely nothing about those big-time teams. There had been no baseball team to follow in Gardner, New Mexico, and I would have been too young to care. My total knowledge of the subject was when I heard about Jackie Robinson, and I didn't even know what team he played for.

Now, in school, after school, everywhere, all the talk was about the hot competition for the American league championship between the New York Yankees and the Boston Red Sox.

Suddenly I found myself intertwined in a scheme, a strange scheme involving baseball and boys and I never saw it coming.

Since the day of our last war, and since my birthday party, Gloria, seemed to have decided I was worthy of being some sort of junior friend. I didn't mind her new attitude; I was beginning to like her. One day she approached me. "Marisol," she said, golden curls and blistering blue eyes confronting me, "do you know about the race between the Red Sox and the Yankees for the pennant this year?"

"Sort of," I mumbled. (Why was a wave of fear whipping through my gut?)

"Well," she said softly, with a very slight conspiratorial tone, "do you know that I kinda like Steven Remson?"

I had to tell her that I didn't. That fear had now traveled to my lower gut.

"Well I do, and I think he likes me, too," she revealed, speaking very softly. Suddenly I felt like a co-conspirator, but of what? "And he wants to make a bet." She cupped her hands to my ear. "Problem is, the bet has something to do with you," she whispered.

"With me?" I blurted, incredulous, pointing my thumb into my chest just a bit too hard. "Except for seeing him at school I don't even know him!"

"I know," she said. This conversation was getting stranger. Gloria continued, "Do you know his friend, Terry?" she asked.

Well yeah, I did know him. I blushed at the thought of my first smooch and my infantile reaction. Terry was Early's best friend, too.

"Weelll…" she said, crossing her arms, light blue cotton skirt sashaying before me just a bit. Now I swore I could smell the intrigue. "Steven is a Yankee fan and Terry is a Red Sox fan, and they want to make a bet."

"So?"

"So if Steven wins—if the Yankees win," she paused, "he wants to give me a kiss."

Next came the punchline. "And if the Red Sox win, Terry wants to give YOU another kiss," she announced, smiling coyly.

I didn't like any aspect of this proposal. I was having trouble actually understanding this entire conversation. I was frightened. And, as I recalled my encounter in Gloria's kitchen, that niggle in my gut began to throb. "But I don't want to kiss Terry," I protested.

"But I DO really want to kiss Steven," she said, smiling demurely. "Please, Marisol," she begged.

Well, what should I do? What could I do? My mind turned into Jello. My head swam. Gloria had just begun to accept me, and I had failed so miserably at this kissing thing.

What I should have done was go home and discuss this with Mama, but I didn't. I kept my secret to myself. I could have discussed it with Cyn, but she wasn't here. What I did was, I relented. I said, "Okay, yes." And within seconds, I regretted it.

But I was committed. Now, I had a reason to pay attention to all that baseball talk. Daily I checked with my radio, hearing what I didn't want to hear—that the Red Sox were on fire and were likely to win the pennant. What could I do? I suspected that the little kiss Terry gave me at the party wasn't what he had in mind this time. I felt trapped. What did a real kiss entail anyway? I wondered.

I began to worry, and the more I worried, the more I was baffled as to how to extricate myself from this situation. Soon, I swear, I saw that boy hanging around everywhere I went. Sometimes he was with Early and sometimes alone. Maybe it isn't fair for me to say that. Perhaps I just happened to wander where he was, but I bumped into him everywhere I went, and when I did, he had this look on his face that reminded me of a sea lion waiting for somebody to throw him a fish gut. Ugh.

What did he see in me, anyway? With pigtails and big feet, pooches hidden under Daddy's old sweaters, and a new worrisome pimple on my forehead, what did he see in me? I felt helpless, bereft of any protection whatsoever in this quicksand world.

So I resorted to the only way I knew to avoid the consequences I so feared; I began to pray. I prayed hard, very hard, whenever I could, many times a day and definitely at night before I went to sleep. I prayed at Mass on Sunday, when I knew the Lord was really listening, and I continued for weeks. My prayers were serious and intense, until the moment when, thank you Lord, the Yankees won the pennant! I thanked the Lord often and over, and over, and over for his kind attention to my plea for help.

The truth is I prayed so hard that as of this year, 1963, the Red Sox have never won the pennant again. In fact they haven't even been close. I feel guilty because I think their bad luck is my fault. But I couldn't help it. Sometimes I think about all those nice baseball players and fans, and to think that I have jinxed their joy because I prayed so hard. Sorry, Red Sox, I didn't want to do it, but I did what I had to do.

***

It wasn't long after that when Mama scrutinized me and gathered that the time had come for her to have the big one, the growing up talk with me.

She handled it pretty well. "After all, Marisol, I've never had a little girl before, so this is new for me, too," she spoke softly, reaching over to pat my hand. It all seemed confusing still, but thanks to her, I was at least on the road to understanding this subject.

This was the perfect time for Mama to explain to me about the glamorous red-headed lady in the Cadillac. She was known as the Spanish Queen, she explained, and provided a necessary human service for the town, one that paid her very well, indeed.

"Mama," I began tentatively. "Mama—"

"What is it, baby?"

"Mama, um, Mama, don't you really miss Daddy? I mean in that way?" There, I had spit it out.

"Oh, honey, you have no idea. I miss him always, and deep in my gut." Her words trailed off, tears spilled over and down her cheeks. She stood and walked away from me, her arms hugging herself. After a pause, she said softly, "Sometimes, when I would touch him, your Daddy, I thought I loved him so much, my hand was going to stick to him forever."

She pulled out a tissue, wiped her eyes, and then took a big breath. "But as for me, kiddo, here is what I feel. Here is what my future holds. These are my decisions. Sure, I miss making love, I miss it a whole lot. I miss your daddy so much sometimes my guts ache. But..." She took another breath and sighed. "I have decided that, as long as you need me, we are a team. I will be here for you and that picture will not be muddled by a new man taking Daddy's place."

"But Mama,"

"No, seriously." Her expression was firm. "After all, I am still trying to understand myself, little girl, and it isn't always easy for me, you know. I'm a practical person, and I am trying to make practical decisions about us. Sure, I like men in my life, and it sure is nice to have them tell me I'm pretty or charming and I appreciate all that very much. But for now, men will not be an important part of my life. It's just simpler that way."

"But how about Major O'Keefe, Mama?" I asked.

"Honey, he is a wonderful friend; he can make me laugh, and really, he spoils me. He spoils us both, don't you think?"

I nodded.

"The truth is, I am not at all in love with him and he knows that," Mama continued. She reached over and pinched my cheek. "I think he loves you more than he loves me. I am grateful for his friendship, but I don't owe him anything except friendship, Marisol, or any other man, for that matter."

"Sometimes I wish he would wait until I grow up," I grumbled.

"I know, but he won't, Marisol," Mama laughed. "And someday he will leave us and look for someone he can share his life with, and that is the way it should be."

Our conversation ceased, but it was clear that Mama had more to say. I just waited because I had no idea what was clouding her face at this moment. "Honey," she began and then paused, choosing her words carefully. "You had so much trouble accepting my decision to come here. And I know that, believe me. I knew we had to leave, but it wasn't easy for me to say goodbye to everybody and leave our little home. But in the end, the decision was made for me. Marisol, your Uncle Kenan loved your Daddy and us so much. He wanted to help us so much."

She paused. "But the problem was, I think he was falling in love with me, and I just couldn't have that; I couldn't let it happen. That was why it was right for us to leave. Do you understand now?" Mama's eyes were tearing up.

"Of course!" I said. "Oh Mama, of course!"

So that was the end of my facts-of-life talk, except for one thing. Sometime later, Mama explained the joke about the man and the shark, and I finally got it.

HALLOWEEN

Fall 1948

I anticipated the beginning of this school year. I would be a sixth grader and we would rule the elementary school. This year started off with a zany twist—the two taxis in town got themselves into a price war. Can you imagine? That meant we kids could call for a taxi to bring us home from school, or take us into town for a chocolate malted milk, for a dime or a quarter. We took advantage of their service on a lot of occasions.

Of course the temperature gauge descended daily, but so far the weather continued to be tolerable. Unfortunately, just as the taxi war came to a close, the wind arrived. Seward nearly always has wind. That has to be expected since it sits at the mouth of a bay. But this wind came in the form of huge, deep gray round clouds, low on the horizon, resembling the huge swirling dust clouds kicked up by the cavalry coming over the hill in a western movie. It remained, a steady, grinding presence, causing us to walk at an angle, if we were to walk at all. It blew through every bit of our clothing, and we chewed the sand and bits that invaded our mouths. Gusts sent us careening and staggering, sometimes planting us on our rumps when that wasn't our plan at all.

There was nothing we citizens of Seward couldn't endure, we thought. After all, we had made it through last winter, didn't we?

Halloween was coming. The PTA made its plans for the annual Ginger Bake Sale. One morning, Cyn and I started across Third Street toward school carrying a load of goodies destined for the Ginger Bake Sale. We pulled our collars up, tucked our chins in, steered our bodies into major thrust and soldiered on, making little progress.

Suddenly, one big gust came at us from our right and knocked us over, cookies and all. As Mama would say, we fell tail over teakettle tumbling all the way down the street toward Homebrew Alley, snacks tumbling along with us. The best we could do was keep from blowing into things. We had no control actually, and for the better part of a block, we were at the mercy of that wind.

At the corner, we were saved at last by Andrew and Early, on their way to school. They helped us find a spot on the curb where we could recover and they chased cupcakes, peanut butter cookies, and taffy, carrying them for us back up the hill to school. Cyn and I sat a little longer, catching our breath, brushing dirt from our jackets, and muttering in indignation.

We saw Sava turn the corner near the railroad station and plow up the hill against the wind. Grasping our predicament, he chuckled and accompanied us to school. The boys put the boxes and bags of goodies on a low wall in front of the school, and we did what we could to salvage the items. We saved a lot of them, actually, but some cookies went to the boys and Sava, and a cookie or two for us. In the bottom of one carton, we peered at the residue, a mass of broken, crushed, delicious, bits and crumbs.

"Lotta cake broke, girls, huh? Better put 'em broken ones under that hemlock tree," said Sava. He smiled, and shuffled his feet while crushing and uncrushing his hat.

"Really? Why?" I asked.

Sava just shrugged his shoulders and gazed up to the hemlock tree. In that tree perched a raven, raucous and nasty as could be, screeching and cawing as a smaller bird cowered, hoping for nothing but to be left alone. Raven nagged and pecked at that poor bird incessantly. He hopped about, fluttered his wings, diving at the smaller bird, yapping and cawing. The smaller bird held on in silence. I think Raven was demanding its nest, which was too small for him, anyway. What a show Raven put on. By now he had our total attention. What a rude creature he was, and downright mean at that.

Sava emitted a sort of guttural sound, ending with a low whistle and Raven ceased his ranting. Instead, he began to look us over, nodding his head. "Girls—meet Hero Raven," Sava announced, chuckling. And then he addressed the black bird, "You stop fussing at that little lady bird and leave her alone."

In response, Raven darted toward the nest and extricated a piece to tinfoil. With the foil in his beak, he looked over at us and then flew away.

We dumped the remnants of our goodies beneath the tree, turned our backs and walked into the school. That was our introduction to the famous Raven, and we were not impressed.

At last, Halloween arrived, and, as if it were waiting for a cue, the wind brought our first powder of snow. We sixth graders would join the bigger kids this year. We planned to meet at six o'clock and go trick or treating together.

It was already dark as we started out, part of a gang of six or seven, led by Andrew and Early decked out as pirates. Early had an eye patch and a checkered cloth tied around his head.

Mama helped me drape a white sheet like a toga over my long underwear shirt and blue jeans. On my feet were Mama's sandals over wool socks. Mama had pinned my braids around my head in a crown and stuck a sprig of hemlock into my hair so I looked like a veritable Roman beauty. She said I could pass for a regal Theodosia any day. Sensible Cynthia dressed warmly as a hobo, with plaid wool shirt, heavy trousers that pooled at her feet, and an oversized pink wool beret perched on her head. Off we trod into the wind, me stumbling over my toga and immediately regretting that I had opted for a costume that demanded no coat. Brrr. Cynthia rolled up her trouser legs and pulled her hat down over her face and ears. My costume and my vanity demanded that I wear no hat and immediately my ears began to ache.

We all headed into town to hit the open stores for treats: jelly beans at the ice cream store, Baby Ruth bars at the grocery store. The group scattered toward different stores and I became part of a trio--Cynthia, Early and me.

"Shall we hit the bar?" I inquired. I wasn't sure they could hear my words in the wind.

"Sure!" they responded. Cyn and I knew what her father would say if he knew what we were about to do. But we had Early with us for protection, we thought.

We brazenly entered Solly's Bar.

Directly ahead of me in the dim light I could make out a round table where five or six players shuffled cards, snorted, and swigged a shot of booze. As the customers in the booths spied us, the bartender looked toward us, slowly wiping foam from a beer mug.

The conversation continued at the poker table where Cowcatcher Charlie occupied the center of attention, regaling the group with one of his stories. Charlie had his back to us. He had stopped for a moment apparently to spit and put another gob of chew beneath his lip. Then he continued his story, bellowing in his best stage roar: "SO I SAID, 'HELL, MAURICE—I'LL JUST CUT OFF MY HEMORRHOIDS, DIP 'EM IN SUGAR, AND SELL 'EM FER DOUGHNUTS!"

Just about every face froze, looking our way, eyebrows elevated, shot glasses in mid-air, the place was dead quiet. Poor Charlie, his lip appropriately stuffed with chew and prepped for a few appreciative laughs from his cronies, turned his head our way.

"Trick or treat!" we shouted. Laughter began anew, and the tension shattered like mirror glass.

We confronted each customer in turn. Our faces showed no shock about what Charlie said; as a matter of fact I wasn't offended at all—my concept of a hemorrhoid was fuzzy, at best. But just the presence of our young faces made them feel sheepish, chagrined. We made a killing in there.

We approached the customers sitting at the bar last, as we headed out the door. One of them was Mr. Lauber, his face flushed rosy red. At the door we turned and thanked everyone and began our exit. But not fast enough.

"Marisol, wait!" The voice was Mr. Lauber's. His elbow slipped off the bar, he grabbed his coat, and headed out the door with us. Lucky us. Once outside, we began to pick up our pace, but if we thought we could out-walk him, we were very mistaken; his legs were long and, even though his gate was unsteady, he kept up with us just fine.

He wanted to talk. He liked our costumes, and asked about school. We answered him in short, quick responses, all the while wondering how we could get away from him without angering him. We were very glad that Early was with us. For a tortured block, we walked and talked. He was chewing on a toothpick, grinding it really, and appeared agitated. I held my breath; I had seen him like this before.

Finally, at the next corner, our agony ended. "Well, Mr. Lauber," Cynthia said, "we have to turn here and head back to school. Our friends are there already."

We stopped; he continued ahead for a pace or two, and then turned back to face us, swaying just slightly. A thin covering of ice was building up on the surface of the recent skiff of snow and we held our breath, concerned whether he could maintain his balance. We watched him carefully. His nose was running and two drips of snot glistened on his whiskers.

"Well kids..." he said, as he tipped slightly forward in the wind and lifted up on his toes.

He reached into his pocket, pulled out three silver dollars, and dropped one into each of our bags. "Here's a Halloween gift for ya," he said.

He then grinned at us, took off his cap, bowed low, miraculously maintaining his equilibrium, and ambled away.

Profoundly relieved, we hurried uphill toward the school, feeling a bit elated. We had escaped from Mr. Lauber and the wind was at our backs for the moment.

The way from town to the school took us through alleys harmless by day, but frightening on this night. By now we had no idea where Andrew and the rest of the group were. We shuffled along the dark street, suddenly aware of the shapes created by shrubs and fences, which lurked, lying in wait for us.

Suddenly two wavy shapes, perhaps twenty feet ahead, lunged at us. Dressed in black, they wore winter caps and sunglasses so that nothing was visible except mouths and waving gloved hands. The larger shape growled and lunged at us. Naturally we panicked, scattering and running for our lives.

I suddenly was alone. I couldn't breathe; my heart went, "Kalunk!" against my chest as I turned and ran, clutching the hem of my toga. I ran as fast as I could, curling my toes in the sandals in vain; they weren't cooperating, sharp gravel stones driving my feet wild. I headed down an alley, bounded by wood fences and occasional low frame buildings, my toes seriously hurting. As I proceeded at my high-speed shuffle, flakes of snow and chipped ice flew up under my toga and they felt like little fire sparks against my skin. My ears throbbed. My sole desire was to survive, to get away from these fearsome shades.

Then, in darkness only the moon mitigated, I encountered an obstacle I could not surmount; directly ahead of me an old, rusty oil tank had blown over into the alley, along with a canvas tarp. They blocked my way. I could now breathe again, just barely; but I had to turn around and face my leering adversaries, to find that I now faced just one huge gloved and growling shape.

When I stopped, it stopped. We both stared at each other momentarily. My lungs heaved as the wind howled. The creature growled, held its hands out making claws of its fists and took a step toward me, laughing a long, icy laugh.

Just then, just behind me and to my right, I heard what in the wind sounded like some primal groans, which disintegrated into a sort of a gurgling. My adversary must have seen what appeared to be a pile of rags come to life. As I turned toward the source of the noise, I saw seated against the fence, a very drunk Garbage John munching on a pork chop bone, a whiskey bottle in his raised hand, and he was singing, "It filled my heaaaaart with tears...They took the ice from off the corpse and put it in the beeer."

If I was stunned; my leering enemy was, too. It moved on, disappearing as fast as it had appeared.

I cannot describe adequately my relief. The beast had released me. I could breathe again. "Thank you, John. I think I love you," I muttered. He responded with a lengthy, satisfying belch.

That had been a moment of truth. Anger and determination overtook me, body and soul.

I didn't recognize the black body or claws, the growl or the roar, but I sure knew that icy laugh. It was Byron, I was sure of it.

I bid goodnight to John and walked toward school alone, cold, angry, grimly contemplating something akin to mayhem.

NORTHERN LIGHTS AND SPOTLIGHTS

Cynthia agreed with me. And if Byron had been my adversary, Louise was surely his companion—the mysterious shape who persecuted Cynthia and Early. Their pursuer had not been particularly brave, soon peeling off from chasing them in search of other, more enjoyable moments. It would seem that Louise's heart wasn't in the game. Even so, after that night, Cynthia mounted a thinly veiled attack on her sister with comments at every available moment, implying strongly that she knew just who that sneaky freak was.

***

As our days went on, Mama began to think about buying a car. Factories in Canada and the U.S. were rapidly retooling from war materiel to new automobiles, but they sold at a premium. Most of Seward's military vehicles had been shipped south. People in town began buying up the leftover military salvage vehicles for use on our elementary road system. Major O'Keefe urged Mama to consider buying a jeep.

"Don't forget they're perfect for life here, and let's face it, we can't ever have fewer roads than we have now," he said.

Already a gravel road had been finished as far as Turnagain Arm. He had come across a jeep, he told her, which would be a fine source of transportation for years. He had his mechanics check it out and the verdict was that the engine was sound, the axle straight and the tires better than average.

So Mama bought it and turned it over to Artie, the body and paint man at the Ogle Garage. He had a reputation for creating wondrous things from his fenders and quarter panels and Mama encouraged him to let his artistic whims prevail.

"That's all I am going to say," Mama told him, "Except that I don't need it until summer, and I want it to be useful, but beautiful."

Mama said that Artie grinned and scratched his head, but couldn't wait to get started.

***

By this time, there was an abundance of snow covering Seward. Sometimes, when the sun managed to show its weakened, slanty rays, the light made big spots of snow look just like pools of gold. At recess, we kids loved to devise games with the long and strange shadows our bodies made on snow and pavement.

It wasn't long before, once again, our minds turned to holiday preparation. Tia Susana was getting married. She wrote Mama and me about every detail of the wedding plans, but Mama and I couldn't help feeling sad that we wouldn't be there for the wedding. She was marrying a naval officer and moving to San Diego. If he was as nice as he was handsome, she was marrying a fine man. Grandfather and Abuelita liked him a great deal and that would have to be good enough for us. I couldn't wait to see the pictures. She would wear Mama's veil and Abuelita's pearl ring during the ceremony.

We had gotten a letter from Maureen recently telling us that Uncle Kenan was engaged to a pretty girl named Fiona O'Neill, and the Downey family was happy about that. So was Mama.

***

We wrote our letters consistently. There was no doubt that we missed our New Mexico family profoundly. Christmas cards to them would be particularly sentimental that year. We tried to write happy thoughts, but our hearts were broken, wanting to be in two places at once. I added a note to the card headed to the Neroli family. I still thought about my friend, but I didn't let those thoughts fill my head with hope. He was probably busy being one of those smart, popular boys who had no time for a lowly sixth grader.

Our church choir sang at one service and at Midnight Mass and I hoped we were as good as we thought we were.

As we unwrapped our ornaments for the year, we admired the special ones and studied our newcomer, the spun glass angel from last year. Its wings were intricate and lacy, and we were fascinated by the musical instrument in its mouth. Was it a recorder? Or a whistle? No matter; we hung it toward the top near a colored light so it glowed soft blue.

On Christmas afternoon, Dotty Etta rapped loudly on our door. From her ample rose-colored bag, she extricated a brand-new copy of *Tales of the Alhambra.*

"Great horny toads, young lady," she laughed, "I thought for awhile you would bring back the library copy in stringy chunks and pieces."

She signed it, "To Miss Sunshine, never forget the magic. Your friend always, Dotty Etta Klein." That book occupies a special spot on my shelf today.

We planned to go to the Officers' Club for Christmas dinner, so our day had been rather quiet. Mama had made eggnog for our tenants and anyone who came by. She poured a cup for Etta and we sat near the heater.

"I have meant to ask you, Etta. Was last winter the evil time you were expecting years ago? After all, it was a doozie, and people died in that avalanche near Moose Pass."

"I don't think so, Marisol. Maybe, but I don't think so," she said, examining a piece of Miss Tenney's fruitcake.

"Well, how about this year's ongoing wind? Have you ever…?"

"Oh no, sweetie. I may be wrong, but my bones tell me it will be very destructive and serious. Don't worry though. I don't think it is coming soon."

Mama and I agreed later that what she had to say didn't alleviate any of our feelings of dread.

New Year's Eve 1948 was my first opportunity to celebrate past midnight. The northern lights had been performing well that year and the word was that they would be something worth witnessing that night. The Bergens came to our house, except for Louise, of course. Aaron brought Matthias along and Major O'Keefe joined us. We played cards and Monopoly all evening and into the night.

The younger ones began to tire. Aaron and Matthias took heavy wool army blankets and fell asleep on our beds. The rest of us played on until our neighbor called to tell us the light show was beginning. Bundled well against the wind, hugging mugs of hot chocolate, we stood in the backyard as a subtle arrow of green appeared, and then morphed into curves and lines. We all saw it happen, but we were incapable of saying when or how the shapes came and went on that background of icy black sky. The shapes were lovely and transient. Once, for tiny moments, we thought we saw a yellow streak or a pink shadow, but it would be gone before we could shape the words.

Soon the wind won the battle; we could stand the cold no more. Weary and content, we trudged into the house, woke up the boys, ate fried egg sandwiches and wished one another a Happy New Year. My bed was still warm where Matthias had lain. I didn't recall even putting my head on my pillow before I was asleep.

Just after New Year's, on another night of tedious gusting wind and swirling snow, our mysterious visitor came by again. But this time we were ready for him. At the first sound, perhaps a snowball aimed at the side of the house, Mama called, "Mary Ruth, bring the spotlight!"

Mama and I ran to our bedroom window, peeled back all the layers of covering, and shone our flashlights in the direction of the noise. Miss Tenney scurried to the window wrapped in chenille bathrobe, curlers in her hair, her fur-lined moccasins announcing her approach. Mr. Larson's mukluks were seconds behind her and they quickly positioned the spotlight, yet another life-saving item from the salvage store, and turned it on.

We all peered out that window and it was as if we were watching the slowest of slow-motion movies. With the considerable help of the spotlight, we could make out the back of a large man, arms outstretched, hands encased in huge, furry mittens.

It was what we saw beyond him that amazed us. The form was lost momentarily in snow swirls. But there it was, the most monstrous bear any of us could have imagined. His form seemed to glow silver in the spotlight, the frozen tips of his fur standing at attention. Seemingly in a torpor, confused, and blinded by the light, his eyes shone back at us quizzically, not comprehending.

It was Old Gnarly, we were sure. The man appeared to be unmoving, frozen by the terrifying sight in front of him. We stared, thunderstruck and speechless. The bear shouldn't have even been there. He should have been high in the mountains, asleep in a cave. But he wasn't. He was right there, transfixed by our lights, looking for all the world like a monster from a movie. Even his claws glowed leaden in the light.

It was Mama who began to formulate a semblance of a plan. "Marisol, go get the box in my drawer and what you find with it," she whispered.

I slipped from the group and did what she asked. In Mama's top drawer, nestled among her handkerchiefs and scarves was the *The May Company* box which contained the Luger and beside it lay a clip of ammunition. With reluctance, I picked up both. She took the gun from my hands and, with hands shaking, she inserted the clip. We all heard a horrid, cold *click, click* as she cocked the gun and placed the barrel on the windowsill, holding it with both hands.

"God knows, I don't want to have to use this," Mama whispered. No more than stifled gasps passed our lips, we the dazed spectators.

"But I will," she said quietly.

This didn't seem to be a solution. We stood for seconds which seemed like hours.

Thank God for Mr. Norman. He broke the impasse.

"That won't solve anything," he whispered softly to Mama. "Just let me open this window a bit."

Mama stepped away; her arm at her side, she walked to the far wall.

We struggled, chipped away ice, pushed and yanked, finally succeeding in opening a very stubborn window.

Mr. Norman yelled to our visitor, "GO AWAY WHILE YOU CAN, YOU STUPID SHITEPOKE! WE WILL COUNT TO TWENTY SLOWLY AND YOU HAD BETTER GET YOUR SORRY BUTT OUTTA HERE BECAUSE WE WILL TURN OUT THE LIGHT. AND YOU ARE ON YOUR OWN. AND DON'T YOU EVER COME BACK!"

All that in a Swedish accent. I didn't know he had it in him. We watched anxiously as the furry parka ever-so-slowly sashayed away, keeping his attention on his menacing adversary. After the count to twenty, we turned out the spotlight and we let the situation take care of itself. At least we didn't hear any growling or groans. Miss Tenney and I looked back at Mama.

Her breathing continued to be fast, the gun hung heavy in her hand. Finally she spoke lowly. "Mr. Norman," she said firmly, "may I request that you disarm this thing?" The glow of the space heater reflected on the pistol. He approached Mama and carefully took the weapon from her hand. She sighed, looked down at her open hands, and wiped them on her bathrobe. Then she looked up, smiled, and together we began to laugh, a laugh of relief.

In the kitchen, Mama made coffee, liberally lacing bourbon into all cups but mine. Even then, we spoke furtively. "Mama," I began to ask the question she was expecting.

"Keith said I ought to be able to use the gun if I had it," she explained. "He got me the ammunition and taught me how to fire it."

Mr. Norman asked, "But just what did you hope to accomplish?"

"I'm not sure, to tell you the truth," Mama said. "But he was—is a human being after all, and that bear…"

Slowly our heartbeats returned to normal. At last we retreated to our beds. I don't know about everybody else, but Mama and I slept the sleep of angels.

The next morning, the police arrived and found only the slightest evidence of footprints in the newly fallen snow.

MY INITIATION INTO A DARKER SIDE OF LIFE

Our confrontation with Old Gnarly contributed significantly to my growing up process. I learned that I could be more terrified than I had ever been before, and I learned how tough Mama could be in a tough situation. I wouldn't have minded if that had been our only crisis for awhile. Unfortunately that was not to be.

I am going to have a difficult time of it, but I will try to tell you this story just the way I remember it. The time was April 1949. A nurse pulled back the curtain revealing Mama, sitting up in a hospital bed, hands seemingly calm, across her lap. She greeted me with a look I had understood for years, the *Marisol, what have I gotten us into*? look. What I saw did not match her expression. A white patch covered Mama's entire left cheek, her eye was black and swollen, and a good bit of Mama's hair had been shaved to make way for a large bandage over her left scalp area.

I gasped and began to bawl.

The nurse restrained me cooing, "Honey, you can't hug her, she hurts too much right now."

She held to my elbow firmly and led me to a chair near Mama's bed.

"But you can hold her hand, and you can stay for a few minutes." Then she left.

I worked to calm myself, but I wasn't doing a very good job of it.

A half-hour before, a booted, over-coated soldier had rung and rung our doorbell and awakened us at 2:30 a.m. Miss Tenney and I arrived at the door at the same time. The porch light was still on, I noticed. Mama was not yet home.

"Very sorry to bother you ladies so late, ma'am," the soldier said, standing carefully on the rag rug designated to catch the residue of winter. "But Major O'Keefe has had an accident, and Mrs. Downey was injured, too. If you can come with me, I'll take you to her right now."

I never put on clothes faster and I was on my way to the hospital on the hill.

It was difficult for Mama to speak, but she did. "Keith and I were driving back from Moose Pass," she explained, alternately holding my hand and rubbing my fingers. "He lost control and the jeep slipped down the embankment on my side of the road. She paused for a few seconds. "Somehow the little door opened, you know those canvas things, and I fell out just as the jeep began to fall over. But, instead, it got caught in really deep mud at the edge of the road, and I kept on tumbling."

She took a sip of water. "As for me, I am just lucky the jeep didn't roll over on me. I landed splat, can you believe, just splat into a little stream that didn't know yet if it was ice or water." She looked to see my reaction. I was not laughing.

"I was unconscious," she continued. "But I guess my head broke that thin layer of ice, and there I was, face and hands in water with the rocks and the mud.

"Keith was still in the jeep, she explained, but his ribs were broken from impact with the steering wheel. He had the breath knocked out of him, but somehow he crawled out.

"The headlights in the jeep were still on, so he saw me in the water, and somehow got to me, pulled my coat around my hands and put his scarf under my head just a little before he passed out, too."

I was sobbing. She stopped talking for a few moments.

"He's in the hospital too, honey. I guess his ankle is badly twisted." She drank more sips of water and continued. "So, there we were, until an army van came by and rescued us." She scrunched her shoulders and tried to smile; her mouth was bruised, her face revealed pain.

"The black eye," she said, "is mainly the result of blood from the bump on my head settling around my eye, honey. It looks worse that in is."

That hardly made me feel better. I put my head on the side of her bed and she rubbed my hair until the nurse returned to send me home until visiting hours the next day.

There is no way to describe how much I did not want to leave her. The soldier drove me home and walked me to the door. "Tell Major O'Keefe that I'm sorry he is hurt, and I am sending a hug," I said, through tears.

He nodded, and was gone. Miss Tenney was there, awaiting my return. I talked to Miss Tenney for awhile until I felt sleepy once more. Miss Tenney walked me to bed and sat with me for a few minutes, but my eyes never closed the rest of the night.

In two days, Mama was home.

I'll bet you think that is the worst of the story. It isn't. Mama still looked terrible, but we adapted, often thinking about Mama's homespun advice. "Just get over it," she would say.

It wasn't until the second day, when she took a bath and needed help that my world as I knew it imploded. As I helped her slip off her clothes, I couldn't miss what I saw, particularly a bruise on her ribcage and a bruise on her right arm in the shape of a man's hand.

I helped her wash those sore areas. I was silent while I helped her out of the tub. Then I declared, with all the force I could muster, "Okay, Mama, I want to hear the whole story."

Anger filled me, body and mind as I contemplated that hand print. I helped her into her robe and slippers and sat on the bed, and sat unmoving until I knew what had happened.

"Oh, Marisol," she winced when I hooked her brassiere. "Now that it is over, it wasn't such a huge thing." I gave her a look of disbelief. "Really. Besides, I'm having a hard time discussing things with you that I don't think you are ready for."

If she thought that would be the end of the conversation she was wrong. "I'm ready, Mama. And if I'm not, I will be really quickly. Like now. What has happened to you?"

"Okay honey." She sighed a very deep sigh, leaned back onto her bed pillows and began.

"Oh, sweet Lord, this is really tough to talk about. I want you to know that Keith is devastated by what happened. His heart is broken and I don't know if he will ever get over it. He is so sorry. It's just as well I tell you because I suspect that he and I will be the topic of gossip around town, and the truth is, we deserve it."

"Mama, I already told him I forgive him about the accident, and what do you have to be ashamed about?"

"No, baby. I don't mean about the accident."

I crossed my arms, and made it clear that I was not giving up.

She sighed and hesitantly began again. "When Keith called to ask me to dinner, he said that he had something very important to talk to me about. I suspected that he was going to tell me that he would be transferred someplace else, so I was prepared for that, and I knew I would be happy for him. We went out to the Black Rapids Road House at Moose Pass, and we drank a couple of cocktails."

Mama swallowed, looked over at me, and spoke again. "He told me, as I expected, that he had received orders for Washington, D.C. and that he would be leaving soon--Marisol, get me a cup of coffee, will you?"

I did and came back, sitting once again in my exact spot. "And?"

She continued as she sipped, "And we talked, and my tongue was loose enough, I rattled on about how much he meant to me, his friendship--that is, his help and his laughter, and his support. Marisol, I had always been very frank with him about the nature of our relationship." She paused and slowly sipped coffee before going on. "Sure, over the years we kissed a lot, and sure we teased and shared secrets, but that was it, and he knew it."

"After all, we cared about each other. We did things people do when they care about each other."

"I get it, Mama. After all, we did just have the Big Talk. Go on." I said firmly.

"You will want to feel that way someday, I promise." She sighed and pretended that she was done talking. At least she hoped she was.

"Okay, Mama, so?" I said.

"And I will be there to tell you that it is all normal and wonderful… Get me somemore coffee, would you please?" I did and returned again.

She took the cup, blew on the hot liquid, and I waited until she accepted that she had to continue. "But, I had drawn the line firmly with him from the outset. Well, you know where I drew the line. It was a firm line. We understood that we were friends, making one another happy by being together, and we knew we could say goodbye any minute without owing anything at all to each other. That was the way it was."

Mama's face showed pain. "Are you hurting?" I asked.

"No, baby. At least not physical pain. It is so hard to talk about this with you." She made a sort of frivolous gesture—a wave of her hand, her fingers danced. "So, I guess we spent a good deal of time talking about the fun we had had, and the laughs, and how much my daughter liked him." She smiled at me and I smiled back, a little. "Anyway, we had a fine dinner. Sirloin steak and all, from the lower forty-eight. We even ordered a bottle of wine and continued trying to have a wonderful time.

"Then, he became more serious and I soon knew what the subject was that he wanted to talk about." Mama leaned toward me, her hand on the bedspread and she looked directly at me. "He proposed, Marisol. He said he wanted us both and he wanted us to be his family now and forever. And he was suddenly earnest. Deliberate."

"Oh." I said, and was silent. It was my turn to consider the moment.

"Well, I didn't know what to do," Mama continued. "I was quite surprised and I think now that I didn't handle the moment very well, because deep down I was a little angry that he was putting me in this spot. I told him that his proposal flattered me and I was humbled by the thought. But I repeated to him what I had said so often, that I had no plan to marry, and only then would I become sexually involved with a man, and that he knew that."

Of course, he said that he wasn't just any man, that he loved me completely, that his commitment was genuine. And he drank from his glass of scotch as he talked. I told him I appreciated his devotion, but I couldn't reciprocate, and, that is when he became angry and I began to worry."

A deep sigh came from within Mama, and her voice held back tears. "You know, he had been so good to us and I had never seen him angry, not ever." It seemed as if it was easier for her to go on, at least for a moment or two. "We didn't talk a lot over dessert. We danced a couple of times, but we both knew that he was deeply hurt, and I was angry.

"So we finally left. We got into the jeep and started home, and the snow was blowing in curls and circles. We both concentrated on the road because the headlights weren't letting us see enough.

"At least that is what I was concentrating on, so I was surprised when Keith pulled over to the side of the road. He put on the emergency brake and reached over for me. He began to tell me, again, how he felt, and suddenly I was sort of disgusted. I told him that my answer was firm, and that now I wanted to go home.

"Instead, he pulled me really hard, as you can see from my bruises, and so, um, so I opened the canvas side door and tried to get out."

Her eyes were no longer meeting mine.

"Somehow the brake released when we were struggling, and the jeep just rolled down the embankment, and, well, you know what happened from there."

"No Mama, I don't know what happened." I was not letting go.

"Honey, this is so tough for me. After all, you are my daughter and I can't tell you these things."

"I think I just grew up a few minutes ago. Go on, I want to know"

"Well…" She just sat silent for quite awhile, and I sat silent with her. Finally she began to speak, softly, hesitantly. "First he was yanking at my coat, and blouse, and I was fighting him, and then he was kissing me hard, so hard I couldn't breathe and all I could hear-- Oh, Marisol, this is so hard."

"Please go on, Mama." My face was becoming a thundercloud.

"Then he was suddenly opening my coat, and ripping at the buttons on my dress, and his hand-- so I-- Oh, Marisol." Her eyes met mine and she started to giggle, "I bit his lip really hard!"

"No!"

"I did, and there was blood all over his mouth, and I think that is when his leg pushed against the emergency brake and we started to roll."

Strangely enough, we both laughed as if that was the funniest joke in the world, desperate to relieve the tension we had just endured, and the laughter did it. We pulled ourselves together. When Mama continued, her mood had changed. "You know, I feel so sorry for Keith."

I said nothing.

"I mean, he was just crushed when he realized what had happened to me. Crushed Marisol!" And she started to laugh again. "Oh boy, was he crushed!" Just thinking about that word made us laugh again, a howling laughter we didn't want to let go of, because stopping meant that we would have to return to the reality at hand. And laughing was better than crying, we knew. "Can you imagine the pain he was in," she continued finally, working to control herself again. "When he scrambled and crawled to where I was in the water? Really, Marisol, and then he tried to help me as much as he could."

"That's all very nice, Mama," I said, still holding back now meaningless giggles. "But all I know is he hurt you. Right now, that is all that's important to me." Laughter extinguished, fury prevailed.

"But, Marisol." Mama spoke quietly, "we need to find a way to forgive him. He is terribly disappointed in himself, and devastated that he has hurt us…" she rattled on.

"I don't care right now, Mama. He hurt you."

"But I hurt him back!" she said. "Really, Marisol, he is in as much pain as I am, I know. Emotionally as well as physically. We are going to need to help him. He is, after all, our friend and a human being."

"I've heard you say that before, Mama. But right now I am not in a mood to forgive."

"Marisol, think about it. He is and has been our friend." Mama managed to pull herself up and get the box of Kleenex from the nightstand. Both of our noses were running from tears of laughter and pain. "I have been thinking. Seriously, I think we both need to talk with Father Paul. Separately, I think. Perhaps he can help us work this out, and help us begin to forgive. After all it was partially my fault."

"Mama! Are you kidding? What if this had happened to me, and I said just what you just said? Mama! You gave him your respect, and you trusted him. I don't want you to blame yourself. You just can't."

"I just feel ashamed…"

"You haven't done anything to be ashamed of!"

"But he's a friend." She began to cry, a sound coming so low from within her that it became a groan.

She needed to be alone, I thought, and I began to realize that some of the experiences I had tucked in the box, in the back of my mind, would now need to be dealt with. "How about if you just lie down and rest for awhile?" I said, and I backed out of the room leaving the door open just a crack in case she needed me.

MY CONCEPT OF CRUELTY DEEPENS

March 1949

Sure enough, Mama's scratches and frostbite healed. Stitches were removed from the bump on her head and her hair grew back. The bruise on her side began to lose its ugly color. That hand print on her arm was fading, too. But each time I saw it, it infuriated me.

Mama began visiting Father Paul. With her goodwill and his support, her heart began to heal, too. Even so, I knew that every moment of that episode would remain indelibly with her no matter how slight the scars became.

Mama was correct when she said that gossip would fly around town. That, alone, annoyed me. But every time she said something about men having certain needs, I would shoot her a sharp look. If I had known how to curl my lip, I would have. She had cautioned me many times about never giving away any personal part of me just because somebody asked for it.

Yet here she was, making excuses for Major O'Keefe's actions. To me that statement about a man and his needs was no more than a simple statement of fact, as in Jane's face is brown, or my socks are dirty, or the flower is dying. So what? Men needed to learn to get over it and go on.

***

One ray of sunshine did bless me during those days. I got a letter from Silvio!

Here is what he said:

> Dear Marisol,
>
> How are you doing? I have gotten your notes and I am sorry I have not written to you. I just am not good about writing but I remember our days on the ship really well. I like Juneau a lot and I love football. I ski too. What are you doing up in Seward? Someday I am going to come there but I don't know when. Father is very busy. He gets to help design buildings and there are a lot of buildings going up here. My mother is not doing so well. The long dark days make her miss Italy. I do have some very big news from our house. I have a baby sister!! Her name is Gianna and she is almost a year old. I really love her, I play with her and she is like a wind up toy. She never stops and never goes where we think she will. I have some good friends at school. Sometimes we sneak over to the billiard hall. Well, Marisol, I better go now.
>
> Your friend,
> Silvio

There is no way to explain my joy. I had actually gotten a letter from him! I could have taught him how to write a better paragraph, but nothing could dampen my euphoria. I kept the letter under my wooden jewelry box and I read it over and over.

With few exceptions, I was still spending two or three hours at the Peterson house every Saturday. Byron would pretend I wasn't there and I would do my best to stay out of his way.

Once in awhile, Byron or his dad still rode the horses to town or beside the lagoon near their house.

I cannot imagine that Mrs. Peterson didn't observe our behavior, but I guess she figured we would work things out in our own way some day. After all, five years did separate our ages. She was wise; we did work things out eventually. It just didn't come about as anyone would have expected.

Sometimes the Peterson family took the train to Anchorage or Fairbanks for a few days, and that meant I could feed and care for

Daisy and Buck. When they were restless, they liked me to talk to them low and slow, without looking them in the eye, gently rubbing their noses and heads. I brushed them, fed them turnips, and told them my secrets. They always listened, nudged my hand and snuffled. I told them that I didn't think much of men right now, and at least Daisy was sympathetic.

As you can guess, my real source of support was my friend Cynthia. She never told me to understand or forgive, she just listened. I think she knew that I would come around to forgiving all by myself.

We spent a lot of time together on those long winter days playing games and trying to figure out just what this world was all about. One day, when I was going on about Rancho San Pablo and the terrifying portrait of Doña Inéz, Cynthia shrugged her shoulders and remarked absently, "I never had a chance to know about those relatives, and I certainly never saw them. My mother's father was born in Bucovina, Romania."

"Romania? I've never even heard of such a place. Where is that?" We were playing rummy and I was dealing.

"It's a long ways away, that's for sure," she said. "It's a country in the east part of Europe, a country that Russia and Turkey have fought over for more years than I can count. Russians, Romanians and Turks, they didn't like each other much then, but there was one thing they could agree on, I guess, and that is that they all sure didn't like Jews. There aren't very many Jews left in Romania."

"Why?" I asked. I thought of my grandmothers, and wondered about Granny Bridey's people still in Ireland.

Cynthia sighed, putting her cards neatly on the bed face down. "All I know is that everybody who wasn't a Jew wanted to kill the Jews."

"Kill Jews? I just can't imagine, Cyn. What caused such horrible hatred?"

Cyn's eyes were now seemingly glued to the rose-blossom pattern on her bedspread. She continued, "Anyway, my grandfather's family home was destroyed, um, and the family had to make their way to Hamburg, in Germany."

"But how? Why?"

"Marisol, I don't know, and I guess I will never know why. It just seems like everybody enjoys hating somebody, and often it's the Jews."

We were both quiet until she continued. "That was my mother's father. My mother's mother left on foot from Vucovar, Croatia. That's the country across the Adriatic Sea from Italy. She and her little brother, my great Uncle Moshe, had to watch while their parents were burned alive in their own home."

"Dear Lord!" I said. I suspect I looked at her as if she were from another planet. How could she speak in such a calm way about this? I couldn't believe what she was saying.

She continued in a cadenced, unemotional tone, "They began walking and, just kept walking, until they got to Hamburg, too, just the two of them. She was fourteen and her brother was ten. They ate scraps of food from fields, or they begged. Their clothes—well, you can imagine, and their shoes, well they just didn't have any, and this was in February when they got to Hamburg."

She looked up, smiling shyly, wiping her tears with the back of her hand. "I'm sorry—and that is where my grandmother met grandfather."

I wondered at her strength, at how she could say these things as if she were telling me what was for lunch at school. The more she talked, the angrier I got and I decided I didn't want to be part of such a mean adult world.

"My dear friend, Marisol, too many people, too many people…" she looked down again. "They died when a big group of people in their town just decided it would be fun to kill Jews. That's called a *pogrom.*"

"But why?" I was incredulous.

"You don't need a reason for a pogrom, and it happens all the time," she shrugged, now pretending to be cavalier. "You just need to hate somebody."

Still studying her bedspread, she gave out a low, choking groan. I reached over, putting my hand over my friend's hands. My eyes were full of tears, too, and I felt as helpless as I did when Byron hit me on the head. But this time it wasn't me, it was my friend who was hurting, and she hurt from deep down inside.

"P-O-G-R-O-M," I uttered. "Put those letters together and they make such an ugly word." I squeezed her hands and tried to speak, but whatever I said was inadequate. "You are my friend, Cynthia," I said, my voice breaking, too. "My best and dearest friend, and I am so very sorry."

From her chest came a low, quiet sob. It came from the same place Mama's came from after Major O'Keefe hurt her. I moved across our dealt cards and put my arms around her, rocking and repeating, "You are my friend and you will always be my friend."

From her chest, the pained sounds continued. So I just held her and let her cry, not hearing any words. When the sobs began to abate, and she was no longer trembling, I pulled away slightly, looked into her face and said to her quietly, "Cynthia,"

"Um?" She said.

"Remember the day I was ready to fall off the grandstand and you reached out and caught me?"

"Yes"

"And if you hadn't caught me, I was ready to land on my head?"

"Yes?"

"Well," I hesitated, trying to find the right words. "What you don't know is that when you grabbed my pants, you, um, you ripped the whole crotch out of my underwear."

"What?" she grinned.

"Yep, you did, you did, and you pulled my panties completely into two pieces, and I spent the rest of the day worrying about this flap of panty that kept moving around. And it may not have seemed cold to you that day, but my bottom was not used to that much breezy cold air."

That did it. She coughed and her sobs becoming a guttural laugh, and I joined in. The tension was broken. We put our cards away and allowed ourselves to think of other things…such as the ever-present subject of ourselves and the changes in our bodies.

We tried on shades of Mama's lipstick and we painted each other's fingernails with Mama's precious Chen Yu polish. We laughed about Cynthia's Toni-induced short bob, and we came upon a terrific idea. We found Mama's sewing scissors and cut off my braids. The tangled result was a mass of undisciplined auburn curls that tumbled around my face helter-skelter. We wet my head down, and combed, and brushed, deciding the result made me look, well, sophisticated.

But Mama didn't think so. Stunned, she stared at my braids as they lay on my dresser top, former extensions of my persona, now lifeless carcasses bound with blue bows. She was dismayed, and beyond my new coiffure, I suspect she was not pleased that we had used her sewing scissors.

Fortunately, her shock was only momentary. Laughing ruefully, she trimmed the ragged edges we had left, remarking that I still looked like Olive Oyl, but with an Orphan Annie hairdo.

We three laughed. It was good to hear Mama laugh about something silly again.

A STUNNING DISCOVERY

One Saturday in April, the Peterson family took the train to see a basketball game in Anchorage. When I arrived at their home, there were a few dishes in the sink, so I washed and dried those, putting them into their proper cupboards. As I had many times before, I ironed and folded the sheets and pillowcases, folded the underwear and matched the socks. Next, I carried towels to Mr. and Mrs. Peterson's bathroom and made up their bed with fresh sheets. Returning to the laundry room, I picked up Byron's socks, lay them on top of his folded sheets and carried them into his bedroom placing the entire pile on his desk. I picked up the four clean pairs of socks and stopped, frozen.

My eye had caught an item sitting on his dresser that caused me to find that my long-held suspicion was fact. He had forgotten his watch, and there it sat resting on top of a small, soft piece of beautiful white fur, a piece of fur I was sure I recognized. It was the fur from the treasure box. I knew it, I was sure of it.

That sneaky, snotty piece of dirt, I thought. Now I knew what I had suspected, but hadn't had the courage to put into words until that moment. Byron had stolen our treasures. He was the one who violated our secret hiding place and left us that stupid message. I could have dwelt on wondering why he would do such a thing, but I already knew the answer. He was mean.

I searched under the bed. I explored the area between his sheets and mattress. I thoroughly scoured his drawers, checked in boxes and sacks in his closet, finding only magazines with pretty girls in skimpy bathing suits and *Tales from the Crypt* comic books.

I sank onto his bed, consumed in anger. My eyes began to systematically scrutinize every surface in his room, looking for any slight clue to the site of our treasured items. Then I examined the log walls of his room. In one corner, about a foot above the floor, I saw that a chink of plaster looked slightly discolored. I crouched, picking at an area about three inches long that looked as if it had been filled in crudely.

Without a speck of guilt, I took Mrs. Peterson's silver-handled nail file from her dresser and headed back to the rough repair in the mortar. I easily pried out the chink and a small piece of blue and white porcelain nearly fell out into my hands. I was thrilled. I cradled it, almost caressed it. As I did, a plan for revenge manifested itself in my churning mind.

For now, I decided, I had to return it to its hiding place. Back in Mrs. Peterson's bathroom I found what I sought. A can of Ipana toothpowder stood in the medicine cabinet. I mixed it with water to the right consistency. I surveyed my work; my spackling looked better than Byron's. With little effort, I found another suspicious spot, and there I beheld the strange plastic-like piece with obscure glyphs scratched on it. I smiled and without removing it, I resealed the chink, admiring my handiwork. I searched his room again, hoping to find the bentwood box, but finally gave up. I would have to be happy with my partial discoveries, I decided.

Doing sneaky things didn't come easily to me, but I was learning. I remembered being Silvio's willing accomplice and smiled. Mumbling unkind words, I made Byron's bed, and got out of there, hoping some malignant shade hadn't witnessed my actions.

As I walked home that day, I was a thunder cloud. I would get him, I knew. I just didn't yet know how.

SOME OF THE MANY SIDES OF LOVE

Mama and I were at the station when Major O'Keefe left, headed to Fairbanks and points south. He was downcast, dejected. His mouth betrayed just the slightest mark where a surgical stitch had repaired the damage Mama had done.

Mama was healing well, both outside and emotionally. She found it easy to forgive. I was not yet at that point. I looked at him, and I felt sorry for him. I looked at him, and I recalled the happy moments with him. I looked at him, and I wanted to smack him and ask him how he could have hurt Mama.

Mama actually embraced him, smiling and wishing him well. I just looked at him, my mouth set, my fists rolled up in my jacket pockets.

But when it came to be the minute he was to board, I suddenly began to cry. I walked straight up to him, hit him as hard as I could on the arm and then embraced him as tight as I could. I wasn't thinking, I wasn't rational, but I am glad I did that. He was crying, too, as he pulled away and climbed the steps into the train.

I wondered why I reacted that way, and I still don't know. All I can say is that I loved him more than I hated him.

He wrote Mama a couple of times, but eventually the letters stopped coming.

When Mr. Norman moved into his own house, Mama decided it was time for me to have my own bedroom and I thought so, too. With paint, stencils, fabric, and determination, we created my own private lair. Pale yellow walls embraced walnut single beds.

I had told Cynthia of my discoveries at Byron's house. She was, at first, astonished, and quickly came around to see that he fit the culprit persona perfectly. Soon we sat cross-legged in my very own bedroom, planning our attack under the watchful eye of my little cloth doll, a wide-eyed, mute witness as our devious plan coalesced.

We decided we would create substitutes for the tiny treasures. A scrap of an Alaska crab shell would be perfect for Cyn's project. Acquiring it down at the pier was easy, but it smelled, awful, an aroma that was hardly ancient. We soaked and scrubbed it with Clorox in our kitchen, squeezed lemon juice on it, and finally buried it in the mushy soil under the snow in our vegetable garden.

In the house, the smell lingered. We thought a batch of cookies would go far toward masking the aroma. Toll House cookies were the new rage in Seward and I recalled seeing a package of those tiny chocolate plops in the bodega. Directions were right there on the package.

Dish towels tucked into our collars and tied around our waists, we scrupulously measured and mixed. We then shoved those cookies into our oven and waited. On cue, that seductive smell filled the air, and we knew we were delivered from discovery.

On the window sill over Mama's kitchen sink she kept a little blue and white flower pot with a pattern of tiny blue flowers and open fans, a birthday gift from me many years ago. I had spied it in the Five and Dime in Gardner and saved my allowance money until I could buy it. On the bottom of the pot was stamped *Made in Occupied Japan*. Inside the pot grew a hearty bunch of parsley.

Not exactly a perfect match for our ancient treasure, we decided, but it would have to do. Mama liked that little pot, but at that moment our plot was paramount. After moving the parsley into a coffee mug, I smashed the pot on the back step. Any qualms lingered for only milliseconds. I salvaged a nice piece and dumped the rest in the trash.

I accidentally dropped the pot, I told Mama. I was acutely aware that I was lying and I was aware of how easy it was. Was that part of growing up too? I wondered. Unfortunately this was not to be the last time I failed to tell Mama something important. But then, I had told her the truth. I had broken the pot, and I was sorry. Sort of.

The next Saturday I had to work at the Peterson house and Byron was seemingly everywhere. I made a point to stay away from him and his bedroom. Around eleven, Mama called Mrs. Peterson asking if she could pick me up. We had an appointment, she said.

Now that was a bolt from the blue. How she was going to pick me up, I wondered. Since Major O'Keefe's departure, we could not count on available transportation. She must have called a taxi, I thought. But where were we going? There weren't too many places far enough away that we needed a car. I waited at the end of the driveway, now curious and impatient.

In minutes, she arrived, but not in a taxi. She was driving our new automobile! I knew it was to be something nice; Mama had visited Artie a number of times at his garage-atelier, but she refused to tell me more than that I would like it. I was dying to see it.

Here she came, white scarf tied to cover her hair. Nothing could cover her smile. Artie sat beside her, his beaming visage complementing hers. What stood before me was an object quite outside of anything I had imagined.

It was simply a thing of beauty to my eyes. The car only remotely resembled its former life. It had a soft, elegantly curved body and its new metal skin gave off a burgundy glow. It now had shiny chrome bumpers, chrome headlights and taillights. The steering wheel was chrome and had its own pigskin cover. It had a new white canvas top, folded down, to reveal plaid seats. Attached to the polished burgundy hood, was an ornament Artie said, from a 1935 Auburn sedan. She was a sleek, chrome angel and she looked as if she were ready to take off in flight, head held high and wings flung to her side, making way for our car. The best word I can think of to describe her is *delicious,* and she belonged to us.

Byron came running when he saw the car pull up. He nearly drooled. His parents were enchanted, laughing at our cleverness and at Artie's artistic talent. I jumped in the back, not inviting Byron to join us, and we took off for the continuance of Mama's driving lesson and our first drive around town.

The next Saturday, Mama called again. Again, she told Mrs. Peterson that she would pick me up at eleven sharp. And, again, I was puzzled. We now had our car, and I thought I had been just about everywhere in Seward, so what was the surprise? This time Mrs. Peterson came out to the car and she and Mama chatted while I sat impatiently in the passenger seat.

Mama cut off her conversation when she heard something, a sound not that unusual in Seward, an airplane engine. "Gotta go now, sorry!" she called and pulled away, headed for the airfield. "I got a phone call just after you left this morning, honey. Dr. Evert is coming in. He can spend the afternoon with us, and the evening, too. And," she said, "he is bringing Silvio with him!"

"Oh my gosh," I sputtered.

"Yeah. And they can stay overnight, so I made reservations for them at the Van Gilder."

"Oh my gosh."

We watched the plane land. They both did whatever needed to be done to secure the plane and walked over to us, grinning. I was thinking in terms of memories, I realized. There was Dr. Evert, looking the same, even to the soft brown and beige clothes he wore—soft boots, dark wool scarf around his neck, smooshy hat on his head. Both of them had rucksacks slung on their backs. Dr. Evert looked our way and I swear I could hear him doing that soft whistle thing he did.

My buddy had sprouted more than I had. He wore jeans and a light leather jacket, a wool cap on his head. For a second, he had his hands in his pockets, and then he took them out. He was thinking about his mother's instructions, I bet to myself.

For the first time that I knew of, I felt insecure. He had only answered one letter, after all. But he didn't owe me any letters. He was just my friend, and a friend I was happy to see. That was all the thinking I had time for before I ran up to him, hands clasped in front of me, bouncing with glee to see him. He grinned back at me, and I was relieved.

"You cut your hair," he said.

"Mama nearly had a heart attack," I responded and he laughed.

"And you are not a peanut anymore," he said.

"That's true. And neither are you!" Suddenly the size of the gravel pebbles at my feet became important. What do I say next?

Dr. Evert held out his arms and I went to him and hugged him.

They fussed over the car and we basked in their appreciation. We drove home to a lunch Mama had quickly put together. Mary Ruth ate with us and Mr. Meninski too. Mama let me do the introductions and they were enthusiastic. "These are our friends from the *Denali!"* I exclaimed. Our tenants were already very familiar with their names.

Dr. Evert explained that he had an appointment at the hospital that afternoon. "But you pick the best restaurant in town and that is where we will have our dinner," he instructed Mama.

"Then I have to do emergency surgery in Eagle Creek and get back to Juneau. My young companion has to get back to school," he smiled at Silvio.

Whatever our initial discomfort, it evaporated rapidly. It was as if we had never been apart. We began to catch up on the news as we ate Mama's chili and corn bread. Dr. Evert's practice kept him as busy as he wanted to be, and he was teaching a class in emergency medical care at the Juneau community center.

Silvio said he really took to life in Juneau. School was easy for him. He liked algebra and French was a cinch. He hoped to be a halfback on the football team next year and skied as often as he could. Mama asked him about his new sister and hearing him tell us about Gianna was great fun. "I know my mother was surprised when she found she was expecting a baby and my father, too. Well, so was I! I wasn't sure I wanted to share my family with somebody else, but I sure have changed my mind. She breaks me up, that baby. She is so cute." He reached for more cornbread and poured honey on it.

We had our fair number of stories to share, too. We showed them the house. We told them that we had just recently used up the last of the powdered eggs and the Ipana toothpowder.

"Next year, we pull this linoleum off and repair the wood floors," Mama explained. "And after that I think we will be ready to move Marisol upstairs."

We told them about our mysterious visitor and Old Gnarly. Dr. Evert asked me about school and I jabbered on that subject at length. We asked them if the northern lights had been so beautiful in Juneau and told them that we anxiously awaited the day the wind would stop for more than one day at a time.

There was one story we didn't tell them, and I thought about the barely visible remnant of that bruise on Mama's arm, now covered with the long sleeve of an orange cotton sweater.

We chattered away into the afternoon. Then Dr. Evert had to get to his appointment, so Mama suggested that we take them down to the Van Gilder. Just before we piled into our car, Dr. Evert remarked, "Don't you think your car needs a name?"

"Well yes," Mama said, one hand on hip. "After all she is a member of the family."

"I'm looking at that gorgeous creature on the hood," Dr. Evert mused. "And she looks like a Victoria to me."

"You're exactly right! Do you agree, Marisol?"

"Sure. Sure, that's perfect," I said.

I opened the car door and, before I could move, Silvio's arm shot out, pushing the passenger seat forward so I could get in the back. A whole bunch of thoughts flew into my head as I crawled in. *He's a gentleman. He's not a kid anymore. That's like what Major O'Keefe would do and I liked it. I'll bet his mother taught him to do that. But that isn't so bad, is it?*

And when he crawled in the back with me I had this feeling that I liked him being there. No big deal, really, I just felt sort of pleased.

Mama and I were like children as we dressed for dinner. She had a closet full of pretty things to wear. But what about me? I had never been to that restaurant and I had this sudden compulsion to look pretty.

What should I wear? We searched through her clothes, finally deciding that I would wear my own wool skirt and her brown cashmere sweater. She begged me to wear a pair of her nylon stockings and I cried foul. The only harness I had given in to was a bra, although I didn't have much to put into it. When I looked at my body in the mirror, I thought that my breasts looked like strawberry cupcakes that didn't rise in the oven. I would wear a slip, but that was where I drew the line. Over the last years, I had witnessed Mama putting on a garter belt and had decided it was the ugliest, most ridiculous piece of underwear I had ever seen. So I wore my new brown loafers and bobby socks. Mama asked if I would like to wear her gold locket and, of course, I agreed.

Mama was beautiful and radiant, as usual.

Dinner ended too soon. I was content just being with Silvio, but I began to think our time was almost over. We walked one block back to the car at the hotel, Silvio walking with me. That's when he said, "Dr. Evert says the weather report isn't so good for tomorrow morning. He says the ice won't be melted, so we can't take off until eleven."

"Good," I blurted. I had been struck dumb, my vocabulary reduced to one word.

"So, how about if I come up and get you and you can show me around Seward tomorrow morning?"

I don't think he had thought this out any more than I had, but at least he had the moxie to say something. "Sure," I said. "How early?"

He smiled then, and said, "Well, I think it isn't light until nine."

"Oh yeah," I said. My mind was still frozen.

"So I'll be there at nine?"

"Okay," I said.

This time he opened the passenger door and closed it when I was in the car.

"So I'll see you at nine?" he asked, looking sidewise to get Mama's approval.

At home, I had a very hard time falling asleep. I was anxious. I was curious. I was a little afraid. But I was happy.

I sat on the porch watching for him a few minutes before nine, and I didn't wait long. When I saw him, it occurred to me that I didn't know what to do. Should I walk out to meet him, or wait here? I just didn't know anything. This was all uncharted territory for me and survival was paramount. I waited, and asked him if he wanted some cocoa before we started.

"Sure," he said.

Mama's presence really helped. She poured a half-cup for each of us and chattered about the fog. "Did you notice that the sister ship of the *Denali* is in port? Maybe they'll let you go on board."

At last alone, we walked about a block without much of a plan, until I heard the whine of the train.

"I know what—let's go up the hill some and we can watch the train pull in." So we rushed to a small park at the base of Mt. Marathon and sat staring down at the valley, the bay, and the mountains beyond. Only the very top of Mt. Ida was wrapped in fog.

The low *waaaaaa* of the train whistle moaned, echoing back and forth across the valley as the train made its entrance into town. We sat there for quite awhile. I talked about Cynthia and Sava and our day at the Home. He told me about his friends and his father and he went on about baby Gianna. "Here, I have some pictures," he said. He pulled out his wallet. She was a sweet baby. Her chubby face displayed a big smile and her huge eyes made her look as if she were always surprised. Dark blonde ringlets danced around her face and on top of them sat a huge bow. In the photo, she sat, her bare feet shot out in front of her, and she played with a white kitten.

"I really love her, Marisol." And I was happy for him. And, I confess, a little jealous.

I felt his arm around me. Tentative, uncertain, I felt he was no more sure of himself than I was. All I knew was that I liked his arm there. We sat quietly for awhile satisfied that we weren't looking at each other. Silvio broke the silence. "My dad loves what he is doing, I think. He loves the challenges and the busyness of his life. He loves Alaska, Marisol. He loves it as much as I do. But the problem is Mother isn't very happy. I think I told you. She really tries, and I feel so sorry sometimes, because I see she is trying. But the darkness and the rain really make her sad.

"Is there anything she can do about it?"

"I don't know. That is grownup stuff, don't you think? I mean, I just don't know what to do. She's very busy with Gianna, and that is a good thing. But that isn't enough. She went back to Boston after Christmas with Gianna. They have just been back a week or so."

"Boston? That's not much better than here."

"You're right. But at least the days aren't so dark. She wants us to move back to Boston. I think she really wants to go back to Italy. Nonna is in her seventies now."

"What do you think about that?"

"I keep trying to put her off. If we can just get her to stay until I finish high school."

"Do you think you'll succeed?"

"I just don't know." He paused and we were both quiet.

"She wants me to go to prep school in New England."

"Oh!" That was a total surprise.

"I don't want to go. I mean she and I are a lot alike, you know. We both love to read, and we both like opera."

I looked over at him quizzically.

"Really," he continued. "I can't say that to any of my friends in Juneau. They would think I was nuts. I understand how my mother is suffering, but sometimes I think I am getting squashed between what she wants and what my father wants. And what I want."

I just didn't know what to say. I knew what it felt like to miss another place, but I had taken to Alaska and I couldn't imagine living anyplace else now. I felt like saying to his parents that they should just let him be a kid. But I was afraid to say that.

The only thing I could do was change the subject. I told him about the treasure and Halloween and Byron, and what we were doing about it. He was intrigued.

"So what now?"

"I don't know. At least we can get some of the things back to Sava and his people. That may be all we can do. But I sure would like to rub his nose in bear scat someday."

I stood up and stretched.

"You'll let me know what happens?"

"Sure," I said. "Let's walk."

We skirted town heading toward the pier and the railroad station, walking wherever our feet took us. His hand now held onto my shoulder, and I didn't mind a bit. We walked out onto the pier and gazed at the ship, dodging workers loading cargo headed south.

"Remember when we…"

"Yeah, I remember," I said. "Weren't we crazy?"

What exactly did I mean by that? Whatever it was, he seemed to agree. We ambled on, walking along the shore where Mama and I often walked, crushing those generations of shells under our feet. Then we stopped, leaning against a large rock.

He took his arm away and that was okay.

"Marisol," he said.

"Hmmm?"

"I wish I had written more letters to you."

I said nothing. It had suddenly become difficult to swallow.

"I mean, I wasn't kidding when I said that it is hard for me to write. You wouldn't think so when you hear me talk. But I have a really hard time writing what I am thinking. I think sometimes that's why I like opera. I mean, all those old ducks up there bellowing out how they feel. I envy them."

"Yeah," I said.

Silvio reached over, took the glove off my hand, enclosed it in his own hand, and slipped our hands into his pocket.

"I mean, the thing is, I don't know how I feel about you. I know I'm too young to be having silly love thoughts. And I won't say that that is how I feel. But Marisol, I want you to know I sure do like you a whole lot."

That did it. I pulled my hand away only so I could encircle his chest with my arms. Even through his jacket, I could feel that he had a very fine chest and my head was buried on that fine chest and I had the feeling I would like to stay there for a long time. "Silvio, I feel so much the same. I mean we both have so much to learn, but all I know is that I like you a whole big..." I jabbered, talking into his chest. He put his finger under my chin and brought my face close to his. Those eyes, I thought. Those brown eyes.

"I think..."

It wasn't the color of his eyes that got me. I had memorized that color long ago. It was what those eyes were saying to me; things I had never experienced before, insistent things, things that made my whole body feel like an Eskimo Pie on a warm sunny day. And then his lips were on mine. His sweet lips were on mine and I was liking it a whole lot.

"Wow," I said, my head returned to his chest. "Silvio...I think...you are beautiful."

We both laughed, and then he said, "Can we try that kiss again?"

We did and we both liked it again. In fact we liked it quite a few times. But then I had to look at my watch. "We need to get you to the hotel to pick up your bag."

We started slowly, dreamily walking toward the hotel, my arm at his waist as his arm was holding onto my shoulder. One more time we stopped. For the first time I felt his entire body leaning into me and I thought, if the Lord was watching us, he would say this was good. Because it was good. We walked on to the hotel, gathered his rucksack and headed for my house. We didn't talk much as we walked. I think our heads and bodies were in a jumbly swirl.

Just one time we stopped; he grabbed my face, kissed my forehead and said, "You know, when you kissed me back there, my socks curled up all the way to my knees." We grinned, both of us holding the other for a moment, and then we moved on.

Just before we got to the house, he stopped again, looked at me intently and said to me, "Marisol, you're my girl."

He was holding my hand again. I have no idea if other people saw us that day. In fact I have no idea if there were any people in town except us. I don't know if Mama saw us walking up to the house. I didn't care. In fact, when I thought about that walk many times during the years, I don't recall that my feet even touched the ground. I think we just floated.

Unfortunately, as we got to the door, reality encroached upon our reverie and the spell was broken. We hurried to the car, to the airfield, and then he was gone.

To this day, I recall those moments clearly. For weeks, I walked around in a happy cloud. I did get letters from Silvio over the years. He was right, it pained him to write what he felt, but he came close once in awhile. As days passed, I began to learn that the only thing I really possessed of Silvio were those memories. When I received a letter I answered it. I felt often that his mother could be reading my letters, so what I wrote was supportive but noncommittal. Because of that, mine were probably as stilted as his.

His mother prevailed; he went to a prep school in Vermont and then he went to Boston College. We wrote steadily for a few months, and then less, and it has been a couple of years since I have heard from him.

We changed: we grew up, our interests multiplied, and in those few letters we talked about that—his girlfriends and my boyfriends. Who knows, he could be married by now. But we both will remember each other always I am sure, with a great deal of respect and fondness.

WE DO SOMETHING VERY SWELL

Days and weeks passed. Silty troughs along the road flowed more each day with what recently had been sharp, deadly icicles If the sun shone just right, those droplets of icicle melt made me think of tears just before they joined the streams of muddy slush running along every road in town.

My thoughts returned to our devious project. Cynthia and I retrieved the shell, now well-stained with black Alaska mud. We shaped it into a pretty good facsimile of what we had found in the cave and, with screwdriver in hand, Cyn etched a number of Hebrew letters onto her counterfeit masterpiece, a stroke of genius, we thought. Next we soaked it in strong tea, and consigned it once more to the carrot patch, accompanied by my piece of porcelain, until just the right moment presented itself. And we were sure it would. We could wait, after all; we weren't going anywhere. Joy of joys, as it turned out, our wait wasn't going to be long.

A telephone call from Mrs. Peterson initiated the next step in our plan. Byron was to play in a basketball tournament in Fairbanks, she said. Could I take carc of the house and horses? Oh my, could I.

I had thoughts about not letting Mama in on our plot, and I felt almost as bad about fooling Mrs. Peterson. But I had to accept responsibility, right? After all, some things took precedence.

Without real discussion, Cynthia and I knew we had to be in this together, and alone.

Freeing up Cynthia on a Saturday would not be an easy matter. We wore her parents down, reminding them of the many exceptions they had made for Louise, and we prevailed.

On Saturday morning, laughing and singing, we trudged along toward the Peterson house carrying in a canvas bag, the tools necessary for our criminal act—flannel doll blankets, Mama's sewing machine screwdriver, our counterfeit masterpieces, and our own can of Ipana toothpowder.

Today Daisy and Buck's nurture was of secondary importance. We fed them and cleaned their stalls speedily, our minds on the impending task. Cyn stayed with the horses, adding hay and keeping watch while I went into the house and went to work.

My heart pounded as I entered Byron's room. With set purpose and downright fear, I dug out the precious items, wrapped them in a flannel blanket, and placed them in my canvas bag. Next, I placed the substitutes each in their places and sealed them into their new homes, using my now perfected recipe for toothpowder spackle. Goosebumps trotted down my arms and back up; my neck felt chilled. Double checking, making sure that I left no telltale debris, I wiped perspiration from my palms and got out of his bedroom.

By now, Cyn's teeth were chattering; from the kitchen door I called to her to come in the house. She would check once more to make sure I hadn't forgotten something—some tiny detail. She pronounced the job well-done and we co-conspirators shook hands. We also took a few minutes for her to admire the entire house.

Next we dove into the chores. I ironed sheets and pillow cases; she made beds and folded clothes. We washed and wiped the dishes in the sink, cleaned the kitchen counters, mopped the floor, and finally exited the house.

Still feeling euphoric, we spilled the beans to the horses. We rubbed their noses, fed each a carrot, and headed down the road feeling that only our heavy boots kept us from flying.

***

Our opportunity, to finally deliver the items to Sava would come soon; his series of stories were to start, and we would be there.

We sat patiently, enthralled in his story of Raven's antics with his friend and adversary, Fox. He related how he tricked old tricky Fox by tempting him with moose meat and teasing him about his lack of courage. All he had to do was ride a toboggan across the lake—a lake Raven knew wasn't frozen enough to bear up to Fox's weight. Not a one of us doubted who would prevail in that contest.

His story over, Sava stood and prepared to go, but before he knew it, we overwhelmed him, trying our best to be the picture of decorum while we really wanted to shout and scream. Outside the building, we sat him down on the low wall by the flagpole and with great ceremony, presented him with a small package wrapped in a small flannel baby blanket. I don't know who was happiest at that particular moment.

On seeing the items, Sava moved his jaw continually, and to us he began to speak. "These are things that are what you say, precious to me, my little sisters. These things my people love, from Qutekcak since before time, before air even. Our hearts been sad for long, long time, because they live we know, but they live lonely so long we don't remember when they left us or how. (His mouth quivered just slightly.) We have stories, they say the death spirit hide them and living rock protect them, but where? We feel shame, we ask living rock to tell us, we always hope, but we never know. Do you understand what you give me, my little sisters? You give us part of our hearts. I say thank you, thank you for all my life, for all of my people."

He put his head in his hands for a few moments, and we waited. Then he looked up, and said in a clear voice, "Swell, so swell. Thank you."

DEATH AGAIN, AND AGAIN

Trees still stood naked against the sky, seemingly hoping for their spring dress. The sun made peremptory visits often now. The promise of life was just around the corner, and the pace of life was beginning to quicken. Indeed, on a certain bright crystalline-blue spring day in the year, 1949, the town's pace sped up a bit more than most had planned, and for some others time froze.

On this particular morning, I saw that the marina was abuzz with patrol boats and police; at the newspaper office, the staff was frantic to change the day's headline. Townspeople congregated, shaking their heads in disbelief.

It was at this time of new life that Gloria's mom set out on a trip, one that she had planned with great care. She spent the morning, after Gloria and her father had parted for school and work, picking up the house, squaring away every detail and leaving dinner already prepared in the refrigerator. She even thought to set the table.

Dressed in smart gray wool slacks, white cashmere sweater and stylish black leather flat-heeled shoes, she carried a large pocketbook that contained all the items she would need.

Her pace was determined as she headed to the dock, greeting the port master cheerily. She boarded their family's thirty-foot sailboat, pulled the engine key from her pocketbook, and turned it. The engine purred as directed and she eased the craft from its berth and into Resurrection Bay. At that moment, the sun hid behind thin wisps of cloud. The boat responded on command, through lead-gray water calm as glass, toward the mouth of the bay and on, into the slightly choppy waves of the Pacific beyond. By then, the sun shone brightly.

That was when Gloria's mom went down to the cabin below, changed into a lovely white satin gown, checked her makeup, adding just a little lipstick to the outside edges of her lower lip. Her eyes saw, but they seemed peculiarly vacant today.

She removed a bottle of pills from her pocketbook and swallowed them all in four bunches, washing them into her system with hefty amounts of Hennessey brandy. She held up the snifter, admiring the color of the brandy and released the pins in her perfect chignon. She then combed out her honey-colored hair, lay on the silk bedspread and ran her fingers through her hair so that it almost resembled a halo. Before she fell asleep, she placed one hand just so, over her eyes.

The faithful motor, well-tuned and efficient, continued to churn through the neighboring waters until its source of fuel ran dry.

After many hours of searching, the Coast Guard found the boat, foundering in a cove of a fjord just north of Seward. One of Gloria's mom's legs had slipped just slightly off to the side of the bed when they found her, but that was the only flaw in the picture. She was still perfectly beautiful, her hair still arranged carefully around her face, although the downward turn to her mouth had become slightly more perceptible. She was, of course, beautifully, consummately dead.

There was no picture of the tragedy in the paper, but Etta described it to me, and I was devastated. I found Mama's arms; she was crying, too, and we held each other for a very long time.

"Why, Mama, why?" I kept asking. How could she be so stupid to take her own life, to prefer to lie in a box, never again to smile, never again to hold her daughter, to love her husband and her friends? She seemed to have everything, Mama, I just don't understand."

"I know, baby. My heart is bleeding, too. She was my friend, Marisol, and I feel I should have been able to help. I did try, but I failed, didn't I? I think she, she just didn't love herself. And without loving herself, she couldn't love anybody else. I think that had something to do with it."

"I failed, too, Mama!" I said. "I may have known something about it, maybe I could have warned somebody. I don't know what to do."

"Now wait just a minute," Mama said, holding my face in front of hers. "Just how could that be? Here I am trying to take blame, but not you, too!"

"Mama, the picture. The picture I saw. I found a bourbon bottle in the cupboard, and I didn't tell anyone."

"Marisol, what are you talking about? What could you do about a bourbon bottle?"

"But Mama, that isn't all." I worked to find the proper words. Mama sat me in front of her.

"Go on," she said. Her eyes narrowed slightly.

"Okay." I breathed deeply and continued. "On the wall in the bathroom is a picture in a teeny gold frame of a beautiful lady. Oh, you can't help but see it when you sit on the toilet, and the lady is in a kind of paradise place and she is wearing a satin dress and lying on a silk bed, and her hair is perfect. Oh, Mama, should I have told someone?"

"So it's your fault because you sat on a toilet and looked at a picture?"

"No, Mama! This isn't funny. I'm not joking," I cried out.

"Let's just say you could have told me, but what could you or I do about a bourbon bottle or a picture? No, honey. Here we are taking on guilt and the truth is it is not our fault. She did this and we don't know why. That's all we know, we don't know why."

"But her daughter is beautiful, and her husband..."

"I know, baby, but it just wasn't enough."

I began to get mad. Suddenly I felt the way I had about Major O'Keefe. "She was selfish, wasn't she?" I stared into space.

"Yes, she was," Mama agreed. She crossed her arms in front of her, her attitude was firm. "No doubt about that. She did something absolutely awful, and caused more grief than she ever intended. We all suffer from this."

Whether I like it or not, that picture is etched in my mind forever. The bed cover, the tree leaves, the vine-covered pillars, the beautiful lady forever dreaming. Some dream. She left us all with nightmares. "If she was here I would tell her off. How dare her!" I stood and crossed my arms, too. "How dare she choose to take her life when my Daddy's very breath had been stolen from him. Shame on her."

***

The fire at the small frame house on Sixth and B seemed to have started in a bedroom. A young father had returned from his night shift at the railroad yard to discover the fire and he managed to pull his wife and daughter from the flames. But his son and a boarder were not so lucky. By the time Matthias and I arrived at the fire scene, the entire house was enveloped in smoke and the flames had reached a spruce tree in the backyard. There we stood, along with scores of other gawkers, horrified and transfixed at what we were witnessing.

That tree was not a young, weak victim. It had a handsome, stout trunk from which grew sturdy branches promising life for years to come. Instead searing fire glowed from within its body. The trunk had burst open revealing a cruel glow. Those lower branches appeared as if they wanted to rip open its chest even more, but they had been caught in one searing moment, rendering them charred, crackled and powerless.

Everywhere there was activity—firemen dragging hoses through char-sooty pockets of remaining snow, lights flashing, searching, hoping for survivors.

Matthias and I had been tasked by Father Paul to wash windows that morning. The Sacred Heart congregation was renovating the basement of the Oceanview Apartments to provide safe rooms for our sourdough old-timers like Garbage John. Just as renovation began, the chimney in the church hall collapsed from heavy snow and old age. The emergency demanded that the entire congregation become involved and our job was at the Oceanview.

We were merrily scrubbing in the sitting room when we heard the wailing siren of the fire truck. We dropped our squeegees and headed toward the noise and the smell. The smoke plume was north of us, black and spreading as it rose. Fire trucks negotiated slushy streets, as roaring flames broke through the roof and steamy hissing sparks shot into the air. Ambulances were already in place. We had heard what the grim news would likely be from fellow gawkers. Stinging, acrid air pervaded the area; tears filled my eyes. I turned toward Matthias; I had seen enough.

We walked back to the Oceanview, morose and downhearted. We took up our chores again, preoccupied by a foreboding feeling that bore fruit. Shortly the news reached us. From the rubble, medics removed the charred remains of a small boy, and a boarder who had been identified as Mr. Lauber.

There was death again staring me in the face, and, again, guilt was my first reaction. I thought back to Halloween and how I had treated Mr. Lauber. Was he ever more than a monster-sized creature bereft of malice? I knew what I had been—a smug kid who gave him no understanding at all. Had he ever been a threat? I would never know. I prayed for his soul, and mine too. But I couldn't help thinking that maybe we would never have a mysterious nighttime visit again.

I thought about Major O'Keefe. He became for us a monster in disguise. But he didn't intend to be a monster I now knew. I was confused. I needed to talk to Father Paul again, I decided.

I would add Mr. Lauber to my prayer list. That was the least I could do. I already prayed for Gloria. I wished that her heart would mend and I wished everything good for her in her life. She seemed to be coping well and I was thankful that Merrylyn was committed to her.

One day I walked by the lunchroom at school and saw Gloria sitting alone at a table. Without thinking, I scooted in next to her, surprising her. "Gloria," I blurted. "I just want you to know that I think you are a terrific person." She smiled at me. "I mean it, I really admire you."

"Thanks, Marisol. Just thank you," she said. Her hand covered mine for just a second "And I know you are my friend."

"Yes, I am," I said, and since I couldn't think of any more words, I mumbled,

"Gotta go now. And Gloria. I love you," I sputtered and I was gone.

I surprised myself, but I'm not sorry that I said those words to her. She became president of her senior class, graduated with honors from Northwestern University, and hopes to become a child psychologist. Who would have guessed?

DRESSING THE STAR

May 1949

Pale green buds on the willows promised that spring was approaching. I hoped warmer breezes would blow away some of our recent sadness.

I had been thinking about digging out that old tin whistle from Daddy's trunk, so I did. Each day I experimented with it, and even those ragged fledgling notes became pleasant scatter shots in the air.

Our house now had new wood floors on the main floor, and a finished ceiling on the second floor. That gave us two more rooms we could rent if we chose to, and the neglected upstairs front window now afforded us an unobstructed view of the bay and the mountains beyond.

In the Bergen household, Louise would turn sixteen in just a few days. The Petersons had invited Louise and her parents to dinner at the Seward Hotel to mark the event. Cynthia would stay home with Aaron; and Cynthia had invited me to spend the evening.

Louise would need assistance for this momentous occasion and Cynthia and I would serve as her minions. She presumed that she was the only girl to be the guest of honor at a fancy dinner at the best hotel in town. I remained mum about my dinner with Mr. Evert and Silvio just a couple of weeks back. Perhaps our restaurant wasn't swank and I wasn't guest of honor, but I recalled the experience and its aftermath as being something akin to celestial.

On the afternoon of the big occasion, Cyn and I stood at attention. I steamed slight wrinkles from Louise's forest green velvet circle skirt and watched spellbound as she began her ritual. Seated before her oval mirror, she surveyed her face and applied the tiniest bit of pencil onto her eyebrows, stretching, pursing, and puckering her lips, she assured herself that every fulsome millimeter of her mouth was covered with bright pink lipstick.

She brushed her hair until every strand glistened and sparked with static electricity. She then curved those strands gracefully around the side of her hand to form a perfect pageboy, that framed her petulant face. I was impressed. My hair was more like a bowl of elbow macaroni which defied any attempts to control it.

Next came the matter of Louise and her nylons. This whole process was the reason why I had worn bobby socks and loafers on my night out.

That was me; this was Louise. What I witnessed at that moment was more a ballet of sorts. She sat on the bed like one of those calendar pinups and slipped her toes one by one into those delicate stockings and gently pulled each up along her legs. She'd had practice.

Her pink silk slip snapped with static electricity and Cynthia rubbed her down gently with a moist washcloth. She slipped into her skirt, a white angora wool short-sleeved sweater and matching cardigan. Around her neck, she tied a small, apple green silk scarf, fluffing it until it was just so. She pinned onto her cardigan a cunning scatter pin in the shape of a letter L.

If ever there had existed a definition for impeccable comeliness, I thought, I was looking at it.

After she slipped her toes into her polished black leather flats, she twirled around a number of times, each time checking her image in her full-length mirror until she twirled herself toward the top of the stairs. For our benefit, she uttered a benediction. "Will you two close my door?" She chirped.

She rubbed her lips together, pinched her cheeks, smiled at her admirers at the base of the stairs and began her descent. Gloria Swanson descending the staircase in *Sunset Boulevard,* I thought.

***

My friend arrived at school the next morning bursting with details about the night, and I couldn't wait to hear them. I imagined the tall tapered candles on the table and waiters wearing jackets and bowties; salmon broiled with a lemon sauce, garnished with whipped cheese, and white angel food birthday cake sprinkled with tiny, shimmering silver candies.

All of that was delicious for the imagination. But Cynthia next divulged information that was even more tasty. "Before dessert, Louise received her gift from Byron," Cynthia began. "It was a silver necklace with a football on it, like the Seward High School award the team had won this year."

I caught myself thinking that I wouldn't mind getting a gift like that.

It was Cyn's next words that set my heart a pity-pat.

"And guess what, Marisol?" We were at recess. I leaned against the exterior wall and Cyn stood in front of me rubbing her hands, her body bobbing slightly.

"The necklace," she paused and hesitated for effect.

"Yes?"

"The necklace was inside a stained, chewed-on bentwood box. Got it? A bentwood box!"

She was jumping up and down at that moment.

I gasped. "No kidding!"

"A box," Cynthia went on slyly, "that Byron said he found over near some old arm equipment on Humpy Cove."

"He what?" I yelped.

"Shhhhhh!" warned Cynthia.

Covering my mouth with her hand, she went on, "So Louise, being Louise, just had to show it off to me when she got home. She said Byron told her it was an Indian relic and worth lots of money."

"Can't you just gag?" I gurgled.

"But it's our box, Marisol," Cyn exclaimed, her hands on my shoulders. "I saw it and there was no doubt in my mind. I watched her wrap up the box in a piece of mother's amber satin, and take it into her bedroom."

Louise would be crazy about the necklace, but we suspected she wouldn't be thrilled about a stained, scratched old box. Our minds went into overdrive. The box was safe and we knew where it was, but darned if we had any idea how we would get it back to Sava.

BYRON'S COMEUPPANCE

A few days later, Mama and I were downtown. Walking our direction were two of our favorite people, Matthias and Sava. It had been some time since we had seen them and we asked them to come up to the house for lunch.

We served some cold sliced chicken and Mama made linguine with a white vegetable sauce. We enjoyed watching the two guests top their pasta with Romano cheese, take their first bite and smile. We talked about news in town, and we asked about Elsie.

"Sava," Mama said as she passed him a bowl of tomatoes, "Please excuse me, but I want to remind you about your promise." She paused, her expression said that she hoped she hadn't overstepped her bounds. Sava looked at her inquisitively and smiled. I knew he was teasing her.

"About our walk into the land where my people walk?" He paused, looked at Matthias, and then looked back at Mama.

"Do not worry, my sister. That day comes soon, I think."

I don't recall Mama's response. I do know she was relieved. She had wanted to hike with Sava for more than a year now and had made plans.

Our lunch complete, Matthias and I began to clear the table.

"Matthias," I asked quietly. "Can you finish this for me? I want to talk to Sava." I led him onto the front porch and asked him to sit on our cane loveseat. I sat next to him.

"Sava," He waited quietly, waiting for me to speak. "I have some news for you. Cynthia and I know who stole your things."

His eyebrows rose, his black eyes met mine.

"We know it was Byron Peterson, and we know where the bentwood box is, too." He smiled and waited. "Sava, we know it is safe. But we don't know how we can get it back for you."

He sensed my frustration, my sadness, and he smiled. "Wait," he said quietly. "Funny how life take care of things."

I hoped he was right. I waited patiently and fervently, but for what I wasn't sure.

***

Our year of being the big shots at school was drawing to a close. At recess, we girls sang *I'm Looking Over a Four-leafed Clover* and wailed: "There was a boy, a very strange enchanted boy," and "The greatest thing, you'll ever learn, is just to love and be loved in return."

And as we sang, I thought about someone who made me feel what I thought might be love. I even hoped there might be a day when he would think I was a pretty lady, like a dove.

Often the recess conversation had to do with boys and, while I didn't say much, I sure did listen. The boys began to slick their hair back into ducktails, and roll up their shirt sleeves. We girls put pennies in the slot on the front of our loafers.

Late May brought the usual string of end-of-school-year activities, and certainly an important one for us sixth graders was our graduation ceremony. Tiny white appliquéd daisies danced on the bodice of the yellow cotton dress Mama was creating for me. I hoped it would not be too short by the time we marched in our graduation ceremony. I would wear new white linen flat-heeled shoes, my legs still white and bare.

The special day arrived; our hearts fluttering, our hands fidgeting, we seven graduates filed in, Cynthia in the lead. To the best of my memory, we all performed our ceremonial tasks, to the enthusiastic approval of our fans seated on hard metal folding chairs. Those included Mama, Elsie and Sava, the Bergens, Miss Tenney, Dotty Etta, Maudie, and Father Paul.

One of our classmates recited from *O Captain! My Captain!* emoting appropriately,

> But O heart! Heart! Heart!
> O the bleeding drops of red

Where on the deck my captain lies,
Fallen cold and dead.

I played one of Daddy's favorite Irish jigs on his whistle, and it wasn't too bad. By now everyone in town knew of Cynthia's prowess and yet they were delighted as she played the guts out of a Liszt Sonata. We received our diplomas, ate little chicken sandwiches, drank fruit punch and that was that; we had jumped another hurdle on our bumpy race toward maturity.

It was another, completely different assembly that brought great joy to Cynthia and me and to others, as well. I shall try to be calm as I relate these details. I assure you I was not calm at the time.

In mid-May, the mayor and the school superintendent announced that a distinguished scholar and expert on indigenous culture would be visiting Seward. School officials were aflutter, and plans were altered so that the esteemed professor, Thomas Fersch, Ph.D. could be our featured speaker at the final school assembly.

Invitations encouraging all parents to attend went home in the fist of each student. An esteemed expert in anthropology from the University of Alaska was coming to town! Posters appeared throughout town, even in Solly's Bar.

The nucleus of a plot sprouted and grew in Cynthia's and my fiendish minds. Just thinking about it gave us joy. The issue was whether we could pull it off.

We expected that Byron, egotistical Byron, moronic Byron would be among the first candidates to show off for the professor, and the very prospect brought glee to our hearts.

On cue, he began to do things that we could only hope for. He would want to degrade us, certainly me. As he showed off the treasures he knew had been ours, we didn't want him to waver for a moment. We would help him; we would bait the trap. He was a rat, after all, and was begging to be trapped.

Louise became our naive co-conspirator; she announced at family dinner one night just what Byron's plans were, and Aaron was happy to relay to Cynthia any activity he witnessed. "I saw Louise bring her box down to the living room," he gloated. "I was practicing on the guitar," he continued, "while Byron pulled stuff from his pockets and Louise packed it into the box. What's the big deal about that stuff anyway?"

We were talking in the schoolyard before school. Aaron was getting very curious about this entire matter. We decided to divulge only what was necessary about our scheme, to prevent him from saying or doing something, anything that would short-circuit our plan. Besides, we needed him to perform just one more task for us—just a tiny task, but one that called for brazen guts.

"Do you know where the box is? Does he have it?" I queried.

"Sure I know. I saw Louise take it up to her room and I know where everything is in her room. It's in her drawer."

At that moment, I declare, I loved that kid.

"Aaron, can we ask you to sneak the box downstairs this afternoon while she is at her dance class?" Cynthia asked, smiling, her hand lightly touching his shoulder.

We had discussed larding the box with more junk and had decided against it. But here we were, with access to the box just hours before Byron's finest hour and the temptation was too great.

"Sure!" said the kid. We could have lit up a cigarette with the sparks emanating from his eyes.

So that was that. Cyn and I waited in her bedroom while Aaron brought us the box, still inside the satin case. The idea of Byron digging out our clumsy facsimiles and not even knowing the difference delighted us. I confess it was pure maliciousness that drove us to open it up and add an additional little item. Then we sent it back to its lair in Louise's drawer.

We could hardly stand the tension until the assembly day arrived. Cynthia and I sat in the bleachers and they rapidly filled with students and assorted townspeople. The Petersons were already seated below us and soon Mama joined them, followed by Mr. and Mrs. Bergen.

We watched as the mayor's wife came in, and Mrs. Vohlman, Maudie, and Etta, along with her hairdresser. The manager of the Alaska Shop arrived with some of the employees from the Brosius Building. Quite a few teachers from the Home arrived. Sava, Matthias, and some of the students from the Home came in, as well as a couple of nurses from the tuberculosis hospital. The bleachers were not packed, but there was a substantial crowd. Some were there to see the high school students perform, but most were there to ogle the esteemed professor and see what he had to say. Byron sat with his class and, in his hand, was a small package enclosed in satin. So far so good.

Before us, the mayor, our school superintendent, our teacher, the Episcopal minister, and the distinguished professor filed onto the stage and sat in the metal seats that awaited them. Before them in the center stood a low dais.

"We meet today," began the school superintendent, uttering all the words that he was expected to say before he introduced the minister, who asked us to:

"Bow your heads please, as we give thanks and bless..." began the minister, who introduced His Honor, the Mayor, who talked and talked seemingly forever to a restless audience, eager to hear from someone other than the mayor.

"And now, it is with real pleasure that I introduce to you the respected Dr. Thomas Fersch, Doctor of indigenous studies and anthropology at the University of Alaska." He paused for coughs, light applause, and continued. "Dr. Fersch will be spending a few weeks in and around Seward as he studies and collects information for his next book. Professor Fersch has received awards for..."

"Get on with it," I blurted under my breath.

"So please give a welcome to Dr. Thomas Fersch!"

Welcomed by polite applause, the distinguished professor Dr. Fersch stepped to the podium. At first sight, Dr. Fersch didn't fit my idea of a professor. To begin with, he seemed to be modest, almost shy. I wondered if he had slept in his trousers, which were topped by a worn brown wool jacket that he clearly loved since its creases matched every movement of his arms. A slight beard curved at the sides of his round head and connected with sandy curls that hugged his head until it met with a bald pate exactly like the heads of Capuchin monks.

Smiling, he surveyed his audience as he pushed his gold-colored spectacles onto the bridge of his nose. The mayor carried a little table toward him and Dr. Fersch covered it with a piece of soft fabric. He then placed a number of items he had brought to share with his audience. As he talked, he picked up and discussed each one, treating each item tenderly and respectfully.

Finally, he closed, inviting people in the audience to share any item they had brought.

"At last, our moment is here," I muttered. Anticipation for what I hoped was to come made my fingers turn ice cold. I grabbed Cyn's arm. Silence filled the room.

"Come on now, it's your turn," the professor smiled, rubbing his hands together slowly. "If there are people who have brought items today that you would like for me to take a look at, I would consider it a real pleasure." And after a long pause, "Really, I don't bite, I encourage you to come forward…after all, I will be grateful for your help."

We gazed about and noticed others with small items, but it seemed nobody wanted to be first. People smiled and looked around at one another. Cynthia and I were not smiling; outwardly at least, we were calm. The strain was becoming intolerable. I felt as if I were a pop bottle, well shaken.

At last, Byron raised his hand, his face the picture of condescension. He would be the brave one.

"At last!" Cyn whispered. He was performing as we expected and had no idea that he had become a puppet and we pulled the strings.

Box in hand, Byron ambled toward the stage, his magnetic smile ignited, his darling errant curl dancing on his forehead. Every eye was on him and he knew it. He mounted the steps to the podium, slid the box from its satin covering and placed it in front of Professor Fersch, with such care he may have been serving a plate of cookies. Stepping back slightly, he clasped his hands behind his back. Oh, he was so pleased with himself.

The professor gingerly examined the box, feeling its surfaces and turning it. At length, he turned to Byron. "Young man," he said slowly, "You have an interesting item here. Tell me who you are and how you came to have this box?"

"I am Byron Peterson and I am in tenth grade, sir," he declared, smiling. A couple of his buddies whistled.

Cynthia looked at me and we both mouthed, "Sir?" That had to be a new word for him.

"And how did you find this box?" continued the professor, his eyes fixed on Byron.

"Well," His arms crossed smugly over his chest, he was now speaking to his entire rapt audience, "I was riding my horse over on the other side of the bay near the Chee Chaco claim at Thumb Cove and, well, there it was."

Professor: "And where precisely did you find it?"

Time froze. My heart thumped.

Byron: "Well, sir, as I remember, I just looked down and, uh, there it was, kinda sitting under a rock."

Cynthia, under her breath: "Sure it was, you miserable pile of fish guts."

Me: "May your nose grow so long you have to support it with a sling."

Professor: "Hmmmm. Under a rock. Well, let's just take a look." He turned the box slowly. "This box may be quite old. Haida bentwood box. Very nice painting, looks like Raven and maybe Bear painted here. Have you examined the contents of the box?"

Byron: "Yes sir. They're real old, too, sir. I thought maybe they were magic Indian things."

The professor carefully opened the box, saying, "Let's have a look."

I wish I had the capability to describe the look on the professor's face...surprise? Confusion? Disbelief?

His eyes went from the items to Byron and back again. At length, he gave Byron a long, quizzical look. Byron met his gaze grinning, and then looked down at the box. Instantly, his self-assured expression dissolved. His face became crimson, his eyes widened, and finally his lush, darling eyebrows furrowed.

Oh, all the work, the worry, the guilt we had endured, the fear and tension while we set up our attack, every moment now became infinitely worthwhile. Nothing could have been so precious as that moment of truth; it was exquisite.

Professor Fersch removed the piece of porcelain from the box as Byron stood, mute.

"This may be old," the professor spoke slowly and deliberately. "But I doubt it. Perhaps prewar Japanese, but I suspect...no I think it's from occupied Japan."

We heard sounds from the audience. Mumbles, chatter. They mouthed the words,

"Occupied Japan?"

Next he removed the crab shell.

"I don't know what to make of this." Professor Fersch held it up, examining the glyphs.

His arm extended the shell toward Byron and Byron flinched. The local high school hero actually flinched.

"Hmmmm," said Dr. Fersch.

He then held up a tiny sock doll with auburn braids, rabbit's foot attached to one arm.

"This does look Indian…"

Byron stared at Naasha's doll, his face displaying shock. His jaw gaped and wobbled; his complexion now bright red.

I too gasped and grabbed Cynthia's arm; I was just as stunned as Byron. She looked back, equally perplexed. We had inserted a surprise, but the professor had not yet found it. I would never have put my doll in that box. Never. How did it get in that box?

Finally the professor smiled and held up a piece of paper, looking at Byron. "This must be part of a joke, young man?" He queried, smiling. The audience began to giggle. Byron's pals made catcalls.

The professor unfolded and held up a piece of white paper and we beheld our very own artwork—an image of Kilroy.

Byron stomped off the stage, his face a thundercloud. I am sure he had never felt so alone as when he marched through the aisles, past the bleachers, and out of the gym. He was followed closely by Louise. I swear I saw smoke coming from his very red ears as the glass door swung shut.

We shared in his confusion, but his anger was his own alone. Fortunately, we couldn't hear their words, but we saw Louise touch his arm, and we saw him pull abruptly away from her. We were witnessing the dramatic demise of a high school romance. Poor mortified, bamboozled Byron, who never saw it coming, and poor Louise, who was blindsided too.

Professor Fersch examined one more item from the audience and in a short time concluded his talk, encouraging anyone to bring up artifacts and questions. We pushed toward the dais in the crowd, hoping to retrieve my precious sock doll in the confusion. Cynthia eased her way into the melee, slipping the doll into her pocket, and we beat feet as fast as we could to get out of there.

On a grassy spot at the base of Mt. Marathon, the very spot where Silvio had sat to survey Seward and the bay, we lay on our backs laughing like puppies being tickled, kicking our feet in the air. Cyn pulled my doll from her pocket and sat her on my lap facing me. I held her tight.

Grinning, Cynthia said, "I don't know how we could have done it better, do you? Ooo, my sides hurt."

"No," I said. "It was really perfect. But we had some luck here, didn't we? I mean, what just happened?" I turned my attention to my doll. "How did you get in that box, dolly? I mean it. How did you get there?" My doll couldn't explain because she didn't have a mouth. She was and forever would be mute.

"I swear, Marisol, I don't know," Cyn declared. " I had nothing to do with putting her in there. But it was just about perfect, don't you think? However it happened."

"Oooh yes, it was. Well, she's safe back with me. But the main thing is, we got him. We really did. Etta would say, 'Glory be!' And I say, 'Amen to that!'"

"Yeah. Just about perfect," Cyn declared.

After a moment of happy reflection, I said, "There just is nothing we can do about that box, darn it, but other than that, our entire afternoon was just about perfect."

We lay there, still, enjoying the moment. I gazed from dolly to crystalline sky, allowing my aching sides to recover from laughter.

"You know, how lucky were we that he just dug those things out of his walls and didn't even realize…"

"That they were fakes!" I said, "Dumb fakes!"

"So, you know, now he thinks he found a box of junk!" Cyn declared. "Oh, Marisol, the very joy of it all."

"You know, Cyn, I actually feel just a tiny bit sorry for him."

Cyn's reaction was immediate. "No way! He asked for everything he got."

We lay there enjoying this delicious moment, hoping it would last forever.

Whoosh! The sudden sound and flash of motion caught our eyes, and there he was. Raven himself, sitting on a tree snag just to the right of us, perhaps four feet away. His tail flicked; he stood in silhouette, amber eyes glaring, his scissor-sharp beak open slightly, checking the breeze. He held our gaze and we dared not speak or breathe. He was so close, and still, I could see the breeze slightly ruffle the delicate pin feathers at the juncture where his leg joined his body. He splayed his tail into a wedge, then tucked it. His body shone silver and violet in the light.

He began picking up his feet and stomping about. With each step, his head declined, as if he were looking at his feet, and he repeated that motion again and again in a deliberate marching rhythm. "Gga… gga…gga…" He said, shaking his head. "Tok, tok, tok." He drew one claw across the tree bark.

We remained still, and he became still; we stared at each other, seemingly transfixed for some length of time.

Then, suddenly in a glint of light, he was gone.

"Now what did that mean?" I wondered out loud.

"Darned if I can say for sure," Cyn answered me. "But I think he was congratulating us."

"Or asking us to congratulate him?"

We would never know. The spell broken, we gathered ourselves together and reluctantly headed home, still rejoicing in our almost perfect retribution.

AT LAST MAMA GETS THE PICTURE

Cynthia and I continued to be so pleased with ourselves that the air we breathed seemed ethereal. Two weeks went by before I went to the Peterson house to work. I don't recall exactly what my excuse was, but it took me that long before I felt I could face Byron after his descent from the heights of teen royalty. I finished in the kitchen, putting away the last of the dishes, when he came home from baseball practice. I watched as he walked to the stable, where he remained, waiting for me to leave. I suspected that his smug, dismissive attitude toward me had begun to morph into something akin to respect, and that suited me just fine. He had to know that we were instrumental in his demise, but he was treating Louise as if she had the plague. Poor thing, I thought.

He was still puzzled over what had happened to him, and I would be the last person to alleviate his confusion and humiliation. Especially since, in one way, I was as confused as he was.

That afternoon, Sava staggered up the gravel driveway under the weight of a huge basket full of writhing, cranky Alaskan crabs. Mama's face radiated delight. She gratefully accepted the basket, placing it on the table on the front porch for the time being. She insisted that he come into the kitchen. Sava sat next to me as Mama heated the teapot, sliced soda bread and pulled butter and jam from the refrigerator.

"Can you join us to help us eat those crabs?" Mama queried.

"No." he said. But something was on his mind. His hands fidgeted in his lap, one thumb pressing against the other, then absently rubbing. "My daughters," he began, speaking slowly and softly. "My daughters, I have much to thank you for."

We waited, silently anticipating his words, and I thought the moment had arrived to tell Mama the entire story.

"My little daughter, you and your friend trick the boy so good." He smiled.

"What do you mean?" Mama asked, her face a map of surprise.

I piped in, "Sava, you are my friend, we were happy to…"

"But you do it so perfect! You make the boy wiggle, wiggle big and long. It was, it was, it was…very swell. But, my sister, you must not be harsh at our Marisol. She has done something very good. "

Mama sat, still confused; and I gushed, "Sava you are sooo welcome."

A look of impatience flooded Mama's face; she was perplexed. "Marisol," she said, "just what are you two talking about?"

Oh boy. I was in for it, I thought. So I told her, starting from the beginning— our secret hiding place, finding the treasure, Byron's theft, finding the items in his house, and making the fake items. I watched apprehensively as Mama's expression changed from fear to comprehension.

At last she broke into laughter and blurted, "So that is why you broke my little parsley pot!"

"You knew?" I said.

Mama looked at me, saying firmly, "You may think you are cleverer than I am, little girl, but you're not. Furthermore, you didn't clean up the mess on the back step very well."

"You know, young lady," she said as she filled Sava's teacup, "you know you put my friendship with Byron's mother in jeopardy."

I had thought about that, but not for very long. I had watched Mrs. Peterson's face as her beloved son fell from his pedestal, and she was dumbfounded.

"That's one of the reasons I didn't tell you, Mama. I'm truly sorry," I said, and I was, indeed, contrite.

Sava smiled. "So now, my daughters, I must do what my promise says that I make many months back."

Mama and I leaned forward in anticipation.

"Soon we go, all of us, on a walk trip into some of the country where my soul lives, the land my people love. At last we will share it together."

"You mean our hike?" Mama exclaimed. Sava nodded his head, still smiling.

"You really mean it? When? When can we go?" Mama was excited and I was relieved. Perhaps the time of my crisis was over. It wasn't so bad after all.

"When you want," he said. "That is when I will go, when you wish,"

So it was that Mama began plotting for our long-awaited hike, which kept her so busy she didn't have time to be mad at me.

WITH THE FINEST GUIDE WE PENETRATE ANOTHER WORLD

June 1949

Mama knows how to get results when she chooses. In just a few days, she had procured permission for Aaron and Cyn to join us, had arranged a release from the Home for Matthias, and had wangled two five-foot square army surplus tents, one for the girls and one for the boys.

I had not seen her so drawn into a plan, her jaw so set, since we started out for Alaska a few years ago.

If only Sava would share his knowledge of the land with us, Mama would do the rest. She volunteered to oversee us all, her own unruly pack of kits. She would plan meals, buy supplies. She would arrange for what went with us; she would plan it all.

By then, our spring-summer had arrived. Over the centuries, each species of animal had adapted sleep patterns to fit its needs amid the peculiarities of Alaska summer and winter. Generally they slept or left in winter. But summer was a completely different matter.

Birds set their own daily timetables; no matter when hours of light arrived, or bronzed darkness descended, they kept their sensible sleep routine. They had been flocking to Seward's meadows and mountains, frenetically preparing their new homes for their new families.

Other animals had barely awakened from their winter slumber, but knew instinctively to begin to prepare for the next long winter sleep. Ground squirrels, hoary marmots, various rodents busily scurried about taking advantage of every hour of their lengthening days, mating and caring for their young households. As they intently scurried about, they were likely pursued by red fox and coyotes, just as eager to feed their broods.

Bears, particularly sows with new cubs, awoke emaciated after their winter snooze. What was their summer schedule? we wondered. When did they sleep in summer? We soon found out—they are driven to eat, and eat, sleeping only when fullness makes them sleep. Then, when they awaken, they begin eating again.

As for human animals, we would arise to a sluggish dullness at a very early hour and toss about in that same dullness before sleep arrived.

To this day, I think the birds have the right idea.

So it was that very early one morning, a morning blessed with sunshine, we set out on our hike along Resurrection River toward destinations chosen and known only by our sage guide.

Snowmelt from Mt. Marathon meandered in myriad trickles toward Resurrection River, sometimes veering into shallow side streams and eventually into the bay itself.

Mama and I wore matching men's small boots from the army surplus store. They would enable us to cope with mud and bits of receding snow. Sava carried a light leather bag on his back. The rest of us carried our share of gear and the equipment that Mama had decided was necessary for our trip.

We met at the mouth of the river. Already Sava waited, bent on his haunches and urging us to make a circle for a meeting. "We make rules," he said. He had a short stick in his hand and he sketched lines in the fine pebbles. "We stay where animals make the roads, but keep eye open for where fish make babies."

That meant that we needed to watch out for the soggy, mossy spots along the way, spawning places for scores of river creatures.

"We talk. Talk okay, but we are in animal place and we not be rude animals. We all have special spirit and we need to show respect," he continued.

"Porcupine is big boss of north wind and cold. We make him mad and if he think we laugh at him, he bring us bad wind fast. He is grumpy. Don't make noise.

"If you see bear, you tell me. Bear mamas want only one thing: feed and take care of babies. But they can get very mad and can change mind quick. Remember we go into their place. We need to ask bear to forgive us in their place.

"So you tell me, and Matthias help me too, if you see bear, okay? You talk good with birds, but you help me with animals too, okay?" Sava said to Matthias.

We looked over at Matthias as he nodded his assent. So Matthias had special capabilities that Sava understood? This was news to all the rest of us, but we soon came to know that his way with animals was real.

"Everybody understand?" Sava looked at each of us. We had been squatting long enough we would have agreed to anything to get going. We trudged single file through the slippery stones and frigid rivulets. I thought about the story of the Pied Piper and his ragtag vagabonds. All Sava needed was a panpipe.

We soon saw evidence of tiny fish making their meals of minuscule wind-borne spores and seeds. River birds watched from shore or in the sky, in turn making meals of the fish.

As we walked, Sava pointed out small gatherings of goose-tongue plant, and farther on, as the water slowed momentarily spilling into a small meadow, we saw baby sculpin and stickleback fish. Birds chattered and darted from tree to shore, flitting into cottonwoods and conifers.

We paused for a break; Sava signaled for us to follow him up a small tributary, its contribution to the river barely more than a trickle. We arrived at the spot he desired, nothing more than a flat spot beside the stream. Sava's finger to his mouth told us to sit in silence. A sharp SMACK! sounded a short distance away, where we spied a beaver scurrying, gathering small branches and diving into the water at the base of his family's dam.

"*K'enuy'a*, beaver," Sava spoke quietly.

"Two more dams, or *etl'*, ahead," he said. Instead of moving on, we retreated slowly, looking down and noting all manner of tiny, delicate plants sprouting amid the slush and soggy soil. At a spot that looked quite nondescript to us, he stepped carefully away from the main trail, leaned down and uncovered a delicate puffball blossom.

Cynthia was astonished at the simple beauty of the tiny plant.

"You say *Alaska Cotton* when it have flower. Our word means, *Raven pops it.*"

We returned to the river where a small family of trumpeter swans fed, and a score of tiny ground squirrels gorged themselves on new cones.

"This look like place for salmon and eggs soon," he said.

We walked along a winding animal path where we were accosted by a gaggle of harlequin ducks who protested our presence while they jostled among their peers and parents.

We ate our lunch sitting on a flat table rock at the river's edge, warm from the sun and worn by ancient waters. Native humans must have used this spot to dip net trout and hooligans in their season for centuries, we decided. While we ate tuna salad sandwiches, Sava shaved a point on an alder branch to stab a nice trout for our dinner. Aaron tried his fish-stabbing skills, resulting in a pair of wet boots. Sava caught two more trout and carefully stashed them, wrapped in leaves, in his pouch.

The sun by now was perfect, its warmth a blessing. The air was pure and refreshing, the sound of the water mesmerizing. It would have been very easy to lie back, soak in the rock's warmth, and take a short snooze, but that was not to be.

Sava signaled silently for us to look upstream. His hand pointed out a black bear sow approaching the water with her two cubs. She had not yet caught our scent. We watched, our noise rationed to sighs and tiny gasps as she caught a trout with her paws, and then another, putting them on shore for her babies, who were busy playing in the water and rolling on the shore. They gobbled their lunch and slowly ambled toward us.

Mama bear suddenly stood alert, her head turning to survey the area. As she spied us, she quickly chased her cubs onto shore and sent them scurrying up a tree, never for a moment losing sight of us. We froze in place. That sow was uneasy. She paced the shore, frowning at us.

Sava very quietly directed us to spread out slightly so we appeared to her as an even bigger group. We scooted on hands and knees very slowly, glancing at her and then at Sava.

As we watched, Sava stood on the ledge, firmly setting his feet, and he commenced to stare at the sow. The two seemed to be locked in a stalemate for what seemed like minutes. The sow took a hesitant step in our direction, and Sava spoke to her in clear, guttural sounds, respectfully but firmly, in sounds certainly not understood by me.

The sow stared at him quizzically and at length. For long, tense moments, we waited. And we watched. At last, still displeased, she turned, gathered her cubs, and in her own good time chased them into a copse of alder, at last looking back at Sava and at us. She finally slipped into the density of the tall spruce trees just behind the alder, and out of our sight.

I heard sighs from Aaron and Cynthia. We began to breathe again, watching Sava and still not speaking. "She is nice lady, that bear," he said, and he spoke no more about the incident.

We picked up our packs and continued on, hoping that the sow was saying to her babies, "They nice humans."

After a few moments, Sava remarked, "Watch out for bees. They kill bears sometimes." That gave us something new to contemplate as we moved on, negotiating paths well-chosen by Sava. Jays and magpies screeched above, and a raven or two careened in the sky, coming to rest near us on the ground and in the branches nearby. In the distance we heard woodpeckers busy procuring their next meal.

Near a tiny pond, in a spot protected from the sun, ice was slow in shattering. In the melting snow we saw traces of footprints, evidence of ermine or a small fox. At one point, Sava identified the footprints of a lynx.

Later in the day, we noticed that Sava's gaze was toward a hillside about forty feet to our right. He stood quietly for a long moment and then pointed to a small clearing nearly covered by fern bracken and young alder trees. With binoculars I could just see a small wood structure, placed there purposefully. A massive splash of pink lupine blossomed nearby.

"That is home where my wife and daughter live," he explained.

We were aware that they had died in the diphtheria epidemic many years ago. We honored his quiet melancholy.

At his cue, we continued, our feet trudging on layers of leaves, mosses, pine needles and, varied kinds of cast off, moldering forest detritus. We were beginning to be weary. The time had come to choose a place to set up our evening camp.

Sava indicated a spot in an open meadow, just a few yards from the river's edge. Here, in the grasses already clipped short by caribou and deer, we found enough dry ground to raise our tents. Cyn and I worked like a team. Pole in the center, four shorter poles inside on each corner, four ropes attached from the corner and pegged in a diagonal line, that's it, keep pulling, straighten that pole, good job; we pushed, pulled, pegged ropes, dug trenches.

Sleeping bags were laid open to absorb mountain air. Mama prepared a site Sava had deemed suitable for a fire while the rest of us followed Sava in search of fire tinder and water, just enough for our use, and no more. "You need to thank the river for water," he said.

For our bathroom use, he led us to a spot where pine needles had collected, rotting at the base of their massive, tall spruce hosts, which would afford cover. There, he explained to us how to use twigs, sticks and leaves in ways I will not describe, but served our use just fine, although Cyn and I giggled as we assumed the necessary squatting position.

Meanwhile, there was no time for us to rest. He marched us into the forest, through patches of thorny, spiky devil's club and skunk cabbage, to a place where he knew we would find wild celery and other plants destined to be part of our dinner that night. We thanked the plants for their sacrifice.

Our fire caught, crackled and spit. Sparks flitted into the dull evening sky. Sava gutted, cleaned and skewered our trout onto the stick he used for catching them. He then jammed the stick at an angle over the fire, where the fish slowly cooked, sending tiny spatters of fat to make fleeting fireworks above the flames. He removed a well-worn pail from his pouch, filled it with water and, into it, he placed a hot rock from the fire. He hung that from another pole fashioned over the fire. Into it went slices of Indian potato, wild onion, parsley, celery, Sava's herbs, and carrot sticks, that became a fine vegetable stew for our dinner. Sava ate from a wooden bowl he brought and drank from a caribou horn which had a deep hollow area scoured from the inside.

"*Adee*" he said as he held up his cup.

"Aha!" said Mama, pointing her finger at Sava. "Something you drink out of! I have an *adee* at home, Sava, that Naasha gave me, but it is made from a gourd."

Sava smiled with pleasure. He was in his territory, talking about his language and he was pleased to share his words with us and his southwestern brothers.

The rest of us ate from metal bowls, first eating our stew that had a somewhat exotic flavor appreciated by the group in varying degrees. Next we devoured the trout, removing the bone and cutting bites with spoons.

We weren't yet ready for sleep. The birds were quiet, not pleased about the racket we made. Insect sounds caused the night air to vibrate just a little. Frantic little critters scurried at our feet as we sat near the fire. Sava spoke of Raven and how sometimes, when he gets crosswise with Grandmother Mouse, he loses. He told us about River Otter and his people, who could live on both water and land. "My wife make pretty things from hair of mountain goat and yellow grass like that," he said, pointing to a clump near the neighboring pines.

We sang a little bit—silly tunes and popular songs. Our efforts were half-hearted however; we had worked hard and were probably getting ready to sleep. There was also a feeling among us that we were intruding on something. We weren't sure just what.

Mama declared she was weary and headed into the girls' tent. Eventually Sava slipped into his tent and curled up onto his own blanket, the tent flap still open. Cynthia, Aaron, Matthias and I sat on a partially decayed fallen log, poking the fire and watching it explode.

After awhile, I asked Matthias, "Do you have family somewhere nearby anymore, Matthias?"

"I don't think so," he said, studying his hands, his nails, the palms, the backs.

"You don't know?" That was not an answer I expected.

"No," he said, still examining his hands. "But there are a lot of children at the Home who would say the same thing. Lots of us lost our parents to diphtheria or flu, or something."

The fire popped and hissed. Cyn's face was grim; she shook her head slightly. Aaron threw tiny pebbles into the fire.

"Do you remember your parents?" I asked.

"Yeah, some. I do remember my father holding my hand once. We were walking out to his fishing boat, but that's all I recall. He drowned when I was four in a storm off Chugchik Island," he said. The tone of his voice, seemingly matter-of-fact, was forced, I thought. "My mother told me as much about him as she knew," Matthias continued, now gazing absently at the fire.

"She said my father had come from France and was a fur trapper. Mink and otter. But, she said my father talked about his people who came from farther east. She said sometimes he called me his *Little Magyar.* My mama was Aleut. When she did talk, and that wasn't a lot, she had a soft voice, like, um, berry juice."

He paused, just continuing to gaze at the sparks and listened to the snaps and hisses of the fire.

"She caught a fever and died suddenly when I was five," Matthias went on.

"I can understand a little bit, Matthias," I said quietly, "I lost my father when I was seven."

We sat in silence, both of us speaking about sad things in matter-of-fact ways, yet knowing they were hardly matter-of-fact. Cynthia gently rubbed a small spot on Matthias' back.

"My auntie found me in the cabin with my mama," he continued. "She had been gone for a lot of days I guess. I was so little, I hoped she was just asleep. But I think I really knew."

"Matthias, I'm really sorry," I said. "My daddy went off in a plane and never came back." I couldn't talk any more about his death at that moment. We were both victims of death that came too soon. I put my arm very tentatively around his shoulders, and he seemed to appreciate the closeness of Cyn and me.

"It is all right now," he said. "I've cried all my tears out for them and they know I love them still."

"I've done the same thing, Matthias. And I know my daddy knows", I said, suddenly interested in the flight path of flying insects as they neared the fire. "But you don't know if you had brothers and sisters?" I continued.

"Where I lived," Matthias said, "if a family couldn't afford to keep a child, they would give it to somebody in the village. We all knew each other. So I don't know if my mama gave away any children. I don't think so, but I don't know," he sighed.

"Anyway if they are still there, they are being taken care of," he said in a way that told me he had said all he wanted about that subject.

After another spate of silence, I asked, "Do you like the Home?"

"Oh, yes I do," he smiled and this time he looked over at me.

"We work hard, and we learn a lot and have fun. Now I have a lot of brothers and sisters."

"Matthias," I said, "what do you like to do?"

"Oh, I like to play chess with Aaron, and I like to run, and swim, and I like the music in church," he said.

"Yeah, and he is pretty good at chess!" Aaron added to the conversation. "And he is pretty good with a basketball."

"You like to sing?" I asked.

"Yeah I do," he said. "I like to sing a lot."

"I thought so," I said, and then, as an afterthought, I said to him, "You know, we have a fun choir at my church. Do you think you would like to come to church with Mama and me sometime?" I asked.

"Sure, I would like that," he smiled and began rubbing his hands together again.

"Deal," I said. At that moment I wasn't sure just how the Methodists at the Home would take to my invitation, but I was sure we could work it out. We'd just have to see.

We picked up long sticks, scribbling in the loose soil the way Sava scribbled that morning. Our sky was actually beginning to take on obscure tones. We were finally ready to sleep.

Suddenly Aaron, for no reason I can think of, let out a howl, "Ow, ow, owwwww!"

To his amazement and our dismay, his call was returned by what seemed to us like scores of similar calls. We looked at each other with wide eyes.

"Coyotes," Sava said, as he scrambled from the tent.

He motioned to Matthias and they walked past the direct firelight where they stood, the two of them, for perhaps a minute, facing the coyote sonata. Sava waved his hand toward us, encouraging us to stand and join them. We all witnessed the glow of many coyote eyes staring back at us, like so many globs of amber.

"Coyotes. They just nosy. But we ask them to go away," Sava said. "So they did."

That was too simple an explanation.

"But what did you say, Matthias?" Cynthia asked.

"Oh...mmm...I just told them if they were our guardians, we welcomed them, that we thanked them for their hospitality and that we would leave soon. Now, that is what I said; I don't know what Sava said."

Sava chuckled, "I just told them they behave bad, not nice hosts, and they gotta stop right now or I use my stick to close their eyes with pine tar pitch."

We banked the fire for the night and snuggled under covers, not so frightened by the coyotes that we couldn't sleep.

In the morning, we packed carefully but sadly knowing that this was the beginning of the end of our adventure. Tents and equipment folded and packed away, we checked our fire to be sure it was dead out, checked to be sure we were leaving nothing to mar the land, thanked the creatures for their hospitality, and began marching toward home, retreating through a grove of tall spruce and hemlock trees. Their branches nodded slightly in the morning breeze, seemingly waving us on.

Our return route was not the exact one that brought us. Just a few yards from the water's edge, we climbed over snags and tumbledown trees, some soft from decay, which gave way to the weight of our boots. Multitudes of insects responded to our trespass. After all, they had work to do collecting and building and attacking new buds for their nutritious treasure and dismembering tiny creatures.

Where the trees fell and sun shone, ferns and baby alders sprouted in proliferation. Warblers and flycatchers zipped about busy at work.

Then, we spied a porcupine—fortunately, before he spied us. We froze, and watched him as he ambled along, snuffling in the moist pine needles and bark. In a few moments he chose to move on into the forest, and we began to breathe again.

Suddenly, it started to rain just slightly, hardly an unusual occurrence in the Kenai. It seems that rain never really starts, or ends. It is just there, sometimes more than other times. Our morning baptism.

Sun reappeared momentarily, drying us slightly. Sava led us onto a small animal trail, so soggy that we couldn't help sinking into the mossy terrain. Spruce branches swept our faces as we came upon another kettle pond. Slight breezes caused its waters to twinkle as the sun shone through branches and onto residual patches of snow that gave off a brassy glow.

The pond's water, filled with generations of decayed moss, leaves, pine needles, allowed for precious little to live in its acid water. Near the pond's edge we saw a spruce, contorted and stunted from its efforts to survive. Another had branches shaped like a human breastbone blackened and bereft of muscle or skin. Another looked as if it wanted to form stunted wing projectiles and fly away to a more hospitable environment. The breeze stopped again, and the water surface became obsidian in its stillness.

Sava led us to a certain spot where tiny sundew plants with nearly microscopic hairs grew. "Hairs catch bugs so plant eats them," he explained. We sat and watched them for a few minutes as the sun moved and the tiny blossom ever-so-slowly followed its rays.

We returned to a path near the river. Suddenly Sava gave us the quiet sign, and pointed across the river. Far to our right, we saw a thick conifer patch, its dark floor comprised of many years' decaying and moist needles. A swaggering shadow moved through the pine copse.

"Wolverine," Sava whispered. That was a surprise for all of us. Wolverines are savvy creatures, and shy, rarely seen by humans. The truth is, he remained elusive for me. While everybody else professed to see him, I saw only the shadow and the waving branches of the shrub.

We stopped for a break; Sava pointed out the thin gray moss hanging from a number of the spruce trees. *"Old Man's Beard,"* he said. "Something to eat for my people if winter is long."

Behind those trees I saw six or seven spruce trees, better said mere skeletons of the trees they had been, silver-gray, eerie, lifeless, frozen in their anguish of slow death. Their heads monk-shrouded and bowed, their sleeve-arms bent before them as in eternal prayer.

We hiked on, passing bearberry and currant shrubs, protected in light thickets of trees—paper birch, and alder, all budded and promising a fine spring. They served as a filter for the sun's mellow rays, allowing alpine azaleas to blossom beneath them in full pink bloom.

We passed another shrub. *"Hey gega,* berry bush," Sava said. "Not good now, good later."

When we could finally see the bay, Sava guided us across the shallows of the river to the other side. He ascended a slight bank and we followed, hiking perhaps a half mile across a meadow cleared of large growth, cupped by low hills. It was here that a swarm of mosquitoes—huge pesky biters—found us and pursued us for quite a distance. As we trudged up yet another slight embankment, a slight breeze blew them away temporarily.

We approached a hill containing long, slim well-camouflaged dugout canals, scratched out of the partially frozen soil. Created to be a military redoubt, to serve as a second line of defense had the Japanese invaded Seward, their edges had degraded to stark scars and were decaying, becoming nature's domain once more.

We retraced our most recent path, and, as we encountered the man-eater mosquitoes again, our pace picked up considerably. We hustled along, swatting at the devilish critters.

"Durn mosquitoes—evil giants," Sava said. He told us as we marched, "Long ago, my people cut open the mossy skin in bog and they hide there. Then at right time, my people jump up, and kill giants. Now just teeny mosquito children still here."

"Not so teeny," Cynthia muttered.

I thought about a moment nearly forgotten, of Andrew and me hidden in the leaves. I smiled. Our cap guns would have been useless against these pests.

At the mouth of the river, Matthias spotted a large gathering of silver, squirming hooligan. Sava's face glowed with delight. "We will dip-net them," he said. "My people will dip-net them. They taste swell and the oil feeds our bodies."

We knew that after the hooligan's arrival, the salmon would return. Salmon, in quantities beyond numbers would soon begin their tortured climb up the streams to the site of their birth. Their struggle, as predictable as the feeding frenzy of their predators, fascinated me. Bear, eagle, raven included, would bedevil them in the sunset of their lives, and devour their cadavers at the culmination of their spawn and death.

That would occur later; for now, we were tired adventurers, eager for our homes, baths, and beds. The moment had arrived for us to part; we all stood, exhausted and trying to find the words to thank Sava, but we couldn't. He smiled and nodded, knowing what we couldn't say. We watched as he began his long walk home to Bear Lake. We walked together until Matthias peeled off for the Jesse Lee Home, and we trudged to our houses, our happy mission accomplished.

FORTITUDE AND HUMILITY

I was being drawn into teenager-hood, and I was beginning to think it wasn't so bad after all. I actually liked wearing that dress to graduation. I certainly liked my few minutes with Silvio, and then there was the time Cynthia and I came upon four of the high school boys skinny-dipping at the swimming hole. I don't think they ever found out who it was who made bear noises and caused them to scatter into the bushes.

I loved singing in the church choir and playing volleyball. I collected pebbles, each of which told me a story, and continued to work at mastering some tunes on Daddy's tin whistle. I came to understand Cynthia's attachment to the piano; nobody was forcing me to play that whistle, it just gave me joy.

Uncle Kenan sent me an old record of his favorite Irish tunes, and I determined to learn all the rolls and strikes the whistler played on the record. He and Fiona, his fiancée, were coming to see us at the end of summer, and we looked forward to seeing them both. As I practiced and played, I began to feel that I was liberating Daddy, too, from any residual anger that dwelt at the bottom of my heart.

We now had a new member to our family. A scrawny black and yellow alley-cat climbed up our back screen door and worried a small rip in the screen until she could slip through. Once inside, she padded into my bedroom and announced that she was here to stay. She more resembled some sort of feral creature than a civilized family pet, but her personality belied her patchy countenance. When she was happy, her purr could be heard throughout the house, her body warmth made tolerable my bed in winter, and she tormented all rodents who had the audacity to enter our house. We called her *Yahgi*, Navajo for little one.

Fourth of July 1949 was to be a memorable one for me, for more reasons than I care to admit. It started off just as we had planned—Mama's tenure as vice-president of the PTA ended with completion of her final duty, to oversee the July Fourth food booth. She and Miss Tenney piled signs, posters, table coverings, and boxes of paraphernalia into a truck she had wangled from the grocery store.

My job was to stay home and stir Mama's now famous chili, slowly simmering in kettles on our stove. The recipe was one of the few recipes Mama held to be hers alone. Begun the night before in the secret lair of Mama's kitchen, we browned bear and deer meat with garlic, onions, and green peppers. To that, we added cumin, chili powder, some of Sava's savory dried leaves, tomatoes, and a secret quantity of strong coffee. Finally we added some of Abuelita's special spice concoction and something alcoholic, the name of which I have sworn never to divulge.

I contemplated the day; it definitely didn't look like rain, but there were low, wispy clouds trying to block out the sun. They hung over the town and bay as if they didn't have anything better to do. Okay weather for shorts, I thought, but I'd better wear one of Daddy's flannel shirts over my T-shirt.

Everybody was excited that the competitors in the Mt. Marathon run this year would include a woman.

I wondered who would be crowned Miss Seward.

Chairs were set out and the streets were probably alive with chatter already. Nothing would be allowed to interrupt the day's events.

I served myself a bowl of chili for breakfast and decided that it was addictive and strong enough to remove the enamel from anybody's teeth.

Mama and Miss Tenney arrived with the truck and the three of us lugged the chili containers into the truck and down to the booth on the corner of 4th and Washington.

Artie, the man who so beautifully renovated Victoria, came by to see if we needed help.

"Hey there," Mama exclaimed. "You can help us get these kettles up onto those hot plates behind us. Other than that, I think we are all set."

"I'm on my way to get the car from your house," he said. "And then I'll go pick up Cynthia and Aaron." We knew we would be busy at the booth, so we had invited them to ride in her in the parade.

"I've also invited Dotty Etta to ride with you, Artie," Mama said. "She is so excited. When she first saw Victoria, she raised her hands and said, 'Lord beat the crows, what a beauty!' She'll meet you where the parade starts."

We served chili and the day's celebrations began. It was Monday, the climax of a three day weekend, and every citizen appeared to be ready to celebrate. I helped, but Mama knew I wanted to see Victoria and she released me from my duties. In a shot, I hurried to find a good spot to watch the parade. The best I could find was in front of Solly's so there I stood as the town cronies shot pool at the Emporium, downed a shot of their favorite flavor of alcohol, and ran out from time to time to see if the parade had started.

The temperature warmed slightly, but the innocuous gray clouds persisted.

I was in the front row when I heard the first notes of Fourth of July music; Sousa tunes played somewhat anemically by the few members of the U.S. Army band still remaining in Seward. As usual, Byron and his father rode Daisy and Buck, tricked out in red and blue ribbons. Next marched the remaining soldiers in khaki Eisenhower jackets, their pants tucked into their boots, caps set just so; the PTA float came next, and then the Seward High School Band, dressed in cobalt and silver. Garnished with gobs of gold braid, the drum major strutted his best. I had a feeling Cyn would agree with me that Raven carried off that step with more class.

Our Coast Guard contingent walked smartly by with their mascot goat, Sgt. Bill.

Urbach's and Moody's Department Store floats came next, and then the usual—the VFW, the Masons, the Teenage Canteen, the tuberculosis hospital nurses, in smart deep blue capes, and sensible shoes.

I was getting downright anxious. The Jesse Lee Home float followed, with little Paulette and Cynthia's pal, Lilly sitting contentedly among the onions and cabbages. Paulette's hair was incorrigible; Lilly's long cocoa-colored hair had been plaited into two braids that crossed over her head. Two sapphire satin bows, perched atop her ears, held the braids in place.

At last I caught sight of Artie and the gang with Victoria, Artie occasionally revving the engine*; vroom, vroom, vroom*! The white canvas top was rolled down, revealing the flashy plaid seats. There was Artie, decked out in green fedora and jaunty scarf, his gloved hands working the leather-covered steering wheel. Etta, wore a red wide-brimmed hat bedecked with daisies and ferns. Aaron and Cynthia sat on cartons in the backseat so they were high enough to wave to the adoring crowd, who seemed to love the car, with its curved body and elegant sleek hood ornament.

I think a bathtub was the next entry (Best Wishes, Sutter's Steambath and Spic and Span Cleaner); Genevieve Sutters, Byron's new girlfriend, sat in the tub, white towel wrapped around her head, sucking on a large pink straw, as I recall. She blew huge pink plastic bubbles from a pink magic liquid, pinched them off, and threw them into the crowd.

I had seen enough; I checked back at Mama's booth, and then went to the Alaska Shop to wait for Cyn. She soon arrived, still flushed and laughing from her ride in Victoria. We plunked down our pennies for two jawbreakers and a half-gallon of chocolate ice cream in a carton, that we cut in half and, with little wooden spoons, began to see if we could consume it all.

The annual grueling, mind-numbing climb up the shard-faced mountain, was just beginning. Otis Meyer, the former postmaster stood among the competitors. From the base of Jefferson Street the starting gun sounded and the runners took off, heading toward the mountain.

Still working away at our ice cream, we ambled near Homebrew Alley for the hog calling contest, and it was there that Andrew and Early spotted us. That day, Early's chapeau was a cowboy hat.

"Where's your buddy, Terry?" I asked Andrew.

"In trouble with his mom," he replied absently.

"Really? For what?" Cyn asked.

"Well, his grandmother is visiting from Seattle. And when she asked him about a bird in their front yard, he told her it was a Hairy-chested Nut Scratcher, and his mother didn't think that was funny. He's housebound for another week."

Couldn't have happened to a more deserving person, I thought.

We guffawed at the story anyway, as only sixth-graders could. We four wandered down toward the diversion channel waterfall, with no real plan in mind, other than sharing our ice cream. We sat with our backs against low rocks, passing spoons and cartons back and forth to one another.

"Hey Early, I like your hat," Cyn said.

"Thanks," he said. "Christmas present from my uncle in Houston."

Directly before us sat a weathered rowboat, oars resting in their locks, bobbing ever so slightly in the shallows, a long rope loosely attaching it to a ring in the concrete wall. Who knows who first concocted the idea, but it was Cynthia who first verbalized it. "Wouldn't it be fun…" and she didn't have to say more.

In a flash, we four were climbing into the boat, struggling not to drop ice cream cartons and spoons. Andrew and Early, feet splayed and bent at the waist, held onto the prow as Cyn and I grabbed the weathered edge and worked our bottoms and legs over and into the boat, canting the boat first to one side and then the other, sea water slurping into our shoes and onto our legs. A rusty coffee can in the bottom of the boat floated in a shallow pool, and was soon accompanied by empty ice cream cartons and tiny wooden spoons. Cyn on the seat in the prow, me in the back, we each grabbed an oar, jamming them hard against the pebbly shore, as Andrew and Early, slipping and sliding, loosed the rope and pushed until they leaped into the boat and sat center where the oarlocks awaited them. Before we realized it, before we even thought, we were afloat and inching out into the current that carried us beside the shore and out toward the mouth of the bay. I didn't think much at all, but I did know I felt free and clever, and I suspect they were thinking the same thoughts.

After a few minutes of enjoying our escapade, Andrew said, "So, what are we going to do? Just row around?"

"Let's stick close to shore 'till we know what we're doing," Cyn suggested.

"Yeah, okay," added Early. He and Andrew were beginning to have a good rowing rhythm, and I picked up the coffee can and began to bail.

"We could head for a beach and look around. How about that?" Andrew queried.

"Sure," I said. "Then we can get home before anybody misses the boat. Or us."

We agreed unanimously and paddled on, enjoying the scenery and reveling in our cunning.

"Rowing's a cinch. Current is helping us," Andrew commented.

Early just kept rowing and smiling. I remember thinking that I had never seen Early be angry or unhappy. Paddles cut almost effortlessly through the serene waters. There was so little wind that we seemed to be moving almost without friction, and we were serene, delighting in the adventure. Cartons and spoons floated free too, with the boat's rhythm.

Every few minutes, I would bail to keep the water at a minimum.

"Do you guys feel like the current is taking us into the middle of the bay?" Andrew asked.

Our attention turned to the water, and he was right. We were headed toward a huge expanse of water and the water became waves and small swells. We didn't worry, we knew we could handle it. Early passed his oar to Cyn and she began using it as a rudder. The boys took turns rowing every few minutes. With the rudder's help, we headed toward shore near Tonsina Point.

We paddled past, and sooner than we thought, we passed Callisto Canyon, and were headed toward Caines Point. There we turned the boat around and, hugging shore, returned to Derby Cove.

We beached the boat in the cove, extricated ourselves, and sank amidst the sand and rocks, which were peppered with layers of tiny, delicate yew tree cones.

The sea birds, angry at our intrusion into their world, screeched and berated us. We watched two minkie whales head toward the mouth of the bay. Movement in the tree branches meant that the wind had picked up slightly.

Early and I hiked back into the trees and followed an animal trail for a short ways where we came upon some debris, a short piece of rusty heavy chain and a leather remnant of some activity during the war, we figured. We also saw some long bones, white and broken. Whatever the remnants had been, animals had chewed them and weather had contributed in breaking them down. We started back. On the way, Early decided to climb up to the top of the cliff. I watched him at first and told him I was heading back to the cove.

We three sat, burying our feet in the soft pebbles and talking, once in awhile looking up to see what Early was up to. He could have scrambled up the center of the cliff, but instead he was climbing the side near us that rose from the pebbles at our feet, but jutted into the bay at its farthest point.

"It's about time for you to start down, Early," Andrew yelled.

"Okay, couple minutes," Early mumbled. He was beginning to work hard, searching for crevasses and snags for footholds. Farther up, the side became a shear wall.

"He's doing pretty well keeping that hat on his head," I remarked.

Within minutes, he was very close to the top, searching for handholds.

"Hey, little brother, you're just about there," shouted Andrew. By then, Early was the center of our attention. He pulled himself up the last foot or so and we applauded.

"Yo, look at me! I did it!" He had taken off his windbreaker and began swinging it around in the air.

"Careful!" Cynthia shouted, just as a gust of wind picked up his hat. Early reached for it and lost his balance, stumbling to the side, slipping off the edge of the cliff and tumbling helter-skelter into the sea. We heard a high, quizzical sort of utterance, and then nothing.

"Oh, my God," Andrew muttered, and immediately traversed the pebbly beach, entering the water, half-swimming, half pulling himself through the water, "Early!" he called.

We two rushed to the water's pebbly edge. To our right, perhaps ten feet from the base of the cliff, we saw Early. Or rather we saw his body face down in the sea, his arms splayed at his sides, and he was not moving. His hat and his windbreaker floated near him and all three swayed in the gently current near shore.

Andrew seemed to be struggling with Early's form in about three feet of water. Very cold water. I waded in to help Andrew.

Cyn immediately shoved off in the boat, scrambling from the side and working her way toward Andrew, who had turned Early face up, cradling his head, holding it up with one arm and struggling to maintain his balance.

Thoughts of a survival lesson in physical education class were foremost in our minds. "Come on, quick." Cynthia muttered. "All we have is twenty minutes." I took off my flannel shirt. "Let's try this," I said as I slipped it across Early's chest and tied it in the back.

"Mmmm." Early made a very welcome noise and opened his eyes for a second, before slipping away again.

"Early!" Andrew began to sob.

"Take off your shoes and pants," I said to him firmly. He looked at me not understanding. "Shoes first. Just do it, and hurry!" As I held Early's head, Andrew reached down for his shoes. Then he unbuckled his belt and pulled off his trousers.

"Don't worry. We saw more than that at the swimming hole," I told him.

I wasn't sure what we were doing was the right thing to do. We were all shivering, and not necessarily from the cold. We were concerned about surviving in the cold water, and I hated to take his clothes, but we had to eliminate nonessential dead weight. Andrew began doing what he, too had been taught—he used his belt to tie off the top of his pants and next blew into the legs, tying them off with his now floating boots. I had gathered Early's windbreaker and I tried to make the arms into another floating aid. Cyn tied the rope to the stern of the boat and threw the end to me. I connected it to my flannel shirt and passed the end back to Cyn, as together we pulled the rope, connected to the back of Andrew, pulling him out of the water as much as we could. Our efforts were meager, but at least it kept their heads and shoulders out of the water. Andrew now held Early about the waist, working blow-up trousers and windbreaker beneath his legs. The buoyancy they offered was minimal but better than nothing. We pushed Early's hat beneath his head, now on Andrew's chest.

Cyn maneuvered the boat to us and I scrambled over the edge of the boat. She rowed to take up the rope's slack, I picked up the other oar and we began to row like we had never thought we could.

Already a lifetime of precious minutes had ticked by.

"Uhh?" murmured Early.

Andrew began to talk, and he talked nonstop for what seemed like a very long time, "Hey, little brother, I got ya. Anything hurt? I got ya and I'm not letting go." He talked about old times, things they had done, funny moments, about their mom and dad, and his buddy, Terry. He talked about baseball and football, and the Marathon race going on at that moment. And when he seemed to be running out of things to say, we gave him ideas. He thought he was doing this for

Early; we knew he was doing it for his survival as well and his voice was beginning to shake.

We continued to row, our faces set and grim from the effort. We sang songs, or rather we mouthed the words, over and over, to maintain some feeble sort of rhythm.

Early's occasional sounds took on a small measure of coherence. He tried to kick his feet a little, but that hurt, he said.

Cyn and I were making almost no headway. Our muscles began to sting. Even so, we rowed, and rowed hard.

"I'M looking Over
A Four leafed CLOver
That I overLOOKed
BeFORE"

We hugged the shore, constantly fighting the wind's insistent push into the center of the bay. The thought of waves and swells terrified us.

Wind now at our backs. Waves lapping at the sides, spilling in, adding to the swill. Foamy ice cream residue and cartons careened about. No time to bail. We rowed, and we stared at those tiny wooden ice cream paddles, taunting us as they floated about in consort with the rowing rhythm.

"CHICKory CHICK
ChaLA chaLA
CHECKaraLOmie
INa baNAnica"

"Hang on guys." Cynthia mutters.

"Sure, okay," Andrew replys, quietly. Too quietly. He reaches for Early' hands, covering them with his.

"Unnh. Unnh," Early gurgles.

Rowing is now an endurance contest—and we are losing. Precious time ebbing away. Thirsty, I am thirsty. I have a jawbreaker in my pocket. I jam the soggy residue into my mouth. Cynthia mimics me.

A thick gray cloud cover still hangs above. Tiny strands reach down like fragile wisps of stringy hair. Paper streamers, I think. They bring no joy.

I'm not shivering, I'm sweating. No longer making a sound except a groan at each attempt to move the oars in the current.

By now, Mama may have missed me, be looking for me.

I'd love to cry, but that is a luxury unavailable at this moment. I look at Cyn. She too looks exhausted, and desperate. That's it, desperate. We have lost the battle.

Her eyes veer from mine for an instant. I sense she sees something.

She mouths the word, "Boat," and grins.

"Coast Guard!" She whispers.

What came from my mouth was my best try at a hoarse shout. Perhaps three hundred yards ahead, the local Coast Guard cutter approached. Then we heard the cutter's engine. We were going to make it. We would be all right.

Magically, we became stronger, our backs straightened.

A smiling face stared down at us from the side of the cutter. "How you doing?" the uniformed man asked. Just as if this was part of a normal day for him.

Only Cyn had the strength to speak. "Help. Help us," she whispered.

Already the cutter eased toward the boys and began the rescue of our beleaguered friends. "Want some help, huh?" The face grinned. The engine geared down and barely gurgled. With what strength we could muster, we gave ourselves entirely into their care, nodding at their clipped instructions.

By the time we girls were aboard, a crew member had wrapped the boys in blankets and propped their bodies so that blood could flow to their heads. "Don't worry, guys, we're on our way home now," he said. Andrew still held tight to Early's hand, and both hands were encased in a crewman's jacket.

Early smiled.

Our initial arrival at the station is now a blur in my mind. My first recollection was warmth—welcome warmth.

My second recollection was shock. Sitting on a black office chair against the wall across the room was Byron Peterson. I was stunned.

It was the officer's moment to speak. "You four are very lucky people."

My face continued to register nothing.

"Do you all know that? I mean, whatever made you think what you did was smart?"

I certainly didn't feel smart. Lucky, perhaps, but I would have felt a whole lot luckier if Byron hadn't been there.

"This young man came to see us not too long ago," continued the officer. He leaned against the desk, his knuckles grabbing the top edge. "He told us that he saw you four set out a few hours ago." He looked around at each of us girls to see if we were beginning to understand. The boys were still too cold to be part of this conversation. "He said that you were in a rickety boat that he thought didn't belong to you. And he hadn't seen you return."

Cyn and I looked from officer, to Byron, to each other, to Byron once again. It appeared that I might have some serious soul-searching to do. That wouldn't be easy for me.

The officer went on, clearing his throat and saying, "Do you realize now that those currents are nothing to fool with, that you may never have gotten back at all?"

We nodded our heads.

"And furthermore, you all owe this young man your thanks. He was riding his horse at the time, headed up toward Caines Point."

Damn. Double damn. Our heads were still bowed and there he sat, his demeanor modest, and human. I didn't know he had it in him.

He continued. "The ambulance is on its way for the boys. We'll get them help at the hospital. We don't know for sure, but we think the boy who fell is all right except for maybe a cracked rib, and some scratches. The extra meat on his bones helped him keep hypothermia away. But the other boy—he'll need treatment too."

Cynthia sighed deeply. I finally cried, sobbing from relief.

"Now, as for you two girls," he continued, "your only injuries are to your egos. I think I am going to give you a choice."

We stared at him, waiting.

"We can take you home in one of our cars, with a siren…"

We waited chagrinned and speechless.

"Or you can walk home through the cemetery and you can explain all this to your parents yourselves."

"The cemetery!" we said in unison.

And so it was that a Coast Guard vehicle drove us across to the other side of town and we made our way home using our last speck of strength to hurry through those tombstones as quickly as we could.

Mama was already home and just beginning to worry about me. I came into the house, sat at the kitchen table exhausted and dejected, drank two glasses of lemonade and began to cry all over again. Mama was already frightened just looking at me. She sat, covered my hand with hers and listened. When she had at last heard everything I had to say, she quietly told me that I should lie down and rest. "Then, when you are better, I am going to let you have it, young lady. What a stupid thing you have done!"

I awoke in time to hear the beginning of the fireworks. From my bedroom window, I saw twinkling bits of glitter fill the sky, and fountains of light shooting high. Cascading balls glowed and flickered as they fell from the sky, their reflection on the waters in the bay sometimes resembling huge, undulating jelly fish times two. I could hear the onlookers' sighs of appreciation, still knowing that I was in for it from Mama.

A sharp pistol report signaled the show's end. After some seconds, a huge dazzling display, actually three displays in one, exploded into the sky. At their zenith, blue and gold bits winked and then, from within, splashed and cascaded a river of deep coppery gold that glowed luminous amber. I was drawn back to those coyote eyes on a certain New Mexico evening with Naasha, Mama and Daddy.

It was no surprise that I was under house arrest. I polished a lot of furniture during the next few weeks, and I talked to Cynthia seldom. She was in as much trouble as I was, and now we had the dubious honor of being the top gossip item for the remainder of the summer, until a prisoner broke out of the jail and frightened the entire town for days.

I did get to visit Early. Andrew was out of the hospital in a few hours, but Early sat grinning in his hospital bed, with a very sad and stained cowboy hat on his head. His hypothermia was mild and responded to treatment. He had had the breath knocked out of him, suffered a cracked rib and a deep scratch on his inner arm, but he would be fine.

I washed and ironed a lot of sheets, baked a lot of cookies and chopped a lot of vegetables. I read books, played jigs and laments on my whistle, and I did it in my home, in my bedroom, all alone. Nearly alone, that is. My cat Yahgi listened to my regrets, all the while purring and digging her claws into my bedspread.

I thought a lot during my imprisonment, certainly about the danger we had put ourselves in. I wrote a long letter to Silvio and I thought about Byron. That was the toughie.

We all wrote letters of apology to the owner of the boat, and I wrote a letter of thanks to the Coast Guard. But I couldn't bring myself to write a letter to Byron.

Meanwhile, he was once more the town hero. This time he deserved it and he was actually acting modest about it all. That was when I knew that the problem was with me. It would have been easier for me if he was bragging all over town about his heroics.

Finally I was sprung from solitude, but only to work at the Peterson's. That morning I took my time walking to their house, gulping the fresh air of freedom.

Byron was there, busy grooming the horses. Summoning all my courage, swallowing every bit of my pride, I sidled up to the corral fence and commenced to chatter, my voice suddenly a high-pitched staccato. "Byron," I sputtered, "I want to thank you a whole lot for what you…"

He turned toward me, brush in hand, cutting off my chatter. Looking directly and firmly at me, he said, "I didn't do that for you, Marisol, or for Cynthia, either."

"But honestly, Byron…"

"You can be very sure of that."

Our eyes met and I found myself surveying that face I knew so well, and realizing that perhaps I didn't know it at all.

His eyes returned to Daisy and he continued, "It's just that Andrew is one of my best friends." He went on brushing Daisy's withers with fervor while I stood there, mute. This conversation was over as far as he was concerned. I turned and walked toward the house, head down, absently kicking a tiny stone off the path.

I didn't have to like him to be grateful. Yet he seemed to be turning everything I had thought about him upside-down. I had a lot to work out. But for now, as for Byron and what he had just said to me, well I still couldn't believe a word that boy said.

MUCH MORE THAN BERRY PICKING

August 1949

As August approached, I sensed that Mama was close to opening my cage. One day at breakfast she told me that she had had a dream. "I was walking through Ida's cabbage patch, not running, but I was watching you ahead of me and we were moving out quickly."

She was stirring her particular New Mexico tomato sauce at that moment. "There is a stack of pancakes I just fixed over there." She pointed and at the same time picked up the butter plate and handed it to me and continued. "I was trying to catch you, but I was not trying very hard. Somebody was coming from my right and he handed me a shotgun, and said, 'Get her, now or never.'"

Mama put her wooden stirring spoon down, sat with me at the table and continued, "So I pulled up the gun, saw you in the sight, kept on raising it and finally fired. But when I pulled the trigger, the gun turned into a bagpipe, and the pipes just flopped and hung there, making gasping noises." She said she woke up laughing. "Eeeeer, weeee," she imitated the sound of the bagpipes, "that is what the bagpipes sounded like. What a silly dream that was!"

I agreed that it was silly, but I don't think she would have mentioned it if it hadn't troubled her. She said she was bothered that my back was to her when she shot, and the dream made her aware that I was growing up and apart from her. Whatever it meant, we became closer after that and we spent a lot of time together the rest of that summer.

One day we walked downtown to the Palace Café for a hamburger. We had ordered burgers, coffee for Mama and a chocolate malt for me and sat down at a booth. As we settled in, Professor Fersch approached us, his thumbs in his front pockets—his floppy cloth hat protruding from the rear pocket.

I made a space for him, and he began to chatter, removing his glasses, squinting at the lenses as he rubbed them with the tail of his shirt. His antics made me smile, and it occurred to me I had not met such a jolly person since Major O'Keefe had been part of our lives.

"I'm about ready to head back to Anchorage," he said. "I'm back from spending a long time with some of the indigenous people in Copper River."

He turned to look at the menu above the counter and we reminded him that he had to order there. He left us to order and was back, continuing, "My notebooks are chuck-full of info about games and songs and I just turned in eight rolls of film at the drugstore. Great summer, great summer," he gushed. "But, you know, I think I'll just spend some more time here collecting info on the old days of the trappers and miners.

"I'm just gonna play some poker at Solly's and see what comes up."

I wondered if I should tell him about Cowcatcher Charlie's hemorrhoids.

"I don't have to go back to teaching this year. I'm just doing research. And I don't think I can leave until I spend some time with the indigenous people in and around Seward."

"Great idea," Mama said. "But this is one of the busiest times for some, right now. They're drying fish, collecting roots, curing meat, picking berries..."

Our food arrived and we dug in. Maudie came in, drank a cup of coffee with us, and then headed back to city hall.

Some minutes later, Matthias came over to our booth. He had sung a solo at mass recently, but we had missed it.

"Hey, Matthias! Little brother, get over here!" I called over to him. "Here, sit next to Mama," I demanded. I told him I had heard that his solo was great. "So what have you been up to?" I inquired, finishing my malt and stealing a French fry from Mama.

"Been training some pigeons at the Home," he said. "And helping Sava dry salmon and make hooligan oil."

I could see the effect those words had on Professor Fersch. He looked up from his mug of coffee.

Mama dove in, taking advantage of the moment. "You know, Matthias, Sava promised to take me berry-picking over a year ago, and we still haven't done that."

Matthias's chicken sandwich and Pepsi arrived and, while he ate, Mama connived. I could almost see the gears moving. "Matthias, can you help us? Can you put a bug in Sava's ear?"

Matthias looked at her quizzically. Mama perceived that he didn't understand what she had said. "Oh, sorry. That just means that you make him think about something, got it?"

Matthias nodded his head.

"So please, young man, see what you can do. And while you are at it, ask if Dr. Fersch can go with us?"

Matthias continued to nod and chew his sandwich.

"I'll tell you what—we'll make a big pot of stew and we can come back to the house and have stew and berries for dinner. How does that sound?"

Matthias nodded his approval, but indicated that he wasn't sure he would succeed in his mission.

As we walked home, Mama said to me, "How about that? How about Matthias walking in just then?" She raised her eyes and hands toward the sky and said, "Wasn't he heaven sent?"

As I have said, when Mama gets an idea nothing stops her. Within a week, Matthias called and said the trip was on, and Dr. Fersch was invited. Sava would be happy to share Mama's stew and he would bring some items that Dr. Fersch might like to look at.

As planned, very early in the morning on our appointed day, Sava arrived carrying, among other things, a lidded basket that Mama put into her bedroom, closing the door firmly. We stood at attention, Mama, Dr. Fersch, Matthias and me, as Sava surveyed our dress—

hiking shoes, hats, and long sleeves to protect us from the Alaska flies and mosquitoes.

"Clothes good. Mosquitoes bad this year. About the bears," he warned us, "they need berries and they can be angry about people there. If we see bear, we talk loud, stomp feet to say, 'Here I am!' Then we back away, so slow, and if we have bear problem, Matthias and me, we care with the bears. You understand?"

We all nodded, except Professor Fersch. His eyebrows shot up and he gave Matthias a look of newly found respect when Sava indicated Matthias was his acolyte. That was respect Matthias well deserved. We knew that already.

***

The air was chilly as we set out, noting seasonal changes in the plants since our hike. We understood that Sava saved the best harvest spots for his people, but we knew he would help us to find plenty of berries.

Gigantic Devil's club leaves flashed *Winter is coming!* in bright crimson, copper and gold. Near a bog where Cynthia and I had seen bearberries and currants in the spring, tangled growth gave shade also to a patch of blushing cloudberries. We invaded their domain with care, collecting the fruit in sacks and baskets that Mama and Sava supplied. A patch of crowberry bushes, nestled within low growth, were our next addition. Sava pointed out a small white berry that looked like glass buttons.

"No, bad. Stay away," he warned.

In a meadow, we picked and picked ripe, fat blueberries, their low bushes growing at the feet of alders and paper birch trees. Then we came upon more, hidden below brambles and stalks of vivid fireweed in blossom, swaying in rhythm in the breeze.

After a short lunch of smoked salmon, sliced tomatoes and green peppers, we plodded up and away from town, toward patches of raspberries not far from Cynthia's and my secret spot. This was my first visit anywhere near the cave since we had been welcomed and dispatched by forces Cyn and I chose not to fathom. Until that moment, I had felt that the area was best left alone, that it almost preferred to be left alone and I honored that. I knew this area very well, and it was with fear that I even approached it. But that day I was with Sava.

I lagged last in the group, uneasy about what was to come. Sava must have known my turmoil, yet he appeared determined to go to that very area. We hiked up paths familiar to me and stopped perhaps two hundred yards short of the cave. There, we found high, strong stalks of raspberries in clumps and I forced my mind to concentrate on the task at hand.

We took a break—crackers, berries from our baskets, and water.

Sava sat next to me. The others talked about matters that seemed trivial as I fought to control my uncertainty. I owed it to him to show him the cave. Surely the live rock would respond kindly to him, I thought. And I was aware that he knew what I was thinking.

"Sava."

"Ummm?"

"You know how hard this is for me?"

"Umm hmmm." He plunked a few berries into his mouth, his eyes dancing.

"You know I'm afraid."

"Umm hmm. But you are with me, little daughter."

And when I hesitated again, he said, "Let's go."

"Okay."

"Swell."

We tromped through the brush, past the sawhorse retreat, which had nearly been reclaimed by the bushes.

"Your place?" Sava asked.

"Yeah"

I had been leading as we headed toward the cave, but he passed me by. Perhaps he sensed my hesitation. Or perhaps he suddenly knew where he needed to go. I will never know which. He picked up speed until we came to the base of the uneven outcropping of rounded rock formations that were home to the cave.

As I started up the slope, I felt resolute, determined at last to get this done. He climbed beside me, each of us searching for snags and slight outcroppings of rock to use as footholds. As we started up the steep, slightly flinty part of the climb, he shot past me seeming to know more than I.

He scrambled up and into the cave. I stood, watching him and catching my breath, looking at a broad ledge to my left, where in times past I had placed my hand as I tried to enter the cave. Somehow the edges of the rock laid down ages past were softer, rounder than I remembered. I turned, leaned against it, rubbing my hand on the rock and surveying the meadow below as Sava slipped into the cave. A few minutes later I heard, "Look, daughter, I find more." He called to me in a low husky voice. He was smiling. He sat at the lip of the cave opening holding the remnants of the ancient basket, a tiny jade fish hook and a hammered copper bracelet, blue-gray and crusty with age. That huge grin never left his countenance as he worked his way out of the tiny entrance and made his way to me.

"My people will have these things again," he said, catching his breath. He wrapped the small items in leaves, then in his bandana that he took from his pocket. Then he put them into the basket as tenderly as he would an infant.

Next he stood up, took my hand, and resolutely led me along the base of the rock outcropping, as it sloped to about a three-foot height. He faced the rock slope, just standing there, looking at the tangle of weeds in front of him for a number of minutes. I stood, a dense, witless creature, almost illiterate as to what was transpiring in front of me.

He was meditating, I knew, and I just stood and waited. For what, I had no idea.

Finally he took my hand again, placing it on the stone to his right, just above a vertical crack in the rock, a crack large enough to be home for some critter— a mouse or rat, or an ermine perhaps. "There," he whispered and directed my hand. "You just rub the rock. Like this. Like you pet Yaghi. Soft and nice."

So I did, and between my rubbing and the afternoon sun, I could swear it came to be a tiny bit warmer.

Meanwhile, to my left Sava rubbed and caressed the rock formation he faced. He was making a very soothing murmuring sound as he rubbed, and he did it for a long time. Minutes. And as long as he did, I did, too.

He began to form a circle with his fingers. His hands were rough and the rock was not smooth, so he made a circle that was, at first, uneven and bumpy. Soon though, his motion became rhythmic and soft. He kept on rubbing and he kept on murmuring, until at last thc beginning of a protuberance appeared. It slowly, slowly morphed into a dome, and Sava kept rubbing. Lovingly, he caressed that spot until it began to cleave, to open, and soon something looked at us, a huge dark gentle eye surveyed us.

Suddenly a wheezing, sniffing sound came from the area at my feet. Stunned and terrified, I must have jumped back three feet. Gasps emitted from the crack, blowing out dried grasses and leaves. Next I heard a cough sound, and from that vantage point I saw the crack widen. Inches from where my hand had been, I saw and heard the rock crack into what I swear looked like laugh lines on the face of a very old lady.

Sava looked over at me and laughed at my fright. He then stepped forward, gently closed the eyelid, patted the face of whatever it was, and stepped back. At last, the creature's mouth sighed, seemingly content and I was left looking at nothing but rock. It had a few more crazed cracks in its patina, but rock, nonetheless.

He then turned to me and, smiling, said, "We are done now."

We turned and made our way back to the others. On the way, I turned back more than once to survey what I had just witnessed, or thought I had witnessed.

"What—was—that?" I finally whispered.

Sava laughed. "That scare you? That rock is body of old animal soul. Animal live here when Raven make world, looooong time ago. She is Alaska native long time before you and me," he laughed. He really laughed and giggled, slapping his hand on the side of his head. "You have print of foot of her cousin in rock at your house," he continued.

"You mean the fossil of thc dinosaur footprint?"

"Sure. You say it come from New Mexico rock. But we have Alaska rock too."

"Sava, is that true?" I asked, my face the picture of disbelief.

"True, true as can be, my daughter. Living rock," he said. "Someday you smart people study about them in university. My people, they know. They know 'cuz animal spirit love and protect us."

Regarding my experience at the cave, you will just have to make your own decision. But regarding dinosaurs in the frozen north, he was spot on.

He led the way back to the berry pickers, still joking and chatting, as if we had never been gone.

"Mebbe good idea we go home now," he said.

We headed for home, everyone at ease and content, but me. It took me months to accept what I had experienced and accept that it seemed to put to rest the affair of the treasure and Sava's people.

I was hungry I knew, and I was ready to put behind me, at least temporarily, what had transpired that afternoon. Mama's stew, soda bread, and fresh berries with thick cream was the perfect therapy. After dinner, Mama retrieved the basket Sava had left behind that morning. Onto the dining room table, now covered with a dish towel, spilled all manner of items beloved to Sava and his people, including the items Cynthia and I had found in the cave.

Mama caught sight of them, looked at me, and she grinned.

Professor Fersch was in his element. He cleared his voice and spoke, "I am profoundly moved that you would share these items with me, Sava. I thank you; I thank you very much."

He picked up the porcelain fragment. "Now, I realize that you consider this item differently, Sava, but what I am doing now, is translating its place into the white man's history."

He pulled from his pocket a magnifying glass, examining the piece with care.

"This is Chinese," he said. "Probably fifteenth-century Ming Dynasty. Maybe 1425 AD?" He looked up, as we expressed surprise.

"1425?" we said. "How could that be? How in the world? How did it get here?"

Sava sat quietly, sipping his tea. At that moment I was still numb. I would have believed anything.

Sava then handed Dr. Fersch the heavy tool, and when he did, Dr. Fersch grinned. He held it, rubbing the soft surface, and at length declared, "This, Sava, is a lovely example of your people's cleverness and artistic capability. This beautiful instrument, as you know, Sava, is a mortar, a *metate* some people call it. Dr. Fersch continued to rub it, saying, " So lovely, so simple, so practical. A lady would use this to grind roots, or herbs. Nobody I know has seen anything like this. Maybe four-five hundred years old?

Sava smiled at his comment, amused at our attempts to put a date on the item.

Beautiful," Dr. Fersch mumbled, placing it back into Sava's hands.

Sava pulled the copper bracelet from his pocket, and then the fine jade fish hook. "Fine old craftwork," said Dr. Fersch, handing them back to Sava. Then Dr. Fersch picked up the piece of shell, which he examined for what seemed like an extraordinary amount of time. He turned it in every direction and looked at it in different light. He squinted and frowned, his face puzzled. He finally took a deep breath, placed the shell piece carefully on the table, paused for a long moment, and said, "As you well know, our communication today with China is nearly nonexistent. Chairman Mao rules and his people die if they argue with him. He says China has no history prior to his arrival."

He examined the item again, almost with reverence, and continued, "I just can't say with any authority if this is what I think it is—but—oh great heaven, it is nearly impossible, but," he sputtered, "recently we have been getting inklings from secret sources—Chinese scholars, whose lives are endangered for even thinking what I am about to tell you."

We couldn't have been more curious as to what was coming. "They say there exist a few ancient tortoise shells with archaic Chinese script on them, and they think that this script is the ancient precursor to the language we now call Chinese"

Oh, I thought. *I can accept that.*

"If these experts are correct," he continued, "they think the writing is a method to prophesizes the future. Amazing. 'Oracle Bones' they call them." He put the glass down and was very quiet. After several moments, he looked up to say, "If this is, indeed, what I think," he paused and swallowed, his voice slightly breathy, "that would mean your piece of shell would be at least 3,500 years old!"

We were all stunned.

"I mean," he stumbled on, "China was making silk by then, and Egyptians were making papyrus. But how in the world did this get here?"

Sava just smiled. Time and space was no problem for him. "It come from Raven's time," he said, "when he roll the ball of mud."

So that must have arrived after the dinosaur, I thought.

Our minds filled with unanswered questions, we concluded the day. The items were respectfully repacked into Sava's basket, berries were divided, and we said our farewells.

Mama and I were too exhausted to do anything more than clean the kitchen and put the fruit into the storage building before falling into bed. Strangely, sleep came to me without a problem.

Early the next day, we began processing those berries in earnest, and soon the aroma of blueberry pies baking in the oven and berries boiling in the kettle filled the kitchen. I took myself and the remaining berries onto the front porch where I sat on our wicker settee, picking over the berries that we would freeze for winter.

I thought a lot about yesterday. I thought about impending fall and winter. I thought about researching Alaska dinosaurs and starting seventh grade. I hoped I would be able to cope with the additional vagaries having to do with adulthood.

I peered absently at the sun's rays shining softly on the mountains across the bay. Something out of place caught my eye and piqued my attention, something on the road, perhaps? I put my bowl down, stepped to the front porch window and peered toward the gravel driveway. Someone was walking up our driveway, all right, but who?

Then I recognized that easy gait. He was back again, wearing the same comfortable slouchy clothes and brown flying jacket, and he whistled the same quiet tune as he approached the house. Would he have news about Silvio? "Mama!" I shouted, "come here quick! Dr. Evert is back!"

DOORS AND WINDOWS

August 1963

We sit on twin wooden stools each on one side of Sava, Cynthia and I. Now you know why my heart is broken; we are here to say farewell to him. Just a week ago, I received a message from Elsie; her brother was dying and he wanted to gather his family around him one last time.

In near death, his body still reflects nobility. His breathing is shallow and tortured. I am fascinated by the skin on his face. Somehow the wrinkles have disappeared and his skin is seemingly pulled tight, thin and veined as a butterfly wing. His worn hands look huge and bony. They are cold to the touch and I touch them as much as I can. He is suffering from what we call pneumonia and he is going to die today. We know that because he told us so.

Sava's people are quietly gracious concerning our presence. We take turns sitting with him; Elsie, Sava's niece and nephew, Cynthia, Matthias and me. Silent sentinels, we are witnesses to what remains of this fine human being, a vaporous wisp of his remaining earthly entity. We wait with him because we wouldn't be anyplace else.

My mind drifts to Rancho San Pablo. I have vague recollections of Grandfather's mother's time of death.

I was a very little girl. *Hay que velarla, Marisol.* I recall him saying, as he lit candles and sat beside her casket. We need to stand vigil.

Hay que velarte, Sava, I say softly to myself. I promise to cherish you forever.

"My daughters, my sons," he whispers, and smiles.

There is nothing that can alleviate the heartbreak in this room. He had already given Matthias permission to pray over him in his Christian way, but he made it clear that he didn't need it. He is going home.

He signals Cyn to put her ear near his mouth; she listens and then rises, walks to the door, her arms across her chest, hugging her elbows, a silhouette in the doorway.

Once more he is in a reverie. I decide to rub his face—his temples, his hairline, his neck, his cheeks, his ears. A little color returns to his face and my fingers feel the slight heat of blood returning to the surface of his skin. I take his hand in mine. He says, without opening his eyes, "Is that you, Marisol?"

"Yes," I whisper.

"I thought so," he smiles, but then his mouth becomes firm, his eyes open and I see for just a moment a flash of obsidian in them. I bend over, my ear near his mouth; his breath not more than a sliver of ether. He struggles to speak. "…God's child. Death always part of life soup. Life is swell, my daughter—drink it and be grateful—hug it hard."

After awhile he awakens, agitated, and whispers to Matthias, "Sorrow so deep—Qutekcak turns over, turns over—living rock, she…"

His fingers make an effort to squeeze my hand; then they release mine and I turn away, sideways on my stool, facing a primitive, worn wooden wall. In the wall is a wooden frame of a window, and within that frame I see the world outside, a vista that may have been ordinary yesterday, but now it has become clear, and handsome and fine, and I smile in spite of my tears.

A few minutes later, he is gone, and we are left to mourn this fine person, our friend and mentor. For me, it is as if I have lost my heart, my hair, my skin. But I have been given my marching orders. Grow up, he is telling me; I may be an orphan, but I am far from alone. Death and life; Frick and Frack; love and hate; the whole is more than the sum of its parts.

Matthias, Cynthia and I leave him to his family and their own particular way of saying farewell to what remains of him. We have been touched by their silent kindness, but it is time for us to depart.

We begin our trek back to the road and to my car, a two mile walk. The rhythm of our steps is the rhythm of our thoughts; not a dirge, but a steady tune in a minor key.

None of us reveals the message Sava shared with us, although I feel sure he wouldn't mind. We just don't. We approach a clearing and, as Cynthia and Matthias trudge ahead of me, I survey Matthias's now-mature body. His legs have lengthened as well as his torso and his shoulders have filled out considerably. I know he is devastated, yet his back is straight and his walk is deliberate. I see his jaw line as he chats with Cyn, close shaved but swarthy even so. Atop his head are dark brown curls, manicured except for the few at the nape of his neck. He carries himself like a king, I think. He stops to pick up something—an eagle feather,

"Golden," he says as he passes it to me.

Without warning, a whirlwind envelops us, its wind blows dust, scraps of leaves and indistinguishable bits of earth into my eyes and I close them, rubbing away grit. I am torn from my companions, no ushered from them really, my feet propelling forward and my body tumbling, captive of some gentle centrifugal force.

I open my eyes. I see a shiny black caisson and behind it a handsome ebony horse, head down, saddle empty and stirrups set backwards. It passes slowly before me and then it vaporizes in the breeze, gone from my sight.

I hear a rhythmic high-pitched *beep, beep,* a white and blue space rocket appears and fades. A vine sprouts in front of me and blossoms, petals curling open; it twists and tangles around stained boots and broken sandals, and then reaches out toward a twirling, beautiful huge blue ball, like a blue marble. A hand pounds a shoe on a table, and then I hear a voice singing, "How the winds are laughing, they laugh with all their might."

Snippets of music unfamiliar to me enter the maelstrom, and I hear them in spite of the storm. I am sitting on my bottom at the edge of our trail and I hear the voice sing, "It's the soul afraid of dying—that never learns to live." I rub my eyes I hear once more, "And I think it's gonna rain today."

Cynthia a few feet away, is on her hands and knees, and she is laughing. "Whee!" she exults. "Marisol, you look exactly like a forlorn ragdoll!"

Matthias, on his belly, pulls himself up and sits.

"I'm not sure I'm ready to laugh," he says, wiping his face with his hand. "But that was sure interesting!"

Matthias crawls to us and we sit right there on the trail for as many moments as it takes to recover from our experience. We gasp, we wipe our faces, we shake our heads in wonder, but we are not ready to express what has just transpired.

Now my friends sit, quiet and contemplative on the front porch of my house and I approach with bottles of chilled beer. We relax on the well-used and comfortable porch furniture, Matthias' thick-stockinged feet resting on the wicker coffee table.

Our attempts to verbalize our very recent experience, fall short. It appears we three might have witnessed similar sights but the music? Just what did happen to us, and why?

Finally Matthias breathes deeply and declares, "I think we have been blessed somehow and we need to work out the meaning for ourselves."

A statement, but also a gentle order from the youngest member of our group. We nod our heads in silence. We don't disagree with him.

But we do, right then and there, promise to remain friends forever.

I propose a toast. "Here's to the life of an extraordinary human being, our friend Sava." Our bottles clink and then we are quiet again, lost in our own thoughts.

Cynthia's voice cuts through the thick silence, "How is your mama?"

"She is fine, really fine," I answer. "She's flown to Chile to visit Susana. Her husband is the naval attaché in Santiago, you know, and Mama loves to visit there."

As an afterthought, I add, "Was she teaching at University of Alaska when I last talked to you?"

"Yes," Cynthia responded. "She was building her log home near Anchorage."

"That she loves," I interject.

"So, Cyn, is teaching filling up your life?"

"Well, she adds, almost shyly, "I'm having a ball playing guitar in a folk band on the side."

"But you still perform with the symphony?" I can't believe she would give up that part of her life.

"Oh, sure," she says. "But that happens perhaps twice a year, and that leaves me lots of time to have different kinds of fun."

Nobody looks at you quite the same way after they have heard you play the piano, my friend," I say, looking firmly into her eyes.

"Funny," she says.

"What do you mean?"

"That is just about what Sava said. He said to me, 'When you make the music sing, you fly to the sky.'"

Matthias and I nod our heads. "So true," he says.

We are quiet once more, contemplative. At last Cyn breaks the mood. "So what's new with you, Marisol?"

"Not all that much; you know, I think I was a precocious kid, but then everybody caught up and passed me by."

We all laugh, but I am serious. "Really, my life is steady and to some, uninteresting, but I am very happy where I am in life. I enjoy my job and my cabin a great deal, and Naasha's coyote blanket keeps me company on the back of my sofa. I have started to draw, and I love to head out with pad and pencils to sketch. So far, I haven't found the right guy for me, but when he does come around, I sure hope he wants to live in a cabin or a fire tower."

"Do you still hear from Silvio?" Matthias inquires.

"Oh yeah. We have written over the years. You know after prep school he went to Boston College but I haven't heard from him for a couple of years. We grew up in those letters, I guess."

"Still…"

"Yeah, you're right. He will always be special to me. But sometimes you just have to know when to let go."

More smiles and silence among friends, more sips of beer.

Matthias asks, "So how is Aaron getting along? I haven't talked to him for months."

"He's fine, Matthias," answers Cyn. "He is so busy working at NASA and playing his classical guitar, I rarely hear from him, the twerp," she says.

"And Louise?" I ask.

"She is fine. Can you believe she loves married life? She has twin boys and lives outside of Albany."

"I'll never forget the day she returned the Haida bentwood box to Sava." I added. "I was stunned."

"Yeah. She decided it didn't really belong to her. I think maybe that was the moment she began to be human," Cyn remarked.

I go to the kitchen and return with a tray of snacks, three wine glasses and a bottle of chilled white wine from Mama's stash that she brought back from her last trip to Chile.

"Matthias," I remark, applying smoked salmon to a cracker and passing it to him, "you have come a long way since you were the master of the dovecote at the Home." I am curious about his recent activities.

He smiles. "How did you hear about that?" he asks, happily accepting my offer of cracker and salmon.

"Well, you made the front page of the Seward paper, kid," I say, crossing my legs and resting my feet across from his on the coffee table. "I happened to be home that week and read about it. The headline read *Local Boy Attracts Collared Doves to Kenai.*"

Cynthia is interested. "My brother's best buddy raises doves?" she remarks, smiling, leaning forward in her chair. "I thought basketball was your center of interest."

"Nooo," I interjected slyly. "I'm aware of at least a blonde Linda in his life, and then a pretty girl named Peg. They occupied some of his time. And of course, Matthias still chants part of the mass at Sacred Heart."

Matthias's face colored slightly; then he sat back and raised his arms, palms up, in a gesture of resignation. "What can I say?"

Then he sits up tall and clears his throat. Somehow Cyn and I know something significant is coming.

"But that's all in the past," he says. "And my life's future is set."

"Oh? Go on," I say.

"The decision is mine, and I have made it. I leave for Europe in a month," he declares.

I look at Cyn and her eyes meet mine; we are surprised and curious. "So then what?" I ask.

"I have accepted the calling to become a novice at the Franciscan Monastery in Melk, Austria," he calmly tells us.

"What?" Cyn and I say in unison.

And then, likely thinking in unison, we both realize how logical his decision is. This was meant to be, I think, even though the thought had never crossed my mind.

"I have considered and meditated for a long time and, yes, this is what I want to do with my life," Matthias says. "My mind is completely made up."

We all silently consider Matthias's news. I stare and swish the wine in my glass, thinking that whatever his contributions to life will be, they will be couched in modesty, courtesy, kindness and humor.

"Well!" I declare, "whatever you do, you certainly have my love." Cynthia voices the same sentiment.

"To change the subject," Cynthia remarks, "what do you think Sava meant about Qutekcak turning over ?" Cyn is well aware of what took place during Sava's and my visit to the cave. "Could he possibly be talking about an earthquake?"

"You got me," Matthias remarks. "Perhaps that was part of the message in the wind." I refill our glasses, our thoughts still too recent and raw. So we revert to happier times. We trade stories about our moments with Sava.

"You know," Matthias says, "Sava encouraged me to become a priest."

"Really?"

"Yes," Matthias continues. "He encouraged me more than Father Paul did. He said that I needed to serve the Great Maker in my own language. He said that my God speaks with flowers in His mouth. And he assured me that his shadow-soul will always be with me."

Then Matthias sits back, stretching his legs, moving his toes. "And he said that his shadow-soul will always be with you two, also."

I suspect we both knew that.

Then Matthias smiles and says, "Remember our camping trip up the river when he showed us all those plants and flowers?"

"And he almost shared the resting place of his wife and daughter, and then we were devoured by the mosquitoes," I added. The rhythm of the conversation picks up, the stories continue amid some tears, but mostly laughter.

I bring out platters of king crab, sliced tomatoes, more wine, and we eat until we cannot eat anymore.

We finally stumble to bed, the pain in our hearts and confusion in our heads mitigated for the time being.

The next morning, we finish the crab with toast and coffee; we hug each other, and promise to write, and wonder when we will ever be together again. Cyn and Matthias head for Anchorage and points far from Seward.

So now my friends are gone, headed toward their homes and jobs and families and I am left to reflect on our time together. I wipe dishes and make beds.

I think again about my assessment of the house when I returned yesterday. It seemed lonely, languishing in its emptiness after all those years of activity. Now its creaks and sounds rarely have an appreciative listener. I saw that Mama had been here recently; the freezer was full of moose meat, a mouse trap was set on the porch, and an opened copy of an oil delivery bill sat on the dining room table.

Upstairs, I plop into the couch in front of the big picture window and wonder what the years have in mind for me. Breezes blow patches of cloud from right to left and, for just a moment, a ray of sunshine shoots through the glass, and I see in its rays all the dust I have just set free, myriad particles dancing a dervish. The dust reminds me of those errant whiskers below Mr. Lauber's lower lip and I smile, remembering how the bread crumbs mesmerized me. I can barely see the mountains; the sky is piled high with even more fast-moving clouds and the aspens are quaking anxiously. Fall is already here, and winter awaits its cue.

Then, without thinking, I pull out Daddy's whistle from my rucksack and head for that hemlock tree where our summer war headquarters had been many years back. I sit cross-legged, and begin to play Daddy's favorite lament, setting the proper mood for today. I play another, and another, and by now my back sways, leaning into the message of the notes as they fly free into the air. I am content, sensing that benign power that encircles me and the people I love.

I don't see him, yet. Instead what I sense is a quick flutter, a vibration. There he is; wings ruffling as he settles in at the edge of the wheelbarrow, tucking wings in at his side and gathering in his splayed, sassy tail. At first, Raven puts his back to me and I see his head undulate up, down, up, down, feathers moving slightly in the breeze. The feathers at his throat show silver in the sun.

"You are getting old, aren't you? And you don't like this wind." I remark..

Slowly, deliberately he takes his favorite silhouette stance again, head facing toward my right. He picks up one foot, then the next, creating a slow cadence.

"You miss him, too, don't you? Did I tell our story to your satisfaction, 'Demanding One'?" I ask.

He sits there still, head into the wind, facing the bay and the ocean beyond. His amber eye catches mine for a moment, and then, just as suddenly as he came, he is gone. Just like that, he is gone from my line of sight. But not out of my life.

I smile, suspecting that he will never fly far from me. I think he will always sit on my shoulder, perhaps now a more permanent fixture.

The truth is there has already been an angel there ever since Daddy died. I have understood that for years now. So sometimes in the future it may get crowded on that shoulder, I suppose. Never mind, I smile. I need all the help I can get, and I feel certain I will have it. Surely they will all work it out somehow.

I gather myself and my thoughts and go back into the house, to hear the demanding jangle of the telephone. "Marisol? This is Carol from the post office. I saw you in the yard yesterday afternoon and thought I should call you. You have a letter here, in your mailbox, and since just about nothing comes here anymore, I thought you might be interested. Besides, if you aren't curious, I am."

'Yes? What's the big deal, Carol?"

"Well, it's from a Silvio person, and the return address is the U.S. Consulate in Madrid."

The End

BIBLIOGRAPHY

Baez, Joan *Joan Baez, Donna, Donna* Vanguard Records 1960

Baez, Joan *Joan Baez in Concert, Part 2, Fennario* Vanguard Records 1963

Barry, Mary 1986-1995. *Seward, Alaska: A history of the gateway city* Volumes l, ll, lll, M.J.P. Barry. Anchorage, City of Publishing

Bruchac, Joseph ed. *Raven Tells Stories* Greenfield Center New York, Greenfield Review Press 1991

Hessler, Peter. *Oracle Bones: A Journey between China's Past and Present.* New York, Harper Collins 2005

Holy Bible, King James Edition 1895. London, Oxford University Press

Kari, J. & Fall, J. *Original Alaska Names by True Original People*, http://www.wilderness.alaska.gov/index.

Middler, Bette *The Rose* Atlantic Records 1979

Navajo Animal Words, http://native.languages.org.navajo words. 5/26/10.

Orton, Bruce "Letter to the Editor", *Archeology*: January/February 2010

Reid, Bill and Bringhurst. Robert, *The Raven Steals the Light* Seattle, University of Washington Press 1984

Simone, Nina *The Very Best of Nina Simone, I Think It's Going to Rain Today* Sony BMG 2006

Smelcer, John *The Raven and the Totem*

Teofilo, info retrieved from http://gamblershouse.wordpress.com. Jan 18, 2010. Info downloaded on 5/26/10 and 6/15/10.

Whalen, Dr. Douglas *Athabaskan Family Tree,* http://www.emeldorg/school/case/navajotree. 6/15/2010.

Yeats, William Butler 1986. *A Treasury of Irish Myth, Legend, and Folklore,* New York, Gramercy Books

BACK OF THE BOOK QUESTIONS

1. Marisol says that perhaps Coyote and Raven are the same in American lore.
   Clearly they aren't the same animal—what does she mean? Do you agree with her?

2. Why do indigenous people have so many superstitions and rules? Do you have some strange phrases or superstitions?

3. Have you ever met someone a bit like Mrs. Neroli?

4. Do you believe that a family could have hidden from the Germany for the duration of the war?

5. Do you think Silvio's stories about Italy could be true?

6. Who is your favorite character and why?

7. Perhaps you would like to discuss "magical realism" as a literary technique.

8. Do Dotty Etta and Maud play a part in the story or are they just silly?

9. What do you think of Byron? What will his future likely be?

10. Does the friendship between Mrs. Peterson and Marisol ring true?

11. What do you think Matthias' heritage is? Any clues in the story?

12. What do you think about Mama's and Marisol's reactions to Major O'Keefe's misbehavior?

13. What do you think of Sava's relationship with Mama, Marisol, and Matthias?

14. Is the close connection between Navajo language and Alaskan dialects really true? Could the Navajo be the builders of ancient sites such as Chaco Canyon? What does the word *Anasazi* mean?

15. Just where and how did Sava's people end up with items from another continent? If you have read Peter Hessler's *Oracle Bones: a Journey between China's Past and Present* you may wish to add comments regarding one of the artifacts.

16. Can you believe that the remains of a dinosaur could exist near Seward?

17. What is to become of Marisol? Silvio? Cynthia?

18. What is Sava predicting about the future of Seward?

Made in the USA
San Bernardino, CA
24 October 2013